W9-BTD-107

Banker's Trust

Sabrina Stephens

authorHOUSE®

NEW HANOVER COUNTY
PUBLIC LIBRARY
201 CHESTNUT STREET
WILMINGTON, NC 28401

AuthorHouse™
1663 Liberty Drive
Bloomington, IN 47403
www.authorhouse.com
Phone: 1-800-839-8640

©2011 Sabrina Stephens. All rights reserved.

No part of this book may be reproduced, stored in a retrieval system, or transmitted by any means without the written permission of the author.

Published by AuthorHouse 2/28/2012

ISBN: 978-1-4685-2496-3 (sc)
ISBN: 978-1-4685-2494-9 (e)
ISBN: 978-1-4685-2495-6 (hc)

Library of Congress Control Number: 2011962557

Any people depicted in stock imagery provided by Thinkstock are models, and such images are being used for illustrative purposes only.
Certain stock imagery © Thinkstock.

This book is printed on acid-free paper.

Because of the dynamic nature of the Internet, any web addresses or links contained in this book may have changed since publication and may no longer be valid. The views expressed in this work are solely those of the author and do not necessarily reflect the views of the publisher, and the publisher hereby disclaims any responsibility for them.

This book is dedicated to the best two-thirds of who I am—my identical sisters, Sharlina and Selina. Thank you for your love, support and guidance. I love you.

Mid-Atlantic Bank: Shallotte NC
Pre-Merger with American One

George Everett
Bank President

Greg Hardy
City
Executive

Rita Miller
Office Executive

Vacant
Shallotte Main
Office Executive

Spencer
Cashwell
Retail Loan Mgr

Ocean Isle:
3 tellers, 1 CSR 1
retail lender

Len Allen
Branch Manager

Viv
Thomas
Branch Manager

Laurel
Meadows
Branch Manager

Shallotte South:
2 tellers, 1
CSR

Holden Beach:
2 tellers, 1 CSR

Calabash:
3 tellers, 1 CSR

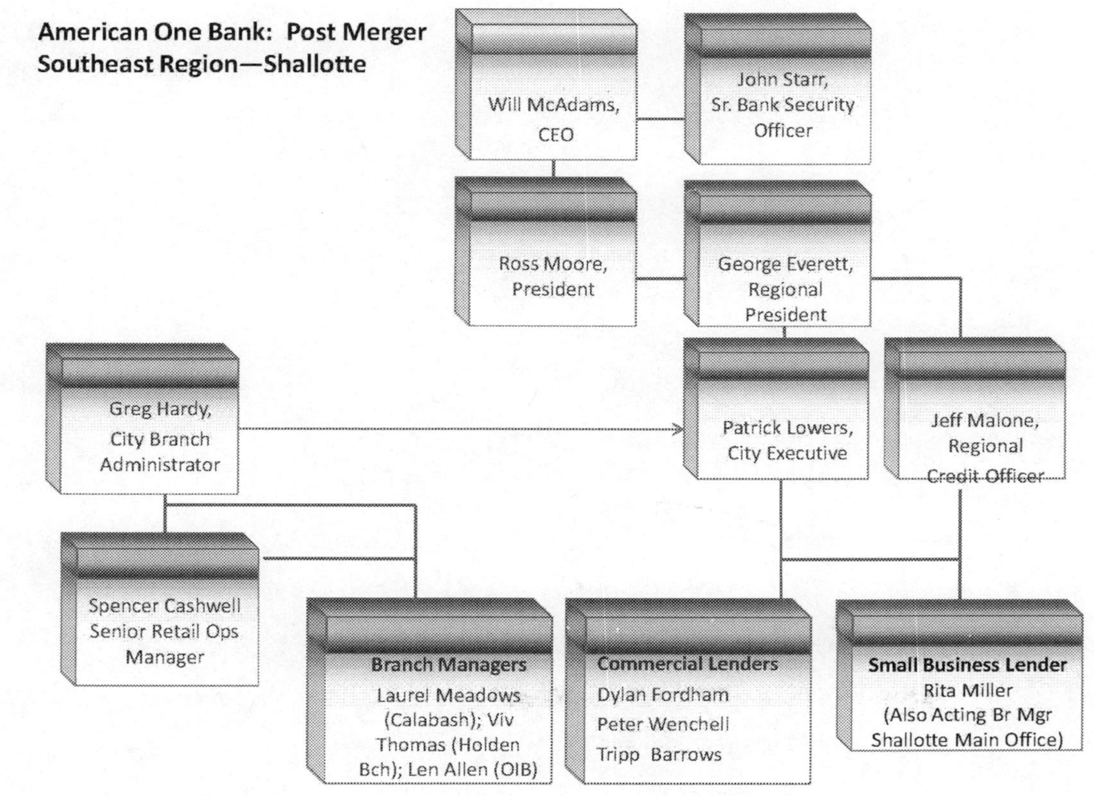
American One Bank: Post Merger
Southeast Region—Shallotte
Will McAdams, CEO
John Starr, Sr. Bank Security Officer
Ross Moore, President
George Everett, Regional President
Patrick Lowers, City Executive
Jeff Malone, Regional Credit Officer
Greg Hardy, City Branch Administrator
Spencer Cashwell Senior Retail Ops Manager
Branch Managers
Laurel Meadows (Calabash); Viv Thomas (Holden Bch); Len Allen (OIB)
Commercial Lenders
Dylan Fordham
Peter Wenchell
Tripp Barrows
Small Business Lender
Rita Miller
(Also Acting Br Mgr Shallotte Main Office)

Chapter 1

The whole sorry saga began with an innocent act, intended to be a personal rebellion, but like so many seemingly mundane decisions, the consequences took the decider, i.e. me, down a road not only less travelled but also more hazardous, reeling out of control. Have you ever played that game called Jenga? We loved to play it in college, cans of beer and a bowlful of plain M&Ms to help sustain us. You take turns pulling the wooden pegs out of the wooden peg tower. Each player employs a strategy to keep the tower intact. The problem with that strategy is that nobody knows anybody else's strategy and so the game becomes a "fly-by-the-seat-of-your-pants" escapade into chance. When the tower finally falls, it never falls slowly. The tumbling is sudden and violent, and ultimately, the loser is the puller of that one fatal peg.

I had come to Greensboro as the victim of a bank merger which wasn't really a merger but more like a corporate takeover. Hell, a cultural overthrow is not even an overstatement. My professional world had been born and shaped at Mid-Atlantic Bank. In retrospection, the eleven years were Utopia. The 400 employees across North Carolina, South Carolina and Virginia almost all knew each other. We called our top executives, later known as the Magnificent Seven thanks to their golden parachutes, by their first names and they knew all of us the same way.

I had joined the bank right after graduating from a state university where I got a wonderful, well-rounded liberal arts education. Not exactly high finance, but what all the banks in the mid-90's wanted were communicators, big-picture idealists who could be taught how to use a HP financial calculator and complete a loan application. Our bank was hopelessly old-fashioned, which was sweet at times like when we were told not to go to the ABC Store in Shallotte to buy liquor, but to drive over the border to Little River, SC. In other instances, the countrified way of doing business was downright infuriating and to some of us "minorities," sexist and racist. The most memorable instance was when I was passed up for a commercial loan officer position because I did not, at least not then, play golf. I'm not exaggerating, that was the reason my boss gave me. He should have been as blunt as he usual and said, "You don't have a penis," but I think even he was afraid to go that far with me.

The guys treated me like, well, one of the guys for the most part. The entire management team—the men—all recognized early on that I was not exactly your shrinking violet or coffee-fetching, sleep-with-you-to-get-to-the-top office female, mind you. I was the daughter of a cattle farmer from the Piedmont. I was raised a devout Methodist along with my brother and sister but probably had broken, albeit contritely most of the time, every commandment short of robbery and murder. Life was always interesting but quite often without money. We played outside all year long and all of us were quite athletic. After a lucky break, literally, my senior year in high school, my sports course changed to sports reporter and photographer from small forward on the basketball team. The teammate who cut my feet out from under me and landed me on two puny and suddenly broken wrists at a practice during Christmas break took my starting position and was offered a scholarship at the micro-college just down the street. I couldn't have been happier. The local sports editor offered me the chance to travel with our high school teams, write a weekly column complete with my mug shot, and submit black-and-white rolls of film that I shot for publication. I was hooked, and from that day forward, I could only be described as a complete sports junkie.

I learned to drive a tractor—and I don't mean a glorified mower—at 10; a four-speed Ford dump truck at 12 and weed a mean row of green beans and tomatoes faster than my mother or my sister by 14. The chores were hard, but I learned early that if I could get my part done quickly, but well, I could go school my older brother in H-O-R-S-E or Football 500 for several hours each afternoon.

Ok, ok, back to the story. So each year, American One Bank, the "Mega" bank that took over Mid-Atlantic, holds what we cynical merged employees fondly call The Pep Rally. This year, the rally was in Greensboro, NC which was deemed central to Mega's network of branches or its footprint. This corporate indulgence is really two-day assimilation into Mega's corporate culture. So year after year all of the bank officers gather to hear the same mission statement, the same corporate beliefs, and the same corporate spin on bank life in general. The sessions stretch for two and, sometimes, three hours with "social" breaks in between to mingle with 2000 of your fellow bank officers. Throw a lot of beer, wine and food into the lobby and we're just having a really fabulous time. Please. The social breaks just allow the cynical majority time for enough lubrication to almost numb the senses in preparation for the next session of corporate group-think philosophy. Even the young, I'm-going-to-be-CEO-someday types cannot keep a straight face and tell you this is a fun time.

Let me say for the record, though, this corporate retreat is not optional. ALL ARE REQUIRED TO ATTEND. That's exactly how the e-mail read, I swear. For me, though, I always ventured, how would they know? Nobody is there to take roll or anything. Every suit looks like every other black/gray/navy suit with just slight variations of exuberance as we reintroduce ourselves for the 3rd, 5th, 10th time, mind you, to CEO and his upper management entourage. I even did an experiment at this, my second and, thankfully, last rally. I introduced myself as "Rita Hayward" even though my corporate nametag correctly said "Rita Miller." No big deal. Except for a chuckle from the dashing bank president Ross Moore, the corporate team didn't even notice.

As we were herded back into the assembly, I knew this was going to be a particularly brutal, three-hour monotony on "our mission." My mission was to arrive early, find the seat closest to the door and find an opportunity somewhere near the middle of the session to excuse myself discreetly for a bathroom break. As it turned out, though, I really did have to go to the ladies' room only 15 minutes or so into the corporate chat and I just felt certain that my boss, Patrick Lowers, would see me leave and expect me back in an appropriate amount of time…whatever that was. So, I left the room as discreetly as possible, hit the head and really took my time washing my hands. I even sang "Happy Birthday to You." Dragging ass, I was almost physically sick at the thought of going back into the session.

Suddenly, like a gatekeeper at hell's door, the CEO's assistant informed me that I was not allowed to go back into the room until a break. I could have kissed the old witch. Faking irritation, I simply turned on my black stilettos and marched off to the parking lot. I had escaped and really not even tried. I didn't know what to do with myself so I went to my car, got in, put my Eagles CD on to play, reclined the seat and closed my eyes.

I was in heaven. That is, until somewhere around "Take it Easy," a rap on my window brought me crashing back to reality. I opened my eyes only to see Ross Moore peering in at me.

Crap.

Chapter 2

Ross Moore hailed from Shallotte, North Carolina. He played baseball on scholarship at Carolina in Chapel Hill but was not quite good enough to be drafted professionally. Besides, he had different plans for his future. He got his undergraduate degree in finance and immediately entered law school at Chapel Hill. After graduation, he moved on to Wharton where he graduated with his MBA, a thoroughly educated Southern gentleman.

He had come to Mega, as the employees so fondly called it, highly recruited after the CEO had seen him speak at a convention in Raleigh on "Doing More With Less—Technology for Banking." He had been at Citizens Community Bank for several years as the Chief Operating Officer only to be supplanted by the granddaughter of the founder who had been working her way up through the ranks for five years. Prior to Citizens, he had been with the FBI in Washington, DC and later, in Charlotte, NC for 15 years, working on white-collar cyber crime.

Ross was 43. He almost couldn't believe it when he heard himself say it out loud. He had married his college sweetheart, Caroline, out of law school. She had been a cheerleader at Carolina. She was friendly, perky and smart. She was also the prettiest girl on the squad…perfect hair, perfect teeth, perfect body.

They had married in her hometown of Roanoke, Virginia, a storybook wedding that was the social event of the year. And while the weather, the ceremony and the reception were splendid, the happy couple was never really happy. Even as they honeymooned in beautiful Hawaii, the lack of enthusiasm, passion and love in their newlywed existence was obvious to the resort staff, the casual onlooker and even the couple themselves. They had nothing in common—no common goal, no common hobby, and no common desire. They also had nothing to talk about.

Ross had tried to make it work, but day after day for the two years he was at Wharton, he could feel the relationship draining the life out of him. When Caroline suggested that it was time to start a family, he realized she was right. He filed divorce the following Monday so she could find her prospective baby's daddy.

The divorce had been hard on him, but even harder on his parents. They had not only lost a daughter-in-law, they had lost hope that their only son would ever have children for them to spoil. For the first time that he could remember, they lost faith in him, believing that he had made a huge mistake.

It would take them years to get back to the close-knit family they once were and the awkward time until then was bridged by many holidays apart, few in-depth conversations and a secrecy that shrouded his day-to-day life from them.

Financially, all he and Caroline owned in Philadelphia was hers—her parents had bought their townhouse, their cars and funded their socially respectable lifestyle while he went to school and she climbed the charity volunteer ladder. When Ross left for Quantico, Virginia to begin his job at the FBI Academy, he had his clothes, a Visa card with a $5000 credit limit and a bank account with a measly $2400 in it.

His only refuge from his pathetic personal life was work, and he threw himself into it with gusto. He volunteered for every weekend computer search, every night audit assignment and every lifestyle surveillance job that took him away over the holidays. His work got him noticed. Ten years and four promotions later, he landed back in North Carolina in Charlotte to head up the Cyber Division in the Charlotte Field Office.

Ross loved North Carolina. His folks were three hours away by car at the coast, a 10-month-a-year garden spot for boating and surfing. The mountains were two hours away, a wonderland for hiking, fly-fishing and camping. Washington, DC was a 30-minute flight away when HQ duty beckoned. Besides, Charlotte, North Carolina was the east coast hub of banking, his specialty at the FBI.

Only a few hours after his arrival in Charlotte, he was smiling and humming to himself as he cruised around the Queen City at night on I-77. Suddenly, a stunning realization dawned on Ross. He was happy. He was relaxed. He was home.

Chapter 3

The changes in the banking world happened very quickly and constantly in the 1990s and early 21st century after changing very little for decades. Computers, faxing, e-mail, scanning, online approvals and internet banking changed not only how the customers did business, but how bankers did business. With the rampant technological changes of the mid-to-late 1990s, banks got bigger, mostly through community gobble, buying out all of the local and regional banks around the country. With the growth, profitability soared as economies of scale kicked in. Employees were given their pink slips, often via an interoffice e-mail. It was a pathetic time.

Many good bankers were on the street, polishing resumes and perfecting interviewing techniques for the first time in years. Most eventually found jobs, and the banking world settled again. In what I thought was a lucky break, I retained my job after Mega's overthrow of Mid-Atlantic. In the years ahead, I looked back wondering why I didn't just take my lumps early and go elsewhere. Perhaps, it was because I had always been the best lender, the best salesman and the best employee I could be and I was naively sure that I would win the Mega management team over. Perhaps, I was just a scaredy cat, too afraid to get out of my comfort zone and start over. Whatever it was, that voice in my gut kept whispering, but I didn't listen closely enough to figure out what it was saying until I was all in.

I made loans and lots of them. At Mid-Atlantic, I was the top lender in the bank and I was based out of Ocean Isle Beach, not Charlotte or Raleigh or Richmond. In our rural market, I did a little of everything—business loans, car loans and mortgages. In our beach markets, every retiree looking for a next or last home or young professional buying a vacation home needed a mortgage and I was the one to make it happen. The bank knew it, the realtors knew it and the local attorneys knew it. I was golden—at least, for a while.

When we merged with Mega, all employees had to become specialists. That meant you did one thing and you did it very well or you did it somewhere else. I was pulled to Shallotte to be a small business banker, the only one in the area. The role really was a dumping ground for what the Commercial Lenders didn't want to do. THEY were the bank darlings now—the three amigos: Peter, Dylan and Tripp. Of course, they all bled Mega blue. They were hired by Mega, went through the Mega management development program or MDP and basically towed the party line 24/7.

All the MDP darlings were brought into the fold with much fanfare each year, touted as the best of the best by Mega. Each was presented to the board and introduced to the upper management ranks as the "next big thing." The fascinating part was watching many of the front-line managers gaze at them in awe. Some wondered how the darlings put their pants on in the morning. Right.

These kids were not outstanding intellectuals or spellbinding speakers. Most were fraternity/sorority presidents or the son/daughter of "somebody." They were the beautiful crowd—impeccably dressed with polished manners and nice cars and pads before ever earning a dime of their own. I know, you think I'm just cynical or jealous--cynical, maybe; jealous, no. I felt sorry for them more than anything. They had no idea what awaited them. Several times during my tenure at Mega, though, a nova stood out in the crowd. A couple of the MDP's were truly amazing. These few were innovators or true entrepreneurs that had landed by mistake at Mega for a short while until they figured out a way to do something better on their own or made the leap to an industry that rewarded radical invention or breaking convention. Besides, the rest of the darlings were only 10 years or so away from being the corporate hacks that the MDP's past had become.

Years ago, when my boss had been one of those corporate darlings, he had had the banking world in the palm of his hand. Patrick Lowers had moved up the ladder quickly, tackling the tough assignments in the armpits of North Carolina and Virginia, handling problem customers with aplomb and problem employees with ruthless abandon. He had made many enemies, but gained the respect of upper management who appreciated his zeal for boosting the bottom line. The bigwigs were also more than a little scared of him.

Lowers was named the City Executive in Shallotte when Mega bought the bank. This plum assignment was to reward his 20 years of grunt work as a company man. Besides, even though Mid-Atlantic had controlled over 50 percent of the banking market in Brunswick County, Mega had to come teach us merged employees how to be super bankers the Mega way.

So after 11 years in the banking world, I was suddenly in the Patrick Lowers' fold. Oh, joy. Pretty simply, Lowers was an asshole, but he was my boss. The best I could pray for was to stay off his radar. In short, that meant produce loans en masse, bring income to the bottom line and forsake all others, literally. He tried early and often in our dance to lead me where he thought I needed to go, but like the type "A" that I am, I kept stepping on his toes. I didn't necessarily want to lead; I simply wanted to dance by myself to my own beat. I was also a better dancer than he was. He knew it, he hated it and constantly ratcheted up his hostility toward me, but I would never give in to his constant bullying. And because of that fact alone, I think I scared him to death.

Chapter 4

God, how do I handle this? I knew I had to think quickly as I turned off the Eagles and rolled down my window before I met Ross Moore's amused gaze head-on. I was, simply, busted. I decided to just shoot straight with him.

Instead of the "What do you think you're doing out here anyway?" that I expected, I got a "Hi, are you as bored as I am?" Easy girl, Mega enjoyed entrapment.

"Mr. Moore, I was not allowed to go back inside," I began.

"Am I *that* ancient? Ross, please," he said and extended his hand into the tiny window of my white Miata. Well this, certainly, was new territory for me--careful…careful.

"OK, Ross. Rita Miller," I said, shaking his hand. I could actually feel my heart racing wildly, and I was sure I was going to keel over.

"Well, now I am disappointed. Where *is* Rita Hayward?" he chuckled, then added, "C'mon. Let's go grab a drink."

Certain that my feet never made contact with the ground, I was out of my car, into his SUV and inside a local restaurant bar with Ross Moore, the pep rally just a distant memory. As he talked, I was enthralled by his good looks and his casual intelligence, but I had to try hard to listen actively enough to engage in conversation, so loud was that voice in my gut screaming, "Why you, Rita? Why now?"

Chapter 5

Patrick Lowers was forty-two, married and the father of two teenage girls. He was comfortable with his life and really didn't have to think too much about anything thanks to his wife, a superior homemaker and caretaker. He had never really developed any true hobbies, so he had built his life around his work. Patrick was a live-to-work kind of guy. He loved the career he had chosen and, admittedly, was intoxicated by the power he had. For the first time in his life, he called the shots and controlled those working for him.

He basically liked the people who worked for him, but Patrick had always been socially awkward. His inherent distrust of everyone only compounded his isolation. He had been raised by God-fearing but child-weary older parents, the fifth of five boys. He was also the lasting realization of the daughter his folks wanted but never got. Five years younger than his youngest brother, much of the time he was left to his own devices, too young to be included in the football games, boy scout programs or bike races that seemed to admit his brothers into a good social set. By the time he started school, he had learned to count on no one, need no one and trust no one.

Patrick's mother, Delores, had ruled the Lowers' roost. She kept a meticulous house, dressed in the finest clothes and wore her pearls even as she swept, mopped and gardened. She paid the bills and organized the household, volunteered at the boys' school and played the organ at church. Publicly, she deferred to her husband, Jim, so that his colleagues at the CPA firm where he was partner, his friends at the local country club and the deacons at church could buy into the fantasy that he was "the man." At home, he yielded to her decisions, cowered at her flashes of rage and fury and paid penance with his checkbook. One Delores diatribe could send the boys scurrying for cover. That is, all of the boys except Patrick. He would curiously sit and watch the family chaos unfold. Screaming voices, slamming doors, Delores wins again. He, however, had figured his mother out early on. Don't give in, don't argue, just do. It was hard to get permission but very easy to get forgiveness. His mother was a mover and shaker. She was the real "man" in the house and that was powerful stuff to Patrick.

As a product of this environment, Patrick was a good judge of character. He took his voyeuristic view of people to social functions, preferring to watch and listen instead of involve himself in mindless, incessant chatter that others needed to fill every second of silence. He had long ago stopped caring who liked him, believing that one was much smarter to be respected rather than liked. He summed up his employees quickly and approached business settings with the personal insight he gleaned from watching them.

For example, he knew that Dylan was an empty suit. Sure, Dylan had polish and charm. He could glad-hand with upper management, work a room seamlessly at community affairs and convince weak-kneed credit officers that every loan he brought to the table needed to be made. Patrick knew him differently, however. He saw a guy that would bend the rules to make his annual sales goals, lie to both sides of a political issue to curry favor and stretch the truth or embellish loan underwriting to get a loan made. He was a dangerous sort, and Patrick knew he would resort to any underhanded tactic to fell the fool that got in his way. Patrick also knew that the downfall of Dylan was coming because as he charged forward and laughed at the people he left behind he couldn't even see the cliff right in front of him. It was going to be a glorious fall.

Tripp and Peter reminded him of his brothers and father. They dutifully came to work and made their goals, primarily out of their fear of him. They were terrified of his booming reprisals if they missed a deadline or fell short of Patrick's lofty expectations. They worked hard for him, hoping it would buy them the promotion that might get them away from him early in their careers. They respected him because he got results, but they often toasted his demise over a beer at the local brewery. They had a standing stool time there every Friday at four, excusing themselves to go call on a client. The poor idiots. He was on to them shortly after his arrival in town. Everybody liked Tripp and Peter because they were basically decent guys, but they were not the brightest bulbs in the fixture. They would end up in middle management somewhere where they were comfortable and let their wives run the household, volunteer at the local school and manage the checkbook. So familiar, so boring.

Patrick liked Greg and when he was alone and honest with himself, he envied him too. Greg was affable and smart and was liked by everybody who knew him. What made him enviable, though, was the fact that even after Greg was basically moved aside and Patrick was brought in to manage the area instead, Greg never once acted bitter, vindictive or angry. Greg moved out of the city executive's office without grumbling. He sponsored Patrick at the local country club for membership and introduced him to people in the community with genuine kindness. In fact, Patrick had never heard him say an unkind word about anybody. Patrick would criticize him, Greg would listen, nod and then comment on how much he appreciated the feedback. Patrick would give him a task with an extraordinary amount of work and a ridiculous timeline. Greg would get the task completed beautifully and on time. All the while, he never complained. How could anyone be that nice? He was probably a closet cross-dresser or functioning alcoholic or something sinister deep down. Being that kind had to be an overcompensation for something. Patrick was sure of it.

Then there was Jeff Malone, the senior credit officer for the Coastal Region of the bank. Shrewdly, Patrick had curried favor with him the first week in the area by taking Malone's over-conservative position on a decision to deny one of the local real estate moguls a loan for an expansion of his motel. The borrower was upset and threatening to call the CEO of the bank. Tripp was the lender and he was irritated that Malone was blowing an opportunity for him to crush his monthly loan goal. Malone was unyielding in his decision. No more hotel loans. The bank had enough. At Tripp's insistence, Patrick stepped in and reviewed the package. The bank had a 16 percent concentration in hotel lending which was over the 15 percent threshold. Another loan in Shallotte would just further skew the concentration. Furthermore, the package was weak on projections for the expansion as well as historical information on the existing hotel. Bottom line was that the borrower thought he would get the loan because he wanted it, not because he deserved it. Tripp had not worked hard enough on the package for Patrick to go to bat for him either. At the end of the day, Patrick sided with Malone, met with the borrower along with Tripp and made it very clear that the loan decision—his decision—was final. Malone, known for being bull-headed and self-righteous, was impressed with Patrick immediately and smugly touted his credit prowess among the sorry, sloppy lot of lenders in the department. Patrick had found an ally against the local real estate hotshots and had reinforced Malone's place high up in the local pecking order. Malone was a blow-hard, but he was useful, and in Patrick's world, a useful friend was much more important than a kind one.

Rita, though, was a breath of fresh air. She was direct, kind-hearted and honest. She had toughness to her that was refreshing, but a softness that made her endearing. She was, in many ways, a paradox. Patrick had tried to bully her early after she came to the bank via the Mid-Atlantic merger. His attempts had failed miserably and he was glad. A less perceptive person would have believed she didn't care about her job, but Patrick knew just the opposite was true. She cared too much. Oh, not about this particular job, but about the job she did every day. She believed that providing loans to people who needed them, who qualified for them, who could then contribute to the community was a noble calling. This woman had been raised right. Still, though, she worried him a little. All of the other guys worked hard and made Patrick look better to the bank top dogs. Rita worked hard and seemed content on her own little island of satisfaction, shunning recognition and reward which certainly she was due. Her nonchalant attitude frustrated Patrick to no end because she wouldn't lobby for her fair share of accolades which would raise her stock in this man's world. Selfishly, he realized that "kudos" to her would help him as well.

He had overheard Ross Moore and George Everett, the regional executive over Southeast North Carolina, discussing Rita and it made him proud that she worked for him. That is, until Everett made the comment that Rita was truly never managed by anybody but herself. Patrick seethed. They discussed her independent streak and her understated intelligence, and agreed on her attractiveness and bohemian nature. Then, Everett had commented that some gal must be really lucky to have her, sure that she was a lesbian. Moore got very angry at the comment and said so. The conversation grew very strained and ended with Everett apologizing, confused at how he screwed up but sure that he had and Moore walking away after telling Everett that his attitude toward women needing some serious adjustment in the twenty-first century. Patrick was livid. Rita could really screw things up for him. She was clueless to how everybody perceived her and couldn't care less.

As mad as it made him, Patrick secretly reveled in her style. The best he could hope for his two daughters was that they turn out just like Rita Miller.

Chapter 6

The afternoon sun was setting when we pulled back up into the parking garage at the convention center. Not sure if I was loopy from the beer or delirious from the body in the seat next to me, I was trying hard to figure out how this situation was going to conclude. Would we walk into the social hour together, fueling speculation about where we had been and what we had been doing? Would he slide in the side door clandestinely while I walked in the opposite way to mingle casually with the banking mass, as if I too had been mesmerized for two hours by spellbinding corporate drivel?

Interestingly, I never considered the real unfolding. He pulled up beside my car, pulled out one of his business cards, scribbled on the back and reached over and put it into my hand. Then his piercing gaze met my eyes and grew very serious.

"Keep your chin up, don't let the bastards get you down and watch your back, ok?" he whispered. I had completely lost my voice so I simply nodded.

"If you need me for anything, my mobile number is on the back of this card. I'm heading back to Charlotte right now so I'm afraid I have to miss the rest of the festivities here," and he broke into a huge, boyish grin, "But you only have the dinner to survive now, right? I'm sure Lowers has saved you a seat, so don't keep him waiting any longer. Good night, Rita. Thanks for keeping me company."

I climbed out, shut the door and smiled and waved slightly as Ross Moore drove away. Sure that I was firmly in a Twilight Zone episode, I walked woodenly to the back door and immersed myself into the sea of black/navy/gray-suited bankers, hoping to find a spot where I could simply plant myself. I plastered a smile on my face, grabbed a beer and turned to go find Ivey Jones to capture as my dinner partner. Unfortunately, my escape was blocked by the glowering face of Patrick Lowers who was moving through the crowd toward me like a bull in a china shop. Ugg.

"Where the hell have you been?" he all but yelled.

"I've been trying to stay lucid after two hours in that room. Why?" I fibbed. I didn't really say *which* room.

"Where were you? I saw you leave and not come back."

"I had to use the facilities. Unfortunately, I was not allowed to re-enter through *that* door," I pointed, "But I walked around to the back and slipped back into *that* door," gesturing to the obscure door by the corner through which I had just re-entered.

He stared at me so hard I was sure he was trying to see the folds in my brain, but apparently, he bought the story. "I've saved our team a table at the front for dinner. Let's go," he ordered.

"Ok, I'll meet you there in five. I want to go track down Ivey Jones first," I said. Without waiting for his smart-aleck retort, I bobbed and weaved into the crowd searching through the sea of faces until I spotted Ivey next to a beautiful, blond Amazon who had surely just completed the MDP. I just laughed and shook my head.

"Hey fool!" I called to him. He smiled broadly and reached up and hugged my neck. "Are you going to eat dinner with me or lure this temptress into breaking some rules with you?"

Well, I might as well have slapped Amazon because she sure acted offended and said, "I'm happily married, thank you!" and huffed off. Ivey and I just disintegrated with laughter. We were so bad together.

"Gee, I wonder what's on the menu tonight," I joked, knowing that banker dinners are famous for a total lack of culinary imagination. Odds were better than 2-to-1 that the fare consisted of some type of baked chicken, some variation of green beans and some kind of potatoes, but it was fun to dream of prime rib or veal scaloppini.

Ivey rubbed his hands together and licked his lips, "Maybe they'll have gravy on the chicken tonight! Come on my brown-haired sister, let's sup!" and he hooked his arm through mine and away we went to the dining hall to graze with the rest of the corporate herd.

Chapter 7

Ivey Jones stood just over 5' 4" and weighed in at about 140 pounds fully clothed, including his shoes. What he lacked in stature, though, was more than compensated by his towering personality, his boyish charm and a cool confidence that came from being comfortable with himself. He was deceivingly smart, wickedly funny and brutally honest.

Ivey Jones was really John Michael Jones, IV. A kindergarten classmate, Shelley Connors, had read "IV" as "Ivy" out loud to the class off of the nametag on his desk and began teasing him to upset him. John Michael liked it, though, and thought the name was interesting. Shelley pouted the rest of the day that she didn't get the best of him and that he was the center of attention and not her. The rest of the class began calling him Ivy or Poison Ivy and the name stuck. He began spelling it I-v-e-y, though, when he wrote it on his paper that year and John Michael became a distant memory.

Ivey was one of the first generation of X-gamers. He could skateboard, surf and snowboard better than anybody at prestigious Davidson University, honing his skills in his spare time in the mountains or the beaches of North Carolina, depending on the season. He was a serious student, though, and spent much of his time in class and in the library during the week. He was sure he would end up as a college professor, engaging young minds and staying forever young by the constant association with the perennial parade of faces that entered the university each year, but his career path changed quickly once he got a taste of banking.

After graduation, Ivey was selected as one of a class of twelve management trainees at Mid-Atlantic Bank. He quickly set himself apart with the devotion to learning and the drive to succeed that was ingrained in him by a father who was one of the top sales representatives in the pharmaceutical industry and a mother who was a professor of philosophy at Elon College. It didn't hurt either that he worked with one of the best customer service banks in the nation. Upon completion of the nine-month program, Ivey had his choice of plum assignments within the bank's footprint. After interviewing extensively, he accepted the assistant manager of the Shallotte Main office. He was a perfect fit.

The other managers and lenders in the area were all young and hip and truly liked each other. They laughed often, goofed off some and were serious about being on top in quality loan production. The area executive was Greg Hardy, and he was the best. His hands-off style gave the lenders room to grow, be creative and make mistakes. He supported his team in the face of adversity and shared praise liberally for a job well done. Ivey, like the rest of the team, would have taken a bullet for Greg.

His closest friends were Rita Miller and Spencer Cashwell. Like him, they were young and single and full of life. They had a good-natured rivalry with each other at work that carried over to thrilling evenings of penny poker with lots of good food and drink. Years later when they were all separated, they would recall these evenings as some of the best times of their lives. They had spirited political discussions, strategized about how to make their sales goals to make more money and dreamed of hitting the lottery so they could live like movie stars. They lived in the same condo project and spent so much time together professionally and socially that their co-workers dubbed them "The Three Musketeers."

Life in the coastal town was perfect for Ivey for about three years before everything began to change. The months leading up to his relocation left him exhausted and burned out. Greg had called him into his office and nonchalantly told him that one of his largest relationships was delinquent and that it was going to be handled by credit administration. He sensed that some type of problem with the relationship had called his credibility into question, but Greg assured him that the problem was not with him, but with the borrower. As Ivey continued to try to help, Greg finally told him to just let credit do their job. Going forward, he was not allowed to discuss the accounts, work the accounts or restructure the accounts. Three loans to a well-known, well-heeled local businessman went into default and were charged off as a loss to the bank. The loss cost him his annual bonus, but also dinged his pride and confidence. Worst of all, he never got the opportunity to defend his decision with the credit committee. Instead, George Everett, the head of the credit committee and the chief credit officer at Mid-Atlantic spearheaded the effort from Wilmington. George had referred the customer to Ivey and apparently, when the accounts went into the crapper, he had taken it personally and led the charge to rid the bank of the scumbag. He never once called Ivey for input, never assured Ivey that everything was going to be okay and never made an effort to take partial responsibility for the accounts, which would have at least given Ivey back some of his pride if not some of the money the mess had cost him.

Ivey railed about the injustice of the situation to Rita and Spencer, but they had a really difficult time understanding why it was such a huge deal to him. Lenders are in the risk management business, not risk elimination business. If you make enough loans, you are going to make a few that go south. If not, you are not making enough loans. They listened to him for weeks, then, finally, told him to get over it. But he couldn't. Something was not right, but he couldn't figure out what was wrong.

About a month later, Greg Hardy, the city executive, approached him about an opportunity to go manage a large branch in Raleigh. The move meant more money, more responsibility in the capital city and a new start. Ivey jumped at the offer. Unfortunately, he had to leave Spencer and Rita and just thinking about that part of the opportunity made him almost want to reconsider. Almost.

As he told them over drinks at Santa Fe Station that Friday night, they had stared at him in silent disbelief for what seemed like ages. Rita teared up, but then Spencer smacked her and bravely choked, “Well congratulations, you fool!” Rita got up and hugged his neck while Spencer hunted down the waitress for Jaeger bombs all around. They celebrated until closing time, stumbling to the taxi they called for a ride home.

When he had packed all of his belongings into his beat-up old land cruiser, he found it almost impossible to keep himself composed when he tried to say goodbye to them. Spencer held onto him then held him away, flashed her big white smile and asked, “Were you trying to feel my boobs again?” With a look of mock horror, Ivey replied, “Those big things? They still scare me!” Then he hugged Rita and knew he would never have her right next door when he needed her, and he wondered how he would survive without her as his sounding board. “Knock ‘em dead, John Michael. I know you will, my brother,” she said then added, “summertime rent is only $200 per day for you! Don't be a stranger, huh?”

As he pulled away, blew the horn, waved goodbye and threw them kisses, he was suddenly struck with the thought that he was leaving his problems in Shallotte behind him, but squarely in front of two of the people that mattered most to him. The feeling that seized him had only one name and that was fear, and it was not until he drove past the Raleigh city limit sign that it loosened its grip. Ivey convinced himself that he was just afraid of all of the changes going on in his life, the challenge of the new job, making new friends and relocating to a new city. He had been through change before, and he knew he would be fine.

When he arrived, he called Rita and Spencer to let them know that he already missed them and to tell them thank you for helping him pack. That deep feeling of fear was still coiled quietly in his gut while they talked and laughed, but he did not say anything to them about it. When he finally hung up the telephone, he made himself admit the problem out loud—something was not only a little off in Shallotte, something was really wrong.

Chapter 8

The pep rally ended after the dinner and while many of the 20-somethings decided to party the night away, I said my "goodnights" and slipped away to the sanctuary of my hotel room. As I unlocked the door with the key card, the toll of the day seemed to seep all the way into my bones. I was whipped.

Worst of all, I knew I wouldn't sleep a wink that night. On top of hating to sleep in hotels, my mind was racing all around the events of the day. Everything seemed just…surreal. I needed to think. I needed to talk. I needed advice. Bottom line, I needed Spencer.

Without a second thought, I dialed my best friend's number and let the phone ring while I kicked off my shoes, undressed and plopped flat onto the bed in my underwear. Spencer picked up on the third ring. "Hey baby! What's up?" she answered. Audibly letting the air escape my lungs, I felt an immediate sense of relief, and I said the only thing I could think of to start the conversation. "I couldn't make up a wilder story if I tried, Spence. You just aren't going to believe it."

"Spill it," she said, and I did.

Chapter 9

Spencer Cashwell was petite, blond and beautiful. She had the brightest, whitest smile around and, by far, the best name in the banking world. She was also talented, grounded and hilarious. Everybody loved Spencer and honestly, she had more true friends than any one person had a right to have. At her 35th birthday party in the fall, hundreds of her friends attended and toasted the milestone with her. Each and everyone had a Spencer story and shared a special bond with her.

Spencer had never been married, though she wanted to be—one day. She had gotten close once, but as they neared the big day, everything began to fall apart. She wanted it all—love, family, career, money. She realized, though, that Jack brought the love and certainly was capable of helping start a family, but he lacked ambition and drive. As a result, she knew she would always be the breadwinner, the caretaker and the provider. Keeping true to herself, she admitted that love was just not enough. She and Jack went their separate ways, parting friends before the bickering over money, time, sex and family ruined what they had had together.

Almost simultaneously with the breakup, Spencer accepted a job with Mid-Atlantic Bank as the retail sales manager. She would be located in Shallotte where she had grown up. She interviewed with Greg Hardy and knew instantly that she was not only going to get the job, but accept it. That day, she met Rita Miller and Ivey Jones, too, and she knew she had found her professional home.

For the first three years, work was a joy and a challenge. She was extraordinarily successful at cultivating her team of young retail lenders. They liked her immensely and respected and admired her vast area contacts that continuously brought in new customers, new loans and new banking relationships. She found exceeding the bank goals exciting, and her enthusiasm was contagious to her team and her friends, especially Ivey and Rita. The three were unabashedly the top guns at the bank, but they also spent many evenings discussing sales strategies, new opportunities and improvement ideas at the bank over pizza and beer in their apartments. Work was a source of energy for all of them and their drive fueled each other to do more and do better.

While many of the bank employees thought the three of them were crazy to spend so much time together, their boss, Greg Hardy, encouraged their camaraderie, often posing philosophical bank questions or outlining seemingly complex situations he needed them to ponder, discuss and solve together.

Work was not her whole life, though. Spencer's mom lived in Shallotte. Penny Cashwell was a realtor with a local firm, but she was passionate about golf. She and Spencer had a standing golf game at the local country club every Tuesday afternoon. Spencer played half-heartedly for years, content to be beaten by her mom who played virtually every day. Then one day, she learned that Rita had just taken up the game, and she asked her to play. Yes, Rita was horrible for the first year, but then her natural athleticism kicked in and she improved remarkably. Plus, they played the same way—quick, with a Miller Lite in hand. Spencer began to improve too, and her love for the game grew. She knew she was finally a player the day she beat her mom by one stroke in a fierce contest, shooting her best round ever, a 79. Granted, Penny did not play particularly well that day and she was put out a little that she got beat, but she was truly thrilled for her only daughter and celebrated the victory by buying everybody in the clubhouse a beer.

Recently, though, her desire to hone her golf game to a sub-10 handicap was not only fueled by her love of the game, but also by an increasingly overwhelming need to get the hell out of the bank. After Ivey's departure over two years ago, the whole bank seemed to be turned upside down. Worse still, after the merger was announced between Mid-Atlantic and Mega, the Mega troops had come in, guns blazing and riddled the organization to shreds. There was no chemistry, no direction and most of all, no fun anywhere in the region that had once been the textbook example of high-growth, high-return banking. Amazingly, the changes happened in a little over one year. The year had been drudgery. Even Rita, the perennial optimist, was being worn down.

The Shallotte area had a new boss, Patrick Lowers, the city executive. Sure, he reported to former Mid-Atlantic chief credit officer, George Everett as the regional president based out of Wilmington, NC, but the real kick in the ass was that Greg Hardy reported to Lowers. The idiots in the corporate boardroom had to be smoking crack. So the pecking order in Shallotte was City Exec Lowers, Regional Sales Manager Hardy, the Mega originals, and last but not least, the Mid-Atlantic plebes. What was worst, though, was that while Spencer's job as retail sales leader had not changed that much, Rita was being called on to not only do her job as a small business team leader (quite hilarious since she was the only one on "the team"), but also manage the Shallotte Main office. The one time Rita had broken away to play golf with Spencer, Lowers had unloaded both barrels on her the next day. A person could only take so many 60-hour work weeks with no reward. Luckily, Spencer reported directly to Greg, not to Lowers, so she just kept doing her job, exceeding her goals by a little and skipping away to the links a lot.

Today was one of those days. Rita had called Spencer last night and told her about everything that had transpired with the handsome Mr. Moore. While Spencer normally would have sacrificed five years of her life to be in that same situation with such a fine specimen of man, Rita was right. Something was off-kilter. As promised, Spencer would keep the events of Rita's encounter in the strictest confidence, but she needed to mull it over—alone. And so, it was just Spencer, the golf cart, the clubs and the beautiful sunshine on the Byrd course at Sea Trail. Here, she could hear herself think. But Spencer knew it was more than just Rita's most recent encounter that bothered her. There had been "things" going on for a long time and with increasing time alone, Spencer was pulling it all together. The more the puzzle came together, the more complicated the picture it pieced together became. Suddenly, upon realizing that she was not only alone but that no one in the world knew where she was, a chill ran down Spencer's spine that caused the hair on the back of her neck to stand. If she and Rita were inadvertently involved in some high-level corporate scandal or cover-up, a whole lot more than their jobs could be at stake.

Chapter 10

It was 7 p.m., and I knew it was time to pack up work for the day and head home. The Monday following the pep rally was finally over but the work that had been waiting on me was far from done. The sun was setting quickly as I locked the door. The days were getting shorter and even in Shallotte it was not safe to leave the bank alone in the dark. Not that I had anything for a would-be robber to steal. Almost universally, bankers never carried cash. I certainly was no exception, mainly because I never had any excess cash. I had the mortgage on my condo, a car payment on my Miata and I ploughed every excess cent I could afford into my 401K or my rainy-day fund. I lived comfortably, but I lived frugally.

Today had been a doozy. I had to approve the overdraft report and, as usual, the same culprits topped the list. When Greg asked me to help with the branch management duties, I said I would, believing this consent would be extremely short-term in nature. Six months later, here I still was. I vowed last week that these overdraft regulars were either going to get off the list or get out of the bank. I personally called all seven of them and told them that they had one week to get their accounts straight or I was going to close them. Well, today was the day.

As I called the five accounts still on the report, I got a litany of excuses from some, pleas from a couple and an idle threat from one idiot, Ricky Jarman of Coastal Entertainment. Before he hung up, he told me he was coming to see me. I told him I didn't have time to meet with him this morning, and I was returning the four bad checks he had written. His "we'll see about that" remark as he slammed the phone in my ear didn't deter me in the least.

True to his word, the big doofus stood in my doorway 20 minutes later. I told him my decision was final and that I was not going to discuss the matter any further. He simply smirked and walked away. Or at least I thought he did. What he actually did was go over my head to see Greg Hardy and that ticked me off.

Greg came by *sans Ricky* to see me after he left the bank. He asked me to give Ricky some more time to straighten out his account because he was going through a rough time. He also said that Ricky had deposited enough money to cover the deficit and that he had spoken with Jeff Malone to approve the overdraft since the total loans outstanding to the bank exceeded my loan authority. After a mild protest, I relented and paid the checks, spending an hour with deposit operations trying to undo my earlier decision. This whole process had taken the better part of four hours of my day.

To complicate matters even more, I was preparing the budget for the branch as well. I was responsible for setting the budget for the new manager's loans, deposits, fee income and expenses and I wanted to get it right. God knows if I set the new manager up to fail I could be doing this job again and that almost made me physically ill.

Somewhere during this madness called branch management, I was supposed to make loans. Alas, the hours between five and seven p.m. had become my lending hours. These golden hours were quiet. There were no employees, no phone calls, and no customers demanding my time.

The sun was setting over the horizon as I walked out that evening, and I noticed that the summer's heat had mellowed into an autumn crispness sometime in the last couple of weeks. I loved the fall and the very thought of it made me pick up my stride as I walked to my car at the back of the parking lot.

I opened the door, slung my bag into the back and started to get in. As I looked down at the driver's seat, I froze. Staring up at me were ten, perfectly fanned out Ben Franklins. I looked around, but I was completely alone. Suddenly frightened, I didn't know what to do. Should I call the police? Bank security? Should I call Greg? Spencer?

I carefully got into the car and sat down on the edge of my seat. As I leaned my forehead into the cool of my window, I suddenly knew exactly who to call. As I dialed the number, I realized my hands were shaking. Before I could figure out why, I heard "hello" in my ear.

"Hello, Ross? It's Rita."

CHAPTER 11

The beauty of a bank merger is the blackout period. This three-month godsend is like a black hole where bad decisions are forgiven and bad loans are forgotten. Write downs become write offs. Problems just disappear. The problem with problems, though, is that the people behind them don't disappear.

When Mid-Atlantic merged with Mega, there were few problems to wipe away. The few the bank did have, however, were huge. The biggest problem loan was in the coastal region on the Sun Runner Business Resort. This multi-million dollar cluster had George Everett's signature all over it. After drawing down 100 percent of the funds for construction, the 30,000 square foot office complex sat completely vacant and still a long way from completion. Two months after the last construction draw, the owners never made another payment. The project had quickly been dubbed the Snort Resort amidst rumors of heavy cocaine use by the jet set owners, Ted and Debi Jarman. The "fabulous" husband and wife had skipped town and probably, the country. Shamelessness was a family trait because their extended family still lived in the area and continued to strut around town bragging about what they had and how smart they were, including Ted's first cousins, Ronnie, Rich, Randy and Ricky. Several of the morons still banked with Mega and for the most part, their accounts were problems.

Having grown up in the Shallotte area, Ross was very familiar with the Jarman degenerates. The three brothers and their families had been in Shallotte for many generations. He had never met people like them in all of his travels, studies and relocations. They were simple and uneducated, but crafty and cunning in business negotiations. They would also pray for you on Sunday and screw you to the wall on Monday. They operated a hodgepodge of businesses that ran the gamut from churches to nightclubs. They were suspicious of other business owners, jealous of each other and bent on destroying any competition by all means possible. They would lie, cheat and steal without conscience. Throw in a little paranoia on their part and success on anybody else's part and Ross was sure the family activities would quickly escalate from petty criminal mischief to serious felonies.

Armed with this knowledge and his own family ties in the area, Ross knew that the Jarmans were in some way involved in the huge historical losses the bank had accumulated in southeastern North Carolina beyond the losses on the real estate loans. He also knew that the corruption and conspiracy reached to the upper ranks of the former Mid-Atlantic Bank management team. He just didn't know who was involved, how they were involved and most importantly, why they were involved, but he meant to find out. A clear picture of the crime would help him map out the scheme to seek indictments, convictions and hopefully, long prison sentences for the culprits.

The most obvious person in the scheme was George Everett, the southeastern regional president at Mega and the former President of Mid-Atlantic. He had signed off on each of the three large loans that went south prior to the merger, including the Snort Resort debacle. The losses totaled almost $4 million dollars collectively, a colossal total for Mid-Atlantic. Many of the senior lenders and most of the senior credit officers believed that these losses alone led to the buyout of the popular regional bank. They weren't far off the mark. Sensing the huge drag on earnings the loss created combined with the need for a massive computer upgrade for the almost $5 billion bank, the opportunity to get a premium on the bank's sale was immediate and fleeting. The deal was struck between the executive management teams of both banks at 25,000 feet in the air, so concerned were the parties that rumors of the merger would leak out before the details of the agreement were finalized. The announcement to the employees of Mid-Atlantic was made on a Sunday morning via conference call for most of the regions but in person for the southeastern NC region. Many were was stunned and some were angry and everybody wondered how the merger would affect their jobs. Only the seven members of the executive management team were thrilled. They had employment contracts. They were also instantly rich.

Everett was one of the magnificent seven, and he became proof that financial success was not always a result of sound decision-making or high integrity. He simply was lucky enough to be in the right place or position at the right time. He now towed Mega's party line. He espoused sound lending principals like they were Bible verses. He preached growth through weighing risk and reward. He was also unbelievably smug.

Even with his history, though, Ross wasn't sure if Everett was the mastermind of an elaborate scheme to defraud the bank, if he was just swept up in the greed as it unfolded or if he was involved in the fraud at all except perhaps unknowingly. Yea, he was that clueless.

Whatever Everett's part, Ross knew that the answers would be found only when he identified the other participants, willing or unwilling, in the plot. Amazingly, the losses continued after the merger, indicating that perhaps Mega employees were involved in addition to Mid-Atlantic managers. His short list of possible players included Ivey Jones, Patrick Lowers, Dylan Fordham, Jeff Malone and Greg Hardy. He also couldn't discount that more than one of them was involved as well as more lower-level employees like vault tellers, loan assistants or account managers. He was just beginning his covert investigation, but he knew time was his enemy.

The more time passed between the fraudulent transactions and the present, the more likely evidence would be lost, forgotten or by design, destroyed. He also knew that with the Jarman boys in the mix, evidence could just as easily include people as paperwork and for the few that had been eliminated from suspicion by asking questions and identifying problems that meant danger. He knew that Rita was one of those few who stood squarely in the clear. She had taken control and accountability for the Shallotte region and questioned everything. She was determined to curb losses and demand repayment from charged off accounts. She was also extremely persistent and wise to foolishness. Ross knew that these two qualities had garnered her praise from the bank's credit team. He was just as certain, though, that these traits could easily garner her attention of a fatal sort from desperate crooks.

Chapter 12

He was back in up to his neck. As he sat pondering how he could have let himself screw up again, he loosened his tie. He had risked everything and for what? To keep up appearances? To live "the good life?" Now, he was down $200,000. This time, he could not only lose his house and possessions, his family and friends, he could also lose his job. Not that he was going to let that happen. He had the one necessary tool for job security—ammunition. If he went down, he was taking the whole damn southeastern NC bank down with him. Still, he ate antacids like candy, took sleeping pills every night to knock himself out and forced himself to eat to avoid looking like a walking skeleton. He was a wreck.

The constant worry that his world was going to come crashing down made him irritable, suspicious and afraid. The path to getting whole again financially was going to be tougher now too since the merger had added new layers of accountability and oversight to muddle through. He had no choice, though. His balls were to the wall and "Fat Ass" was calling him every day demanding cash he didn't have.

As he reached for the phone, he let out a loud sigh. He was too old for this crap. On the first ring, Mary Ann's familiar "sing-songy" voice answered, "American One Bank, how may I help you?"

"Hi, Mary Ann! How are you on this perfect October morning?" he asked. Sometime he even amazed himself at just how friendly he could sound.

"I'm great, handsome. How are you?"

"Good. How's your family?"

"Great! Hang on, honey. Let me see if the big guy is in."

As he waited on the line, he caught his reflection in the mirrored glass of his bookshelf. He looked tired, haggard and almost crazy in a desperate sort of way. He immediately closed his blinds, popped another Tums and waited for a voice that he hoped would help him take the first step out of this mess he had helped create.

Chapter 13

The day after my "grand" discovery was nerve-wracking. When I spoke to Ross on the telephone the night before, he instructed me to put the cash into a blank envelope with "Deposit for Ricky Jarman" handwritten on the front and drop it into the night deposit. Of course, I did just that. No one would know about the attempted bribe except Ross and me and that included Ricky himself. Not only could he probably not balance a checkbook, he might not have even passed second-grade math. I was still jumpy and paranoid, though.

To make matters worse, this budget business was about to drive me to drink. I was having a whale of a time budgeting fee income, interest income and charge offs due to loan loss for the office. I had pulled histories on each account for the last three years which included the last full year the branch operated as Mid-Atlantic. The disparity in each account over the three-year period was astounding. I realized I needed help and a second set of eyes and I knew just who to call.

Before the phone rang one full time, Spencer's loud "Yo!" sounded in my ear. I began to laugh.

"What are you doing?" I asked.

When she muttered her nothing, I felt the tension in my shoulders loosen. "Can you come help me with this budget? I really need another perspective."

Spencer snorted, "Damn, woman. You must be desperate then! I'll be right there."

When she rounded the corner, I could tell her brain was already working on how we could escape this madness and hit the links. So before she even uttered the words, I counted the two words on my two fingers as I said them to her, "Pipe Dream."

She sighed, "Okay. What's going on?"

So I began by showing her the huge spike in fee income, interest income as well as loan charge-offs in year one and the subsequent plunge in year two and the flat line for year three. I also showed her the chart where I had graphed the timing of each. Loan fees would go up for a month then plummet. The following month, NSFs would spike in tandem with interest income for a couple of months. Within four months of the spike, a charged-off loan would cause the loan loss general ledger to spike. Within a month, the whole process would start over. This cycle happened three times the year before the merger with Mega.

As we stood contemplating how such a cluster could unfold unnoticed, the look that passed between us was one of shock and fear. The whole picture suddenly became clear to both of us. Ivey had been the manager for the full year. This mess was no accident. This situation was huge.

Blankly, Spencer said, "Let's blow this joint" before she even noticed that I had grabbed my purse to do just that.

"C'mon, you drive, I'll buy," I said, and without any more discussion we hit the road to find our favorite anonymous watering hole.

Chapter 14

Ross woke with a start. He rolled over and looked at the clock. It was only four a.m. Resisting the urge to turn over and try to go back to sleep, he pushed back the covers and forced himself out of bed. He went to his kitchen and started the coffee that he hoped would clear the cobwebs out of his head. Or, more importantly, clear Rita Miller from his mind.

"What is wrong with me?" he said out loud to himself and an amused Jinx, who sat nearby. He was officially on vacation for a week, and in about two hours, he would load his trusty chocolate lab, his kayak and his packed suitcase into the SUV and head east to his parents for a week. Not that this week was going to be particularly restful.

He couldn't get Rita out of his brain. Her piercing green eyes and long, curly brown locks had invaded his life day and night. Last night, he dreamed she was a gypsy beside a fire in the woods. She wanted to tell his fortune and when he reached his hand out to her, her touch was hot and electric. When he looked into her eyes, they were troubled and wide as she stared at his palm. When she looked up, her eyes were dark and serious. She leaned over to him and whispered, "Don't let your career interfere with your destiny."

Before he could ask her what his destiny was, she stood and walked into the darkness, glancing back at him, wordlessly beckoning him to follow. As he entered the blackness, he called her name over and over, louder and louder. He could hear her walking, but couldn't see her. He could hear her breathing, but couldn't catch up to her. Suddenly, a gunshot pierced the night and he heard her scream. At that point, he sat straight up, breathing hard and sweating.

He knew heading home to Mom's and Dad's would help him sort out the trouble brewing in and around the bank in Shallotte. As soon as he arrived, he became a local again temporarily and that gave him the cover to discreetly keep tabs on the Jarmans as well as the Mega bankers, including one Rita Miller. As his brain was working, he poured himself a cup of coffee and caught himself grinning like an idiot. He turned again to Jinx and repeated the question that had started his day. "What is wrong with me?"

Chapter 15

My alarm clock roared to life at 6:00 a.m. I was exhausted because I had slept very little last night after Spencer and I had pieced together the huge, well-designed web of fraud at the bank. The more we examined the reports, the clearer the situation became. We had a crook working with us, among us. Apparently, we had for a long time, going back to Mid-Atlantic days. I wondered who it was.

Spence and I had stayed at the Sand Bar, a locals-only watering hole across the border in Little River, SC for almost four hours unwinding the tangled mess. According to our napkin calculator, just in the two years prior to the merger and the first year post-merger, over $2 million had been charged off in small unsecured loans and overdrawn checking accounts just in Shallotte. That was huge. Furthermore, all of the accounts had several common denominators. First, George Everett had approved all of the loans. Second, all of the loans were unsecured, single-pay notes. Last, but certainly not least, all of the borrowers or depositors were in some way related to that fat-ass Ricky Jarman. His involvement was surely not a coincidence, and he was one scary lunatic.

By the time we left, we had decided to keep the information to ourselves with one exception. I would go lay out the findings to Patrick tomorrow morning, feigning confusion and soliciting his help in finalizing the budget. That way, he could draw his own conclusions from the information and go after the culprits by involving audit and internal fraud. Spencer wouldn't let on that she knew a thing. This secret was to keep her safe and to help keep Patrick honest. If he tried to pin anything on me or tried to sweep the information under the rug and not do anything, we would know that he could possibly be in on the take. The scam had spanned from Mid-Atlantic to Mega.

After our initial shock at the realization that Ivey was the branch manager when the fraud was going on, we agreed that there was just no way he figured it out. We also discussed what we could remember about the circumstances behind his decision to leave. We were both convinced that there definitely was a connection to our discovery but equally sure he did not know the scope of this mess. For now, we decided to keep it this way.

So, understandably, I was nervous and a little scared when I put on my best "confused" look and stuck my head in Patrick's door in the morning. He looked up, irritated that he was interrupted from whatever he was doing and asked, "What do you want?"

Ah, that Lowers charm. "Good morning to you too," I beamed to his now scowling face. "I need your help," I continued. I knew that would butter up his ego.

"You've got two minutes," he said and looked at his watch as if he were timing me.

So over the next almost two minutes I gave him bits and pieces of what Spencer and I had discovered veiled in uncertainty as to how to budget with the confusing and fragmented history of numbers. I was cautious not to sound suspicious or accusing, forcing myself to control my voice in speed and tone. When I finished, I sighed and said, "So, that's it, but your budget is due on Friday and I don't want my part to hold you up. Have you got time to help me?"

I don't know for sure what part of the spiel of information tidbits did it, but something piqued his interest. He woodenly reached across the desk and asked me to hand him all of the pooled reports. As I did, I was watching him carefully to gauge his reaction and he suddenly looked up and met my gaze. Then I saw as clear as rain that he knew he was going to uncover something damning and his face showed both intrigue and excitement. He quickly looked away and told me he would look at the budget and see what he could figure out. "I'll just enter the information into the budget for you since you couldn't pull it together," he tossed at me as I was leaving. What a peach!

I muttered, "Thank you," and turned the corner to go back to my office, relieved of the burden and glad that I had thrust it upon the pit bull of banking that was Patrick Lowers. It was just like him to see this as an opportunity that would catapult him into the upper ranks of the bank. At least Spencer and I could surreptitiously watch how the process unfolded now without being involved. It was sure to be quite a show.

CHAPTER 16

It was Monday and Greg was tired to the bone this morning. He and his family had spent a wonderful week of vacation in Ocean Isle Beach at a condo on the Intracoastal Waterway. While the condo was a short eight miles from his home in Shallotte, it seemed miles away from the reality of banking. He and his son, Grant, had taken the boat out several times to fish, catching enough Spanish mackerel for dinner one day. His wife, Kendra, and daughter, Sydney, stayed on the beach and basked lazily in the sun until the boys returned. Then they would all pile into the boat, anchor at one of the unpopulated spoil islands and swim until the sun slipped slowly below the horizon. The week sped by and Greg savored every minute with his family away from the stress and drama at work. Before he was ready, he realized it was Saturday and the dread of the coming week returned with a vengeance as they were packing the car up to return home.

Since the merger, work had been drudgery. He loved his employees but detested his manager, Patrick Lowers, with a passion. Quite frankly, Lowers was just an opportunistic, brown-nosed idiot. How someone so dumb could advance so far up the ladder was telling of the organization that now employed him. Furthermore, motivation was very difficult to muster when he knew that he was so intellectually ahead of a simpleton like Lowers. Greg constantly felt that Lowers was working to undermine him, taking credit that was not his and making small decisions into career-threatening issues. Work was a challenge just anticipating the next shoe to drop. It was petty and demoralizing. Weren't they all on the same team after all?

So as he turned the key to enter the bank, he sighed deeply, breathing in all of the positive and confident vibes he could in those last seconds outside. He put on his upbeat face and went inside. He knew half of his job was to keep the producers in this area motivated and challenged. For Rita and Spencer at the main office and the handful of managers in the beach offices, that meant protecting them from Lowers' bullshit and deflecting the attention most of the time to Dylan, Peter and Tripp, the commercial buffoons on Lowers' team who funneled their loans through Jeff Malone, the senior credit officer. It also meant staying off Lowers' radar personally. His only personal protection came from George Everett who had insisted that Greg stay on the management team after merger. Not that George really would protect him if the going got rough. Greg knew that George would take care of George first and everybody else second. He had proven that fact by not raising hell when

Lowers was named City Executive. George had always been overconfident, though, and Greg was sure he didn't even see that Lowers was a threat to his job security.

As he walked through the empty lobby, the silence was welcome and only after he rounded the corner did he see Rita walking into her office, a half-smile on her face. Before she saw him, he stood watching her from the doorway stacking paper on her credenza with her back to him. She was always so even-keeled and satisfied. "Good morning," he finally said.

She turned, smiling broadly and genuinely, "So you DID decide to come back from Shangri-La, huh? Welcome back!" and she walked around the desk and casually hugged his neck.

He said, "So you DID miss me a little, huh?" Rita's raised eyebrow was all the answer he needed. "Is Chief Lowers in the office yet?" he asked by pointing his head in the general direction of his office.

"Yea, and methinks he is on the warpath, too. This budget has got him in a tizzy because, like everything else he controls, he wants to be the man of the hour with the big dogs on Friday. Not that he gets any help around here, right?" she snorted.

"Tell me 'Welcome back' again, huh?" and he winked and let her get back to work.

Breathing deeply one more time, he rounded the corner and went into his office and sat down. He began opening mail and checking messages as he waited to be ambushed with Lowers' "crisis of the week." As always, Greg was certain that the second Patrick knew he was back, he would hear those pounding footsteps coming toward his office to begin the process of punishing him for taking vacation. Within the hour, all the rest and relaxation accumulated in the prior week would be drained out of him, drop by drop. It was going to be a very long day.

Chapter 17

Ross arrived in Shallotte right around eleven o'clock and headed straight to his folks' house to unload Jinx and his luggage. He hoped his mom had a pot of her coffee waiting for him and that they could sit outside on the porch and catch up. It was a glorious late summer day, and the humidity and oppressive heat of the dog days of just a few of weeks ago were long gone, replaced by a deep blue sky, a light cool breeze, 75-degree temperatures and abundant sunshine.

He couldn't wait to kayak down the Shallotte River to near Windy Point. There, hidden from the world and the crazy development of the past few years, was a fresh-water lake where snowy egrets and blue herons flocked by the hundreds to nest, mate and just perch without human interference. The property was owned by the Bellamy family, and thank God they couldn't get along. A family dispute had kept the real estate from being chopped up into pieces for two generations. As a result, the Point was about a 125-acre peninsula with only a double-wide trailer at the entrance and an old log cabin that had served as a hunting lodge since the 1800s. Being there was truly like stepping back in time. It was serene, awe-inspiring and unspoiled.

When Ross was in middle school, old man Earl gave Ross permission to camp on the property so he could sit and watch the birds or fish in the river. They had struck up a friendship the instant that Earl caught him sitting on a blanket with his camera, a bag of boiled peanuts and a thermos of hot chocolate. When Earl asked him what his business was, Ross "shushed" him and pointed to the huge blue heron stalking a fish just a couple of feet away. Earl respected the land and immediately saw the same quality in the young man trespassing on his land. After the bird was long gone, Ross and Earl talked until the sun was setting over Bacon Island. Ross asked if he could come back and camp sometime. Earl told him that he could as long as he shared the fish he caught and printed him up a couple of the pictures Ross took. For years to come, Ross would stop by with a string of fish, cleaned and ready to fry and check in on him. Sometimes, he would fry the fish up for Earl, especially when the arthritis gnarled his fingers and hands so badly that it made even picking up the frying spider painful.

Earl died about five years ago, having lived to just shy of his 90th birthday. Ross missed him dearly and every time he docked his kayak on the banks at the back of the Point, memories of Earl flooded back. Earl was buried within sight of the lake and Ross knew that there was no more peaceful place, nor perfect place for the old codger to spend eternity.

Chapter 18

The information in front of him was so damning, so exciting, that Patrick had to work diligently to curb his enthusiasm. Finally, he could see his path to the top without the roadblocks of intellectuals, prodigies and second-generation favorites. Besides, he had proof of criminal activity that would not only rid him of his competition at the bank, but could put the crooks behind bars… for a very long time. Serves the bastards right.

He had worked for years to move to where he was right now while the handsome, connected, and brilliant seemed to be on an express track. Well, today was the day that everything changed for him. His gravy train was pulling into the station.

Focus, Patrick. First, he planned to organize a meeting after hours to lay out the information. Then, tomorrow morning, after the future jailbirds got to try to sleep knowing they had been exposed, he would call John Starr. Starr was the head of the bank security department, and he was a barracuda. A former CIA agent, he was a hulk of a man with a piercing stare and a cunning intuition. He was also extraordinarily bright. Having worked with the perpetrators for years, he would be after blood because he didn't uncover the activity himself. Finally, Patrick would take his place among the top management at the bank, having rooted out the network of criminals who had cost the bank millions of dollars. He would be labeled a hero, and it was about time.

Better yet, he would organize a staff golf outing as a cover for the unveiling, waiting until the end of the evening to corner the rats responsible for the fraud. He picked up the telephone and called Sea Trail to organize the event.

After he booked the Byrd course for the afternoon, he composed an e-mail to the management team, the commercial team and the sales team, all ten of whom played golf. Then, before he hit send, he picked up the telephone and called George Everett. He, of course, had to be present to watch the saga unfold.

Mary Ann answered the phone on the first ring and her irritatingly chipper voice sounded like nails on a chalkboard to his ears.

"American One Bank, how may I help you?" she said.

"Mary Ann, I need to speak to George," he all but barked.

"I'm sorry, Patrick, but he's on the phone with Greg."

"Then tell him I'm on the phone and I'll tell Greg to call him back later," he said.

"Hold on, please," and she put him on hold before he could answer.

Patrick immediately shot Greg an e-mail telling him to get off the phone with George and to call him back later. After what seemed like ten minutes, George picked up on the other end of the call.

"What's got you in such a dither this morning, Patrick?" he asked.

"Nothing, George, it's just that I've scheduled a team outing at Sea Trail Friday to celebrate the completion of the budget, and I wanted to give you as much lead time as possible to get you here," he fibbed. "We've had a good year, but I know next year is going to be even more exceptional and we can't celebrate without the head honcho, can we?" he added.

"Patrick, what's gotten into you? You're actually rewarding your team? You must be ill," George said as he unleashed his hyena-like laugh. "I'll be there. Send me an e-mail invitation with the details. I'll see you then," and he hung up the receiver into Patrick's ear.

Smug bastard, Patrick thought. This whole affair went down on your watch, asshole. Well, sayonara.

Patrick reviewed the e-mail invitation to the whole team and added George to the list. He hit the send button, sat back and smiled to himself. The anticipation for Friday was going to kill him.

Chapter 19

The electronic invitation flashed up on his screen while he was in the middle of reading the latest market share report. Why in the world was he invited to play golf in Shallotte when he was here in Raleigh? Some idiot must have forgotten to take his name off of the distribution list, Ivey thought. He looked at the organizer and quickly composed an e-mail to Patrick Lowers to point out the error.

Not even 20 seconds passed before his telephone rang, a Shallotte number popping up in the caller-id screen. Spencer or Rita? Which sister was playing a trick on him? He decided to call the culprit out immediately. "Do you miss me that much?" he said as he picked up the receiver.

"Ivey, this is Patrick Lowers," was the reply from the receiver. Crap.

"Sorry, did you get my e-mail, Patrick?" he asked as he tried to recover his professionalism.

"I did, but the invitation was not sent by mistake. I want you to be here to celebrate the last year and the completion of the budget, and before you say no, I have already cleared it with Micah Brand. You certainly had a hand in everything that's happened here in Shallotte," Patrick finished.

Trying not to let his utter contempt for the controlling bastard come through, Ivey took a deep breath before responding. Furthermore, Patrick's conversation with Micah Brand, the regional president for the Raleigh/Triangle, positioned him so that he couldn't say no and not be a heel. "Well, then, I'm flattered to be included. I would like to ask a favor, though," he said.

"What favor?" Patrick asked, amused that he would be so direct.

"I want to be in the golf foursome that includes Rita and Spencer. They know exactly how bad my game is, plus we can catch up that way. Think you can fit me in there?" he finished.

"Sure," Patrick said. "I'll see you Friday. Eleven a.m. sharp," and he hung up before Ivey could accept the invitation or even say goodbye.

Suddenly, the pit from years gone by was back at the bottom of his belly and it was deeper and darker than before. Ivey had an eerie feeling that his mounting fear meant that Shallotte had a big pile of trouble and, most disturbing, he was sure that this trip was somehow going to propel it right into the proverbial fan.

Chapter 20

The Shallotte main office was buzzing with gossip, excitement, confusion and surprise no more than 15 minutes after each invitee had received and opened Patrick's invitation to play golf on Friday, as in three days away. Spencer buzzed me on the phone immediately.

"Have you had breakfast?" she asked as soon as I picked up the receiver.

"No, but I'm not sure I can get out for an hour this morning," I sighed.

"Baloney, woman. You are going with me to the Waffle House if I have to drag your skinny ass there," she said. "To the car before we're missed."

I had to laugh. Resisting Spencer really is futile. Besides, going MIA meant not having to face any questions that might betray our secret. I gathered my purse, told Mary, the teller supervisor, that I would be back in an hour and hit the front exit, just seconds behind Spencer who had already made her escape out the back door.

As she drove down Main Street, Spencer said, "Well, he didn't waste any time, did he? Damn..." She expressed my sentiments so exactly that all I could do was ape the one word.

"Damn is right. Did you see who was invited?" I asked, and she turned to me and simply nodded. I sighed, a mix of fear and apprehension. "What have we done, Spencer?"

"The right thing and you know it," Spencer said as we pulled into the crowded parking lot. "Come on. At least we can eat since we can't drink or be merry" and she held the door as we walked into the local morning hotspot for fresh-brewed coffee, awesome pecan waffles and what we called "in-the-open privacy." Waffle House always had two televisions blaring, each on a different channel, a large group of retirees, yelling at each other because none of them could hear and they were all too vain to wear hearing aids, and two or three families with screaming toddlers and rambunctious kids anxious for food.

We sat down in a corner booth and ordered our usual. Diet Coke, scrambled eggs, crisp bacon and grits for Spencer, black coffee, a pecan waffle and sausage links for me. We didn't even need to look at a menu. While we waited on the food to arrive, we tried to figure out what the power crazy, ever-conniving Patrick Lowers was planning.

"I mean, *golf*? What is he thinking?" Spencer started. "What's he going to do, club the culprits with his five-iron? He's an idiot."

"Don't underestimate him, Spence," I said. "He is one of the craftiest, most devious idiots around and that makes him dangerous. I'm sure he has his plan for attack perfected. What do you think he's been doing in his office since I left his office on Friday morning? He's lying in wait, hoping to blindside his prey when they least expect it."

Our waitress appeared for refills and we asked for the check, wanting to get back to the office before we were missed. "Already taken care of, girls," she said and as she moved to the next table, Spencer's eyebrows raised so high I thought they were going to get permanently stuck in her hairline. Before I could turn around, I felt a hand on my shoulder. Busted, I thought.

Suddenly, Spencer was smiling. I looked up and saw Ross standing beside me, pretending to zip his lips. "So *this* is where you come to make your great escape? Sad, but effective. Mind if I join you?" and he slid in beside me, the answer a foregone conclusion.

I could hardly breathe so intoxicating was his presence, and I had to pinch myself to make sure he was not just a figment of my imagination. "What are you doing in Shallotte at the Waffle House?" I managed to get out without sounding like a complete dingbat.

"That sounds like a line from a movie, you know," he said and I blushed from head to toe. Amused, he looked over at Spencer, including her in the conversation. "So what are you women over here planning? And the bigger question, how can I horn in? I'm down at my folks on vacation for the week and I've got to have some kind of contact with the banking world, right? How about a round of golf? Spencer, I've heard that should be right up your alley," and he smiled at her and I knew that she, like me, was captivated completely.

Suddenly, I remembered Friday's tourney of terror devised by Patrick Lowers and I had an idea. In a split-second, I volunteered, "You could keep Spencer and me company at the local bank golf outing on Friday!" Spencer's shock was priceless. "I know Patrick would be thrilled to include you or better yet, rub elbows with you. Come on, say you'll come."

I could see the wheels turning in his head, but all he would offer is, "Well, we'll see, okay?"

Knowing that I could spend all day just looking at and listening to him, I was sure if I didn't get back to work I would convince him that I was as empty-headed as the conversation I seemed to have around him. "I've got to get back to work. I hope to see you Friday, Ross. Thanks for breakfast," I said, tearing myself from the booth. He held his hand out to help me up and when I took it, the electricity that passed between us took my breath away. When I looked up and met his gaze, he smiled broadly.

"I hope to see you Friday too. I'll make Rita buy you a beer, okay? She has a bank credit card for a reason, right?" Spencer chuckled. "Let's go Ri. Thanks for breakfast, Ross."

I think I floated out the door and into the car. I got in, closed the door and looked over at Spencer who was laughing at me. "What?" I said.

"You, my sister, have got it BAD," and she cranked the car and laughed at me the whole way back to the bank.

CHAPTER 21

When the e-vitation first popped up on his computer screen, his gut told him that more was going on than just some end-of-budget celebration. The gathering felt much more like an ambush. Lowers was the hunter and he was the prey. He could feel his palms sweating now just thinking about being shot down by such an idiotic prick.

But just watching Lowers prance around so sure and cocky, and he knew. Patrick Lowers had a secret. Furthermore, the secret had to be huge, bad for somebody else, good for Lowers because nothing else fazed the heartless bastard.

Well, he was not going to go down without a fight. He picked up the phone and called in some reinforcements and some favors. He had worked too long and too hard to get to where he was right now. The sins of his past had been erased, and he had long since purged himself of the guilt of being involved in such a scheme. It was an elaborate play and he had his part. He had been handsomely rewarded for his role too.

So without any maudlin thoughts or concerns, he called in his muscle. Mr. Lowers needed a reality check about how the bank in Shallotte worked and his proper place in the pecking order. After a two-minute "you-know-what-to-do" conversation on that front, he placed the next call to his "shield." After all, if the whole plan came to light, he certainly was not the general. Not by a long shot.

After he hung up, he felt better. He had scanned the list of invitees on the e-mail again. All of the troops were out of the foxholes and would be in place should the golf outing become a battlefield. And while right may not be on his side, might certainly was. "Strength in numbers," he thought. How ironic. Numbers got him into this mess up to his ass and, now, numbers would surely save it.

Chapter 22

George Everett was what most people would coin "a player" at Mid-Atlantic. He was one of the largest individual shareholders at the bank, having bought up tens of thousands of shares in the fifteen years when he was coming up the ranks at Mid-Atlantic. He also amassed thousands of stock options, 63,500 shares to be exact, some at $2 per diluted share. When American One announced its acquisition of Mid-Atlantic, George was thrilled. In his role as president of the banking subsidiary, his 270,000 shares became 360,000 shares and, at $30 per share, he became a big man in a big world, assuring him of a plum assignment in the American One banking hierarchy. Sure enough, when the merger happened, he was named the regional executive. He moved to Wilmington, but kept his ties strong in Brunswick County where he spent a large percentage of his time.

George was a good ol' boy of the highest order. He learned early in his banking career that to get to where he wanted to go, i.e. the top, he had to give the people who could help get him there what they wanted. He had never wasted time on the masses and their silly, petty dreams of achieving the ordinary. No, he instead concentrated on the movers and shakers in town that were one loan shy of hitting the big time. When they made it, and many of them did, George never let them forget that he got them there. He "owned" the local state senator, a large portion of the deputies at the sheriff's department, the head of the North Carolina Department of Transportation Board and the chief district judge in Brunswick County.

His one failure, a total lapse in judgment, was trying to help bolster the Jarman family. They were the biggest collection of social degenerates imaginable. He had tried over and over to help them find success in a string of failed ideas—real estate, amusements, and restaurants. The ideas were sound, but the family had the customer service skills of a grizzly bear. Why, over the years, George had loaned them upward of $11 million, most of the time $250,000 or less at a time to stay below the review threshold at the bank and within his loan authority, and they had repaid less than one quarter of it back, not including the interest. The bank had only recouped $2.8 million back from the sale of real estate collateral that had originally been valued at $10 million. The huge office and retail development in Shallotte never got off the ground and the loan proceeds ended up the noses of the Jarman family.

Quite frankly, he hated the bastards, but if he was honest with himself, he knew that his association with the boys of the family had saved his ass more than one time. He still owned them because he refused to seek judgments against them when all of their loans went bad. So now the Jarmans were like his own personal bodyguards. Well, his and the dream team of guys with whom he had surrounded himself at the bank. He had tied up all of the loose ends by helping along a crew of young bankers in whom he had seen much of himself over the years. He promoted them early and often, paid them handsomely and provided them with perks that the other bankers envied. In return, he only demanded loyalty.

Over the years each time he moved up the corporate ladder, he pulled his crew up with him rung by rung. After he was promoted beyond a direct lending role, he still wielded his power to help people who could help him obtain the money they needed. He simply picked up the phone and called one of the guys to get the loan done.

The process had worked smoothly for almost fifteen years until the merger with American One. For a long while, George had sat idly by and observed the people in the new hierarchy and the processes over which they held sway. Before long, he had pulled several of the American One guys under his wing and he was once again able to resume his influence throughout southeastern North Carolina by providing the cash needed to make things happen.

Several times in the past threats to his system would crop up. None to date had proven too serious because he had been able to nip the problems in the bud through relocation, resignation or retribution. Whatever it took, he thought. Several people had happened upon information on the loans, questioned it and then let it go. Others had tried to undermine some of his guys when a few of the loans to the Jarmans had gone sour, unable to see a pattern but complain loud enough or often enough that they had to be removed from the area, most of the time through a wonderful new opportunity elsewhere in the banking network. Finally, one fool resorted to blackmail, so badly wanting to bring him and his successful entourage of wonder bankers to their knees. Blackmail, though, is a funny business because everybody has something to hide and what can't be uncovered can certainly be manufactured when you have deviants like the Jarmans on your team. The poor fool in question loved easy women and it wasn't long before he not only lost his wife when she learned of his infidelity, but was pulled over after leaving a bar and given a DWI. The next morning, he blew his brains out in his garage, a broken failure of a banker, a husband and a man.

Collateral damage, he thought. Only one more year of this business and he was out. Everybody was envious of his planned retirement at fifty-five, but quite frankly, it scared George to death. He loved his job right now. For example, he was excited about the golf tournament in Shallotte this week. He got to be the big man in town for the day-- press the flesh, have a few beers, flirt with Spencer, ogle Rita and check in with his crew. Besides, the weather was supposed to be a perfect seventy degrees and sunny with a light wind. What a life! After retirement, that power, that presence would be gone. Oh well, every plan has to have a conclusion and the close calls over the years had convinced him that banking was changing so quickly with added regulations that the party was coming to an end. That's okay, he thought, his last year was going to be a helluva last hurrah.

Chapter 23

I knew I should not have come into the office today, but if I am responsible for the daily reports, I am going to get them done. "Take a deep breath, Rita," I said to myself. I had one hour to get the reports completed and get over to Sea Trail for the bank golf outing. Besides, I was already dressed and ready to go. I looked to the picture of my grandfather Miller, positioned to the right of my computer since I had been in banking, for inspiration. He was the first Miller banker. I had followed in his footsteps. I had big shoes to fill. He always reminded me that a career is built one day at a time. Right now, I was living minute to minute.

Working quickly but carefully, I was a woman on a mission, trying to beat the clock. Finally, as I hit "send" I stood and stretched to the ceiling, my golf shirt slightly rising up my midriff.

"Wow!" I suddenly heard from my doorway. Startled, I quickly composed myself and turned to see Dylan leering in at me.

Yuck, I thought.

"Dylan, what are you doing here?" I said, knowing the jerk had robbed me of several years of my life.

"Just tying up some loose ends, that's all. Hey, you want to ride over to Sea Trail with me?" he asked.

Well, I would rather have eaten sand than ridden with Dylan the three-and-a-half miles to Sea Trail. He wore his department store cologne so strong that I was sure if I was not in a coma by the time we arrived, then I would at the very least feel like I needed another shower. He was a modern-day lounge lizard trapped in a banker's suit. *Be nice, Rita*, I told myself.

"Thanks, Dylan, but I have already made plans to drive home and ride over with Spencer," I gladly said. "I'll see you there, though!" And I turned around, hoping he would just go away.

"Okay, but I hope you're in my foursome so I can enjoy that pretty little skirt all day! See you shortly," and mercifully, he left.

Where in the world was my Lysol anyway?

Chapter 24

Dylan Fordham was 37 years old and twice divorced. He had been in Shallotte for five years having moved here as the commercial banking manager with American One. He brought his two buddies, Tripp and Peter, with him from Laurinburg where he was the area executive. Some of his co-workers thought he was crazy to take what seemed like a title demotion, but Dylan knew he would be a superstar in Shallotte which was experiencing unprecedented growth. He had also known George Everett for about ten years since he went through the Advanced Commercial Lending program at East Carolina University. George had taken an immediate interest in Dylan and told him that he reminded him of himself in much younger days. George also told him that if he ever got the opportunity to move to the area, he should take it. Five years later, that opportunity came and Dylan jumped on it, leaving behind two ex-wives and his bad reputation as a playboy.

He loved Shallotte immediately and joined the local country club at Sea Trail where he purchased himself a patio home on the sixth fairway of the Jones course. Dylan also fell right into the dating game in the area, asking out the hottest arm candy in the county.

He would wine and dine each for several weeks and occasionally months, promising fidelity and excitement long enough to get in her pants. Then, without any explanation, he would move on, leaving some heartbroken and distraught, others angry and vengeful. He just didn't need the hassle of being tied down. Besides, you don't have to pay for an ex-girlfriend like an ex-wife.

When he was younger, he had longed for a wife who would tend his house, cook his meals and put out for him on demand. After he graduated from college, he married his high school sweetheart, Jenny, ready to set up house as he began his career in banking. She never worked, having dropped out of the cosmetology program at the community college, after they wed.

For about six months the marriage was great. He would come home to her, sometimes greeting her with flowers. Dinner would be on the table and after they ate, they would retire to the bedroom for an evening of sex.

Then, things began to change. Jenny complained about being bored, complained about not having what the neighbors had, complained about housework. She put on weight, withheld sex when she was angry and quit cooking altogether. Life sucked.

He thought Jenny was an ungrateful bitch and he found her less and less attractive each day. He increasingly sought refuge at the local country club, honing both his golf game and his flirting skills. He would tell her he was going out of town on business, he was going golfing, he was going hunting, he was going anywhere but home. Finally, after a weekend of steamy sex with a young waitress at a condominium in Myrtle Beach, he went to the house, packed his bags and walked out of the marriage after just 13 months.

Eager to move on, he offered Jenny the house, her car, their savings account and $1000 a month for living expenses. Against the advice of her lawyer, she just laughed at him. She wanted to string him up by his jewels in public with a nasty divorce. In the end, she screwed herself. The court ordered them to sell the house, each keep a car and divide the savings. He was also required to pay her a flat $50,000. He borrowed the money from the bank, paid Jenny through her attorney, and he was free.

He lived life recklessly for two more years until he met Lucinda, a local attorney who, by any fool's standards, had a smoking hot body and exuded sex appeal by the way she walked, talked and looked at you. Dylan was smitten by her instantly.

She flirted with him shamelessly, but coyly resisted his advances. When he asked her out, she said, "No, not now" and smiled as she tossed her hair and walked away. She was driving him crazy and she knew it. Even so, Dylan couldn't help himself.

One afternoon at the club, she came up to him completely unexpectedly, put her hand around his waist and leaned over and whispered, "Now" in his ear. As she pressed her breast up against him, he wasn't sure he was going to make it to his condo he was so turned on. She began ripping his clothes off before they got to the door and they fell on the floor just inside the door. She straddled him right on the floor, humped him until he came and aroused him again and again begging him to give her more. She was insatiable and he was her sex slave.

The sex was always wild and hot, with Lucinda whispering illicit fantasies in his ear, begging for it harder, faster, each and every time. The night he asked her to marry him, she asked Dylan to do things to her that would make even Hugh Hefner blush, but he did.

They got married at town hall, and they flew to Las Vegas for their honeymoon. For a wedding gift, she brought in a prostitute for a threesome and when he was exhausted from servicing both of them, Lucinda serviced her some more and made her service him and then her again. He never thought he would tire of sex with her, but damn, he was spent. He was also a little more than concerned that while the threesome turned him on, Lucinda seemed to enjoy the girl-on-girl action just a little too much.

For the next three years, they would return again and again to Vegas for these ménage-a-trois encounters. In between, the sex at home never stopped either. He was one lucky bastard and he knew it, but he became crazy with her flirting when they were in public and the jealousy took its toll on his sanity. She would bate him with stories of rubbing up against another woman's breasts, accidentally backing into a male co-worker in the elevator, and realizing that he had a hard-on, she would smile at him over her shoulder as she left. She was maddening.

Finally, he came home sick one day and found her in their bed having sex with another woman. She was unapologetic and begged him to come join them. Sick before arriving and sicker now, he left with a suitcase and went back to his old condo. He just couldn't do this anymore.

The divorce was amicable and quick. He wanted nothing from the relationship. She just wanted confidentiality from him. He agreed to pay her for his half of the house and he was free. Or so he thought. For years, she would taunt him in his dreams. When he saw her in public, she would secretly lick her lips, touch her breast, or touch a co-worker, male or female, intimately to tease him. As a result, he increasingly left home on weekends for the beach where he didn't see her or hear her name. During the week, his best friends, Tripp and Peter, helped by playing golf with him each evening. He cut his handicap to a six and met a whole new group people with whom he could socialize.

It took a year, but he got over Lucinda. Dylan began dating again, but after being used so heartlessly, he was detached and uncommitted. The women he saw ate it up. They wanted him even though he gave them nothing. The sex was satisfying, but hey, after Lucinda, everything paled in comparison.

Two years later, he moved to Shallotte and coaxed Tripp and Peter to do the same. The bank here was poised for explosive growth and professionally, he knew he could be a superstar here. Personally, he left the past behind him and turned to a clean page where he could write his own rules. Women were a diversion but never a distraction. His work was his wife now.

One day, he was going to call the shots here. After five years, he knew that he would have to climb over Greg, Jeff and Patrick when George retired next year, but he was ready and waiting. Nothing and nobody could stop him now.

Chapter 25

Ross arrived at Sea Trail an hour before the first of the local bankers rolled into the parking lot. He had unloaded his clubs, eaten breakfast and was positioned strategically so he could feign reading the newspaper and take in 100 percent of the conversations, actions and attitudes of everybody when they arrived. Only Patrick Lowers knew he was coming today. Well, he was sure Spencer knew he would show, and he hoped Rita hoped he would.

The first of the crew to arrive was Greg Hardy. He had pulled up and was having a congenial, warm conversation with the course superintendent about his son's hole-in-one at a teen tournament the week before. Greg seemed like a decent sort but Ross had been unable to find much in the way of background on him in not only his years at the bank, but the years prior as well. He had definitely kept a low profile.

Greg was well-liked by the bank's management and well-respected by his peers and subordinates. He was also well-read which allowed him to discuss with ease a variety of topics that were interesting to virtually anybody he encountered professionally or socially. He was self-assured but not overconfident and cocky like so many of the wonder bankers at Mega.

"Speaking of cocky…" thought Ross. Wheeling up in his black, look-at-me-everybody BMW convertible was Dylan Fordham. He was surely one of the slickest, most self-absorbed individuals in the employ of the bank. Dylan got out of his car, tossed the keys to the cart attendant, pointed his finger at him and told him to be careful with his baby. Next, he sauntered over to the snack bar to use his latest pick-up lines and compliments on the bar maiden. She saw him coming and had a look on her face that said, "I'll throw your sorry ass out again if I must." Yep, he was a regular here.

Dylan had been successful in banking, though. He consistently was one of the top commercial lenders within the organization. He primarily made acquisition and development loans in the area, but as real estate slowed, he was quick to adjust his portfolio to include long-time operating companies and some owner-occupied construction/permanent loans.

Outside of banking, Dylan had a full social calendar, too. He dated many of the daughters of the local, well-to-do businessmen, many of them divorced once or twice as well. He was active at the local chamber of commerce, had headed up the last two United Way campaigns and managed to keep his golf handicap at a respectable six.

Now, he had found Greg and was bending his ear about the teams and how he always got put together with Peter, Tripp and Laurel Meadows, the manager at Calabash. Greg pretended to be listening, but it was evident to Ross that he had gone into "screen-saver mode" two or three seconds after Dylan walked up.

People were starting to arrive fairly steadily now. The manager at Holden Beach, Viv Thomas; the manager at Ocean Isle Beach, Len Allen; and Peter Wenchell and Tripp Barrows from the main office were now crowded around the carts outside, checking the pairings. Jeff Malone, the senior credit officer, strode through the clubhouse with his putter, quickly saying hello to everyone so he could get to the putting green before the round began.

Suddenly, like a bull in a china shop, a black SUV roared up, crammed full of people and equipment. He smiled and thought, "That must be Spencer Cashwell," and she and Rita and Ivey Jones poured out into the small crowd building in the lobby, the whole place taking on a party-like atmosphere with their arrival. Ross knew that Spencer had spent hours choosing out the perfect golf outfit and shoes for today, not for anybody here, but for herself. She looked like a cross between an LPGA professional and a movie star when she hit the links, choosing to spend her money to fit the part. The guys swamped her like a wave, fighting to carry her clubs, get her a drink, and park her car. She was genuine and funny, not to mention blond and beautiful. How could the fools resist her?

Rita was her usual carefree, gorgeous self this morning and while the masses clung to every word out of Spencer's mouth, Rita almost bowled Ross over by her understated glamour. She was almost always smiling, and the warmth from her smile made her green eyes electric. Her long, curly brown locks had been slightly pulled back and showed her long, ivory neck. She was a stunner, and he knew he had to work diligently today to keep his eyes off of her or else, he would be lost.

Walking toward the clubhouse together from the parking lot, Ross saw Patrick Lowers and George Everett huddled together, deep in serious conversation. Lowers just did not know how to let his hair down. He was the type that wanted to talk banking at weddings and funerals mainly because that was the only world he knew. To the casual observer, the two appeared to be friendly and walking quickly to join the fun. Ross knew, though, that George had no respect whatsoever for Patrick and that he was really racing to the clubhouse to get away from him before he died of boredom. On the flip side, Patrick could barely veil his contempt for George but also never missed an opportunity to brown-nose with him either. Patrick thought George was an idiot and a buffoon and it infuriated him that George was nonetheless outlandishly successful, well-off and connected.

As they hit the door, George broke ranks with Patrick, visibly hurrying away to greet Dylan and Peter at the bar. Patrick, on the other hand, took in the whole room and immediately spotted Ross in the corner. He walked over quickly and shook hands. "Ross, I'm so glad you could join us today. What a nice surprise that you were in town and available to play on such a beautiful day, huh?" he gushed.

"The pleasure is all mine, Patrick," he said. "I just appreciate you letting me crash your celebration while I'm down visiting my folks. Thank you again for the invitation. Looks like quite a turnout. Is your whole team here?"

"They're all here," he said and looked at his watch. "Well, let me round up the crew so we can get started. Did you find your pairing? I put you with Rita and Spencer like you wanted. Ivey Jones, from Raleigh, is your fourth."

"Why is Ivey here from Raleigh?" Ross asked curiously.

"Well, he was the manager here right before the merger so I felt that he had a hand in all of the things that have happened here," Patrick said coolly, "so naturally, I wanted him here. Have a great round and I'll talk to you afterward."

"Naturally..." Ross finished as Patrick yelled to everybody to listen to the rules of the round. Ross had truly been taken off guard with Ivey Jones's inclusion into the celebration. He would have to consider why Patrick *really* invited Ivey later because across the room, Rita saw him and was walking toward him with a smile on her face. He considered his objective for the day and as she drew closer, he realized that his decision to join the celebration certainly included being near Rita Miller. He was suddenly glad he was here and smiled back at her. Yes, Patrick, he thought as he blew out the breath he had unconsciously been holding, thank goodness I'm available on such a beautiful day.

Chapter 26

Everything was perfect, Patrick thought. Today, Patrick had four teams of four. He and George would play together as a twosome, isolated from the rest of the team. He and George would start on hole 5 so they could finish on number four, a long par five where he would lay out what he knew and get to watch George squirm as he realized that his scheme, his career and most importantly, his freedom were finished. Then, as they rolled back up to the clubhouse, George would dismiss himself from the group, a broken man, faced with spending the night trying to sleep knowing he was going to prison. Furthermore, he would probably be on the telephone half the night forewarning his co-conspirators of their imminent professional and personal demise.

To protect himself, Patrick had already outlined in writing the evidence of the scheme that included borrowers, loan numbers, loan officers, and dollars lost. He had even traced the deposit accounts where the proceeds had been funneled on a couple of occasions via wire transfer to Southeast Bank. He was certain the activity in and out of that account would pinpoint every customer, employee and beneficiary of the long-running take. All of the information had been packaged up and sent via U. S. Mail to John Starr, the head of security at the bank. He had also hidden another copy of the information on a disk where he was certain none of the idiotic clods could find it if something happened to the first copy. Trust no one, he thought.

But then again, he did. He trusted Rita. After all, she was truly the one who uncovered the massive fraud whether she realized it or not. Patrick was not sure she did, but he knew one thing for sure. She had trusted *him* with the information and that really meant something. She was wise beyond her thirty-five years as of tomorrow and seemed to relate to everybody by the whole of their character not the balance of their bank account. She often admired the leather-bound, complete volume of Shakespeare at his office his mother had given him when he graduated from college. She had praised his mother's wisdom and asked him if he appreciated the significance of the gesture. When he said that he learned a long time ago there was a correlation between the comedies and tragedies of those ancient works and the current state of the world of banking and bankers, she had nodded and he knew that while Rita Miller may not like him, she trusted his judgment.

Patrick wondered how George Everett would react once his professional demise was at hand. Would he break down and beg? Hardly, Patrick thought.

Maybe he would offer to "cut Patrick in." Oh, please, let me have the chance to turn him down. Finally, if he thought about trying to start a physical confrontation on the course, Patrick was certain he could take the 55-year-old chain smoker hands-down.

He took a deep breath, satisfied that today was the last time he would ever have to answer to George Everett again. As Patrick walked to the cart, George was already seated in the driver's seat. Naturally.

"Patrick, you want to make today interesting?" George chirped.

"Today is going to be *interesting* anyway, George," he replied. "What did you have in mind?"

"I was thinking a dollar a hole, even head-to-head. You in?"

"Make it five dollars a hole, George. I'm going to start a hot streak today," Patrick said smugly.

George bellowed his hyena-like laugh again. "That's just the feeling you get before you go down in flames, boy! You're on. C'mon, let's roll!" and away they rode to tee off the day.

Chapter 27

"Okay, Rita, do you want to drive or do you want to ride?" Ross asked me as we walked together to our cart. I never drive because Spencer, my golf partner ninety percent of the time, thinks I drive like a bat out of hell and have no sense of direction. She's right on her last point, but she is the one who almost put us in the pond while she was driving, talking and texting on her phone at the same time this summer.

"Do you mind driving?" I asked. "I get lost at the supermarket so if you want to get back for the barbeque this evening, you don't want me at the wheel."

"And if I don't?" he asked. "The alternative could be much, much better, you know?" and as he grinned, he faked a huge sigh. "All right, I'll drive today. Let's get out there before Spencer and Ivey send out a search party."

As we drove to hole number three, I looked over at him and tried to figure out what he was really doing here and how I could have been lucky enough to have been noticed by such a smart, successful, handsome man. As hard as I had worked to protect myself from getting hurt, I realized that I was now standing at the edge of a cliff, ready to jump headfirst and enjoy the fall. What in the world is wrong with me?

"Penny for your thoughts?" he asked quietly.

"How about a dime? Inflation, you know," I countered, smiling into his eyes that met mine. "I was just wondering why you were really here?" I said honestly as we drove up behind Spencer and Ivey.

"Hold that thought…" he said as he got out at the white tees and introduced himself to Ivey and spoke to Spencer.

"Oh, I knew you would be here," Spencer snorted. "I saw those wheels turning in your head as soon as Rita mentioned today to you. Everybody has to escape the folks after three or four days of reunion. Let's get this round started. Mr. President, we'll let you have the honor of teeing off first today," and she bowed dramatically. Ivey was stunned, I laughed and Ross just shook his head, smiling broadly as he walked up to the tee box. That Spencer was a hoot.

As I suspected, Ross was a beautiful golfer. He had a natural, easy golf swing that threatened to rip the cover off of the ball as it sailed easily over the water hazard and landed right in the middle of the fairway.

"Nice shot, Pres," Spencer said, "When do you have time to play golf?"

"I don't anymore except when I visit my folks," he said. "Even a blind hog finds an acorn now and then. That shot was probably my best of the day."

"Sounds like my shoulders are going to be sore this afternoon from carrying you people all day," Spencer said.

"You love it. Besides, you have an excuse now for getting your weekly massage," I teased. "Not that you ever need an excuse."

After the first hole, we settled into a comfortable repartee, enjoying the camaraderie and the picture-perfect afternoon. When we made the turn after the ninth hole, Ross and I sat in the sun alone to wait for Ivey and Spencer. Without any preamble, he said, "Why I'm really here is because I like to play golf and I wanted to spend time with you. I really have enjoyed getting to know you. Is that direct enough?"

"Yes," I managed to say.

"But…?" he added.

"But why me?" I blurted and looked him right in the eyes. "Why me?" I asked again, this time more softly.

He sighed and said, "I guess the corporate meeting was just my lucky day, Rita. C'mon." As he stood, he extended his hand to me and pulled me up to him. His eyes never left mine and I knew without a doubt that I was no longer standing on the edge of the cliff. I had jumped and was falling, consumed by the exhilaration and oblivious to the landing.

Chapter 28

When I first moved to Brunswick County, I was twenty-three and full of myself. I was certain that I was the key to transforming the backwater locals into modern-day business men and women with my university education and liberal sophistication. That is, until I met Caleb Capps.

Caleb was a retired high school principal and current real estate broker who sat on the local advisory board for Mid-Atlantic Bank. I met him the first day I worked at Holden Beach and we developed an immediate friendship. In my mind, he was a mix between Aristotle and John D. Rockefeller.

A world traveler and avid reader, Caleb had settled down in Holden Beach after his wife died from cancer, leaving him to raise his son and daughter alone. What began as a trip to the beach from their home in rural Robeson County to grieve and begin healing as a family, ended with his retirement after 20 years as principal to move to the sleepy island permanently to begin a new life as a real estate broker.

He was immediately successful through diligent study and hard work. Some would argue he was just lucky. Others hoped to copy his style. Caleb had two sayings that he repeated to me often. He said "Hope is not a strategy" and "Luck is just a series of decisions, good or bad." I have never forgotten either.

Ten years after he arrived and with both of his children graduated from high school and enrolled at the university in Chapel Hill, Caleb married a wealthy widow from Ocean Isle Beach. He was in love and happy. Over the next two decades, he and his wife, Rena, quietly built a real estate empire that spanned the whole of Brunswick County, from the beaches to growing towns and even tracts of timber and farmland. Caleb wielded influence without applying political pressure and shrewdly negotiated the sale of property with an eye toward bringing business and industry to the county. He championed county-wide infrastructure and planned growth and was instrumental in helping obtain funding for beach renourishment even when state and federal budgets tightened. He was truly progressive.

During the winters of my first two years as the manager of the Holden Beach office, I would visit him almost daily in his oceanfront office and sit and listen to him spin yarns of people and places near or far. He would give me books to read, wonderful books that I had somehow overlooked as an English major at the university. We would ride all over the county and Caleb would tell me the history of each town, the local families and the long-time businesses we passed. I listened intently to his business philosophies that would later shape many of my own. We discussed politics, national and local and even delved into religion, comparing and contrasting Judaism, Islam, Buddhism and Christianity. Interestingly enough, I couldn't tell you if he was a Republican or Democrat or a Baptist or Catholic after knowing him for over 10 years.

Mostly, though, we talked real estate. Caleb fully believed that the ownership of real property was the first big step to financial success, but that every purchase had to be measured for return, sometimes for financial return like return on equity or return on investment but sometimes for return in the emotional sense like enjoyment. Caleb believed that a vacation home and a primary home purchase came back to the same question. When your head hits the pillow each night, are you happy here? Caleb always equated wealth with happiness in life and a sense of satisfaction with and pride in the decisions you make.

When Caleb died last year, he was truly a wealthy man. Thousands of people turned out for his funeral, each sharing a story of his generosity, his kindness and his wisdom. His children and grandchildren listened to each affirmation of the man they loved, smiling and nodding through their tears. As I waited in line to talk to the family, I looked around at the A-list crowd. I could almost see the twinkle in Caleb's eye as I heard him say, "Funerals reveal the character of the living not the dead."

Yep, they were all here glad-handing today, Caleb. The county's slick young sheriff was here making sure everybody saw him. The owners of the other big real estate companies were all in attendance, some out of respect for Caleb, some just relieved that one big competitor was gone. The old name families were here too—the Warrentons, the Carsons and of course, the Jarmans.

Ricky Jarman and his brother, Roger, were right behind me in line to greet the family. Ricky crowded up behind me so close that I could feel his breath on my hair when he talked. I'm sure that was no accident and I quickly moved forward every inch I could to avoid him. Ick!

As I hugged the neck of Caleb's daughter-in-law, Connie, she whispered, "He thought the world of you, Rita."

Moved to tears, I choked, "I'm a much better person because of Caleb. I'm glad he was a part of my life."

As I moved away from the family line, Ricky came up behind me. Not today, I thought. Quickly, I turned and found him leering at me. Trying not to act completely creeped out, I said sweetly, "Did you need something from me, Ricky?"

He chuckled and said sarcastically, "Well, Rita, now that your sugar daddy is gone, I was hoping I could be his replacement."

Without missing a beat I replied, "Well, Ricky, it's too bad for you that hope is not a strategy, huh?" and off I walked leaving him to decipher just what in the world I meant.

Chapter 29

Patrick had played his best round of golf since high school, sure he was buoyed by ending George's run as head honcho. George was down fifty bucks, having lost thirteen holes outright, tied one and won three. As they approached the last hole of the day, Patrick knew that win, lose or tie, George Everett would never forget hole number four of the Byrd course at Sea Trail.

George couldn't wait for the round to be over and be back at the clubhouse enjoying a cold beer with people he actually could stand. "You're up, Patrick," he said. "I'm not sure what's gotten into you today. I've never seen you play so well."

He opened the door, so in I go, Patrick thought. "You want to know what has gotten into me?" When George nodded carefully, he continued, "George, I know your secret."

"My secret? What secret? You beat the crap out of me!" George bellowed.

"Oh, no, not that kind of secret. Your *big* secret. You know, the secret to your success," Patrick stated.

When George looked over at him, Patrick smiled coolly looking him right in the eyes. Then very slowly he said, "Yeah, I KNOW."

George was unflappable, though, and the revelation of his scheme didn't ruffle him whatsoever. He simply stared back at Patrick and calmly said, "You're up, Patrick."

Patrick was thrown a little off-guard by his response, but he knew that George's run as the regional banker in chief was over. George was probably too stupid to realize that someone was thorough enough to piece twenty years of fraud together.

He sliced the ball off the tee around a stand of long-leaf pines and directly into the retention pond. George just chuckled. Patrick took a step back, took a deep breath and realized that George was just trying to throw him off of the scent of the brick now in his pants. He readdressed the ball and put his third stroke three hundred yards down the center of the fairway. Who's laughing now, you old bastard?

George did not speak again until they pulled up to the cart return. He stepped out and walked around to Patrick's side of the cart. "Patrick, thank you for today," he said, extending his hand.

"The pleasure was mine, George. All mine," Patrick said, this time more forcefully, "because I KNOW."

George pulled his hand away and stepped right up to Patrick's face.

Without so much as a blink, he stared coldly into his eyes and whispered, "Sometimes what you KNOW is better left in that gray matter between your ears, Patrick."

"Not this time, George. You're done," Patrick said.

George just shook his head, and with a smile on his lips, he turned and let loose an evil laugh as he casually walked back to the clubhouse.

Chapter 30

As we finished up our round, I was amazed at how quickly the afternoon had passed. As we pulled up to the clubhouse, the room was already teeming with a rowdy excitement. The warm weather and the cold beer were a powerful combination that brought out the playfulness in the group. The barbecue buffet was being set up when we arrived and the rest of the players had crowded around the bar, watching the sports news on the giant flat-screen television in the corner. With only the dinner banquet ahead of us, I didn't want the day with Ross to end there, but I wasn't sure how to move the evening along without coming across easy or foolish.

I needed a second opinion so I asked Spencer if she needed to go "freshen up." All women know the code for "I need to talk to you in private." Why do you think women travel to the ladies' room in packs? Ivey knew the drill, so he turned to Ross and said, "Ross, want to join me for a drink at the bar? We'll save our ladies a seat," and he winked at Spencer and me and walked toward the back of the clubhouse with Ross.

Alone in the bathroom, I asked Spencer what she thought I should do. "Ask him if he can give you a ride home," she said. "Ivey and I are going to stick around here for a while then head out to the Station with Peter, Tripp and Viv. That is, unless you want to join us?"

"No, not that I wouldn't enjoy your company, but…" I just let the sentence fade away, not sure how I wanted to finish it anyway.

"Enough said, ok? He's as hot as lava, woman!"

"He's also the president of the bank," I reminded her.

"God, don't go all conventional on me, Rita! Just do what feels right. You've got good instincts," Spencer said.

I snorted, "And look how well that has worked out for me so far, right?"

Spencer came over and gave me a hug, "So far, you've never met a man worth trying to make it work out well, Rita. I have a good feeling about Ross. Hey, come outside and let me smoke a cigarette before we go back to the table, okay?"

I hated the fact that Spencer still smoked. The rest of us had given up the habit several years ago trying to be healthier, but not Spencer. She smoked when she drank and when she played golf and of course, that would include today. "Okay, sure," I said as we slipped out the back door of the clubhouse to keep from being noticed.

It was a beautiful evening and the sun was setting in the west, slowly slipping behind a big pink cloud on the horizon. As we sat quietly listening to the sound of the cicadas, we suddenly heard angry voices on the other side of the fence beside us. I looked wide-eyed at Spencer and she nodded put her finger to her lips, knowing we needed to be invisible to the conversation.

"...just make it end, you hear me? I'll show that sorry son-of-a-bitch how much he knows...," the voice whispered forcefully.

"Consider it done. He won't know what hit him," the other voice answered.

"I don't want to know. Just handle it, okay?" And with that the side door slammed shut. We could see two large boots walk toward the end of fence. Without a thought, I reached up and opened and shut the door beside us quickly, acting as if we just walked out.

"What a day, woman!" I managed. "That round was one of your best," I continued just as I pretended to sit down. Suddenly, Ricky Jarman came around the fence. He stopped and stared at us, undressing us with his eyes in the cover of dusk.

"Hi, Ricky," Spencer and I said in unison.

"Ladies," he said suspiciously, "What are you doing out here?"

"I just came out here to sin so don't you tell anybody, Ricky," Spencer said. "I do have a reputation to keep up now, don't I? What are you doing here?" she asked.

"I came to have a drink at the bar, but I was turned away because of your get-together. What time are y'all gonna be done?" he asked.

"We just have to eat then we are headed to the Station for a drink if you want to join us," Spencer continued, knowing that he couldn't because he already had plans to put into motion.

"Thanks, but I got to get home tonight. I'll catch up with you another time, though. Ladies," he said and he tipped his dirty baseball cap to us as he disappeared around the edge of the clubhouse. The hair on my neck could not have stood up any straighter.

I turned to look at Spencer and she, like me, knew we had witnessed the beginning of something bad. Suddenly, the cool autumn air caused a chill to run the full of my body and I shivered and stood. I grabbed Spencer's arm and without one word, we quickly went back into the clubhouse, scared to death.

Chapter 31

Ross sized up all 64 inches of Ivey Jones fairly early in the day, and he liked what he saw. Ivey was genuine and intelligent and truly cared about Spencer and Rita like he was their older brother. He was self-deprecating in his humor and did not have a bad thing to say about anybody all day long. Still, Ross wondered why Patrick invited Ivey to the celebration. After the waitress brought them their drinks, Ross sat facing Ivey at the corner table of the bar, waiting on Rita and Spencer to return.

Preferring to be direct, Ross said, "So, Ivey, why do you think Patrick invited you today?"

Without any discomfort, Ivey smiled and said, "I have no idea, but I know there must be some reason. Patrick Lowers always has a plan. Besides, I've never considered him to be one of my biggest fans. He said it was because I was here last year as manager and had a hand in the success of the area, but I'm not really sure. He hasn't said one word to me yet."

Honesty was a trait that Ross admired above all others and he knew Ivey was flush with it. Wanting to find out more, Ross continued, "So did you ever work for Patrick after the merger? Perhaps he wants you back in the Shallotte area in a management role."

"I doubt that!" Ivey said. "I worked for Greg before the merger and left for Raleigh long before Patrick was named the market executive. I, like everybody else, was stunned that Patrick got the position over Greg. Greg was not legacy American One, though, like Patrick." Suddenly, fearing he had said too much, Ivey added quickly, "…not that Patrick didn't deserve the job, though…I'm sorry if I offended you, Ross. I probably have said too much."

"Ivey, I asked your opinion because I wanted it. I understand exactly what you mean. Remember," he chuckled, "I'm not legacy American One either," and with that statement, he quickly put Ivey at ease.

Suddenly feeling trusting, Ivey wanted to open up about the irregularities he discovered in the last couple of months before his departure, but just as he started to speak, he saw Spencer round the corner, white as a ghost with Rita behind her looking quite jumpy too. He stood suddenly and put his hand on Spencer's shoulder, "Are you okay?"

Subtly trying to calm her nerves, she smiled, grabbed her beer from the table and took a big swallow. "I'm just about to die of thirst, that's all. Besides, I just saw Ricky Jarman on an empty stomach. That'll make anybody feel queasy," and she plopped down beside Ivey.

Ross also noticed the expression on Rita's face as she came into the room. She was a little harder to read than Spencer, but she was shaken up too. He saw chills on Rita's arms and asked her if she wanted his jacket. When she said yes and looked into his eyes for the first time since returning, he knew the temperature outside couldn't cause what he saw lurking there--fear. Before he could ask if she needed anything, though, she drank deeply from her red wine and turned to him and quietly asked, "Ross, would you drive me home tonight? Spence, Ivey and a couple of the others are going to the Station and I don't feel up to going. Do you mind?"

"I would be happy to drive you home, but first would you ride around with me while I take a trip down memory lane," he asked and reached his arm around her to wrap her in his coat.

"I can't think of anything I'd enjoy more. Now keep me out of a coma while Patrick wraps up the evening with his speech," and she sighed and casually put her arm on his leg seeking security. As much as it turned him on, he had become very protective of one Rita Miller. Ross knew the lines between his work assignment and his personal life were becoming impossibly tangled. He wasn't sure how this situation with Rita would be resolved, but he knew for certain that as he untangled the problems here step by step, day by day, they would know each other a lot better by the time he wrapped up his case. American One in Shallotte was a powder keg, ready to explode with one careless spark. Normally the impatient type, Ross knew this assignment would take time. He had to be methodical as he carefully tracked down all of the culprits and criminals involved in the long history of financial fraud perpetrated here and all the while keep Rita out of harm's way. Time, he thought as he looked at Rita again. The very sound of the word was like music to his ears.

Chapter 32

After Patrick finished his wrap-up of the prior year, he was walking around the room having individual discussions with several of the people on his team. His presentation had been vague and harped on themes like "a new era for banking in Southeastern North Carolina" and "learning from the mistakes of the past to improve the future of banking." I watched him closely as he strutted around the room, seemingly seeking out various team members for a one-on-one. He had pulled Dylan, Greg, Tripp and Peter aside and now I saw him walking in our direction. What was he up to?

As he approached the table, he looked me squarely in the eyes and smiled the most genuine smile I had ever seen. Oh my. Patrick was on a professional safari and having the time of his life. He was positively giddy and he knew that I knew why. He leaned over and whispered, "Why then tonight let us assay our plot!" and he put his hand on my shoulder in as close to a kind gesture as I had ever seen out of him.

"'All's Well That Ends Well,' right?" I said. He nodded slowly.

Taking his attention away from me, he turned to Ross and extended his hand. As Ross shook his hand, Patrick said, "Ross, I hope you had a good time today. I ordered this weather just for the occasion."

"It has been picture-perfect, Patrick. Thank you again for letting me horn in on your party. You had a great year here in Shallotte and I'm glad I was invited to your celebration," Ross commented.

"We're always glad to showcase Shallotte and its team for the bank's executive management. Ivey, I hope you enjoyed being back in town too. Do you mind if I have a word with you privately?" Patrick said as he held his hand toward a different table, not waiting for Ivey's answer.

Spencer and I looked at each other. Was Ivey involved in the problems in Shallotte in a way we didn't see? As quickly as the thought crossed my mind, it left. No way, no how.

As I watched Patrick and Ivey huddle in the corner, I became keenly aware that Ross had seen our exchange of glances and was gauging my reaction closely. I was ready to go and as I turned to say so, Ross asked, "You ready?"

I simply nodded to keep from screaming an over-eager, "I thought you'd never ask." I turned to Spencer and said, "I'll see you and Ivey tomorrow morning. I'll call you to see what time you want to go to the Waffle House, ok?"

"Ok," she said, "But call a little later than normal since we may not get back from the Station until late."

"You've got it," I said and I stood to go. "Hey, and be careful tonight," I added, the events of the evening present in the look that passed between us.

"You too," she whispered then added, "And don't do anything I wouldn't want to hear about." I smiled. Yep, that was my best friend.

As we turned to go, I looked over to Ivey and waved goodbye. He smiled slightly and blew me a kiss. I suddenly relaxed, knowing Spencer would be out with Ivey tonight. A, Ivey was driving and he drove like a granny, and B, he was staying on her couch tonight. It almost felt like old times. That is, until I felt Ross's hand on my side guiding me to the door. I was suddenly exhilarated, slightly nervous and somewhat breathless as I said my goodbyes and we headed toward the door.

As we walked alone to the car, he asked, "Are you cold?" and without waiting for an answer, he pulled me under his arm and closer to him. I wasn't sure if I was going to collapse or hyperventilate or break out in song. It really could have gone in any direction. Whatever, I never wanted now to end.

As we got to his SUV, he opened my door and went to the driver's side and got in. With a smile as he cranked the engine, he said, "Let's ride, my lady." I sighed and wondered if he had a full tank of gas.

Chapter 33

Ivey got it now. He was in Shallotte to be probed by Patrick Lowers. Actually, interrogated was a more accurate description of the conversation they were having. Patrick was trying to get ammunition for something and Ivey was trying to be diplomatic but not effusive. Patrick began by asking, "So, I know you must miss Rita and Spencer, but do you like Raleigh better than Shallotte?"

Ivey answered honestly, "They are very different markets, Patrick."

"How? I imagine it is harder to get things accomplished in Raleigh as opposed to Shallotte, right?" Patrick probed.

Ivey began to tread lightly, but looked Patrick square in the eye and said, "I'm not sure what you mean."

Seeming to change direction, Patrick asked, "You were hired by George and Greg, right?"

Ivey stated, "Actually, Rita hired me." With that response, Patrick seemed to relax and slid over closer to him discreetly.

"When you were manager, did anything here really bother you, Ivey? Don't hedge your answer, just be direct, ok?" Patrick urged, his voice quieter but much more serious. He looked hard at Ivey, completely silent waiting for an answer.

Ivey instinctively knew Patrick had picked up on the scent of the trail of trouble he had stumbled on just before he left and without any words, he answered with a slight nod of his head. The conversation had taken on a dark, almost dangerous, tone.

"Let me ask you a question," Ivey said. "Why don't you say something to management about the situation, Patrick? I was afraid that nobody would listen to what I had to say."

"I'm not going to SAY anything, Ivey. John Starr will have the written PROOF on his desk tomorrow," Patrick stated quietly but acidly, "Then all the king's horses and all the king's men won't restore their king or their kingdom again, ok?"

Ivey just nodded once more. Nodding back, Patrick shook Ivey's hand firmly, stood and simply said, "I'm glad you came, Ivey. You've got good friends here," then he disappeared into the crowd that was now milling around, ready to move on to a bigger and better place for nightlife. From Shallotte, that destination was the Station.

Ivey, unnerved by Patrick's words, fled to the comfort of Spencer's company. She immediately made him smile when she asked, "What the hell was that all about? He hasn't spoken that much to me in the year he's been in Shallotte. The man is killing my momentum tonight. The Station beckons me brother…let's roll!" Ivey laughed, hooked his arm through hers and headed toward the door.

Chapter 34

As the last of the employees headed for the door, Patrick made sure he made the rounds to talk to almost everyone who was at Mid-Atlantic in Shallotte prior to his arrival. In some he noted curiosity and confusion, in others disdain and discomfort. The whole evening had proven to be extraordinarily interesting to him in a somewhat detached way now that he had figured out the whole scheme, documented his findings and turned it over to security. He sighed, satisfied that while the executive management team may not hail him as a hero, they certainly would admit that he was smart to have pieced together such an elaborate, long-running fraud.

As he headed over to the bar to settle the day's tab, he glanced out the picture window that framed the parking lot. He saw George walking to his car with three or four people tagging along. George appeared to be casually talking to the crew, his left hand comfortably in his pocket, the right subtly moving in rhythm with whatever conversation he was having. There was no urgency in his manner, no panic in his motions. Patrick ordered another Grey Goose and OJ from the bar and turned again to watch George. Now the bastard was laughing as he got into his car and coolly waved goodbye to the remaining employees. Bye-bye, jailbird. I hope your new cellmate takes a real liking to you.

Irritated now, Patrick turned back to the bar. He signed the receipt for the evening and looked down at his watch. It was late. He finished his drink and stood to go. Suddenly, he realized he had had too much to drink. He felt light-headed and strange.

As he made his way to the car alone, he felt sick. He wished he hadn't ordered that last drink. He stopped at his car door and bent over, trying to catch his breath. Okay, Patrick, only two miles to the house, he thought as he opened the door and climbed inside.

His breathing labored now, Patrick cranked the car and drove out of the parking lot onto the highway. He was sweating, shaking. What is wrong with me?

Gasping now, his vision started to blur, but the blue lights behind him were unmistakable. God help me, he thought. As he slowed the car and pulled off the road, he realized he was much more relieved to have help arrive than be scared of a driving-while-impaired charge.

He leaned his head against the headrest and put the window down, praying hard for a breeze against his skin. As he looked up and tried to focus, he tried to form the words, "Help me" as the flashlight hit his eyes. He couldn't speak, he couldn't breathe.

As the light shown around his car, his eyes focused long enough to recognize the face at his window. Then, panic set in. His eyes widened, he wheezed for air. He couldn't move his arms, his legs now.

The car was rolling now and he saw the bridge over the lake at Oyster Bay ahead of him. Suddenly, Patrick knew he was going to die and he knew why. His wife and his girls flashed before his eyes, but the last thing he processed in his conscious mind was his mother, Delores, telling him, "You're not as smart as you think you are, Patrick."

Boy was Mama right.

Chapter 35

Ross stopped the car and we got out to sit by the edge of the Intracoastal Waterway at the end of what is, arguably, the most beautiful road in southeastern North Carolina. Gause Landing Road is a narrow, winding dead-end lane, lined on both sides with enormous, century-old live oaks. The street abruptly ends before a high, grassy bluff that juts out into the water. To the east, the Ocean Isle Beach bridge towers forty feet at the crest of the span that connects the mainland to the eight-mile long island. Tonight, the crash of the ocean waves sounded deafening as it bounced off the concrete behemoth and reflected back toward the mainland.

The autumn air was crisp, gently blowing from the south directly on our faces. I shivered and Ross reached over and pulled me closer to him. I looked at the multitude of stars and spotted Orion almost directly overhead. I broke the silence by confessing to Ross, "I thought the constellation Orion looked like Rudolph the Red-Nosed Reindeer when I was little."

He laughed, looked up and shook his head, "You must have been an interesting child."

"And now...?" I whispered.

He fell onto his back and pulled me over him. He intertwined his fingers in my hair and seriously studied my face. "You've bewitched me, Rita."

I leaned down and kissed him softly, resting on top of him as the waterway, the waves, the breeze and the stars all disappeared from my mind and the world was just us, right now. Ross ran his hand down my arm and I shivered again. Then he pulled me beside him and rolled over on top of me. He kissed me again and this time, the softness was replaced by a raw desire for more.

I felt him against me and I pressed back against him, wanting more, all. He left my lips and explored my neck, my shoulders and the yearning almost consumed me. My hands moved over his chest and his arms, both strong and lean.

Suddenly, the ring from his cell phone pierced the silence, startling me and irritating Ross. He sighed heavily and said, "I've got to take this one. Sorry."

I nodded as he answered the phone and thought how my bewitching talent really lacked timing. I watched him in the moonlight and I saw his face take on a very serious look and heard disturbing, one-word questions and responses like "who?" and "when?" and "yes" and "now." Sadly, I knew the evening was over.

As he ended the call, I asked, "Ross, what is it?"

Without any preamble, he answered, "Rita, I've got to take you home. Patrick Lowers is dead."

Chapter 36

Spencer and Ivey laughed as they walked back into the Station. They were the Cornhole Masters tonight, having been crowned the champions of the outdoor beanbag game by the crowd of drunken fools who were having a hard time picking up the beanbags let alone throwing them the 10 yards into the hole in the wooden target. The Station had a full house tonight, many of its patrons Mega employees congregating to continue the day's festivities. As they grabbed two seats at the bar and ordered another beer, Ivey said, "Man, I wish Rita was here like old times."

"Brother, she is whipped. I'm sure she is having plenty of fun of her own with President Hotstuff," Spencer said.

"You sound and act like you know him well enough to know if he is good for Rita, Spence. Do you?" Ivey asked.

"How do you get to know somebody like him 'well enough' in so short a period of time? I mean, Rita has good instincts, she trusts him and she is attracted to him. It's not like she's bowled over by every good-looking banker, you know?" she replied. "And besides," she continued, "he is charming, available, and successful and he seems to be very protective of her."

"Protective? Why?" Ivey asked. "I saw that flash of fear on your faces when you came back inside from your smoke at Sea Trail. What's going on, Spence?"

Spencer sighed and spun the barstool around to face Ivey squarely. She looked into his face and reached her hand over and brushed his. "There is some heavy duty crap going on at the bank in Shallotte, Ivey," she said seriously.

He grabbed her hand, squeezed it hard, and said, "Spencer, it's been going on a long time…I mean, since I was here. Why do you think I had to get away from here?" He blew out a relieved burst of air. "C'mon, let's ride, sister," he said and pulled her to her feet. He closed out their tab and they made their way to the door, quickly telling everybody they passed goodbye as they made their way toward the door.

Outside, the beautiful autumn day had slipped into a clear, crisp night. As they walked to the car to leave, Dylan and Greg were just arriving and stopped them to try to persuade them to come back in.

"C'mon, Spence," cooed Dylan, "I've got to have a dance with the hottest blonde in the two-state area!"

"You're full of it, Dylan. Besides, I'm tired and I've got to meet Rita at the Waffle House tomorrow morning, bright and early," Spencer said.

"Where is the third musketeer, anyway?" asked Greg.

"She got a ride home with Ross Moore," Ivey said simply.

"Ivey, I haven't even had the chance to catch up with you. How've you been? Is Raleigh treating you well?" Greg asked.

"It's going great. I'm as busy as ever, just working a little harder on underwriting and working out problem loans since the market has slowed, you know?" Ivey stated.

"Yeah, I know. Things are tough right now, but these are the times that you learn lessons that allow you to shine later, Ivey," Greg commented.

"Well, we're going to hit the road back to Shallotte. I've got to get some shut-eye. Rita's probably already in bed asleep a couple hours ahead of me. Good night, guys," Spencer finished.

"Tell Rita I missed her. I hope she's not doing the horizontal tango with Mr. Moore instead of me," quipped Dylan.

"You don't have to be an asshole, Dylan," Greg stated. "C'mon, let's go" and he tugged him toward the door. "Good night and be careful on your way home."

"Ivey, I hope you know you've got it made, man," Dylan whined.

"Yeah, I got that. Good night," Ivey said and he and Spencer got in the car.

"Jeez, hose me off when we get home, Ivey. He's such a sleaze ball. Why the hell does Greg put up with his crap?" Spencer asked.

"That's a very valid question, Spence. There's a lot of valid questions that come to mind about the bank in Shallotte, though," he said as he pulled out on to the highway and headed north back to her condo. "I mean, think about it. Why has Greg not moved on to a bigger role? Or, why has George not retired? Finally, how can the loan losses in Shallotte total more every year than, say, Wilmington or Raleigh and NOBODY lose their job or at the very least be accountable like Jeff or even George?" he finished. He glanced over at Spencer who was watching him curiously and nodding her head.

"So you did know there was a problem? Why didn't you say anything, Ivey?" Spencer asked. "Rita stumbled onto the trail of this mess when she was doing the budget last week. She brought me in and we pulled reports from the last three years. This crap is BIG, brother, BIG," she said.

"I did say something, but I didn't know enough about what was going on to report anything. Don't you remember me complaining when George threw me under the bus with the whole Jarman family fiasco? I mean, I got railroaded royally," he said.

"Ivey, this situation is a whole lot bigger than you knew. The loan charge-offs are just the tip of the iceberg. We found a ton of overdraft losses too and all of them seem to be tied somehow to the Jarmans. There's this whole *cycle* of debits and credits that span a long period of time," Spencer explained.

"Who else knows?" Ivey asked.

Spencer let out a huge sigh. "The three of us…and Patrick," she said.

"Patrick? God…that explains his interrogation tonight," Ivey muttered.

"Yeah, Rita and I thought that he carried enough weight with Mega that he could be a more effective whistleblower. Besides, once he gets his teeth in something he has a tendency to draw blood," Spencer stated.

"Well, he's definitely blown the whistle. He told me today he sent evidence to John Starr," Ivey said. "I guess it is really going to hit the fan now, huh? I'm damn glad I'm in Raleigh, but I sure wish I could be here with you and Rita to help you get through this mess."

Spencer reached over and kissed him on the cheek. "I love you, John Michael. You are always here in spirit, okay?"

Spencer then detailed the conversation overheard outside the Sea Trail clubhouse earlier in the evening and wondered out loud whether Patrick had said anything to anybody today.

"I sure get the impression he did," said Ivey. "He was almost vindictive in his tone when we talked, like he was going to nail somebody to the wall. Patrick implied that there is collusion here on a grand scale. Do you know who is involved, Spencer? Does Rita?" he asked.

"No, we didn't dig after we pieced together the general scheme, but Ivey, it has to be huge to have gone undetected for so long," Spencer said. "And you know if the Jarmans are involved, this situation is not just illegal, but dangerous, right?"

"Right…" said Ivey as they pulled up to the condominium complex. "What the hell...?" he stuttered as he saw Rita crying on the front porch, pacing back and forth.

"Something is going on," said Spencer as she rushed to unbuckle her seatbelt and get out of the car. She and Ivey shouted "Rita" at the same time and in a single step Rita bounded down off the porch and into the safety of their arms.

Chapter 37

I was in shock. I was devastated. I was scared. The feelings just piled on top of one another as I tried to stop crying and tell Spencer and Ivey the bottom line of what I knew. Patrick was dead.

While I knew none of the details, I knew as sure as I knew my own name that Patrick's discovery of the details of the long-running internal bank heist was the real cause. I had opened the door. I had bated him with the information. I had gotten him killed. Oh my God.

Worse still, I didn't know who knew what. I had pulled in Spencer and Spencer had pulled in Ivey. I knew as soon as I saw him run his hands through his hair, or what was left of it, when I delivered the news. We were a collective wreck for a few minutes before we pulled ourselves together. We climbed into Spencer's car, drove to the Skymart, bought six king-size bags of plain M&Ms and a twelve-pack of Miller Lite, and headed back to my condo. Our legendary brain drain sessions had always resulted in idealistic sales methods and larger-than-life bank plans, but never before had they revolved around such horrible madness or begun with such a terrifying situation.

Patrick was dead.

So I jumped right in by asking, "How is this going to end?"

Ivey was next. He asked, "What do we know for sure about the scheme? Who is involved? What proof can we put in our hands?"

Spencer chimed in. "I'd rather know who knows about who knows. So, who knows what we know?"

For two hours we debated, planned and argued the "who, what, when, where and how" of the situation until finally out of sheer exhaustion, we fell asleep on the couches in my den at about 2 a.m.

I awoke at daybreak to the sound of my phone ringing. It was Greg. He wanted us to be at the bank for a meeting at 9 a.m. I asked him why and he told me that he would rather not discuss anything over the phone. I never let on that I knew the awful reason. He asked me if I would call Spencer and I told him I would and hung up.

I went to the kitchen and made a pot of coffee, poured myself the largest mug full and walked out onto the back deck. It was going to be another chamber-of-commerce autumn day. I stood against the railing and peered into the forest behind my home, alone with my thoughts as the birds awakened and the tears fell silently down my cheeks.

As the sun gradually rose above the horizon, all of my sadness was replaced with a resolve and a slow, simmering anger determined to expose the bastards involved. Today was my day to be an Oscar-caliber actress so I would not betray what I knew. Today was my chance to begin to separate the innocent from the involved. Today was my thirty-fifth birthday.

Chapter 38

Ross stood on the deck of his parents' riverfront house quietly contemplating his strategy. The sun was just beginning to rise above the horizon. A new day was underway. Not that he could tell this one from the last one since he hadn't seen the back of his eyelids in over 36 hours. He was exhausted, mentally and physically.

He sighed. Yesterday had held such promise when he got out of bed. After a day as close to perfection as he could imagine, the death of Patrick Lowers brought him back to the harsh reality that he was responsible for heading up a high level, highly confidential criminal investigation. Criminal investigations involve criminals and the criminals involved were now potentially guilty of not only federal bank fraud, but murder. The stakes were getting higher and the crooks were getting more desperate. He knew Patrick Lowers' death was not an accident. He knew the outing yesterday was not an arbitrary celebration. The two were connected and he didn't need an autopsy report to tell him what he knew was true.

By positioning himself to solicit information about Shallotte, he had gotten to know Rita. Now, he was afraid that he might not be able to find out what she knew without blowing his cover. For her sake, he couldn't reveal his professional background. That revelation could not only jeopardize her objectivity in the matter but endanger her even more than any knowledge she might have of the bank fraud. Besides, she was already skeptical of his motives and his interest in her.

And that interest was the problem for him. He was insanely attracted to her. She consumed his dreams, his thoughts and even his actions. He wanted to protect her from danger and shield her from the ugliness of these criminals, but he was helpless to stop her involvement since she was a bank employee.

He desperately needed her to trust him, to let him help her, but he was running out of time and she had to reveal the information to him voluntarily. He was the president of American One Bank for this assignment. Such a high-level post made his effort to obtain assistance, information, and history from a regional, "merged" employee like Rita difficult because her loyalty was to her office, her town and her co-workers, not to corporate officers like him who were viewed as completely out of touch with the line employees who made the bank money.

He sighed again. God, he wanted her. Behind him, he heard the screen door close and he turned to see his mother coming to join him on this glorious fall morning.

"Good morning, handsome," she said. She smiled at him and he leaned down to kiss her cheek. At 70, Marian Moore was still a beauty. She did her own cooking, cleaning and gardening and was rarely resting without a book.

"Good morning, mama," he replied, "I hope I didn't wake you."

She tipped her head slightly and said, "Are you kidding? I've been awake for hours reading. You look worn to a frazzle, son. What is it?"

"Ah, it's just work. But it's always just work, isn't it?" he sighed.

She studied him quietly for a second or two then said, "Not this time. Who is she, Ross?"

Somewhat startled, he looked her right in the eyes and shook his head, and asked, "Am I that transparent?"

"No, but a mother knows," she stated.

He sighed again and reached over and grabbed her hand and kissed it. He smiled lightly and simply said, "You would love her, mama. She's a remarkable woman."

Knowing that his end of the conversation was over, she squeezed his hand and simply said, "Then she's smart enough to know that you are remarkable too, Ross."

She rose and said, "Those camellias aren't going to prune themselves now, are they? I'll see you tonight, son," and she walked down the steps to get to work.

As he watched her go, he looked down at his watch. It was 7:15 a.m. He had work to do to prepare for the 9:00 a.m. meeting in Shallotte to inform the local American One employees about the death of Patrick Lowers. The day was going to be difficult working to comfort a sea of upset fellow employees. The day was going to be even more difficult trying to identify the face of an unknown, cold-blooded killer.

Chapter 39

Morning had come even earlier than usual in Wilmington for John Starr today. On a normal Saturday, he would be up early and headed out to the Gulf Stream for some great autumn fishing. Instead, he was headed to his office before dawn to prepare to go to Shallotte to go through the office of the suddenly-departed Patrick Lowers. What a fiasco Shallotte was shaping up to be.

When he got the call from George Everett in the wee hours of the morning, he was irritated at first. "What now?" he thought. Then after learning about Patrick's death, he sat straight up in bed, suddenly awake and interested in the conversation.

He had known Patrick for years and knew that he was a troublemaker for Shallotte and a darling of upper management at American One, but John also knew that he would never over-indulge on alcohol at a bank function then drive home. Patrick was a too much of a straight-laced prick.

Ten years of work at the CIA and fifteen years as the head of bank security for Mid-Atlantic and now American One told him that Patrick's death was no accident. Oh, boy. He knew he would never have survived the merger with American One with his same position if it had not been for the influence of George Everett, but this situation could knock the wheels off the wagon and he did not intend to ride this wagon on the way down.

He arrived at his office downtown before 6 a.m. The street lights were still on and the stoplights all were blinking yellow. The building was deserted. As soon as he turned the key to his office and opened the door, he saw the package and he knew it was from Patrick.

He pulled out his personal laptop, turned it on and inserted the disk. Ten years of bank fraud, wire fraud, mail fraud as well as conspiracy and blackmail were documented completely and concisely by the late Mr. Lowers with names, methods, accounts and amounts. John sighed. The disk was a copy. The original must be found.

Patrick would never take anything from the bank home that would potentially threaten his family. No, the disk was in the office. John would find it. He had to find it.

He pulled his shredder out from under his desk. Then, he took the small white trash bag out of his pocket. He carefully shredded the disk into the bag followed by the package in which it was sent. John turned off his computer, packed up his briefcase and left for the 45 minute trip to Shallotte. He crossed the Cape Fear Memorial Bridge to Brunswick County. He stopped at a service station in Bolivia, the county seat, to smoke a cigarette and grab another cup of coffee. As he finished his cigarette, he walked back to his car, grabbed the trash bag and tossed it into the huge green dumpster at the back of the property.

Only the original disk remained now, thought John as he pulled back onto Highway 17. Rest in peace, Patrick Lowers! Before this day is through I am going to bury your disk deeper than they bury your lifeless body.

Chapter 40

I woke Spencer at 7:30, handing her a huge glass of diet Coke as she sat up. She drained the glass, reluctantly got up and went next door to shower. Ivey rolled over and went back to sleep, the entire couch now available for him to stretch out now that Spencer's feet were out of his way. I had showered an hour ago but couldn't decide whether to be casual and wear jeans and a sweater or to put on my khakis, white shirt and navy blazer. I poured myself another cup of coffee and decided on the more professional attire.

I was ready to go and walked over to get Spencer. She, of course, had opted for jeans and a black long-sleeve shirt and her black booties. She looked coolly casual. As she closed the door, she said, "God, I'm wearing black..." and simply let the rest of the sentence hang unspoken in the air between us.

The six-mile ride was quiet until we rolled up into the parking lot. I sighed and looked over at Spencer. "I hope I can get through this meeting without crying or cursing, Spence," I said.

"You'll be fine. Besides, I'll be beside you at the table. Don't give me a reason to kick you," she countered and immediately made me feel better. Today, she was my rock.

"Remember, we know nothing. We had a great time last night and for all we know, we are here to be introduced to the new manager in Shallotte, Spencer. We have GOT to be convincing. We are going to be watched as much as we are watching," I reminded her.

We put on our best Saturday smiles and got out. For the first time in over ten years in Shallotte, I locked the Miata, surprising myself as much as I surprised Spencer. She shrugged and we walked nonchalantly to the door of the bank and went in.

Inside, the mood of the co-workers already there was subdued as if everybody had had too large of a time the night before. Out of the corner of my eye, I saw George Everett talking to John Starr at the door of Patrick's office. Greg was off to the side with his head down, his eyes hooded by the shadow cast by his ball cap. He didn't look as if he had had a shower. As if he felt me staring at him, he looked over at me. I smiled at him. For a split second, he didn't respond, as if he was studying me. Then, as if he flipped a switch, he smiled at me slightly and threw up his hand. Look away, Rita, I told myself.

As the rest of the local management team arrived, the individual conversations rose to a crescendo that when heard collectively was loud and chaotic. I was suddenly claustrophobic and almost sick to my stomach. To my rescue, Spencer came up beside me and handed me a Pepsi Max she had taken out of the mini-fridge in my office. She put her hand on my shoulder and hugged me and whispered into my ear, "Happy birthday… We'll have to drown this meeting out and celebrate later today, okay?"

To keep from choking up, I simply smiled and nodded. "You got a gift in there you need to take home today too," she whispered.

Of course, I was interested in my birthday and the gift waiting in my office, but what really piqued my interest was the man who walked into the bank lobby. President Ross Moore's arrival had whipped the small crowd into a frenzy of commentary and speculation. I tried to be coolly detached and keep my feet rooted firmly to my current spot not wanting to appear interested or eager to anybody that might have seen us leave together last night.

Ross moved through the crowd and around to the door of Patrick's office where he was greeted by John Starr and George Everett. Greg excused himself and walked to the front of the crowd and asked everyone to have a seat. I threw one last glance over my shoulder to Ross who was looking at me as he listened to John Starr. They walked inside the office door and I turned my attention back to Greg.

Greg cleared his throat and took a deep breath before he broke the news to the crowd simply and straight-forward. "Patrick Lowers was killed in a single car accident last night on the way home from our golf outing," he said, pausing only to let the enormity of the statement sink into the minds of those in attendance. Surprise, shock, even horror was etched on the faces in the room. "While the family has not had time yet to make arrangements, we will be bringing in some temporary employees to fill in so that many of you will be able to attend the services," he continued. "Understandably, this time will be very difficult for all of us that worked with Patrick, but we will get through it together. I especially ask you to keep his wife, Sharon, and his two daughters in your thoughts. They are going to need a lot of support from us."

Patrick's long-time secretary, Tamara, who had followed him to the area from Laurinburg, broke down and sobbed quietly at the check-writing station. Peter and Tripp quickly helped her to a chair in the lobby and sat on each side of her, consoling her quietly, Peter with an arm around her shoulder, Tripp holding her hand gently. Jeff Malone stood still, looked to the ceiling and just shook his head. Without thinking he jiggled the change in his right pants pocket and rocked back against the wall as if he had been punched. Dylan stood solemnly looking down at his feet. He was quiet and appeared almost afraid to look up, as if he might not seem sad enough, upset enough to the rest of the crowd. He didn't appear at a loss for words, only at a loss for somebody to listen to them. He looked uncomfortable, like somebody might think that

Patrick's death was an opportunity for him. He caught my eye. I tried hard not to telepathically send the words, "It *was*, asshole" to him. I simply walked out of the lobby and into my office. I slipped the gift on my desk into my handbag on my shoulder. I steadied myself on my desk and sighed out loud.

"You okay?" I turned and saw Jeff Malone in my office. I nodded and smiled at him graciously.

"Yeah, I'll be fine. How about you? You were probably closer to him that anybody else here. Can you believe it? The whole thing just seems so surreal," I babbled.

"That it is, Rita. God, those beautiful girls...just awful," he said. "Is there anything here at work I can do for you on the credit side so that you can help out on the management side?" he asked, suddenly very professionally focused.

Mentally knocked off balance, I stammered, "Uh, I'm not sure, Jeff. Can I wrap my head around that question later?"

"Sure, Rita. Hey, I'm sorry. I'm just not very good at handling a situation like this," he continued. "I'll talk to you later," and he walked away quietly to the credit department.

Chapter 41

Jeff Malone was single, childless and a classic geek. He lived alone and liked it that way. He kept his personal life private, preferring the solitude of his home fortress to more social settings like the local country club or even church. Crowds just bothered him.

He loved to play on the computer, though, and had embraced the internet age eagerly in its infancy. The anonymity of the space, the enormity of the information and the informality of the content there thrilled him. He was transformed online. He had moxie, he had confidence.

Not that he lacked either of those at the bank by day. He had risen through the ranks quietly from a credit analyst to a credit reviewer to a credit officer to the regional credit manager. He was now the top cat of credit in Shallotte and admittedly, he loved the power it brought him. In general, he worked well with people one-on-one, but occasionally, he would butt heads with strong-willed lenders who didn't get the memo—Jeff Malone called the shots on credit in the region.

He was a certified public accountant or CPA as well as a banker and he had always taken comfort in the fact that if he ever got the axe at the bank, he could always hang out a shingle to earn a living. But, man, did he ever earn a living at the bank!

He had squirreled away excess earnings for years in his 401K, his securities portfolio, certificates of deposit and even, savings accounts. It was easy to save because he never spent any money. Now, that sizable nest egg gave him the freedom to expand his horizons—online anyway. He had grown increasingly more daring over time in his pursuits.

Last year, he bought an airline ticket to Las Vegas, hired a gorgeous young escort for three days and spent money like a drunken sailor. He screwed the pretty bitch all day and night in every way imaginable. She liked it rough, and she liked it everywhere he gave it to her. She was his sex slave as long as he bought her fancy drinks, lavish dinners and expensive gifts. He obliged her and she obliged him.

Jeff won modestly at blackjack and lost a little at the slots. The trip was a great breakeven financially.

When he returned to Shallotte, he brought with it the intoxicating power being in charge of another person gave him. He stayed on top of everything in the region by surreptitiously minding everybody's business. He realized that he could make other people do things for him by just asking, as long as control was established. Unwittingly, his buddy Patrick helped him cement that control by taking his side against the always pompous and never prepared Tripp Barrows on a loan decision.

The loan was *not* going to be made, he told Tripp, but instead of moving on, the idiotic Mr. Barrows tried to go over his head—big mistake. When Patrick got pulled into the process, he recognized immediately the benefit of taking Jeff's position. They became powerful allies from that day forward and eventually, even became friends—or as close to friends as Jeff had known in many, many years. He had been a loner since childhood when his brother, three years his junior, died after a freak bike accident on the street behind their home. He jumped the ramp they had clumsily fashioned, landed but then lost control at the curb. The bicycle hit the curb and stopped, but his brother didn't and he was thrown right into the trunk of a huge elm tree head first.

He had smiled at Jeff and said, "Cool, huh?" but never regained consciousness again, the swelling of his brain was so severe. Jeff was traumatized by the event, but he persevered. The death of his brother left a vacancy of emotion so deep, he had long ago quit trying to fill it.

Now, many years later, he was truly alone. His parents were both dead since his father's death last year, and while Jeff knew they had loved him and subtly appreciated his accomplishments, academically and professionally, neither had ever fully regained a desire for living after the loss of their younger son.

Now, with the death of Patrick Lowers, Jeff felt a genuine sadness for the loss of his friend personally and his ally professionally. He ached for Patrick's family because he knew first-hand, they would never be the same. Their lives would always be defined as "before the accident" and "after the accident."

Jeff lived in the same condominium complex where Rita and Spencer lived and where Ivey Jones used to live before he moved to Raleigh. He arrived back home last night after the golf outing before they did. He didn't hear Rita arrive, but when Ivey pulled up in Spencer's loud gas guzzler, he left his computer monitor and watched them from his perch on the second story of the building across the huge common area in the middle of the complex. There was a lot of commotion as Spencer got out of Ivey Jones's car and both ran to hug a crying Rita. Jeff watched them together, huddled in private conversation. Ivey casually touched Rita's arm as Spencer patted her back to comfort her. He envied that kind of closeness.

The three left briefly then returned to Rita's condo. Then, Jeff had secretly watched them for hours last night, sitting around the dining table drinking, talking, collaborating, planning…what? Jeff wasn't sure, but they were animated in their gestures, but quiet in their conversations. He never heard a sound from the condo. They talked until after 2 a.m., very late for Rita and Spencer who were usually in bed by 10 p.m.

Even more interesting, Rita was as nervous as a cat in a room full of rocking chairs this morning when he talked to her. She was scattered and suspicious, both of which were out of character for her. It was almost like she was afraid to talk to anybody because her words or her actions might betray a secret.

Jeff wondered what her secret was. Time would tell, he knew. Everybody had some kind of secret and he was great at figuring them out. It was just like reading cards. Observe and wait. He knew almost all of the secrets at the bank. Knowledge was power, and Jeff Malone loved power.

Chapter 42

I knew I had to go around the corner to Patrick's office to see Greg. I walked slowly, taking deep breaths as I saw people all around me falling to pieces. Not me, not today, I reminded myself. As I walked around the corner, I saw Ross talking to Greg and George. The conversation sounded stern and strained. I looked into Patrick's office. Books, papers, manuals, even pictures and mementos covered the desk and floor in disarray. What the hell?

I looked beseechingly over at Ross. He stopped talking and walked over to me. He looked me in the eye, put his hand on my arm and said, "We need your help, Rita."

"Ok, what do you need me to do?" I asked and looked into his eyes for some unspoken assurance and there it was. His eyes flashed concern and a softness that made me believe that he cared. God, I wanted him to care.

"I need you to get the budget information you prepared for Patrick to Greg on Monday so we can finish the budget by the middle of the week," he said softly. "I also need you to help go through Patrick's city-wide budget with Greg and Jeff to make sure it is complete before we roll it into the corporate budget that must be approved by the board of directors one week from Tuesday."

"Okay, sure," I said, trying not to eat a hole in my stomach with worry over what might be gleaned from the budget information I had given to Patrick in the hands of a person involved. When I looked back up at Ross I knew he suddenly saw my worry, my fear.

He patted my arm and said loud enough for everybody around us to hear, "Right now and the rest of today we are not going to do anything, though. We are all going to go home. We'll all be better equipped to handle the budget on Monday, okay?"

I nodded and turned to go find Spencer. As I passed Patrick's office I was almost sick at the destruction wrought in his normally well-kept domain. The office felt strange, off-kilter. I knew that everything had changed last night for our bank. The decisions made had suddenly turned a long-running financial fiasco into a deadly criminal conspiracy to keep the ugly truth hidden. While potentially several of my co-workers were white-collar criminals, at least one of them was a desperate, cold-blooded killer.

I found Spencer talking with Peter just around the corner and asked her if she was ready to go. "God yes," she said and left good old Peter's head spinning like a top. She looped her arm through mine and we walked to the car quickly to put space between us and the office before we started talking. As we approached the car, I noticed a small piece of paper peeking out from under my windshield wiper. Before I tugged it free, Spencer said, "Let me block you from sight so no one can see you pull it out."

When she stood and pretended to be talking to me face-to-face, I grabbed it and stuck it into my blazer pocket. She talked a few seconds more then walked casually to the passenger side of the car and got in. As we shut the doors almost simultaneously, I cranked the car and said, "Where can we go?"

"Well, we gotta eat, don't we? Navigate to the Waffle House. I'll get Ivey to meet us there. We'll have birthday waffles all around, okay?" Spencer asked.

"Perfect. Now grab that note out of my pocket and read it out loud," I said.

Spencer pulled the note from my pocket. It was a scrap piece of paper with three words written on it. "Call me—Ross," Spencer read.

Before she had finished and put the paper down, I had already hit the "send" button on my mobile. He answered before the first full ring and said simply and softly, "I'll be there before your waffle is on the table, okay?"

"Okay," I barely managed, and he hung up. I turned to look at Spencer and she just chuckled and shook her head.

When I turned my eyes back to the road, a beat-up old pick-up truck turned right in front of me and I had to slam on brakes to avoid him. Thank God for anti-lock brakes, but everything behind the seat lurched forward and my purse, the size of a small tote bag, fell behind my seat and the contents—lipstick, brush, wallet, etc.—were everywhere. I pulled into the parking lot and sighed.

Spencer started laughing. "Happy birthday to you," she crooned as we parked the car, got out and walked to the door. I closed my eyes and wished for…him. "Rita Miller, you better make one hell of a wish because I've got nothing to salvage this day for me except hearing all about your birthday present from President Hotstuff! Let's go eat, woman!"

Chapter 43

He was pacing, pacing. God, where was that disk? For sure, it was not in Patrick's office. He had all but ripped up the carpet and torn the upholstery off of the chairs. Prior to the 9 a.m. meeting, John Starr had called George Everett and recounted the information contained on the now-destroyed copied disk. George had quickly called his crew together and relayed the information to them. The initial reaction was a silent shock. Slowly, though, the shock turned to fear as the enormity of the consequences filled the room, consequences that could destroy each individual's life, career and family. Furthermore, if the trail was traced, the monstrous scheme might possibly destroy not only the bank but the entire Shallotte community, so far-reaching were the tentacles.

Interestingly, no one in the room had spoken Patrick's name or mentioned his death during the 15-minute gathering. For the congregants, this meeting was all about the disk. Recovery by them guaranteed preservation; recovery by anybody else ensured certain destruction.

So where was it? Desperation was creeping into his psyche, making him frenzied, almost maniacal. After Patrick's office was dismantled with no results, plans were made to search his car, his locker at the country club and his safe deposit box. Teams were drawn to scour each location. Each search was another illegal endeavor, but hey, they were all in. Criminals already through fraud, embezzlement, and now murder, they had risked everything. Finding the disk was their only out.

And out he would be if they found it. He just couldn't take the pressure anymore. He had settled up his last deficit with the most recent haul. He hadn't gambled in two months, having promised himself he would turn his life around, but now he realized it was too late to be good. He had crossed a line long ago and now, he couldn't go back.

His charge was to check the safe deposit box. Normally, this particular task would be next to impossible because of the many layers of protection put in place to protect the box owners. The boxes were kept in the vault which was under time lock. After a dual-controlled combination to get the vault open, the door key was handled by one employee, the bank box key by another. In addition to the bank box key, each box owner had a unique key that opened his box only when used in tandem with the bank box key. Once the door to the box was opened, the owner of the box was required to take the box to a private room out of the sight of bank employees before opening it. The system was convoluted in order to ensure complete security for the box owner's prized, private contents.

He sighed. Luck just happened to be on his side this week. Rita Miller, who was acting as the branch manager, was on vacation and headed to her parents just outside of Charlotte. Furthermore, Patrick had left his personal keys, including his flat, safe deposit box key, in his top desk drawer. After the vault was opened at 8:00 a.m. on Monday, he would enter the vault before the bank opened with one of the crew who manned the teller line. They talked after the meeting and had arranged all of the details.

He would ask to enter *his* safe deposit box, sign the entry log then they would enter the vault together. Once inside, he would open Patrick's box with Patrick's key and the bank box key. They would shut the door to the box so that no one could see from which slot the box had been pulled. He would then enter into the customer room with the box. Once inside the room, he would open the box, locate the disk, put it into his pocket, close the box, return it to Patrick's space, lock it up and leave the vault.

When the clerk of court arrived at 9 a.m. to seal the safe deposit box, the last record of entry would be Patrick's. The entire contents would be logged and detailed for the estate *sans* disk. The plan was foolproof. The disk would be destroyed off-site and he would be free from the criminal scheme, the ever-consuming guilt. Free. God, he couldn't wait for freedom. He couldn't wait for Monday.

Chapter 44

Ross was seething when he left the bank in Shallotte and he turned off Village Road and onto Copas Road and headed down to the Shallotte River to collect himself before he headed over to the Waffle House to see Rita, Spencer and Ivey.

As he drove, he passed River's Edge, a fantastic Arnold Palmer golf course that followed the curves and twists of the wild and beautiful Shallotte River all the while challenging even the best golfer with natural water, swamp, trees and sand hazards on every hole. When he was a child, he would come here with his dad and his scout troop and camp beside the freshwater pond where the trees were teeming with snowy egrets, blue herons and sandpipers. The water was probably filled with alligators and water moccasins too, but he, like the rest of the boys, was oblivious to such dangers as he wandered in the woods playing hide-and-go-seek and flashlight tag.

He turned onto Middledam Road and stopped at the dead-end of the street and walked to the bank of the river. He slowly inhaled the air, taking in the smells of salt, marsh, mud, bay and pine and let all of the stress and the anger from the day fade away. Today had been a long day and it was only 10:45 a.m.

He was struggling to cope with the pure idiocy of John Starr who was in charge of security at the bank. Starr was seasoned and street-wise, having been with the CIA for many years before he was hired by the bank. Today, however, he had behaved like a modern-day Barney Fife, coming in and ransacking Patrick's office to secure the bank's proprietary and sensitive information before the family could come in and collect Patrick's personal effects. The whole scene this morning was disgusting.

When he arrived, Starr had the local management assemble all Patrick's manuals, folders, files as well as his Blackberry, paper calendar and computer and box them up. At the same time, Starr went through every drawer, cabinet, shelf and book to make sure he hadn't missed anything. To the untrained eye, they looked professionally thorough, as if they understood that the bank must go on. To Ross, though, they looked like they were conducting a search for something. Ross pondered what the something could be and whether or not they found it.

No matter the result or the reason, the timing of the security detail was inappropriate and insensitive when other employees were called into the office to hear about the sudden death of the city executive, their boss, their co-worker. Could anybody really be that heartless or that stupid? After reading George and Greg the riot act, they promised to make sure the office was back in the orderly state in which Patrick kept it before they left today. Sharon, Patrick's wife, was coming in on Tuesday to collect all of his personal items—his pictures, books, awards, diplomas.

The moment she took the mementos of Patrick's personal world away, that office became the office of the next city executive. Monday morning, the bank moved on. Sure, Patrick's death was a personal loss for a few of his closest colleagues, but it was also a career gain for his professional rivals. Meanwhile, the family was left with the much larger and deeper loss, the all-consuming grief, the task of coping without him at every event, holiday and occasion after dealing with the funeral, the burial, the estate. Death sure was a sorry business.

Ross took one more minute and closed his eyes to listen to the songs of the riverside—the flow of the water, the birds in the trees, the rustle of leaves. As he walked back to his vehicle, he felt much better. Besides, he was going to see Rita in a matter of minutes and he hoped she would include him in her evening plans tonight, his last day of vacation before heading back to Charlotte tomorrow. As he pulled back onto the road and headed to the Waffle House, his mood had brightened considerably. The thought of being alone with her made him hunger for her lips, her hair, her body. Dammit man, settle down, he told himself. As he pulled into the parking lot, he saw Rita through the window and she saw him. Her green eyes beckoned to him; her smile consumed him. His stomach growled suddenly and he sighed as he got out of the car to go inside. There was not a waffle in the world that could satisfy this hunger.

Chapter 45

When Ross pulled up in the parking lot, I could tell immediately the last 12 hours had taken its toll on him. He looked tired and troubled. He also had a faraway look in his eye as if he was mentally searching for an answer to a question that had not been asked yet.

Still, he was maddeningly handsome, rugged and manly, and when he smiled back at me through the window, I thought for certain my body had liquefied and I would splash right to the floor in a puddle. Even as I was trying to get a grip on my emotions, I couldn't take my eyes off of him as he confidently got out of his SUV and walked in the door. He casually threw his hand up and said good morning to Janelle who had to be the oldest waitress in the world or at least looked like it. She blushed so hard I was afraid she was going to spontaneously combust. He sure was a lady killer.

When he got to our booth, I instinctively moved over and he slid in smoothly beside me, bumping his thigh to mine. He said, "Good morning, again," and smiled gently as he looked first at me then Spencer then reached across and shook Ivey's hand.

In unison, we all three said, "Good morning."

"What's everybody having for breakfast this morning or is that a ridiculous question to ask at Waffle House?" he asked and immediately quashed any awkwardness and we laughed together good-naturedly.

Spencer said, "We're making Rita eat chocolate chip waffles with whipped cream and a cherry for her birthday."

Ross immediately turned to me and questioned me with mock horror, "You had a birthday party planned and I had to invite myself? That's cold, Rita, cold. I didn't even bring you a present."

I nudged him and smiled at his teasing and responded, "Well, you wrapped that guilt up pretty nicely, Ross Moore!"

Spencer and Ivey laughed and the depressing day ebbed away, leaving in its place, what was it? Happiness? Satisfaction? Whatever it was, we reveled in it and when Janelle put the enormous birthday waffle in front of me, I pushed it to the middle of the table and we dug in, dueling forks and stuffing our faces with the gooey sweetness.

After we had devoured everything on our plates, we sat back and talked about the morning, what we could expect from the coming days and on a lighter note, how Ross had spent his vacation.

He detailed his morning kayak excursions down the Shallotte River, across the Shallotte Inlet to Windy Point and talked fondly of helping his mother harvest her pumpkins from the patch and choosing one to take home with him to carve for Halloween. The conversation was animated and took off in many directions, Ivey and Ross discussing the merits and deficiencies of open versus closed kayaks, as well as the dimensions of every kayak and canoe each had ever paddled. Meanwhile, Spencer and I talked about the Halloween street party at the condo complex, begging a disinterested Ivey to drive down and join us. Finally, Ross sighed and said, "Well, it's almost over now and I only have the rest of today since most of tomorrow will be devoted to packing up, going to the funeral and driving home."

As he spoke, Spencer caught my eye and I knew she was up to something. "You know Rita is picking up where you left off, right? She was supposed to be on vacation starting today for a week. She is going to work Monday, but is heading up to her folks in Misenheimer after the funeral to work on the farm, which to me sounds about as thrilling as mopping the floor or cleaning the toilet, but hey, she can't wait."

Ross turned to me again with his contrived look of shock, "You are just determined to withhold vital information from me, aren't you? Aren't you even going to let me try to convince you to come keep me company while you're there? Rita, I'm shocked, shocked," he teased gently.

"Well, boohoo for you and here you sit wasting time when you could be taking Rita on a birthday cruise in your canoe," Spencer deadpanned. "I'm going home, people, but only if you will get up and drive me there, Mr. Jones," she continued and playfully bumped his hip with hers to reinforce her request.

They hugged my neck and wished me happy birthday and picked up the tab, then my two best friends in the world made their grand exit at the Waffle House.

I shook my head and turned myself around to give Ross Moore my full attention now and found him staring at me, a crooked, satisfied smile on his face. His smile was disarming and I blushed and said, "What?"

"You sure are lucky to have friends like those knuckleheads," he chuckled. "They have your back."

"And I have theirs," I said.

"No doubt about it," he finished. He stood and held his hand out to me and pulled me to my feet, then grandly said, "Now if you will indulge me, lovely Rita, birthday girl, I will take you to the most beautiful place on earth. Are you ready?"

I was enthralled by him and fantasized momentarily about a variety of beautiful places where Ross could entwine his body with mine. My breathing was shallow as we walked with my arm casually through his to his car. By now, he had to know I would have followed him anywhere and having momentarily lost my voice during the intimate conversation, I just nodded to answer his question.

As we drove down Highway 179 toward Shallotte Point, I noticed that the chill of the morning had faded, leaving a bright blue sky, a very light southern wind and a perfect 72-degree temperature. We let the windows down to enjoy the day and I breathed the air into my lungs and let it escape slowly, smiling over at Ross as he watched me curiously.

"How did an obvious nature nut like you end up working inside all day in a business suit?" he asked.

I laughed and said, "Oh, that's an easy one. My career choice was simple economics. I realized that I had to have income in order to feed myself. Farming with my dad and working for the sports department at the local newspapers sure didn't accomplish that feat collectively. My grandfather was a banker for the local First National Bank by day and a farmer in the evening and on weekends. He was one of the most respected people I have ever known. When the opportunity came to interview for Mid-Atlantic, he encouraged me to interview. He said, 'Rita, it's a good career and a noble profession.'" I stopped for a minute to collect myself, hoping that my grandfather wasn't spinning in his grave at the recent ugliness I had revealed on the underbelly of my bank. I sighed and continued, "I didn't know how to use a financial calculator or an Excel spreadsheet when I started, but I immediately loved banking. The people you can help, the people you get to know and the knowledge you glean about such a variety of businesses, careers, and professions is incredible. Each day is just…exciting, you know?"

As I finished and looked over at him, he was smiling and shook his head in agreement and said, "Yeah, I know. Banking is always interesting."

A little embarrassed all of a sudden, I realized that telling the president of my bank that banking was a great career choice was like telling a Warren Buffett that wealth gave you plenty of investment options. I sure hoped Ross didn't think I was an idiot. No matter, my feelings were my true feelings so I finished by telling him, "Besides, I found that when I started working at the bank, I began to enjoy sports and outdoor pursuits much, much more because I had to plan them ahead of time. The planning gave me time to anticipate the activities beforehand, appreciate them while they lasted, then savor the memories of them afterward. Not to mention, I had an income to afford them. So, to make a long story a little bit longer, I am glad even 13 years later I chose banking or at least, most of the time I'm glad. This whole awful situation with Patrick sure makes me wonder if I made the right decision…" and I stopped before I said anything further and looked out the window to keep my emotions in check. There was more to his death than "a single-car accident" I was certain.

As if sensing my feelings, Ross said, "Rita, I hate that I asked you to go to work on Monday to help finish the budget, especially since you're supposed to be on vacation, but you are the only one who worked close enough with Patrick on the local budget process to get it done."

"It's okay. Patrick would want the budget, like everything he did, done on time. He never missed a detail," I said.

"Except getting a designated driver to drive him home," Ross commented. I simply shrugged and looked out the window, a gesture that he didn't miss or gloss over. Looking at me for every facial expression and listening to every inflection of my voice, Ross asked, "Rita, do you think that Patrick's death was an accident?"

Taking a few seconds to let the enormity of the question sink in, I knew the answer was amazingly simple and stated, "No," as I met his eyes.

He nodded his head as if he understood or agreed or thought I was ready for a padded room. I wasn't really sure.

I was sure all of a sudden that we had arrived at our destination because Ross had stopped the car and turned the motor off and said, "Come with me."

We were at a beautiful, secluded residence. The house and surroundings looked as if we had stepped back in time to a much earlier era. The cottage was set up on a bluff on the banks of the Shallotte River and had white clapboard siding with an oyster shell stucco foundation. The old oaks on either side of the driveway were covered in beautiful Spanish moss and had to be hundreds of years old. The air was filled with bay and lilac and pots full of mums and pansies overflowed with a myriad of color all around. Everything looked well worn, well kept and certainly, well loved. What is this place? I thought to myself.

Uncertain as to whether or not my mouth was gaping wide open, Ross stepped up to the front porch ahead of me, opened the screen door and with a dramatic bow said, "Welcome to my childhood home, Rita."

I walked through the door and took in the view. Across the river in front of us was Windy Point with Holden Beach peeking out to the south. The riverbanks were dotted with blue herons and snowy egrets and the sounds of nature were wild and constant and brought the house and land to life. I walked to the railing and took it all in. Finally, to not seem rude, I simply said in wonder, "Wow. How could you have ever left this place?"

Unexpectedly, a woman's voice answered, "Well, he is a man even if he is my own flesh and blood, dear," and I turned to see a beautiful, older woman obviously related to the man to her left smiling at me.

Her smile was warm and welcoming and I stepped forward to introduce myself, but Ross, like a gentleman, did the honors for us. "Mom, this is Rita

Miller. She works at the bank and today is her birthday," he began and I blushed at his ease of poking fun at me so sweetly. Then he continued, "Rita, this is my mother, Marian Moore. She is full of stories that would embarrass me and entertain you all afternoon if I'd let her, but out on that dock is a canoe that is calling our names first. Mama, do you mind making us a thermos of tea and one of your famous snack sacks while I ready the ride?"

"Of course I don't mind, but you get down there and clean that canoe up before Rita gets in it. I don't want her coming back here looking and smelling like the Brawny man after a week in the woods," and she winked at me, gently grabbed my arm to follow her and led me to her kitchen. "Besides, I won't tell her anything that is not true," she said over her shoulder with a chuckle as the door closed behind us.

Ross sighed audibly and said, "That's what worries me! Rita, she's a bad influence so be careful," and I heard him laugh as he bounded down the steps toward the dock.

Chapter 46

As we walked through the foyer down the hall through the den and past the dining room to the kitchen, I noticed that the interior of the home was just as beautiful as the exterior. Original watercolors of local scenes hung framed on the walls and the clean lines of the furniture gave the den and the dining room timeless appeal. The kitchen was amazing with the modernity of stainless steel appliances and granite countertops, but was balanced by the warm elegance of an antique pewter collection filled with apples and pears from the trees outside, homegrown herbs drying by the cupboard and a wreath of red peppers from the garden perched beside a collection of cookbooks that showed years of use. The house was a showplace worthy of *Southern Living* or *House Beautiful*, but the house was very clearly a home for the Moore family.

I spoke to her with a church-like reverence when I said, "Mrs. Moore, this house is one of the most beautiful I have ever seen. I can tell you love this home," and I turned to see her looking with loving eyes around her kitchen.

"Thank you, Rita. This house has been a source of joy for the last 50 wonderful years of my life since I married Charlie, Ross's father. First, though, Mrs. Moore is my former mother-in-law. Please call me 'Marian.' Everyone else does. Second, let's figure out what you like to eat so I will know what to pack. I have homemade fig bars, pear preserves and crumpets and some of the most succulent local goat cheese in the world."

I felt like I had landed in a fairytale and laughed as I told Marian so.

"Well, I grew up on a farm where my mom's favorite saying growing up was 'You don't have to like it, you just have to eat it' so none of us, my brother, sister or me, is picky. As a matter of fact, I eat anything and figs are one of my favorite fruits. I guess I have canned more fig preserves in my life than any one person could eat in a lifetime, but I love them," I said, remembering fondly all of the wacky fig preserve combinations we tried over the years—strawberry fig, blueberry lemon fig and raisin fig.

The nostalgic moment made me miss my family and I was really happy that I was heading home Monday. Snapping back to the present, Marian was looking at me and smiling. I smiled back and felt comfortable in her presence and her home. "What about Ross," I said quietly. "What will he want to eat?"

"Again, he is a man, right? As a boy, he ate like a goat in a garden all day long," she laughed. "He won't eat just anything, he'll eat everything."

And so the conversation continued for a while, with Marian asking me more about my home in Misenheimer and my family and me asking her more about Ross and his childhood. I filled the thermos with sweet tea, fresh lemon slices and crushed ice while she packed the knapsack with food and handed it to me to sling over my shoulder to head to the dock. As I headed toward the door, I stopped, walked back to the kitchen, hugged her and said, "Thank you so much, Marian," then I let her shoo me out of her house to the dock where her son awaited my arrival.

On my way, I passed a beautiful rose garden and spotted the infamous pumpkin patch around the other side of the house. What a glorious place, I thought, and I forced myself not to skip or belt out "Oh, what a beautiful morning," as I strolled down the shell path to the dock. I really liked Marian Moore, and I knew I had made a good impression. Even better, I knew I had made a good friend.

Chapter 47

Ross finished wiping down the long, green canoe, the paddles and the life preservers and stood back to make sure everything was in ship shape. The conversation on the trip back to his folks kept replaying in his head as he worked. Rita believed that Patrick's death was no accident. Rita believed that Patrick was murdered. Even hearing the word between his ears rattled him. How did she know? The results of the autopsy wouldn't be available until tomorrow morning. Furthermore, what did she know? If Rita knew what Patrick figured out and that information had gotten Patrick killed, Ross knew that Rita was in real danger. God, he had to protect her.

He sighed loudly and knew he had to find the answers to both of those questions today somehow. Maybe she knew enough to implicate the killer or at least knew enough to pinpoint the parties involved in the scandal.

This mess was worse than a ponzi scheme, he thought. In the news constantly lately, a ponzi scheme is when a financial manager or broker takes money from a group of investors, produces false reports that show wildly favorable returns on fake investments. Then, the manager takes more money from new investors to pay interest and returns to the first investors. The whole scheme continues, bigger and bigger, until the whole house of cards collapses because one large investor or a group of small investors ask for their money back. A ponzi scheme is possible because of a desire for higher than average returns. A ponzi scheme is possible because of the inherent greed of both the scammer and the investor being scammed.

Internal bank fraud was different because it was only possible when an inherent trust in a banker existed. Bankers were important citizens in their communities. They made loans to fund the construction of churches, build offices and stores and provide working capital to small business owners to purchase inventory and equipment. Bankers were embedded in every chamber of commerce, every civic and social club and every board at the local hospital, community college or university. Bankers were neighbors, coaches and golf partners. Bankers were friends and when they asked you for your business, you trusted them with your money. People don't bank with a bank; they bank with a banker. Bankers often had the trust of an entire community and at the end of the day, the breaching of that trust was not only despicable, it was destructive to the entire fabric of a town, city or even region.

Shareholders lost money, communities lost leaders and families lost sons, daughters, dads, moms and siblings who got caught up in the greed of the scheme. When the trust of the banker was lost, the trust of the bank was at risk of being lost soon after. The bank at risk here was American One Bank, an eighteen billion dollar organization and the subject of a covert federal investigation sparked by an anonymous letter by a former Shallotte NC bank employee to an examiner at the FDIC who immediately contacted the FBI. As a result, Ross was now an official American One or "Mega" employee as well as the head of the investigative team responsible for deciphering the who, how and how long questions surrounding the fraud. Mega was his bank now.

Ross sighed again and looked over at Windy Point, seeking counsel from above from Earl and comfort from the serenity of his surroundings. He turned as he heard Rita coming down the path from the house and said a small prayer that she would trust him enough to confide in him today so he could get her out of harm's way. He watched her approach with interest, amusement, and desire. When she saw him, they exchanged smiles. God, I am lost, he thought. Now, more than ever, he was determined to win justice for American One Bank as well as the heart of one beautiful banker.

Chapter 48

Ivey and Spencer took the scenic route back to the condo, down highway 179 past beautiful Bricklanding and the hairpin curve. They passed Big Nell's place and laughed as they reminisced about walking in on the last day of the month to find a large collection of past due customers eating breakfast there. Upon their entrance, the delinquents quickly scurried to pay their tabs and leave rather than answer to their bankers whose calls they had avoided because they were looking for a loan payment. Two minutes later, the three of them--Rita, Spencer and Ivey--had the place virtually to themselves.

That month proved to be one of the best collection months of the year. The delinquents' hidey-hole had been discovered, albeit by accident, and they quickly made payments to avoid a repeat on an ongoing, monthly basis at their favorite gathering place.

Further down the road, they passed the planetarium and Sea Trail, the sobering events from Friday heavy in the air between as they passed the road to the clubhouse. What was left to say? Patrick Lowers had made this same fateful drive Friday night for the last time. As they approached the Oyster Bay Bridge, Spencer sighed and wondered what happened on the slow, winding road. Ivey, sensing her mental questioning, asked out loud, "How do you get yourself killed on a road like this, Spencer?"

"I don't know, Ivey. I was thinking the same thing myself," she said.

"I mean, he couldn't have been *that* drunk. I spoke to him five minutes before we left and the accident happened less than an hour later. Does anybody think he stayed there alone and poured screwdrivers down his throat? Look, I'm doing 25 miles per hour around the curve. Even if he was doing, say, 45 miles per hour, would that have caused a mortal injury? I don't know…" and he let the rest of his musing fade away.

"I wonder if he just passed out. Or did he drown? I guess all of those questions will be answered at some point with the autopsy. Perhaps, the findings will help us understand better. One thing is for sure, though--nothing can undo what's been done," she finished.

As they got to the end of the bridge, Spencer looked back in the passenger-side rear-view mirror and all but yelled, "Holy crap, Ivey!"

"What?" he asked.

"Just keep driving, keep driving to Bonaparte Retreat then turn in…" she said, almost breathless with what sounded like panic.

Ivey drove the mile or so to the next subdivision, turned in and pulled to the side of the road. He looked over at Spencer who was visibly shaking and pale as a ghost. He reached over and put his hand on her arm and said, "Spence, what is it? Are you okay?"

Breathing deeply to try to compose herself and verbalize the thoughts between her ears, she shook her head several times then turned and looked at him wide-eyed. "Ivey, back there on the bridge, down below at the culvert… Ricky Jarman was there, looking for something, digging around on the bank. I saw him. Even worse, I think he saw me too. He saw me too, Ivey," Spencer said with pure fear present in her voice.

Ivey grabbed her hand and tried to reassure her. "Spencer, he couldn't have seen you. He wouldn't know my car, okay?" he said.

"Ivey, he was looking right at me in that mirror, I'm telling you. God, everything just seems so surreal! What was he doing? What was he looking for in that ravine? He may be a scary lunatic, but he was down there for a reason, I'm telling you," she said.

Ivey stared out the windshield, drumming his thumb on the steering wheel as if spurring brain activity into high gear. Suddenly, he stopped, patted Spencer on the hand, put the car in reverse and turned around. "I've got it, Spence," he said.

As he drove back toward US 17 across Georgetown Road, Spencer calmed down. Ivey had a plan and with the determination she saw in his face now, she was confident they would get some answers to their nagging questions, fears and concerns. "Do tell," she said.

"If Jack and Mack Grissett can't shed some light on this mess, nobody can," he said as they crossed the highway and turned into the brothers' auto salvage and repair business. "They don't call them the Grissettown G-men for nothing, do they? Come on."

Chapter 49

Jack and Mack Grissett were movers and shakers not only in Brunswick County, but inside both beltways in the capital cities of Raleigh and Washington, DC. They were politically connected, university educated, and technically gifted. They were white-collar business men in a blue-collar business. They were black men thriving in a white man's world. They were small business champions. They were civil rights activists. They were horse traders.

Mack was the older of the two. Quiet, introspective and observant, he had been a college basketball star who valued his academic studies far more than his athletic pursuits. When he finished at prestigious Brown University, he had completed not only his undergraduate degree in education, but his master's and doctorate degrees as well.

As if a foregone conclusion, Mack returned to his home in Brunswick County to be near his family. He was the assistant principal for many years at the local high school, having passed up opportunities nationally to make a difference locally. He worked in the position for 15 years until the school principal retired. Before he could even lobby for the job that he knew he so roundly deserved, the county superintendent named the head of the long under-performing northern county high school as the replacement. Mack wasn't even interviewed. The new principal was a good ol' boy and well-known F.O.T.S. or friend of the superintendent. He was also a bigot and an intellectual midget. Refusing to lose his temper, Mack simply retired too—at age 40.

He was asked by the governor to join the state board of health. He was humbled and thrilled to be involved in such high-level policy influence. He was passionate about advocating funding to reduce smoking in the black communities in North Carolina where a black man was more than two times as likely to smoke and almost three times more likely to die of lung cancer than a white man. He knew because it had robbed him of his father when he was just nine. Through the appointment he had found his calling but not his funding.

Jack was three years his junior. He was an extrovert of the highest magnitude. He could captivate you for hours with his stories of amazing people he had encountered as well as entertain you with the funniest jokes that poked fun at everybody but offended nobody. He was the life of the party.

Jack graduated summa cum laude with business and finance degrees from a large state university. He was wooed heavily by every major Wall

Street firm, but ultimately settled on a management trainee position with the almost-local Mid-Atlantic Bank. He finished the nine-month program at the top of his class and was given first choice of placements within the bank. With opportunities in the metropolitan markets of Charlotte and Raleigh beckoning, he stunned the other eleven trainees completely when he chose Shallotte.

He began as the manager of the part-time but influential Bolivia branch of the bank. Bolivia was definitely not the social hotspot in Brunswick County, but it was the county seat and within shouting distance of the county's municipal complex. Every influential politician cashed a paycheck or made personal or county business deposits there. Bottom line, he got to know everybody that was anybody in Brunswick County.

More and more connected to the political scene, Jack was encouraged by the local Democratic Party and the young, influential district attorney to run for the county register of deeds. He was clearly the most qualified since he was going head-to-head with a local never-do-well whose only qualification was that he was the son of the retiring, current register of deeds.

As the election drew near, vicious rumors were circulated in the community, accusing Jack of secret liaisons with white women, harboring hatred of white men and most disturbing, supporting local reparations for former slaves in Brunswick County through a local property tax proposal that he had never seen, let alone endorsed.

In the end, he lost in a landslide and overnight, became ostracized by not only many of the local politicians, but by most of the regional management at the bank as well. When the office manager position became available at the prestigious Southport location, he was told that he just wouldn't fit in with the customer base and that the bank needed him to stay in Bolivia. They filled the position with a young, blond management trainee whose biggest qualification was the size of her professionally-sculpted breasts.

Jack was angry. He was devastated. He was through. He tendered his resignation after 12 years and never looked back on his days in banking. He was going to play in a much larger ballpark.

Six months later, Jack was named to the powerful state Department of Transportation board that virtually allowed him to call the shots with respects to all of the roads in southeastern North Carolina. He pushed through a US 17 Bypass that went around the towns of both Bolivia and Shallotte. Two car dealerships and two convenience stores failed after the road was completed. Both were owned by the Robertsons, the former and current register of deeds.

Coincidence was a wonderful thing for Jack and he let talk of retribution solidify his reputation even if it was unfounded. He made decisions by simply asking himself the question, "Is it the right thing to do?" At the end of the day, the people of Brunswick County were well represented and he could sleep at night.

Jack and Mack opened a large car salvage and repair business on land in Grissettown, just south of Shallotte, that had been in their family for two generations. With Mack's management skills with the mechanics and Jack's sales skills, they earned a respectable income, pursued their political passions, and found the flexibility to have successful side businesses of their own—Jack in sports photography, Mack in writing computer software for the school systems for scheduling and lesson-planning.

The brothers were legendary for needing very little sleep. The worked 15-hour days routinely and were on call for vehicle accident towing the other nine. Their business and political connections allowed them to move seamlessly among every sector of the county, region and state. They saw the good, the bad and the downright evil underbelly of every aspect of society.

They loved to be discounted as merely mechanics or junkyard kings. People loved to talk when they thought they were smarter, better or richer. And when people talked, the Grissetts listened. They learned to help the honest and downtrodden, to overcharge the greedy, and to reveal the corrupt. They picked their battles well and by doing so, they won most of the battles they picked.

Mack had responded to the Patrick Lowers accident on Friday night. By the time he had arrived, the posturing and posing by a large number of people was already in progress. He knew the scene was much more than an accident and that Lowers was much more than an innocent victim.

The people on the scene told him that much. There were bankers, highway patrolmen, Ocean Isle Beach and Calabash policemen, neighbors and ordinary bystanders. One of those was Ricky Jarman. He hung back in the crowd, smug, disinterested and almost impatient. When the county coroner arrived and pronounced Patrick Lowers dead, Jarman hit the road. His presence at the scene was no coincidence, thought Mack.

After the body was taken away, Mack hooked the car up to the pulley on the tow truck and hoisted the car out of the deep ravine. Once the car was on the rollback, he surveyed the now-deserted scene. Lowers had "missed" the bridge altogether and had careened straight down into the culvert.

Even the incredibly drunk could have navigated the wide, cement-railed bridge. According to Barry Fipps, the investigating officer, Lowers was passed-out drunk and had no seatbelt on. Mack knew Lowers through the community college board of trustees on which they both sat. Lowers was an uptight, driven perfectionist. He was also a family man. Everything he heard and saw here was out of character.

One plus one never equals three, Mack thought. That is, unless there is another one hidden in the equation. No matter how many times he did the math that night or the nights that followed, he knew that Ricky Jarman somehow figured into the equation. For Mack, figuring out how Jarman was involved was the only way to answer the question of what really happened to Patrick Lowers.

Chapter 50

George was still in his office. It was 3 pm. It was Saturday. He wondered how his life had sunk to its current, sorry state of existence. He stood and walked slowly to the window. Outside, cars slowly made their way down Third Street in Wilmington, heading to Wal-Mart to shop or Elijah's to eat. So many ordinary people found joy and contentment in ordinary lives with so little everything—money, time or possessions. Yet, they were living and he was in the office alone at 3 pm on a beautiful, autumn Saturday coping with the death of Patrick Lowers.

His life began unraveling last night and not because of any silly, sentimental sense of loss for the man. No, in his attempt to contain the havoc that Patrick Lowers threatened to wreak, he had pushed people much more desperate than he was across a line from which there was no return.

As a result, he was no longer sure he would see retirement slated for just under a year. He was no longer sure because he was no longer in charge. The finely tuned machine he had created, enhanced, and perfected over the last twenty years now had a mind of its own and was spiraling out of control.

He walked back to his desk and sat down. On Monday, the results of the autopsy would be announced, and he was worried. His team was loyal to a point, but at the end of the day, most of them would throw him to the wolves to save their own skins. No doubt.

John Starr had assured him that he was on top of the damage control and that they would find Patrick's damning original disk. George didn't know what was on it, but he did know one thing for certain—all the evidence led back to him.

He sighed and thought to himself, *I've got to find that disk and then I'm going to retire—immediately.* It had been a great run, he had had a ball and no matter what happened, he was going out on top.

Chapter 51

As I approached the floating dock, I saw Ross waiting for me. His smile was spontaneous, authentic and incredibly sexy. My stomach did a somersault as I smiled back, my body anticipating his body nestled close, not to mention hot and naked, next to mine. Girl, get a grip, I said to myself.

He reached up and took my hand to help me into the canoe with one hand, while the other deftly took the sack of food. Through it all, the canoe never rocked in the slightest. Smooth operator, I thought. His gesture was so chivalrous I had to laugh. He surely can't think I need fussing over. Maybe he just wants to impress me. Maybe he just wants the sack of food. "Your mom said you would go for the food first," I said.

"What other deep, dark secrets did she divulge?" Ross asked, mocking suspicion. "She is a first-class trouble-maker, you know," he continued.

"Uh, I could say something about an apple and a tree," I teased, "but I won't. What's said in the kitchen stays in the kitchen."

"Mmm-hmm, she's already gotten to you with her quaint, Southern charm, I see," he said and I smiled and nodded like I was under her spell with my eyes wide and my head moving robotically. "I'm sure she offered to feed us tonight too." He laughed heartily and finished with, "She's a dangerous woman, that Marian Moore."

"Let's embark to Paradise, okay?" and he said it so reverently that I'm not certain he heard my whispered "okay" reply.

Ross paddled the canoe like an old pro and I felt like Cleopatra riding the river Nile. The sky was almost navy it was so blue and there was not a cloud visible anywhere. As we moved toward Windy Point, the breeze blew my long locks back behind my head and I leaned my head back to let the sun warm my face. I looked over at Ross. He smiled at me, but I could see he was focused on navigating the Shallotte Inlet across the mouth of the Shallotte River. "Would you like me to help paddle?" I asked. "I've certainly canoed enough in my life to assist your effort."

"I thought you'd never ask," he said. "Grab that paddle under the seats. We'll dock just to the north of the Point."

I grabbed the paddle and put my muscles to work. They responded naturally and I remembered fondly how much I had enjoyed my childhood canoe trips with the Boy Scouts Explorers. My best friend, Susan, and I had canoed on Badin Lake, High Rock Lake and Lake Tillery just to name a few. We were the only two girl boy scouts I had ever known. We loved every minute of it.

We canoed in silence taking in the sounds of nature—the splash of the water, the breeze blowing lightly in our ears, the laughing gulls screaming overhead. Too quickly, we reached the dock. I held the canoe still while Ross stepped easily onto the dock. I threw him the rope and he secured the canoe to the dock. I reached down and grabbed the sack of food and turned to find him smiling at me appreciatively.

"You've done this once or twice before, haven't you?" he asked.

"Uh…yeah—a couple dozen times or so. Didn't I tell you I was a boy scout?" I asked.

"You never cease to pleasantly surprise me, Rita Miller," he said, and he walked over, wrapped his arm around my waist and kissed me lightly.

Suddenly breathless, I opened my eyes and struggled to find the right words to describe the moment. "Wow" sounded ridiculous and "damn" sounded confusing. I simply said, "Thank you," and immediately regretted sounding like I was practicing my customer service skills in a dreadful bank role play.

He stayed close and whispered, "For what?"

"For making my birthday beautiful," I said.

He continued to study me for a few more seconds with a slight smile on his lips. Then he said, "C'mon, birthday girl. You haven't seen anything yet!"

We climbed up the bluff and turned left onto a sandy trail through the woods. We meandered around ancient live oaks dripping with Spanish moss and through native wax myrtles, bay trees and long leaf pines. The scent was intoxicating and I breathed it in deeply.

We were walking northwest, the river on our left, the Intracoastal Waterway behind and to our right. We hiked for about a mile, Ross leading the way, me behind until we came to a long, high dune. Once we got to the top, the view dropped suddenly downward to a freshwater lake, teeming with waterfowl. The sight was breathtaking.

The mallards and their ducklings swam placidly on top while the enormous blue herons fished expertly all along the water's edge. The snowy egrets filled every branch of every tree around the lake, some sleeping, others grooming themselves. Our presence didn't seem to disturb them at all.

While I was watching, Ross pulled a blanket out of the back of his jacket and spread it along the high bank. As I continued to stand and stare, he walked several yards away, and began snapping digital photos of everything. He was serious, observant of both light and angle and discerning of everything potentially filling his lens. "Where did you hide that camera?" I whispered.

"I never leave home without it," he said quietly. "Besides, I can't think of a better birthday present than your expression when you topped the dune."

Well, maybe I could think of a *few* things better, but he was right—this place was amazing, serene yet wild.

We both walked to the blanket and sat down. I rested my head on his shoulder and sighed as he put the camera back into its bag. What a fantastic day! I reached over and took his arm and laced my fingers through his. He put his arm around me and leaned down and kissed me on the top of my head.

"I've been coming here since I was a child," he said. "After all these years, I never grow tired of this place. I'm glad you came to share it with me. Most people wouldn't appreciate it like we do."

I was speechless and looked up at him, searching for…what? Perhaps, I looked for tenderness, and it was certainly there. Maybe I was searching for a whole lot more. As I searched his eyes, he reached over and kissed me, slowly at first, then increasingly, more passionate.

I lay back and pulled him with me, insisting that his lips not leave mine. He moved on top of me and I could feel his arousal against me. God, I was way past the point of no return. I reached down and unzipped his jacket and he helped peel it off. He then slowly unbuttoned my shirt and seamlessly took it off with my blazer at once.

He momentarily pulled away from my lips to look at my almost naked body. Then, he intertwined his fingers in my hair and swooped down suddenly to devour my necks with kisses, nipping my flesh occasionally. He was driving me insane with desire and I was sure I was close to self-combustion. Every flick of his tongue, touch of his teeth shocked me with pleasure and I moaned as the heat of his body, his touch swamped my control.

Time was lost. Somehow, the rest of our clothing was removed and I ran my hands urgently up and down his tanned, muscular back. I needed him. I wanted him now.

As if sensing the height of my desire, he ran his tongue down my breastbone and devoured my breasts. I moaned with the touch of his tongue and begged him to take me and he did.

I gasped with the overflowing desire. I was on fire. I was rolling away. I was possessed. We rode together on what felt like a tidal wave until the energy of the crest built higher and higher until it finally toppled explosively, washing over us, leaving us spent and sated.

We lay quietly for what seemed like hours. While I slowly recovered but struggled for breath, I sat up slowly and looked down at his sculpted, long body. He smiled up at me, still out of breath himself. Never one to mince words, I said exactly what I felt. "That was incredible. Damn, man, how old are you--18 or 19?"

Ross laughed. "You are beautiful, you know that? Crazy, but beautiful," he said, kissing my chin. "You know what? I'm starving. Come, woman, let's eat!" He reached over and grabbed the knapsack, pulled out the tea and the food as I sat up, and we had a wonderful birthday lunch completely naked and sweaty with only the birds and the trees for company.

Chapter 52

The disk was not in the car. No matter how many times the damn bankers asked the question, "Are you sure?" the disk was not in the car. Ricky Jarman had all but torn Patrick Lowers' Toyota apart searching for it—the glove box, the trunk, under the seats, in the console.

Granted, he had broken into the car under the cover of darkness last night after Mack Grissett towed it over to his lot. Using night vision goggles from across the road, he watched Mack unload the car, take the rollback to the shop and lock it up. Then, he went into the office to prepare his report. It didn't take long. In fact, Mack never even sat down. Once he was done, he turned off the light, locked the office door, got into his car and left.

When he got to the car, Ricky fully believed the disk would be found in an obvious place. After checking all of those places with no luck, though, he looked harder—behind the back seat, with the spare tire, in the owner's manual, but there was nothing.

The disk wasn't in the ditch, the culvert, beside the road or in the shallow waters around Oyster Bay either. He had checked and double checked himself. The disk was not in the car.

But now he knew that somebody knew he was looking for something. There was no doubt that the blonde he saw in the side mirror this afternoon was Spencer Cashwell. She had seen him and he had seen her. She knew it and he knew it.

He would know those eyes anywhere. Spencer was a hot piece of ass. She turned him on. She was also scared to death of him, and that turned him on even more.

Chapter 53

Ivey and Spencer pulled up to the garage and parked at the edge of the dirt driveway. As Ivey put the car into park, he saw Mack walking up to the car, interested but not over-eager. Ivey got out of the car and yelled, "Mack Grissett, what is going on!"

"Well, aren't you a sight for sore eyes! A small sight, but a sight nevertheless!" he replied and they shook hands heartily and amiably before Spencer could even get out of the car.

"Let me get Jack! Hey, Jack!" Mack yelled as they walked back toward the office. "Where is Jack's green-eyed goddess anyway?" he asked, referring to Rita.

"Brother, she is whipped! Rita has been whisked away from the land of the available by a suave, cool local," Ivey joked.

By this time Jack walked up having heard only Ivey's comment about Rita. "Say it ain't so, Ivey," Jack said. "My gypsy has gone over to the light side?"

Ivey sighed good-naturedly. "Well, she is on her way, at least," he said.

"Who is he? You said 'local.' Does that mean I know him?" he asked suspiciously.

"I don't know—maybe. Do you know Ross Moore? He's the culprit," Ivey continued.

"Oh my God," Jack and Mack said simultaneously, Mack quietly shaking his head with a smile on his face, Jack with his head straight back laughing out loud.

"I should have known. I should have known," Jack said. "That man always was a lady killer!"

"Yeah, the school girls hung on every word he said, but he never gave them the time of day. He was more interested in logarithms and soliloquies than sex. Crazy bastard," Mack said fondly.

"He was a hell of a good baseball player too," added Jack. "That's what Rita knows. She knows when a man's got game. That's why she loves me so much," he finished and chuckled at his mock vanity.

Mack had been watching Ivey and Spencer closely during the exchange and he knew they were here about Patrick Lowers. "What brings y'all here today?" he asked. "I'm sorry about Patrick. He didn't deserve his fate." As he talked he motioned for everyone to sit down around the picnic table under the oak beside the office.

"No, he didn't," Ivey said. "Did you respond to the accident?" he asked.

"Yeah, and man, it was a sorry sight," he said and shook his head at the memory of the scene.

"God..." Spencer answered, "What a mess," and she walked around beside Jack and sat back on the edge of the table.

"It's just crazy, Mack. I mean, we left him not even an hour before the accident and he wasn't even remotely intoxicated then," Ivey stated.

Mack commented, "He *missed* the bridge altogether. Drove off the edge and dropped straight down into the culvert," and he demonstrated the accident with his hands. "He may not have been drunk, but something sure wasn't right. *And* he didn't have his seatbelt on.

"What?" Spencer all but shouted. "No, no, no—Patrick Lowers has never in his life gotten into a car without buckling his seatbelt," Spencer said. "He was anal retentive that way. There is just no way..." and she let the rest of her comment just fade away.

"That drop sure tore the car up," Mack said.

"Where is the car now, Mack?" asked Jack as he got up and surveyed the property for it.

"It's over behind the shop next to the Parker's blue Volvo," he said.

Without anything further said, they all got up and began walking to the car. As they approached, Mack realized that someone had been in the car since he left it here last night. "Damn, somebody has been meddling here," he said and he trotted quickly up to the side of the car.

"How do you know?" asked Ivey as Mack looked inside but did not touch the crumpled wreckage that was Patrick's Toyota.

"The driver's side window was shattered but not broken out like this," Mack said.

"Let's call the police," Jack stated and he pulled out his cell phone.

"I'll bet you find Ricky Jarman's paw prints all over it," Spencer commented uneasily.

Mack turned abruptly and looked at Spencer inquisitively, and asked, "Why do you think Ricky is involved, Spencer?"

She sighed audibly and said, "That degenerate is involved alright..." and she recounted how Ricky was at the golf outing and what she and Rita had overheard last night behind the clubhouse. Then, she told them what she saw at the crash scene as they passed in the last hour. She finally added, "He wasn't there looking for bait fish, that's for sure."

Mack nodded as Spencer talked. When she finished, he told them that Ricky was at the scene when he arrived with the wrecker and was lurking warily in the background and he added, "You're right. Ricky Jarman is no casual bystander in this wreck."

After Jack had dispatched the sheriff's department, they all agreed to keep the discussion they just had confidential. Ivey and Spencer left before the sheriff deputies arrived. Jack and Mack promised to keep their eyes and ears open to see what they could find out about the events of the night before. They all agreed to talk quietly after the funeral tomorrow and Spencer and Ivey would make sure that Rita was up to date on what they had seen and heard.

What was unspoken was the growing uneasiness that the death of Patrick Lowers was more than just an unfortunate accident. The wreck was like a bomb, undetonated, but ticking. They were like the bomb squad—in harm's way from the shrapnel the impending explosion would create unless they could dismantle and disarm it first.

Chapter 54

The sun was barely visible above the western horizon as we canoed across the Shallotte Inlet back to the Moore family's dock at Shallotte Point. We shared an easy quietness in the dusk of what I considered an extraordinary day. After we crossed the torrid currents of the river's mouth, the pace was slow, easy and relaxed.

Ross smiled over at me and finally broke the silence when he asked, "So, how is your birthday shaping up so far?"

"Today has been…spectacular," I said, pausing for effect. "I wish it never had to end."

"Well, it is not over yet. I'm sure my parents have been deviously planning a spread that would impress Julia Childs. You need to watch them. Once they have designs on your soul, they are relentless in their pursuit to capture it," and he laughed at his over-dramatization of his folks.

"Again—apple and tree, Ross, apple and tree," and I smiled back at him because I knew it wasn't my soul in danger of capture, but my heart instead. I was a lost cause now.

He suddenly took on a more serious tone and leaned toward me. "Do you trust me, Rita?" he asked and he waited silently, looking for the answer in my face, my expressions, my reply.

I was almost stunned at the question. Did he really think I would bare my soul, my body, my heart to just anybody? I sat quietly and finally whispered, "Yes, I do. Isn't it obvious?"

"No. I don't take anything for granted, but good. Can I ask you something about Patrick?" he questioned, and I nodded.

"You said you didn't think Patrick's death was an accident. Why do you believe it wasn't?" he asked.

I was suddenly conscious of the stillness of the moment. There was only the two of us in the canoe drifting slowly toward his parents' dock on the western bank of the river. The wind had died down, the birds had nested for the evening and the paddles were silent, motionless and out of the water. I breathed in the air to calm my fears about the local bank. I was one of them. Ross was the president of the Big Bank, of Mega. Would talking to him label me a traitor? Would it cast suspicion on innocent local employees? Would it tarnish his opinion of me? I wasn't sure, but I knew that the fear of the answers to those questions paled in comparison to my fear of the danger of what was happening, what had happened in the Shallotte office, apparently for years, even before my employment.

"Ross, I'm afraid I've uncovered a mess, quite by accident," I stated quietly and looked off toward the horizon where the sun had left only a bright orange-pink glow in its disappearance. "I think what I touched on, Patrick completely figured out, and I think it got him killed." I breathed out loudly, then continued, "I saw a problem and gave it to Patrick to solve because I was too…too afraid of what digging might find. I was a coward. *I* got Patrick killed," and I looked at him intensely, afraid that if I said anything further, I might just fall to pieces.

He leaned forward toward me and took my hand. He put the index finger of his other hand under my chin, lifted my face to his and kissed me gently. "You know that's not true, Rita," he said. "Who else knows what you found?" he asked.

"Spencer and I figured out the general scheme last week and I gave the outline of information to Patrick by pretending I was confused by it and couldn't finish the budget because of it. Last night after you took me home, Spencer told Ivey. That's it…besides you. God, and you're the president of the bank…" and I shook my head at the thought of how inappropriate it was to take a local problem to executive management directly.

I steeled myself and continued to make sure he understood the situation fully or as fully as I did, "This situation is not some 'I'll take a twenty for the weekend and pay it back on payday,' okay? This fraud is long-running, complicated and widespread. There is collusion here on a grand scale and there has been for *years*. At least three or four employees are involved and the participants have funneled millions of dollars from overdrafts and loans into accounts all over the place over the last three years…and that's just what *I* know. Patrick knew much more," I finished.

"Do you know who is involved?" he asked quietly.

"No, but I know who isn't," I stated. "I'm not, Spencer is not, Ivey is not and, of course, Patrick was not. Everybody else is in play and under suspicion."

"How are you so sure Ivey is not involved?" he asked and firmly held my arm and continued, "I mean besides just…knowing?"

"Because he knew something was wrong when he was here. He started digging after he got railroaded on another Jarman loan charge-off that had been assigned to him. Suddenly, voila—an opportunity arises out of town, out of market, out of the way," I stated. "We didn't piece the connection with this mess together until last night after we got back to my condo."

Ross silently contemplated the information Rita just gave him. "Okay, there is fraud on a massive scale. The people you named all knew about it. What makes you think the knowledge got Patrick killed?"

I sighed and told him about the exchange between Ricky and some whispering male bank employee outside the clubhouse after the golf outing. I also told him about Ivey's conversation with Patrick as we were leaving, including the part where Patrick told Ivey he had sent documented evidence overnight to John Starr. As I finished, I felt a chill run up my spine. Telling the story out loud made the scheme even more real, more sinister. I realized I was shivering.

Ross got up expertly and moved over beside me. He kissed me lightly and searched my face for something. His face was etched with worry and I wondered if he thought I was some mad conspiracy theory nut-job or just a bank drama queen. He pulled me closer and said, "I'm glad you're going to your folks for a week, Rita. If you are right about Patrick, the murderer is desperate to conceal the fraud and anybody that gets in his or her way is in danger. That means you," he said quietly.

"I'm right and I know it. Spencer and Ivey are in danger too. Now I've involved you, the president of my bank…God, what a screwed up mess…" I finished.

"Hey, don't you worry about me, okay? We're in this together—you, me, Spencer, Ivey and the other 2000 innocent bank employees," he stated determinedly. "Do me a favor, though."

"Anything," I stated honestly.

"When you go into the office on Monday, I want you to be very careful as you work on the budget with Greg and Jeff. I don't want you to show them the pattern you uncovered, simply budget for each of the problem areas exactly what was budgeted last year. Then, I want you to give them the historical information while you are there and let them look at it. Your job is just to observe every reaction, action, comment, facial expression, body language… well, you know what to do, Rita," he said quietly. "Then, I want you to make me a copy of exactly what you gave Patrick. Call me on your way home to your folks in Misenheimer and I'll meet you in Albemarle where we can have dinner, look the documentation over and talk about it, okay?"

"Okay. Let's meet at the Board Room in downtown where we can sit in a quiet booth," I said, knowing that the privacy was for professional reasons, not personal ones.

Ross smiled at me slightly and said, "After Monday night, the dinner dates will be much less business and much more fun. I promise," he said and he held his fingers up in the boy-scout sign that totally lightened the tone of the evening.

I laughed and hoped it was a promise he would keep. I mimicked the sign back to him and said, "I take boy-scout promises very seriously."

"You should," he said. "You'll be in my town for the next week and I'm going to show you the Queen City like you've never seen her before. Of course, that's assuming I survive the dinner table with my parents sharing horribly embarrassing stories about me to you. I only hope they leave some vestiges of my dignity intact," he said and he sighed heavily, handed me my oar and moved back across from me. "Help me row, woman! My punishment for being such an entertaining child awaits," he added, and I laughed at his melodrama the rest of the way to the dock.

Chapter 55

Marian and Charlie stood at the screen door watching Ross and Rita laugh and banter with each other as they brought the canoe to the dock and walked casually back to the house up the oyster shell walkway. They stood close to each other, holding hands and talking with their heads close together, all the while smiling and laughing. They saw a budding relationship that had a fondness and closeness that neither had witnessed before in any relationship their son had ever had, including Ross' two-year fiasco of a marriage that ended years ago.

As Ross approached the porch, he saw his parents standing in the doorway and smiled up at them with genuine happiness as he said, "Uh-oh, Rita, they just can't wait to begin their stories. Mom is bad, but she is much worse when Dad chimes in. Beware, I tell you," and he laughed as he opened the door.

After the introductions were made between Charlie and me, Marian whisked me off to freshen up and wash my hands. Alone now in the foyer, Charlie turned back to his son, put his hand on his shoulder as they walked back out onto the porch and told him matter-of-factly, "Son, don't screw this one up, okay?"

Ross was a little confused and turned to face his dad and said, "What do you mean, Dad?"

"You are stupid over her," he said. "And quite obviously, she is stupid over you too. Now, come on, let's go fix the drinks for supper, I'm starving."

Ross was totally surprised by his dad's candor. Two sentences summed up and spelled out personal feelings he had never before shared with Ross. Charlie Moore was a man of few words, but when he spoke, Ross listened.

Ross followed his dad to the kitchen and they put ice cubes in the glasses, poured the tea and took them to the table. At the same time, I came around the corner and asked what I could do to help.

Charlie walked to chair facing the window and pulled it out for me to sit so I could see the water in the fading light of the evening. "Sit down right here, young lady," and he pushed me up to the table.

Marian brought the food to the table along with her men and finally, we all sat down to eat an absolutely fantastic dinner of Jamaican shrimp with peanut sauce, black beans over orzo, and fresh steamed greens. All the while, the funniest stories of Ross' childhood and adolescence were shared and laughter filled the room.

After dinner, coffee was passed around to complement Marian's chocolate cheesecake that would make any New York chef green with envy. She brought the dessert to the table with one candle lit in the middle as the Moores sang a three-part harmony version of "Happy Birthday" to me. Any outsider looking through the window would have sworn I was just another member of the family. The conversation was relaxed and comfortable as we wound down after an extraordinary day.

I offered to help do the dishes, but Marian and Charlie wouldn't hear of it. We walked out on the porch and said our goodbyes. I hugged each of them and thanked them for a wonderful birthday dinner and a memorable evening. Marian said, "I will be very upset if you don't come back to see me soon."

I answered, "I will, I promise. How else will I get that chocolate cheesecake recipe?"

The crescent moon had risen in the east and was reflected off of the water as we got in the SUV and pulled away from what I was certain was as close to Shangri-la as I had ever been. I sighed contentedly. "What a perfect birthday, Ross. Thank you," I said, and I leaned over kissed him squarely on the cheek. He reached over, grabbed my hand and kissed it.

"You are welcome, birthday girl. Now I better get you home so you can pack your bags to head west," he stated matter-of-factly.

"I can't wait," I said. "Tonight made me realize just how much I miss my own insane family. I hope you get a chance to meet them."

"I'll be disappointed if I don't," he replied. "Is that an invitation?"

"You bet," I stated. "I'll give you the full tour of the town in the first two minutes of your arrival then my parents can bore you for hours about what a problem child I was…am—you'll see." The thought of going home to Misenheimer broadened the smile on my face as we rode back to my car. I was sure my parents, sister and even brother would acknowledge a change in me within 15 seconds after I hit the door—happy, confident, and head-over-heels in love.

Chapter 56

When we pulled up outside of the Waffle House, night had fallen, heavy and deep. Ross leaned over and kissed me deeply. The kiss held the promise of the week to come alone with him in Charlotte. I had a fleeting thought of inviting him back to my condo and locking him in my bedroom for the rest of the night and half of Sunday, but I knew we both needed to pack. With him in my room the only place clothes would wind up would be on the floor as we raced to undress each other.

Besides, Ross was leaving tomorrow right after Patrick's funeral and he had a week of packing to do. So, as hard as tearing myself away from his touch, his kiss and his smoking hot body was, I did the right thing. I got out and unlocked the Miata. He waited for me to get buckled into my seat. I looked back over at him and smiled. He smiled back and rolled down the window and said, "Happy Birthday, Rita. Remember, the Board Room in Albemarle, Monday night. Call me on your way to your parents."

I nodded and replied, "Thank you again for a perfect day. I'll see you Monday evening." I rolled up the window and backed out, raised my hand to say goodbye and pulled away.

As I made my way home, I turned on the XM Radio to Carly Simons' "Anticipation." A cold chill went down my arms as I thought, "Exactly…" Monday seemed like an eternity away.

Get a grip, Rita, I scolded myself. I was acting like a silly, hormonal teenager. Besides, I would see him at the funeral tomorrow. As sad as I was about the funeral, I was glad he would be there even if he would be sitting with the bank's executive management team. I hoped to at least catch his eye, but I knew I had to be careful. He was in a powerful position as the bank president and I was just a mid-level manager. I had to protect him from gossip and rumors that could threaten his reputation.

I didn't want to be that threat to him, but that bell had already rung. Dammit! I had had sex with the bank president. Correction—I had had hot, consensual, fabulous sex with Ross Moore. What do I do about it now, I thought, besides keep our secret? The answer was nothing.

As scary as the implications of an affair were to our professional reputations, the thought of never getting another opportunity to be with him again was terrifying. Somewhere in the last month I had fallen in love with Ross Moore and I couldn't—and quite frankly, wouldn't—change that fact.

But other facts wouldn't change, either. Fact one, Patrick Lowers had been killed and his killer was on the loose. Fact two, I had uncovered a web of fraud and embezzlement that could implicate many powerful people both within and outside the bank. Fact three, I had shared the damning information with Spencer, Ivey, Ross, and Patrick which led right back to fact number one—Patrick Lowers had been killed.

As I pulled up to the condominium, I parked my car and reached into the back to retrieve the contents of my pocketbook from earlier in the day. Lipstick, checkbook, wallet, pens, paper—crap was everywhere! After making sure I had everything off of the floor, I locked the door and went inside. Once there, I put my purse down and walked upstairs to pack quickly so I could get a shower, make some hot tea and watch an old movie on television.

As I packed I was humming the Eagles tune "Best of My Love." As I walked around the bed to my dresser I looked out the sliding glass doors and paused. I could have sworn I closed my curtains on Friday before I left for work, but hey, the last two days felt like two millennia. I walked over to close the curtains. As I stared out into the courtyard, I looked around. The night was quiet in an eerie sort of way. I looked at the other condos with lights on and seeing nobody, I felt exposed, almost vulnerable standing in full view. I felt the hair on the back of my neck stand. My heart was beating hard enough for me to feel it in my ears. I was alone, but I felt like someone was watching me, staring at me through the darkness. I quickly closed the curtains and zipped my suitcase. I bounded down the stairs and out my front door. I walked next door and knocked. I heard footsteps and suddenly, Spencer opened the door.

As I blew out the breath I had apparently been holding, she said, "Are you okay? You must have had some birthday to still be out of breath," but I could tell she knew I was scared. "What's up, Rita? You look like you've seen a ghost."

"I don't know what is wrong with me, Spence. I was home packing when I felt like somebody was watching me, staring at me…which is stupid since the door was locked and nothing was out of place, really…" I stammered. "I'm losing my shit, woman!" and I half-heartedly laughed.

Spencer wasn't laughing though. She asked, "What does the 'really' mean?"

"Only that I thought I closed my curtains in the bedroom before I left the house this morning," I said. "I know I didn't sleep up there but I did take a shower after I got up. I don't remember opening the curtains back up… unless I just forgot to close them with all the craziness from the night before. I mean, we didn't get to sleep until after two or so in the morning. I don't know," I rambled.

"Huh. It's certainly not like you to dress with your curtains open, but you were operating on about four hours of sleep after a long day with a horrible ending. Go get some sleep. I'm right here," she assured me. "I'll come over tomorrow morning about 8:00 and we'll go eat some breakfast. Okay?"

"Okay. Hey, where's Ivey?" I asked.

"He's crashed out upstairs in the guest room. He came back here and packed up so he can leave for Raleigh after the funeral tomorrow. He's like you, and yes, me too. We've all had a long couple of days," she said.

I hugged her neck. "What in the world would I do without you, Spencer?" I asked.

"You'd be dull…and old! Happy birthday! Now, get out of here and go get some sleep. I'm giving you a break tonight and it is killing me to wait to hear all about your day with you-know-who until tomorrow. You better go before I change my mind!" and she opened her door to let me out. She stayed on the front porch until I opened the door to my place.

"Good night, Spencer," I said.

"Good night, John Boy," she snorted. "Go! I'll see you at 8:00."

I laughed and closed the door and made sure it was locked. As I checked the back door and turned off the lights, the serenity returned to the quiet and I relaxed. I went upstairs and climbed into the steamy, hot shower and let the water wash away the rest of my stress.

While wonderful in many ways, the last few days had rattled me. The discovery of fraud, the death of Patrick, and the search for the people connecting the two had left me jumpy, suspicious and scared. Rightly so, I thought to myself. This situation is going to destroy careers and lives when it is finally uncovered. The uncovering had just begun and already the process had proven to be much more than just dangerous: it had cost Patrick his life. Conversely, my, uh, relationship or at least my time spent with Ross had been idyllic. I was physically, intellectually and spiritually attracted to him. I was getting to know his family and he would soon get to know mine. I certainly had gotten to know him, well, in the biblical sense as my grandmother was fond of saying. Intellectually, he challenged me. He trusted me in banking matters and truly wanted my opinion on the people and processes at the bank.

As I crawled into bed, I was satisfied that at the very least, Ross respected me and liked me, but God, I wanted so much more. I wanted him beside me; I wanted him with me. Hell, I just wanted him period. I was suddenly exhausted and I thought about making love to him that afternoon. The memory temporarily satisfied my yearning. The memory made me smile. The memory faded into a deep, dreamless sleep.

Chapter 57

Dreadful is the only word that describes the heart-wrenching cries, moans and sobs of Patrick's girls and wife at the funeral the next day. I was almost physically sick to my stomach and I wasn't sure I was going to get through the service. Between the music that played to evoke fond memories and the touching photo DVD that ran along with it, the service captured the surprising, simple happiness of Patrick Lowers as a family man that we never knew, never saw at the bank.

Trying to detach myself from the overwhelming sadness I felt for his family, the service was an interesting, strange gathering. Filled to capacity, any casual observer who didn't know the man would believe that Patrick Lowers was roundly blessed by the gift of friendship. Unfortunately, the pews were not filled with friends. Instead, the congregants were almost entirely executive management, colleagues, co-workers and employees at Mega and other area financial institutions. Peppered among the bankers were customers, community leaders and most of the members of the bank's local advisory board. The "who's who" gathering would have impressed even Caleb Capps, but I found it antiseptic, impersonal and completely devoid of warmth for the man being remembered.

Perhaps, though, the service was more perfect than I cared to admit for a man that many people loved to hate and somebody hated enough to kill. Feeling the hair stand on the back of my neck, I looked around and caught Dylan staring at me. I pierced my gaze into him unflinching until he turned away. I made him uncomfortable and I wondered why.

Trying to be casually cool, I clandestinely looked for Ross. He was somewhere in the left alcove of the sanctuary mixed in among the executives of our bank. My stomach lurched at the thought of seeing him, of him seeing me. I had completely lost myself in wanting him. Ok, focus, please—funeral.

Spencer was to my right and Ivey to my left. I was so thankful for good friends—true friends who I was certain would be just as relieved as me when the service was over. Spencer hated anything emotional, especially when the dominating emotion was sadness.

Apparently reading my mind, she walked her fingers up my shoulder as she put her arm on the pew behind me. I looked over at her and she patted me on the back twice and smiled. I returned her smile and felt the tension in my back and neck ease significantly. We were all going to get through this together.

As the service came to a close, we stood and the family left the church to go to the graveside. They let the alcoves exit first since they were at the front of the church. As the management team somberly filed out, Ross passed our pew and looked over at me. He smiled slightly and nodded his head. I smiled back and sighed. I heard Spencer quietly laugh behind me, and I bumped her with my butt to let her know I heard her.

We filed out of the church into the bright sunshine of another beautiful fall day and worked to adjust our eyes. As I rummaged through my purse to find my sunglasses, Ross walked up to Ivey and was talking to him quietly. Spencer joined them and I watched them talk together with the fondness of old friends. The sight made me exceptionally happy. As I headed to join them, Jeff Malone stopped me.

"Hi Rita," he said quietly. "That was quite a service, huh?"

I nodded and tried not to appear annoyed. "Yes. It's easy for us to forget that Patrick was a husband, son and father and not just our boss or co-worker."

"Well put," he said and then continued, "Hey, I was thinking that you really don't need to come into the office tomorrow since you had planned to go out of town on vacation. Do you want Greg and me to just handle the budget?"

Stunned at the question, I paused to restrain myself from asking him if he was smoking crack or trying to push me out of the process when I remembered that he did not know what I knew and calmed myself from answering by sighing loudly. I could see he thought the budget process was upsetting because of Patrick's death, so I simply said, "That is a kind, generous offer, Jeff, but I've done most of the legwork and it won't take me long to give it to you and Greg and let you go over it after I leave."

He looked me in the eyes silently for a few seconds that quite frankly felt like an eternity and then patted me on the arm and said, "Okay, Rita, but just don't wear yourself out."

I nodded and said, "Thanks, Jeff. I'll see you tomorrow."

I walked over between Spencer and Ivey. Ivey put his arm around me and I leaned my head into his. "I'm glad you stayed, John Michael," I whispered.

"Me too," he said.

Spencer leaned over and said just loud enough for Ross, Ivey and me to hear, "What was *that* all about?"

"Oh, he offered to let me go ahead and go on vacation without going into the office tomorrow to assist with the budget," I said and lifted my left eyebrow to Ross.

"Interesting…" was all Ross said.

"He seemed to be concerned that it might upset me and ruin my vacation," I continued.

"Yeah, you're a real puddle of nerves, Rita," Spencer retorted. "I think he's hiding something or knows something."

"Maybe," I said, "But he didn't seem put out when I told him no either. We'll see. Can we just get out of here now?" I asked.

"Let's go, sisters," Ivey said, and he offered each of us an arm to escort us. "Ross, I hope to see you soon," he said and offered Ross his hand and Ross shook it.

Ross smiled at me and said, "Ivey, you are a lucky man. I will see you soon. Be careful on your way back to Raleigh. 'Bye Spencer, keep 'em straight while we're away, okay?" and he looked at me and continued, "I'll see you tomorrow, my lady," and he quickly winked and walked away.

"Breathe, Rita," Spencer teased. Ivey bumped her with his hip.

"You're mean, Spencer, mean," I laughed and we walked arm-in-arm back to Ivey's beat up, old FJ to head home.

Chapter 58

Unbelievably, Monday came quickly after rushing to pack late Sunday night. After the funeral, Ivey, Spencer and I lingered at Roberto's Pizza to discuss the week behind us, the week ahead and generally compare notes to make sure we were all on the same lesson. Ivey agreed to come back for the Halloween party in less than two weeks at least partly to check on us and to stay connected with everything happening in Shallotte.

It was difficult saying goodbye to him for both Spencer and me. I guess after such a sad, mournful ending to the life of Patrick Lowers, we needed each other and the closeness you can only feel among best friends. Finally, after a many hugs and I-love-yous, Ivey left for Raleigh.

Spencer twisted my arm after Ivey left and talked me into having a beer over her house and watching a movie. As much as I complained and half fought the idea, I was so glad she invited me over. We chose a comedy and laughed until beer came out our noses it was so funny. When I walked over to my place, I was in a great mood, happy and relaxed, but it was late and I was beat.

Forcing myself upstairs, I packed quickly and lightly. I still washed clothes at Mom and Dad's every time I visited for two reasons. First, Mom washed clothes almost every day anyway. Second, I hated to pack dirty clothes. As a habit, I always limited myself to one suitcase and my bag of toiletries no matter where I went and it never took me long to pack.

I think I was asleep before I hit the pillow and I slept like a rock. I was still fast asleep when my TV came on to awaken me in the morning. I was also still tired, but once I got into the shower, I emerged re-energized about leaving to go see my family and excited about seeing Ross. First, though, I had to get through the budget fiasco with Greg and Jeff, manage not let on that I knew there was a problem and judge each of their reactions once they saw the same information I presented to Patrick. Ugh, what a task. Yep, I was dreading it.

I put on my khakis and a pullover, refusing to dress in a business suit on my day off and lugged my suitcase and toiletry bag downstairs to the car. I poured myself the largest travel mug of coffee I could find in the cabinet (automatically-programmed coffeemakers are the best invention in the world in the mornings!), started the loaded dishwasher, and locked the condo on my way out the door.

I looked over at Spencer's as I got into my car and saw the light on in her upstairs bedroom. She was getting ready for work. I was thankful she would be in the office today so we could talk after my one-act play with Jeff and Greg was over.

As I drove the short five minutes to the office, I listened to the radio to drown out the chorus of self-doubting voices in my head. I wanted to arrive early to get the budget information together, rehearse my spiel for the "presentation," and use a critical eye on the documentation to see if anybody could overlook the pattern. I knew the answer and the answer was no. Crap, here we go again…

I opened the car door when I arrived at the bank and breathed in as much of the crisp autumn air as my lungs would hold. As serene as the morning was outside, my insides were stirred up like a storm. I was the first to arrive at the bank which meant that I had to disable the alarm, check out the premises and set the morning glory signal—an alert to the subsequently arriving employees that the coast was clear for entry. The process is methodical and mundane—which is good—and actually helped settle my churning guts.

I sat down at my desk and got to work on the preparation needed for the meeting. Somewhere in the 30-minutes that I had the bank to myself, I decided I was going to present the budget situation to Greg and Jeff the same way I had to Patrick. I would go through the deposit projections, retail and small business loan projections and fee income projections quickly and easily, then I would present the three "confusing" areas to them and tell them that I didn't understand them—overdrafts, loan charge-offs and commercial loan projections. I would give them the historical numbers from the last three years and tell Greg and Jeff that Patrick suggested that he handle those accounts for me. I would appeal to their respective areas of expertise—commercial lending for Jeff and regional management for Greg—and ask them to handle the budget in those areas. I was sure Greg would help because he was a great manager who worked well in collaborative settings. I thought Jeff would help because he was the region's senior credit officer and now had dominion over his budget for the first time ever. At that point, I would be finished with the budget—free at last—and I could go say goodbye to Spencer and hit the road. The entire presentation would take me 30 minutes. I would be on the road by 10 a.m. Oh, how I longed for 10 a.m.

Chapter 59

Ross had arrived back in Charlotte around 8 p.m. on Sunday night. While Jinx went into the back yard to stretch his legs, Ross straightened up the house and unpacked. He was finished in less than an hour and went into his home office to answer e-mails and get a head start on tomorrow's workload. His office was more like a library. It was filled with shelves stocked with books of every genre—fiction and non-fiction.

Ross loved to read. Unfortunately, when he was on assignment, which he was now, he rarely had time to read for enjoyment. Reports, ledgers, internal memos and e-mails filled his time and took him away from his life-long escape mechanism from the world—reading.

He walked over and pulled down one of his favorite books about George Washington, his historical hero. As he ran his finger down the spine of the book he thought about the courage and leadership Washington had demonstrated to help him withstand the challenges of 1776. He was an incredible man and Ross worked hard every day to emulate those attributes. This assignment, this placement was much, much harder than he imagined it would be. He had gotten to know the executive management team on a personal level and considered several of them friends. He had grown fond of many of the regional employees and management teams and respected the front-line work they did every day to allow the bank to operate. Then there was Rita...wow, she blew him away. She was a smart, dedicated, honest, beautiful and sexy banker. She had seeped into his veins, captivating him with her goodness inside and out. She was in danger because of her integrity and he was going to protect her if all else failed. Rita claimed ownership of American One Bank and took her responsibility there very seriously. So did the vast majority of the other two thousand employees. So did Ross.

Ross replaced the book, sat down and got to work. He had a report to write. He had a bank to protect. He had a killer to catch.

Chapter 60

Greg, Jeff and I sat around the small round conference table in Patrick's office. It was still too awkward, too emotional and too daring to sit behind his desk. Doing so by any of us would seemingly convey, "I'm in charge now. I've taken Patrick's place." None of us wanted to seem that bold or insensitive.

I breezed through the lion share of the budget information in record time justifying each budget entry with three years of historical data and facts. Greg and Jeff asked very few questions and nodded in agreement with the decisions. Then, I pulled out the three budget items at issue. I feigned confusion and told them that I had given the historical data to Patrick because I didn't understand how to budget given the volatility in the three accounts.

I shrugged my shoulders and finished, "Patrick agreed to do these entries himself because he said he didn't have time to educate me on how to budget properly." I sighed and continued, "I didn't even know where to begin…"

Greg reached over tenderly and said, "Everything is fine, Rita. Jeff and I will look over this information and plug in the numbers. Then, when you get back, you and I can sit down and go over them if you'd like to understand what we did, okay?"

I was speechless. Apparently, so was Jeff. I struggled to find my voice and finally managed, "Okay, Greg. Thank you. It is hard to admit you don't know how to do something."

Jeff never took his eyes off of me and snapped out of his budgetary coma long enough to say, "I agree with Greg, Rita. We'll finish the entries today. Commercial loans are very difficult to budget. With lines of credit and refinancing, volatility is a given. Don't be so hard on yourself, okay?"

I smiled and added, "Okay. I can't tell you how much I appreciate your help. I can go on vacation knowing the budget is in very good hands." I stood and grabbed my purse. I put my hand on Greg's shoulder and squeezed it slightly and said, "Thanks again. I'll see you next Monday."

"Bye, Rita. Be careful on your way there and back," Greg said.

Jeff nodded, smiled slightly and added, "Take care."

As soon as I turned the corner, I breathed a huge sigh of relief. I hurried around to the other side of the office to say goodbye to Spencer. I walked in and closed the door softly.

I decided not to sit down so I would appear to be just casually saying goodbye. As soon as the door latched behind me Spencer said, "Well...?"

"I think I was fairly convincing that I was confused and needed help on the three items where the problems are embedded," I stated. "They even offered to share the new entries with me and help me understand them when I return."

Spencer looked skeptical. "I'm not so sure they weren't playing you as well as you think you were playing them. I mean, *I* figured it out," she said. "Or maybe they are not involved. I don't know."

"I know what you mean. I hope we're wrong and this fiasco is not as vast as we think. I want to believe my co-workers and managers are honest and good," I said, "but at least one of them is not." Patrick's death hit me again. We had a killer among us.

"Be careful on your way to Misenheimer, okay?" Spencer said. "I'm going to miss you while you're out hitting the town with President Wonderful and picking corn and watch the hay grow and crap!"

I laughed. "Just don't shave any more strokes off your golf handicap while I'm gone. You're making me look bad on the links, now."

Spencer snorted, "Woman, you don't need my help looking bad out there! Now get out of here!" and she came around the desk and gave me a big bear hug.

"Promise me you'll be careful, Spencer," I said seriously and she nodded and rolled her eyes. "I'll see you on Sunday," and I kissed her on the cheek and turned to go.

As I headed to the car, I was almost giddy with excitement to be leaving the bank and heading home, heading to see my family, heading to see Ross.

Just as prominent, though, was relief. I had managed to get through the budget session. I felt like I was convincing in my ignorance and naivety of the ramifications of the information I presented.

It was behind me now. I was finished. I was free.

Chapter 61

Greg and Jeff continued sitting around the table in silence after Rita left the room. When Greg could take it no more he stood and began pacing back and forth in the office. He ran his hand through his hair and said, "God, the information is stark, obvious, damning…" and stopped pacing, breathed a huge sigh of relief, looked over at Jeff and added, "Thank God Rita didn't figure it out."

Jeff appeared amused at the situation. He stood casually, pushed the chair back to the table, and leaned over toward Greg and calmly said, "Do you really think she is that ignorant, man?" He just nodded, refusing to wait on Greg to answer and slowly smiled when he stated, "We're talking about Rita Miller here, Greg. She knows. And let me tell you what else—if she knows, Spencer knows and if Spencer knows, Ivey knows. Those are the facts here whether you choose to believe them or not. "

Greg sat down, almost collapsed on the chair behind him. Jeff packed up his papers, stacking them neatly and turned to go. When he got to the door, he stopped and walked slowly back over to Greg. "We know the situation here, buddy," Jeff said. "We know who knows what. The question is how we're going to deal with it."

"I'm not going to 'deal with it' at all, Jeff. I'm going to get my part of this budget done. I adopted a 'don't ask, don't tell' policy a long time ago here and I'm not about to change it now. Excuse me. I have to prepare to meet Patrick's widow tomorrow morning." And Greg walked past Jeff and abruptly left the room.

Now alone, Jeff chuckled to himself. Greg is so gullible, he thought. Oh well, he figured out Rita's secret anyway. She knew there was a big problem in Shallotte and the Southeast Region of the bank. She might fool Greg and she may have fooled Patrick, but she can't fool me. First of all, she is too smart to have ploughed through all of the budget details she did and not identify the problem. Second, she would never have gone to Patrick to help her figure something out. If she truly didn't understand or know something, she would have gone to Greg or even to him before being treated like crap by the condescending Mr. Lowers.

No question about it. Rita knew. The only question was what she was going to do with what she knew. *Oh, Rita. I hope you're careful*, he thought. They don't say ignorance is bliss for nothing. Turning a blind eye to management problems had been his specialty for the 15 years he had been here. He didn't want any part of it. He was required to review loans, approve loans up to two million, and coach the team on credit policy and banking regulations. He didn't touch the big loans—and never had—even when he knew they were a cluster of crap and destined for being charged off to loss.

Jeff sighed. She could really screw up Shallotte, but God, what a fun time watching the rats scurry in the meantime, he decided. Sadly, she wouldn't even mean any harm because Rita Miller didn't have a mean bone in her body. She was tough, she was fair, and yes, she was incredibly intelligent. From an IQ standpoint, she was by far the smartest in the region, but the best part was that she had cunning common sense too.

No doubt, she intrigued him but Jeff was just as sure Rita scared some of the other idiots in the region to death. To death—what an unsettling thought, but he was sure if she chose to disturb the status quo in Shallotte she might get hurt. Worse still, she might not survive it.

Let sleeping dogs lie, Rita, he thought. He picked up his papers to go back to his office and plug in the commercial loans budget. As he turned off the light in Patrick Lowers' old office, he sighed. Patrick had been hell-bent on vengeance to get what he wanted—power, position and prestige. In the end, it had cost him his life. Was it worth it, buddy? He looked heavenward for an answer he knew would never come. Patrick was dead.

His secret wasn't though. Rita knew. Logically then, Spencer knew and Ivey knew too. With Rita gone for a week, there would be damage control and clean-up going on at the bank in Shallotte. Things should be very interesting for a change around here, he thought.

He walked around the corner and good-naturedly began whistling "Hard-Headed Woman" by Cat Stevens. He was going to go visit with Spencer. She was hard as hell to read, even harder to get her to give up information and impossible to compromise. She never hesitated to question why someone wanted information. He loved a challenge.

Chapter 62

The disk was not in Patrick's safe deposit box. He had to find it. He had to destroy it. *Where is that damn disk,* he questioned himself silently.

He and Angie, the teller supervisor, signed the box entry log under his name and his safe deposit box and entered the vault. Angie inserted the guard key into the lock of box 218. He removed Patrick's box key from his pocket and put it into the lock beside the guard key. The lock turned and they opened the box vault and removed the long, gray box. They closed the box vault door behind them and pulled out both keys.

He took the box to the small, private contents room adjacent to the vault. Once inside, he rifled through the contents piece by piece, document by document. The documents were a summary of the important things in the life of Patrick Lowers—his house deed, his car title, stock certificates, life insurance policies. The box also contained those things that mattered to Patrick, things that defined an important moment, person, or achievement—old coins, a gold pocket watch, a small silver spoon--all the things that mattered except the one that contained the information that cost him his life.

He sighed loudly. He methodically placed the contents back into the box in the same order he had removed them. He left the room with the box. Angie met him at the vault door. They entered together and replaced the box quickly in the same manner they had removed it. He placed the key back into his pocket and they left the vault together.

Angie looked at him; he shook his head. She squeezed his arm to comfort him. He walked away quickly. He hated to be pitied.

He went to his office and closed the door. He felt angry. He felt desperate. He felt like crying. The disk was not in the office. The disk was not in the car. The disk was not in the box.

He put his head in his hands. *Think, man, think!*

The thoughts started to come to him then—maybe the disk was at Patrick's house, maybe there was no disk, maybe Patrick had sent it to the police, the SBI, the FBI. *God, is my hair on fire yet?* Thinking scared the crap out of him.

He closed his eyes and tried to calmly think again. Maybe Patrick gave the disk to somebody. He suddenly opened his eyes. The answer surprised him in its simplicity. Patrick gave the disk to a friend. Whoa—Patrick didn't have any friends, he thought.

Back up, he told himself. He didn't have friends, but Patrick did like people at the bank. Who did he like? Who did he trust?

He closed his eyes again and mentally narrowed down his choices. Jeff? Don't be ridiculous, he thought. Jeff was useful to Patrick, but Patrick probably suspected he was somehow involved. He counted out all of the regional management—Patrick's competition. He quickly discounted the commercial team because Patrick loathed them. He eliminated all of the retail folks—Patrick would never stoop so low.

Suddenly, he opened his eyes. This new-age, meditation crap had merit. He thought about Rita Miller. She was high enough in the local bank hierarchy, smart enough to understand the problem and so completely honest that even if Patrick was jealous of her, he would trust her to get the information into the proper hands.

Yes, Patrick would trust Rita with the disk, but where was it? Rita was gone all week. He had to search her office. He had to be careful. He had to find that disk.

Chapter 63

The drive to the Piedmont was dreadful, encompassing every driving nightmare—rain, fog and wind. A cold front was passing through, promising cooler, drier weather in its aftermath. I just wished the aftermath would have coincided with now. Even with the harrowing weather elements, the drive was scenic as the oaks, maples, hickories and dogwoods put on a colorful display of leaves across the rolling terrain. Somewhere around Ellerbe, the dirt had become a bright red ribbon of water in the ditches adjacent to the winding road through the Uwharrie Mountains, clay turning to mud from the torrential rains.

Despite the dreariness of the day, the homecoming drive always felt good. As I turned onto Highway 24/27, drove over the Lake Tillery Bridge and crossed the Stanly County line, I honked the horn—a time-honored Miller family tradition—to welcome myself back home. I was approaching Albemarle now and the excitement in my gut grew as the time to see Ross drew closer. Taking a deep breath, I pulled into parking lot of the McDonald's to call Ross.

He answered on the first ring and I steadied myself so I didn't sound like some crazy, lovesick stalker.

"Ross? It's Rita. I'm finally in Albemarle," I stated as calmly as I could.

"What a hellish drive," he said. "Do you feel like getting together at the Boardroom or do you just want to go on home to Misenheimer?" he asked.

Is there really a question here? I thought to myself. "No, I'd like to meet if you've got time," I said casually. Meanwhile, my guts were churning.

"Wild horses couldn't keep me away," he said with a sure smile in his voice.

"Me either," I replied almost breathlessly.

"I'll be there in forty-five minutes. Will you go on and get us a table?" he asked.

"You bet," I said, "I'm five minutes away, but I'm going to stop across the street and '*Parlez Francais'* with my high school French teacher. She owns the antique mall across the street. I'll see you around 4 o'clock. Be careful, Ross," I finished.

"I will. I'll see you at 4."

Venez vite, quatre heures!

Chapter 64

What a damn weirdo, Spencer thought as she headed out of her office to the ladies' room. She needed to clear her head after a "Twilight Zone" encounter with the credit creep otherwise known as Jeff Malone. He made her skin crawl and she wasn't sure why. He was single, successful and well-dressed. He was handsome, too, in a worn, rugged kind of way. She was sure of her intuition, though, and rarely was it wrong. Today, her inner Spencer told her there was a skunk in the bank and the odor appeared to be emanating from the general direction of Mr. Malone.

He was asking questions like, "I saw Rita at your house late on Sunday night. What in the world were you doing all evening?" and "Did you help Rita with the budget she prepared for Patrick? She seemed to have her hands full with it." All the while, he kept that sly smile on his face as if he was amused at her reaction to the questions he posed. Spencer knew Jeff really didn't give a rat's ass about what she thought or how she felt about anything around the bank. He wanted information. He wanted validation for what he suspected. Quickly, she surmised he suspected that Rita knew more than she revealed at their meeting this morning.

But she was on to him more than he was on to them. Jeff Malone had the warmth of an abominable snowman, but Spencer long ago perfected her "ice queen" persona. She flashed her snow-white smile at him and gave him the vaguest, uncaring answers available. A couple of "nothings" and "not me's" and she sent the information miner slinking away, hopefully frustrated, but the tight-lipped smile never left his lips.

Was he involved? *Who the hell knew*, Spencer thought. He was an enigma. Jeff Malone was emotionless, unflappable, and antagonistic. She had never really met anybody quite like him. Nothing seemed important to him—not power, position, or paycheck. So if he was involved, what was his gain? He had no family, he had no friends and he had no obvious hobbies. He drove a boring sedan and lived in the same condo complex as she and Rita, a respectable but far from prestigious address with the abundance of waterfront mini-mansions and gated communities in the area. He didn't even own a boat.

As she washed her hands at the sink, Spencer concluded she just couldn't be sure of anything related to Jeff Malone because she didn't know enough about him and nobody else seemed to know him either. That conclusion bounced around the back of her mind then suddenly boomeranged back to the front with frightening clarity. Ignorance is power. Jeff had walled his world off completely from everybody at the bank. What was he afraid of? What was he hiding?

Perhaps Spencer didn't bring the intellect of Ivey and the business savvy of Rita to their roundtable discussions, but what she did bring was tenacity, intuition and cunning. She looked herself in the eye in the mirror and saw a steely determination. She would decipher Mr. Malone. She would break him open. She just prayed he had a warm, kind center instead of a cold, black, empty core. The shudder that ran down her spine only slightly slowed her down as she left the ladies room and headed around the corner for round two with Jeff Malone. She was not going to be deterred. She was not going to sit idle and do nothing. She was not going to let her bank get taken down without a fight.

Chapter 65

I walked in the door of Judee Jones' antique store and smiled. I heard her before I saw her over near the furniture section haggling gently and good-naturedly with a customer. She is good, I thought to myself.

She was telling the dapper, older gentleman about a pine pie safe in which he was obviously interested. She had done her homework. She also read the buyer like a book, lyrically describing the piece's history as one of intrigue and prominence. She talked about the maker, his family and their reluctance to sell such a beautiful heirloom. The man was enthralled. The man was sold. His checkbook never had a chance.

Judee shook hands with him, patted him on the arm and walked the price tag over to the register for another employee to ring up. She was ready for the next customer, but all she got was me. When she looked up and saw me, though, she visibly hurried over to me and wrapped me warmly in her embrace. I returned the affection. I loved this woman dearly.

Ms. Jones was one of the most remarkable people I had ever known. She was one of the most well-read teachers I had ever known. She taught French at my high school. She also taught Classical Literature. I had her for French from my sophomore through senior years. Classical Literature was an elective for seniors that only nine "readaholics" like me dared to choose for course credit. The class was the most exciting, stimulating and educational course I have ever taken. Ms. Jones exposed me to the enormity of the world through literature. She taught me to reach for my dreams, to question everything, to trust my instincts. She taught me how to speak French remarkably well in three years, and even more amazing was how she brought the French culture, people and countryside to life in my mind. While my mother instilled a love for reading in me, Ms. Jones taught me that classical literature was timeless, that fiction could be as true to life as non-fiction and that the best characters are those that are defined by defending what they believed.

And Ms. Jones was one of those characters. She had been vilified late in her career for defending the separation of church and state, i.e. the school. In doing so, she was dubbed a "demon worshipper" by a very powerful parent of one of her students. The parent also happened to be the president of the P.T.A. and the brother of the county school superintendent. Both were quoted in the paper as they worked to condemn her in the court of public opinion. They tried to embarrass her by posting graphic, obscene flyers all over the county and sought to intimidate her by organizing a protest before the homecoming football game where she was pelted with eggs as she walked through the mob to go work the concession stand.

Then she fought back. She hired the top civil rights attorney in the country, not county or state or region. She sued the brothers, the school board and the county for defamation of character, libel and slander in federal court. Exhibits A through Z included flyers, newspaper articles, photographs, and recordings of interviews that the brothers had given to the local radio and television stations. Bottom line, the brothers and their assets and the county and school board and their liability insurers were screwed.

The lawyers tried to negotiate a settlement in private, but Judee would have none of it. This fight was about what was right, what was just. She took the case over a five-year period to federal court and the court of appeals, winning every step of the way. She never let principal get in the way of her principle. She prevailed with a twenty-five million dollar judgment, the highest at the time ever awarded to a plaintiff against a municipality in the state of North Carolina. The brothers were ruined financially and finally moved away from the county which they jointly all but ruined financially as well.

Judee never looked back, choosing to leave a 25-year teaching career behind. As a former student, I realized that her absence from the halls of my alma mater was the greatest disservice the idiot brothers did to the subsequent seniors in Classic Literature. I was fortunate to have learned under her tutelage. I was even luckier to have gotten to know her. She introduced me to journalism and she served as my advisor with the local newspaper. She was my mentor.

Today, though, she was my friend and she took my hand and led me back to the furniture section where we sat down on a Chippendale sofa and caught up. The years melted away and we reminisced fondly about the school, our work, and our lives. She said she was doing well at the antique store and had been able to travel to Europe extensively to purchase some beautiful pieces to sell. She said that her stay in the French Alps was wonderful and that a handsome gentleman from Grenoble made brushing up on her French very enjoyable. The highlight of her trip, though, was her visit to Stratford-on-Avon where she walked in William Shakespeare's footsteps. We truly were kindred spirits.

I told her that my work at the bank was going well but that times were stressful as I juggled dual roles as a small business banker and a branch manager. I also told her about Patrick and voiced my concern about the circumstances surrounding his death. I told her the trait I admired most about Patrick was his love of Shakespeare, but that he was a nightmare of a manager.

"And what else?" she asked suspiciously, "What are you not telling me?"

and she raised her eyebrows and cocked her head slightly. She knew me too well.

"Ross Moore," I stated emphatically. "I'm crazy about him. He's the president of the bank." I looked at her beseechingly.

"Well, it's about damn time, Rita. You sure aren't getting any younger," and she laughed heartily and lovingly as she squeezed my hand. She rose and looked at her watch. "Don't keep him waiting," she said and she pulled me easily up off of the couch and kissed me on the cheek.

"How did you know I was meeting him?" I asked intrigued as we walked to the door.

"I've seen you look at the clock on the wall at least a dozen times in the last fifteen minutes!" she teased.

"God, I'm so rude," I mumbled quietly. "Will you forgive me, Judee?" I begged. "I didn't even realize I was doing it."

"Woman, you're not rude; you're in love. Now go!" she insisted and almost pushed me out the door. I couldn't help but smile and after I crossed Main Street, I turned and blew her a kiss. She rolled her eyes and shook her head all the while smiling while she motioned impatiently for me to open the door and go inside.

Teacher knows best.

Chapter 66

Ivey hung up the telephone after talking to Spencer. He began pacing back and forth in his office that overlooked Capital Avenue in Raleigh. He was worried about Spencer, he was worried about Rita, and he was worried about not knowing who else he should worry about. And here he was 150 miles away, powerless to stop the impending train wreck.

He stopped pacing and returned to the chair behind his desk. He grabbed his telephone and dialed the number he knew by heart and listened to it ring in his ear. On the third ring, the familiar baritone answered, "J&M, this is Mack, how may I help you?"

Ivey breathed a sigh of relief. "Man, am I glad to hear your voice, Mack. This is Ivey. Have you got a minute?" he asked and hoped Mack did.

"For you, of course," he replied good-naturedly. "How is the capital city today?"

"Wet, windy and cold," Ivey stated. "More importantly, how is Shallotte? What is happening with the investigation into Patrick's wreck? I feel completely disconnected here," he said.

"Well, the detectives have been interestingly silent. I get the feeling that the feds, or at the very least, the SBI guys are calling the shots. I did talk to the coroner, though. He said that Patrick did have alcohol in his blood but that he was not even close to being legally drunk. Nobody's told me so, but I believe this is more than an accident investigation at this point and my guess is that the local oversight for it has been wrested away from the locals," he finished.

"Huh," Ivey answered. "Do you think they suspect murder or at the very least foul play?" he questioned.

"I think they do and I also believe that any investigation might be compromised at the local level. I can't imagine how they found out about the break-in here at our lot since not one of the local detectives filed a report after our call," Mack stated sarcastically.

"You're kidding, right?" Ivey said amazed. "That has to mean that somebody involved has some powerful influence with the police force."

"Maybe," Mack replied, "Or it could just be one bad egg in the bunch of policemen who wields power over the others, you know? Whatever, the reason—corruption, incompetence or laziness—this investigation has gained some traction with much bigger wheels than the Shallotte PD or the Brunswick County Sheriff's Department."

"Hey, Mack, will you go by and check on Spencer over the weekend for me?" Ivey asked. "Rita is on vacation in the Piedmont, I'm up here in Raleigh…well, will you just check on her for me?"

"No problem, Ivey," Mack reassured him. "I live just down from there you know. I'll also keep an eye on Rita's place until she gets back."

"Thanks, Mack," he said, obviously relieved. "Spencer just doesn't have anybody else to protect her and she thinks she's invincible a lot of the time. I don't think she is nearly as worried about her safety as Rita and I are."

"She's on my watch now, Ivey. Relax, okay?" Mack said.

"Okay, Mack. I just feel like the lid has come off of Pandora's Box and instead of backing away and being cautious, Spencer is up to her elbows digging around inside," Ivey said.

Mack agreed and added, "And nobody grabs attention like Spencer Cashwell."

Chapter 67

Spencer walked around the corner toward Jeff's office. She was going to put on her most irritated attitude and walk back and confront Mr. Malone again. She was going to go at him headfirst. She rounded the corner, slowed her walked substantially and walked to the frame of Jeff's door. He was on the telephone.

Instead of walking back to her office, she backed up slightly to give him a little—very little—privacy and impatiently and noticeably tapped her foot. She knew without seeing him that she got his attention and she heard him hang up the phone. As soon as he did, Spencer brazenly waltzed into his office with her arms crossed and sat down. Yeah, he was stunned.

In his silence, she looked at him with an inquisitive look on her face, but she paused for effect, acting like she was searching for words. Finally, before he could muster a "what" or a "did-you-want-something," she spoke.

"What do you really want to know, Jeff?" she questioned suspiciously. "I mean, you've never given me the time of day before you came into my office earlier. Why are you suddenly so curious about my conversations or what I do at night? Or is it Rita who's got you preoccupied?" and she waited, silently, for him to respond.

As if a cloud cleared from the sun, he smiled slowly, but broadly, and walked around the desk, closed the door, and walked over to where Spencer sat, leaned back against the desk beside her and sighed.

He looked amused. He looked down at her with his arms crossed and asked, "Would you have noticed if I gave you the time?"

Damn, she thought, *he's pretty bold too.*

Instead of being intimidated, she stood and leaned back against his desk beside him, her arms still crossed. Then, she slowly turned her head to look at him, searched his face for a second and answered cautiously, "Yes. It doesn't take an Einstein to figure out that I already noticed that you had never given me the time before, does it?"

He chuckled and held her eyes. "Touché'," he said.

She took an exaggerated sigh. "Okay," she said firmly and turned and smiled at him. "My place at 7 p.m. Wednesday—I choose the food, you bring the movie—and don't disappoint me, Jeff Malone."

His wheels were turning as he looked at her, seemingly trying to figure her out for what felt like ages before he met her smile and answered, "I may surprise you, but I won't disappoint you, Spencer."

The hair on the back of her neck stood so tall she was sure she was six inches off of the floor. Spencer had never seen this side of Jeff before—aggressive, confidently relaxed. Before she ran away like a maniac or collapsed because her knees went to mush, she managed to stand and walk coolly to the office door. She glanced over her shoulder and softly said, "Good, because I know where you live!"

As she strolled out into the hallway and walked back to her office, his quiet laughter followed her. She headed back to the restroom, almost out of breath. When she got to the mirror, she was flushed in the face and her hands were shaking. She took several deep breaths.

Am I excited? Am I scared? Spencer thought. *Am I CRAZY?* She suddenly but silently asked herself in the mirror. She had just invited this man, this co-worker, this stranger to her house. She wasn't bold, she was reckless, she thought.

Spencer took one more deep breath and splashed her face with cold water. She would call Rita and let her know what she had done—no, not a good idea. Rita would discourage her, and Spencer was going to figure out who was involved. She could. She would.

And she would start with Jeff Malone. After all, her invitation was innocent and neighborly. Okay, not so much, but maybe there was an interesting side to the credit man, she thought. He was surprisingly funny and witty in conversation today. Wednesday would be interesting—no bank professionalism, no business protocol—as they got to know each other socially. She wanted to be pleasantly surprised by him, she admitted to herself.

Strangely, the inner Spencer was silent now. She was more comfortable with Jeff than she imagined she could be. Perhaps he wasn't involved in the bank fraud at all, she thought. "You better hope not," she told herself out loud. Otherwise, she had befriended a definite crook and even a possible killer and he was coming to her house for dinner on Wednesday, alone.

CHAPTER 68

The Boardroom was virtually empty, in part, because of the afternoon downpour, but mostly due to the early hour. The downtown crowd was still at work at the banks, the offices and the shops that catered to the professional workforce. I was glad. I wanted to unwind from the drive and mentally disappear into the Stanly County Rita for at least a few minutes. The reminiscing journey was easier alone. Thankfully, I didn't know the hostess today and she took me to a corner booth with a window that looked up toward the town square. I ordered a drink as I settled in to wait for Ross. The sun had appeared and warmed my face as I took in the town.

Gone for over 15 years, I still knew residents in every town in the county. Furthermore, I had gone to high school with many of the guys and gals who never left home as well as those who relocated back to the quaint and family-oriented county seat of Albemarle after college, law school, med school. I knew many others from church, sports, and the YMCA where I spent at least several years cumulatively of my childhood in the big pool learning to swim and dive. Bottom line—Stanly County was rarely conducive to anonymity or privacy.

But that is one of the many reasons I loved it. Nestled in the shadow of the Uwharrie Mountains, Albemarle's streets had hills and curves and character that mirrored the citizenry. Fiercely protective of our native population, Stanly County was also amazingly welcoming of new residents; at least as long as they didn't come here to try to make it the miserable, less desirable places they left. The county appreciated its proximity in the heart of NASCAR country and could tell you about the local drivers, their histories and all of their "kin." Albemarle also celebrated the success of native Kellie Pickler, the country singer who overcame a meager childhood to capitalize on her hauntingly beautiful voice in front of millions of American Idol fans. Located less than an hour from Charlotte, we claimed ownership of our Carolina Panthers and Charlotte Bobcats as well, rejoicing in their successes or anguishing over their shortcomings each season. It was a great place to be.

For bankers like me, I had always been proud of my profession and could point just up the road to the Charlotte headquarters of both Bank of America and Wachovia as evidence of the national prominence, influence and prestige their success had bestowed on the Queen City, the Piedmont and the entire state. Not that I wanted to work for the financial behemoths, mind you. The current banking environment had brought many of the "too big to fail" to the breaking point. Wachovia, a historical bastion of sound banking, was no more, having been saved from complete failure by the left-coast Wells Fargo. B-of-A, a survivor of the current crisis so far, was hardly recognizable as a "bank" now, having evolved into an enormous financial institution that derived much less of its income from main street banking than it did from its Wall Street investments, credit cards and capital markets divisions. The divide between the international financial institutions and the community banks continued to widen, but the term "banker" was applied to us all—investment, national, regional or community—without distinction. Bankers had become the poster children for financial irresponsibility, greed, corruption. I sighed. I loved what I did, but even Mega was not immune from fraud, internal crime and fiscal dereliction. The banking world seemingly had gone mad.

Well, aren't you a bundle of sunshine, I chided myself. *You are home. You are on vacation. You are waiting for Ross Moore. Snap out of it, will you?* The internal conversation made me smile just as a shadow crossed over me. I looked up and saw Ross and smiled broader. As great as Stanly County was on any given day, the arrival of Ross gave it a luster of perfection today and without a doubt, there was nowhere else on Earth I wanted to be and nobody else with whom I wanted to share it.

Chapter 69

Dylan sat facing the window, staring intently outside but seeing nothing. He was deep in thought. He had lost all bearings of place, time and players. *Spencer and Jeff? Ridiculous,* he thought. *What in the world was she doing flirting with an ass like him?* He couldn't reconcile what he had seen and heard as he stood in the copy room adjacent to Jeff's office with reality—hot, cool, blonde chick with dull, dry, old dude. Spencer was not one to dumpster dive, after all.

The fact was, though, she had invited Jeff to her house on Wednesday to dinner. Dylan heard her—the words and the tone. *Man, that lucky bastard, Jeff, won't even know what to do with a woman like Spencer,* Dylan thought. He stood and began pacing slowly in front of his credenza. He would just have to watch this whole situation unfold and see how buddy-boy Jeff handled the attention of the sexiest banker at Mega. He probably would take over some sappy flick like "Steel Magnolias" or "Beaches," both of which Dylan was certain Jeff owned. Dylan's choices would have been "From Here to Eternity" or "Wild Orchid" with their steamy love scenes. He had seen both movies so often that when he watched them with a date, he no longer watched the scenes, preferring instead to watch his date's reaction to them—a flushed face, a lick of the lips. Now *that* was hot.

Dylan stopped pacing and sat back down. Spencer had just changed everything going on in Shallotte, especially with her gal pal, Rita, out of town for a week. He hoped she didn't get in the way, but clearly, a chummy Jeff-and-Spencer was a complication for him, for them.

Personally, he was surprised he didn't feel the least bit jealous since he had been quietly pursuing Spencer, and even Rita, for the last several years to no avail. Today, all he felt was curiosity. *Strange,* he thought. He was all but certain that Spencer would not put out for Jeff because he didn't think she put out for anyone. After all, Spencer's reputation was as a flirt, not a slut. Damn, he wished she was. *A good lay might make Jeff a lot less uptight,* he thought.

Dylan stretched and looked at his watch. It was after five o'clock. Almost everybody had left for the day. Greg and Jeff loved to work late like he did. Peter and Tripp stormed the door at 5:01 to go have a beer before they headed home to their wives and kids. He would go by Greg's office before he left. Greg had known Spencer and Jeff far longer than he had. Perhaps he could make sense of this twist and help Dylan figure out what this potential alliance, this budding liaison could do to change things at the bank in Shallotte.

Chapter 70

The ride into Albemarle was far quicker and much less stressful than he had imagined when he spoke to Rita earlier in the afternoon. He was across the county line in less than 30 minutes from his house in Charlotte. The rain with all of its ferocity and bluster had vanished, leaving a crisp, autumn sky in its aftermath.

He found a parking place down below the restaurant and walked up the hill to the door of the restaurant. As he walked in, he saw Rita to his left staring serenely out her window. A dark curl hugged her right cheek and she tried unsuccessfully to tame it by pushing it gently behind her ear. She was relaxed and faraway in thought as he walked up to the table. She didn't even hear him coming across the hardwood floor.

Ross slid easily into the booth in front of what had to be the sexiest woman in Stanly County, past or present, and when she smiled the whole room got brighter. God, she was a vision.

Today, she was his date. He couldn't wait to get the banking crap out of the way so they could just enjoy each other and be themselves, not bankers, manager and president, whistleblower and agent. Not that Rita knew everything he was, every role he was being asked to play in this convoluted investigation. He felt duplicitous. He felt like a user.

When he returned home after his week in Shallotte, he had reviewed the autopsy report on Patrick Lowers' death. The results showed a blood-alcohol level of 0.04, below the state's impaired threshold of .08. No trace of illicit drugs was found in his system either. He had trauma to his forehead, presumably from striking the windshield when the car made contact with the concrete culvert at the bottom of the Oyster Bay Bridge. The blow to his head was the likely cause of death, but the report was inconclusive and the death was labeled "suspicious." Bottom line, the autopsy was in line with what Rita feared. Patrick was not drunk or high and could not have just "missed" the bridge without a major distraction or some kind of help in doing so.

The investigation into Patrick's death was proceeding rapidly and other agents in the field were working around the clock to uncover evidence and document every movement of the long list of suspects in Shallotte. The agents simply had to find the connections, the proof, the players. The fraud investigation had been going on even before the merger of Mid-Atlantic and American One. The probe had been painstakingly slow as area and embedded agents pieced together bits and pieces of data only to be thwarted with deleted files, changing information, transferred employees. The cover-up inside was thorough, intelligent and complicated. The murder investigation into Patrick Lowers' death had accelerated the process, though. Suddenly, there was desperation, sloppiness and stupidity involved and evidence of cover-up in the local law enforcement as well. The investigation had to tie the fraud and the murder together, and quickly, or any remaining evidence would be destroyed. Ross and his team had to work fast.

He had also been completely surprised by the state bureau of investigation's revelation of their embedded agent. He had certainly included the agent into the pool of likely murderers before his briefing. The fact that the agent had fooled Ross meant that he was very good in his role and that he had been inside the bank for years gathering information, blending in, becoming one of "them" to implicate the participants in the crime spree. Ross was convinced the agent had been very close to having enough information for arrests in the fraud scheme until Patrick was murdered.

Since the FBI got involved and embedded Ross in upper management, the electronic evidence was being untangled and restored after a very sophisticated and concerted effort to purge accounts, information and offsets by the culprits. No real break in the elaborate scheme had had been made, though, until they compared notes with the NC SBI. Collaboration had helped piece most of the methods and means together. The SBI had identified many of the players with their agent banker but had not gotten to the meat of the scheme—i.e., the money. Now the entire, enormous internal criminal organization was coming into focus.

They only lacked the account numbers and paper trail of the dollars. Patrick Lowers had sniffed the scent and followed it like a blood-thirsty wolf. Ross was sure he had figured out the details—the dollars, the accounts, the players, and most of all, the mastermind—and it cost him his life. If he had documented his findings, and Ross was sure he had after what Patrick had ominously told Ivey about sending the proof to security, the evidence had either been destroyed by a party to the fraud or it had not yet been found.

If the criminals, at least one of which was a murderer, thought Rita was on the money trail too, she was in danger. The less she knew from him, the safer she was. As soon as this sorry fiasco was over and she was out of harm's way, Ross would tell Rita the whole story of his involvement. For now, though, he had a job to do and he was going to do it well. He had to protect Rita from the almost mafia-like organization of criminals inside the bank in Shallotte, especially in light of the recent escalation to murder. He hoped she would forgive his secrecy. He hoped she would continue to trust him. He hoped … right now, that's all he had.

Her smile quelled the battle raging inside him and when he said, "Hello, sunshine," she beamed.

When she replied, "Welcome to my childhood world, Mr. Moore," he returned her smile.

He felt himself relax even more as he answered, "I can't wait for the grand tour."

"This *is* Stanly County, Mr. President," she teased, "A leisurely stroll qualifies as the deluxe package around here. Let's talk and eat and then the touring can begin."

He sighed and said, "You've got a deal. First, tell me about the meeting this morning."

Chapter 71

The disk was not in her desk drawers or her credenza. He had waited until everybody else had gone home for the evening before he began his search of Rita Miller's office. He managed to easily pick the cheap lock on the cheap office furniture then search every nook, cranny, book and folder inside. The disk was not there.

He caught himself breathing hard, almost out of breath, his heart racing, as he logged another failure to find the disk. *Rita, Rita, where would you have hidden the disk,* he asked himself silently.

He moved her mouse pad, he looked under her keyboard, and he pulled the backs off of her pictures. He went through every page of every personal book between her fleur-de-lis bookends. Nothing.

The disk was not in Patrick's office, his car, his safe deposit box. It was not in Rita's office either. Then he had another idea. Perhaps it was in her house.

"Yes," he said out loud. Conveniently, Rita was out of town for a week. He could discreetly search her home while she was away. Hold on, Cowboy. Breaking and entering is a big step up from picking a desk lock. Perhaps it was time to call in somebody to help with this job.

Knowing that the "help" answered to the name Ricky Jarman was enough to make him physically ill, and the thought of that lowlife's paws all over Rita's nice things almost made him want to reconsider. Almost.

Having exhausted this search, he carefully tried to put everything back in its place in her office. Rita sure was a neat freak, he thought. Satisfied that he left it as he found it, he turned the light off, grabbed his briefcase and went to set the alarm.

As he left the bank, night had fallen and he reveled in the darkness. He felt invisible, invincible and determined. His breathing was returning to normal and his heart rate had slowed down. He had a plan. He had hope. He had to find that disk.

Chapter 72

So I told Ross every detail, every gesture, every word of the meeting with Greg and Jeff earlier in the day, now seemingly a light-year past. I described the information in the packet I had brought with me since it was an exact duplicate of the information I had given them this morning, and Patrick before them, to complete the area-wide budget. I highlighted the suspicious areas—overdrafts, commercial loans and charged-off accounts. I detailed the history of the rise in overdrafts followed a rise in commercial loans followed by the amount of the loan being charged off to loss. The numbers were small enough not to be noticed at all individually or over a short period of time. Collectively, though, over the most recent three-year period, the numbers were large and, quite frankly, astounding.

As I talked I looked at Ross' every facial expression and listened closely to every word he said. Did he see something I didn't? Did I have enough information for him to piece together such a complex fraud? I just wasn't sure.

I was sure, though, that this very information had exposed an ugliness that threatened to shatter American One Bank, the town of Shallotte, and the lives of numerous employees, their careers and their families. How did such collusion on this grand of a scale begin, let alone, thrive? Think about it! Did the participants sit around a dinner table or a bar and talk about how easily they could steal millions from their employer if they could just all work together? Or did one bad apple rot the rest by secretly funneling money to the others when a child was sick, an aging parent needed help, the kids were heading off to college? Who knew?

Patrick apparently did, that's who. What had Ross found out about his death? Did I really want to know? I realized I didn't want to know but I needed to know, not to validate my suspicious instinct but rather raise my guard to protect myself, Spencer and Ivey from danger. Not one to beat around the bush, I took the direct route and fired the tough questions at Ross.

"What did the medical examiner find out about Patrick?" I asked.

Ross didn't pause when he answered, "He wasn't drunk."

"What killed him?" I continued.

"Rita, the report is not conclusive. Most likely, the cause of death was the blow to his head where he hit the windshield after the car slammed into the culvert. The finding was labeled as 'suspicious'," he stated quietly.

I sighed. God, I wanted to be wrong.

"Where does it go from here?" I questioned. "Will they do a toxicology report or something?"

That question apparently surprised him, but he looked me directly in the eye and answered, "Probably nowhere without some definitive idea of what substance for which he needed to test. A toxicology report just measures levels of certain substances. Patrick didn't have any illegal drugs in his system or any prescription meds like pain killers, sedatives or amphetamines either." He finished by saying, "But we're still looking at the reports."

Finding that choice of words odd, I asked, "Who is '*we*'?"

Ross paused for a split second, ran his index finger down my pinkie, then answered, "The investigators—from the medical examiner to the North Carolina SBI to the feds. They will provide all of that activity to the executive management team. The golf outing was sponsored, sanctioned by the bank, after all."

"I didn't realize this situation was so huge," I admitted.

"On the surface, a car accident wouldn't get so much attention," he said. "But there are factors in play now—collusion, fraud, embezzlement, and possibly even murder—that trigger a federally-insured institution the size of Mega to hit the radar. Patrick's car was broken into on the Grissett's car lot Saturday night too. Somebody is looking for something, Rita. You saw Patrick's office...complete destruction. Again, somebody's looking for something," he finished.

I let his words sink into my brain as I remembered the nauseating display of plunder in Patrick's office on Saturday at the bank. Finally, my voice returned and I asked "Like what?"

"A disk, a paper, a flash drive—something with all the information Patrick found on it," he said. "The good guys need to find it before the bad guys do."

"How do you know the bad guys don't already have it? Patrick told Ivey he sent 'proof' to John Starr. Maybe it never got there," I wondered out loud.

"Perhaps Patrick's package never arrived or perhaps it did and it was a copy or a print-out," he said firmly.

John Starr was involved? God, how big was this mess, I questioned silently.

As if sensing my inner turmoil, Ross added, "Remember, Rita, the bad guys here don't know whether the good guys have the information either. If they find it, they will destroy it. If they don't have it, they will stop at nothing to find it." He sighed and looked at me with what was clearly relief. "Have I told you yet how glad I am that you're here?"

I smiled softly into his eyes, "No, but it sure is nice to hear." Just for a moment the churning in my guts stopped and the butterflies of desire took over. "Can I buy you a drink, cowboy?" I said coolly.

"I thought you'd never ask," he said. "Would you share an appetizer with me?" he asked.

Are you thick, man? I thought. *I would share a kiss, a bed, a lifetime with you, idiot,* and I chuckled out loud at my thoughts. "Anything," I said quietly.

His eyebrows went up and he teased me gently, "On the menu or not?"

I leaned forward, touched his arm softly, looked him straight in the eye and whispered, "Yep."

CHAPTER 73

Jeanne Miller made up the bed in the guest room, fixed a fresh pitcher of tea and checked on the stew she made for dinner. Lonnie would be home soon, filthy from working on the farm, and he would be hungry. He will have to wait on Rita tonight, she thought, and she wondered what time her middle child would be home.

Rita had been quite mysterious when asked about her arrival. She had given some cryptic answer involving a work meeting then asking if it was okay if she possibly had a friend over for dinner. Then she said she might also have one-day delay in her arrival home if the meeting ran late in which event she would be home in the morning. The conversation was as interesting as it was amusing.

Jeanne knew the clues—"friend" was Rita-speak for "man" and "ran late" translated to "got interesting." She sure hoped Rita had finally met Mr. Right. She had certainly taken her time. Jeanne was glad.

Rita had always been the nomadic one of her three children. She wandered, never aimlessly, but with purpose and enthusiasm. She had travelled to see great wonders on the Earth, sometimes alone. Rita had also gone into the very gates of hell at times to help the unfortunate with the Red Cross where she had been a volunteer since she was in high school. She had travelled to Mexico to help provide the basic necessities of life after a tremendous landslide killed thousands and decimated dozens of small communities and towns. She had also gone to New Orleans to help feed the hungry after Hurricane Katrina. Both trips had been mentally taxing, but Rita returned home both times energized by the efforts of volunteers and exceedingly thankful for everything she had.

At 19, Rita had fallen madly in love with a young teacher and coach she met at a basketball tournament at the local university while she was home on Christmas break. She gave her heart to him and he obviously loved her very much. They were inseparable for a short time, traveling on weekends to see each other, going to basketball games, football games, or baseball games. They were both sports nuts. They had everything in common—family, religion, and the Tarheels. Rita, though, always came home with a foreboding sadness that their torrid love affair wouldn't last. She was right.

He abruptly ended the relationship by just never calling again. No note, no phone call, no break-up—just nothing. Jeanne was sure the whole situation was going to destroy Rita. At night, Jeanne would hear her cry, sob, softly moan with a pain so deep, an ache so raw that Jeanne was afraid it might destroy her too. By day, Rita acted like she was fine except she rarely smiled, rarely ate and never mentioned her lover's name out loud. Jeanne thought Rita would never get over the hurt, but she did. One weekend, Rita came home and announced she was flying to Colorado on a $99 round-trip ticket with a friend and she was going to see the Rocky Mountains. She had moved on.

Rita had friends everywhere, but had never found another special someone, a soul mate, like her sister found in college and her brother found at the local grocery store. Until, perhaps, now.

Jeanne looked out the window again. She heard Lonnie's work truck turning into the gravel driveway. It had to be nearly six o'clock. She decided they would go ahead and eat. A mother knows, she thought. Rita wouldn't be home until tomorrow.

Chapter 74

Spencer unlocked the door to her condo, kicked off her heels and plopped down squarely in the middle of her huge brown couch. She picked up the remote control and turned on the television, not even vaguely interested in anything on at this hour, to let the talking heads drown out the mental conversations between her ears that were driving her crazy.

She thought about Wednesday night. What would she say, what would she do? Was she attracted to this guy or was he just mysterious enough to intrigue her? *Woman, you've gone mad*, she told herself.

She got up and went to the kitchen. *Yeah, like I'm going to cook him up a big, fancy dinner*, she thought. Nope, she would order a pizza and put some beer on ice. He drank Samuel Adams like Rita—she saw him drinking it at the golf tournament and thought the same thing she did every time she saw Rita drink one—yuck. She would need some of her Miller Lite on hand too.

With dinner decided, she wondered what movie he would bring. She hoped it was not some embarrassingly complicated, deeply emotional drama that was guaranteed to send her straight into screen-saver mode. She hated that kind of crap. She loved comedy. She loved to laugh. Jeff didn't seem to be the yuck-it-up type, though. *He might surprise me again*, she thought.

She thought about their discussion/meeting/encounter…whatever it was… today. His voice almost held a promise of surprise in it. Spencer realized she was both turned on and apprehensive. He seemed to be completely straight-laced on one hand yet borderline dangerous on the other. This is crazy!

Spencer grabbed a bottle of water out of the fridge and walked upstairs to change. She slipped into a pair of jeans, a tee shirt and her flip-flops. As she was heading downstairs, she looked out her balcony window across the square to where Jeff lived. She could clearly see into his den downstairs because his light was on and night was beginning to fall. He was sitting in a chair reading.

As if he sensed her eyes on him, he looked up, almost right at her. She froze and wondered if he saw her watching him. Thank God her light was out. He stood, walked to the window, stretched and went back to the chair and began reading again. She let out a huge sigh, unaware she had been holding her breath.

She closed her blinds completely and went downstairs. She grabbed a frozen dinner out of the freezer, momentarily putting it to her forehead to cool herself down. She had jumped right into the frying pan with her invitation today while the huge fraud conspiracy simmered underneath. She wasn't sure if Jeff was her fire escape or the accelerant that would take the simmer to a raging inferno. Either way, it was going to get hot in here.

Chapter 75

Nightfall was rolling in quickly as we walked around downtown Albemarle, past the square, the library, and the courthouse. I pointed out favorite places from my childhood—The Sweet Shoppe that made the best cream horns in the world; Yingling Furniture Store where Mom and Dad bought the picture of a German Shepherd that looked exactly like my childhood dog, Taurus, that still hangs over my bed today; and Lambert's Barber Shop where I got my first and probably hundreds of subsequent haircuts over the years. We strolled, I reminisced, and Ross listened. The streetlights flickered to life as we made our way back down the hill past the beautiful, old cinema, long closed and finally to Ross' SUV parked just past the recently refurbished old depot. The dwindling light softened the old town, giving her a nostalgic, not tired, aura.

I sighed and smiled up to him and he pulled me closer and whispered, "Who says you can't go home again?"

"Thomas Wolfe," I deadpanned then added, "but he wasn't from Stanly County, was he?"

Stopping at his car, he turned me to face him. "Come to the city with me tonight, Rita" he said. "I'll bring you back early tomorrow."

God, it was tempting, but I knew he had to work at the bank downtown tomorrow and I couldn't possibly ask him to drive me back to Albemarle tomorrow morning. I was the one on vacation this week. What to do? I couldn't bear him leaving just yet. Finally, I said, "Let me follow you so you don't have to drive me back before you go to the office tomorrow morning."

I could tell he was thinking that I had driven enough already today so I added, "C'mon, it's only 45 minutes."

"Okay, let's go," he said, and he walked me back to my car just up the hill. I got in, my heart pumping from exhilaration, happiness, excitement. I watched every step he took back to his car and as he got in, I cranked my car and drove over to where he was, stopping to let him in front of me. We were on our way to the Queen City.

The drive was beautiful as we headed west on Highway 24/27, the horizon still a blaze of orange, fuchsia, and gold. Stanly County is deceiving high in altitude and at a special point on the way west, the tree line opens up at the zenith of the trip and you can see the uptown towers of Charlotte, beckoning to you in the distance. Charlotte was my Oz when I was a child, big and shiny, foreign and magical. We would travel to the city several times a year to the old coliseum for the Barnum-Bailey Circus and The Southern Christmas Show and to Eastland Mall for our annual back-to-school shopping that always included ice skating on the huge ice pit below the hundreds of spectators' eyes, watching for a beautifully-landed jump or a particularly nasty spill. The city was the source of so many Miller family memories.

Traffic started to build as the highway became Albemarle Road, indicating that we were now in Mecklenburg County and on the cusp of our arrival into the city. My, how the city had grown over the years and it was hardly recognizable to me as we crossed over Independence Boulevard, travelled down Sharon Amity Road and made our way south. It dawned on me that I didn't ask Ross where he lived so I kept his vehicle clearly in my view, perhaps riding too close to him so I could keep any mobile intruders from coming between us. As we drove, Ross turned off the roads onto smaller streets, tree-lined and amazingly quiet, within the bustling mass that was Charlotte.

We finally turned into a driveway at a beautiful, old Tudor house and Ross parked at the back and opened his car door and pointed to a space right beside his SUV where he wanted me to park. We had, apparently, arrived and I became a little nervous. His house was his home, evidenced by the huge terracotta planters overflowing with mums of every color at the side door and beds of beautiful pansies and begonias around the home's foundation, blooming in the crisp air of autumn. The knowledge that he was the bank president seeped back into my brain—he had done very well for himself. I hoped I didn't look like the country mouse coming to the city or a man-miner looking for gold. I knew I was neither, but what did Ross think?

I grabbed my overnight bag out of the trunk while he unlocked the side door. He held it open for me to go inside then passed by me, deactivated the burglar alarm and turned on the lights in seemingly one motion. The interior was lovely, perfect and very Ross Moore. Hardwood floors peeked out from under obviously antique Persian rugs and the tables and chests were an eclectic, early-American collection of various woods and styles from Chippendale to primitive. Nothing was out of place, but his home had a very lived-in feel and a good-to-come-home comfort that made me sigh.

"Ross, your home is beautiful," I said finally. "Marian must be extraordinarily proud of your fine taste," I added playfully.

He laughed and said, "Yeah, but she thinks my walls are woefully bare since they aren't bustling with Cassatt or Monet. My taste is all over the spectrum. I tend to go for comfort and color over period and style. Mom thinks I'm hopelessly male in that regard, I'm afraid." I saw no regret in him, though, as he took in the house through his eyes. It was a home he loved.

He turned his attention back to me and walked over and took my bag and put it beside the stairs. Then, he led me by the hand to the kitchen where he grabbed a bottle of red wine, a bag of grapes, a box of Triscuit crackers and a block of smoky Gouda cheese. We stood shoulder to shoulder at the granite-topped island working together, Ross instinctively handing me a tray and knife for the cheese and crackers and a colander to wash the grapes while he opened the bottle of wine and grabbed two glasses. We walked feast in hand back to the den and I sat down on the floor. Ross turned on the gas logs in his fireplace and wasted very little time deciding on Marvin Gay as his music of choice.

Was I dreaming? God, I hoped not. "Are you Superman?" I teased.

He chuckled and lay down beside me and answered, "Nope. I can't fly alone."

I rolled onto my back and groaned, "God, you are killing me, man," and I pulled him over on top of me. He kissed me then and I realized there was no need to escalate the level of passion because we were both already at the tipping point. Perhaps it was the long ride to Charlotte. Perhaps it was the two days in between. Whatever it was, I felt like a Jezebel, blazing with heat and almost crazy with desire.

Quite frankly, I probably scared him a little and I certainly surprised him a lot as I pushed him onto his back and climbed on top of him. I peeled off my top and camisole in one motion and he sat up, holding my breasts to his face while he tasted, teased, tortured me with his tongue. I ran my hands almost maniacally down his back and begged for more. He unfastened my pants, then his, and we stripped them away, leaving nothing between our bare bodies. Ross scooped me easily back on top of him and I moaned as I felt like he was all the way in the center of my being. We rocked, rode and climbed together and I hung on the edge of the tidal wave for what seemed like hours until finally I was flung into the ocean below, wet, rolling, consuming. My pulse raced, my breathing was ragged and I turned my head toward him, my hair a swirling jumble of sweaty brown curls. He was breathing heavy, slick with sweat and grinning like a Cheshire cat. "What?" I asked coyly.

"Wow..." was all he could manage.

"Too much?" I taunted gently.

He let out a deep, out-of-breath laugh, leaned over and kissed me slowly and whispered, "You're in trouble, woman, because that was just the warm-up."

Man, trouble never felt so good.

Chapter 76

The breaking dawn slipped between the blinds in his bedroom and fell softly on Rita's face. *God, you are beautiful,* Ross thought as he watched her sleeping soundly beside him. He deemed himself invigorated, but tired this morning and he had awakened before the clock radio turned on. He was glad and he reached over to turn the alarm off to let his princess sleep.

He rose and went downstairs, put on a pot of coffee and whipped together his pumpkin waffle batter and heated up his ancient waffle iron. He opened the back door and let Jinx in the house. Jinx went all around the kitchen sniffing and pawing while Ross filled his bowls with dog food and fresh water. Jinx looked up at Ross with a questioning look on his face as Ross washed his hands and pulled the last four waffles off the griddle. "What?" he asked his furry companion. "I told you she was coming!"

In a split second, Jinx took off and before Ross realized where he was headed, he knew he was too far behind to stop the beast's dash up the stairs to the bedroom. Ross rounded the corner of the bedroom just in time to see the dog mid-air before he landed like a cannonball on top of the soon-to-be-wide-awake Rita. "Jinx," he yelled, helpless to stop the onslaught.

Rita was stunned awake, her green eyes wide and she squealed as the damn crazy dog licked her face like a lollipop. Ross disintegrated with laughter and jumped on to the bed beside them as the sounds of happiness filled the room. "Good morning," he managed.

"Good morning...Jinx," she laughed and hugged the dog to her then said, "And you too," and tussled Ross's hair playfully. She was happy here, he thought. More importantly, the dog sure loved her and a dog's opinion of a person was never wrong.

"What time is it?" she asked.

"Time for breakfast," he said. With that, Jinx was through with them, much more excited about the food downstairs and he bounded off the bed and out the door. "C'mon, Sleepyhead," he added and pulled her to her feet, wrapped her in his extra-large tartan robe, and steered her down the stairs.

Ross had brewed a fresh pot of coffee to complement the stack of pumpkin waffles that sat on the counter, waiting to be eaten.

Rita breathed in the smell and smiled as she exclaimed, "God, I love coffee!" Then she saw the waffles and wheeled around to face Ross with a look of mock-suspicion on her face and asked him, "Are you trying to fatten me up or spoil me rotten so you can have your way with me again?"

He just shook his head. This woman could stir him up over waffles at 6:45 a.m. in the morning. Incredible. He chuckled and sat her down at the island bar and borrowed one of her favorite lines when he answered, "You are killing me, woman."

"Good answer," she replied as she drank her coffee. She patted the barstool beside her and Ross sat down and together, they devoured every waffle on the plate.

Rita made herself at home and got up and poured herself a second cup of coffee then asked him what time he needed to leave to get to the bank headquarters uptown. The thought of leaving her made him long for another week of vacation just to be with her, but he knew he had important work to do and a bank to run. He sighed, looked at his watch and sadly said, "I need to leave in about 45 minutes to get ahead of the traffic."

Rita sighed too and said, "I need directions out of your neighborhood maze and the quickest way to Highway 49 so I can get home at what my mother would deem a decent hour." After a second, she added, "Want to share a shower?"

"You've got it," he said, "but you don't need to hurry. Stay until at least 9 a.m. so you can enjoy the ride home without the hassle of traffic, okay? You can lock up when you leave," he added. Ross looked at his watch, suddenly eager for his morning shower. "Come, temptress, we have a rendezvous with my shower. I hope you like yours long and hot," he said and before he could retract the words, she was all over it, and they began laughing uncontrollably as they climbed the stairs.

"I do long and hot very well," she teased behind him as he went to turn on the water. She dropped the robe and walked into the bathroom, the steam already wafting above the glass door.

He turned and took in her whole naked being and wished again for another day to spend alone with her, but he knew today was not that day. He opened the door, walked in and pulled her in with him. As they let the hot water roll over their bodies, he realized that his primary focus in the criminal investigation under his command was Rita's safety. He pulled her closer and she rested her mass of curls on his chest and ran her hands down his back. She is safe here, he thought. Then she rubbed up against him and stirred him to life and he wondered if he would survive the day without her.

But first he had to survive the physical demands of their seemingly insatiable appetite for each other. After she asked him just how much hot water he had time to use, he leaned down and kissed her and said, "You are killing me, woman, killing me."

Chapter 77

Tuesday roared to life at the bank in Shallotte as each of the employees circled the bank by car, observed the morning glory signal, parked, then unlocked the door and got to work. Greg watched as everybody went about the day to day business of running the bank—his bank.

He loved his work here and he admired the team that he had had a major part of assembling. He walked around the corner and said "Good morning" to everyone he passed. He was in a particularly good mood today. He felt light on his feet, carefree in his manner.

The oppressiveness of the last couple of years had evaporated, vanished into thin air. Greg knew why and as sad as the loss was for the family, Greg felt only relief. Patrick Lowers was dead and his rule over the bank in Shallotte was over. His widow was coming this morning to pick up his personal effects and clean out his office. Then, all vestiges of Patrick Lowers would be gone from American One Bank. Good riddance.

As he rounded the corner, Greg felt like kicking up his heels, dancing a dance, and singing "Ding Dong, The Witch Is Dead," but he contained his glee appropriately. He stuck his head inside of Spencer Cashwell's door and she looked up and smiled at him broadly.

"Well, it's about time you came out of your hidey hole, Mister," she said as she got up to come around her desk. "All work and no play makes a very dull Greg," she finished as she hugged him warmly.

"How are you?" he asked with genuine interest. "How are you surviving without your partner in crime?" he teased her.

"Are you kidding me? She…" and suddenly Spencer stumbled as she tried to contain Rita's relationship with Ross Moore. "Uh, she's busy doing whatever it is they do on a farm like racing tractors or watching the pumpkins grow. It all sounds so…so awful," she said, recovering remarkably well.

Greg laughed and said, "You two are like a female odd couple—completely different but with so much in common. By the way, when is the office princess set to return?"

"Oh, she won't be back until Sunday afternoon or evening. Why are you asking? Can I help you with something?" she asked.

Greg smiled and shook his head then he answered, "No, I just miss her around here. So, Spence, how are you filling up your time?"

Greg had a playful air about him today and one look at his grin told Spencer that he knew about her "date" with Jeff tomorrow. She sighed,

"God, do you people not have enough to do around here? You must not if my personal life is the most exciting topic of conversation. You know about my plans for tomorrow night, don't you, Greg Hardy. How did you find out?" she asked suspiciously.

"Dylan told me. He overheard you invite Jeff to your house. I think he's jealous," he teased gently.

"God, he's pathetic," Spencer said. "Greg, Jeff lives in my condominium complex. I invited him over for beer and pizza, not for hot sex and a marriage proposal. You people need to get a life," she finished exasperated.

Greg laughed and pulled her close for a hug. "Just don't break his heart, killer," he said.

Spencer bumped him away with her hip and shook her head. "Yea, Greg, I'm a real heartbreaker," she said. "What about my heart?" she asked.

"I think your heart is safe with Jeff. With him, it's your head that worries me," he said as he walked out the door on his way around the bank to finish making his rounds.

The last couple of years here had begun to feel like going to work in the salt mines. The atmosphere was oppressive, intimidating, and cold. Today was a new day, though, Greg thought. He was free from the iron grip of the tyrannical Patrick Lowers. Greg Hardy was back on top and the world of banking, at least in Shallotte, felt right once again.

Chapter 78

I rolled up to mom and dad's back door just before 10 a.m. on Tuesday morning. They were obviously expecting me since the garage door was wide open and Maggie, their chocolate lab, was running wild in the front yard to greet me. I parked under the huge red oak and opened my car door to get out, but not before Maggie ploughed me over, licked my face and nuzzled my neck. She smelled Jinx on me and eyed me suspiciously like I was some kind of traitor before she backed away. In the next second, she was distracted by a squirrel in the woods and set off in full chase. Maggie had the attention span of a toddler.

I laughed at her foolishness, grabbed my bag and purse from the seat and headed into the house to see Mom. I was sure she was up to her elbows in the "task of the hour" by now. There was never any shortage of things to be done at the Miller house. As expected, Mom was toasting pumpkin seeds left over from the pumpkins she had carved for Halloween, now less than two weeks away. She had also made a crock pot full of chili for dinner, had cake layers cooling to make a pineapple cake and had already washed up the measuring cups, the mixing bowls and the beaters from the mixer. Again, it was only 10 a.m.

At 62, my mother, Jeanne, was a beauty—always had been, though. She was Jackie-O sophisticated, Martha Stewart handy and Carly Fiorina smart—not that I am biased or anything. I walked up behind her as she was singing to a CD, dropped my bags and wrapped her in a huge bear hug. She turned as if she had rehearsed her reaction a thousand times, kissed me on the forehead and returned my hug, rocking back and forth to the beat of the music. Mmmm, home.

Now most families would stop doing whatever it is they were doing before these Kodak moments and "catch up" before they resumed any tasks that demanded their attention. That way was most decidedly *not* the Miller way. Mom handed me the bowl of pumpkin seeds, now washed and cleaned, the recipe for the spice mixture and marched onto her next task of icing the cake while we talked. Two hands meant twice the work would get done after all.

She asked me about Spencer and Ivey, the bank in general, my job in particular, the condo, the beach, and my car. Mom was very good at marching around your life like the Biblical Hebrews did Jericho to make the walls come tumbling down. Finally, she asked about my meeting last night and how it went. "The meeting was fine," I said honestly.

"What time did you get finished?" she asked.

"Late," I answered. "I decided to stay in Charlotte instead of driving back at night."

"What's going on in Charlotte?" she asked. "Did you have to go to the bank headquarters for your meeting?"

"No, I didn't go to the headquarters for the meeting, but that's where the bank's president lives. There is a lot going on at the bank…the bank in Shallotte, Mom," I said finally.

She stopped and looked at me. I could see that my tone worried her and she was trying to figure out what to ask to quell her concern. "Is everything okay, Rita?" she questioned cautiously. "You're not in any trouble are you?"

I looked her square in the face and said, "No, Mom, I'm not in any trouble, but there is trouble at the bank in Shallotte and I stumbled upon it. I half-ass blew the whistle on the trouble to the City Executive—"

"You mean that dreadful Mr. Lowers, don't you?" she interrupted.

"Yes ma'am. The short part of this very long answer is that Patrick Lowers is dead and I believe that information I gave him was the starting point of a much, much uglier path he followed that got him killed," I said and bowed my head to recover my composure.

"I'm sorry," Mom said. "I didn't know the man and I should not have called him dreadful," and she reached over and squeezed my hand and pierced me with her sky blue eyes. "Rita, are you in danger?" she asked softly.

"I don't think so, Mom," I admitted. "I think the people involved believe that their secret is safe now that Patrick is dead."

She continued looking at me for a few seconds more, then breathed a sigh of relief and said, "Enough sadness and gloom, let's get done in the kitchen and ride over and see your dad. He'll be thrilled to see you."

"What's he up to this morning?" I asked curiously.

"Who knows? I'm just glad to have him out from under my feet," Mom answered as she stacked the second layer of cake onto the first and continued icing.

"Are Jan and the boys coming over for dinner tonight? What about Mark and Shelley?" I asked, referring to my sister, her family, my brother and sister-in-law.

"Of course they are. It's your birthday, after all! Do you think your brother would miss out on a piece of this cake? Jan has just about made me crazy asking when you were coming home, like I had some kind of GPS to track your coordinates or something," she said. "I figured we'd have some chili for lunch and then roast a chicken with some vegetables and mash some potatoes for dinner."

"What about tomorrow night," I asked.

Mom stopped and turned around. "I haven't gotten that far, Rita. Why do you ask?" she questioned.

"I wanted to have a guest over tomorrow for dinner if that's alright," I said.

"Ok. We'll plan something nice," Mom stated.

"Nothing fancy, Mom, just good like always, ok?"

"Ok. So…who's coming to dinner?"

"A friend—he works at the bank. Actually, he runs the bank. He's the president of American One," I rambled.

"I see," Mom said, "So, no presidential feast then?"

"Very funny, Jeannie," I retorted using our lovingly silly name for our mother.

"Lord, your dad will have to shower twice before dinner to be presentable," she deadpanned.

"*Mom*," I warned.

"Let's go see what the King of the Cattle is doing," she laughed. "He could use a break."

Without missing a beat, I added, "I could too," and Mom's infectious, lilting laugh echoed around the room as she finished icing the cake, opened the oven door for me to put in the pumpkin seeds to roast and set the burglar alarm for us to head out on the farm to see Dad.

Watching her move like a whirling dervish, I knew I was going to be exhausted every single night when I hit the bed. I sighed contently and followed her out the door.

It was sure nice to be home.

Chapter 79

The first task Ross tackled when he arrived to the office was a telephone call to Jack and Mack Grissett to see what they were hearing and learning from the local police, the Brunswick County Sheriff's Department and the people on the street. Jack answered the call.

"Hi, Jack. It's Ross. How is everything in Shallotte?" he asked.

"Hi, Ross," Jack replied easily. "Shallotte is very uptight right now. The feeling on the street is that something big is going to happen or is happening and very little can be done to stop this train coming down the tracks."

"So, what names are you hearing?" Ross asked.

"That's just it, there's no talk," Jack added. "The whole chain of talk has gone silent since the coroner dubbed Patrick's death suspicious."

"Why do you think that is?" Ross questioned.

"I think your band of thugs is circling the wagons, cleaning up details, tying up loose ends," Jack said ominously. "Nobody on the outside of that circle is safe, Ross."

"Who is at risk? I mean, who do we need to protect, Jack?"

"First and foremost, my girlfriend Rita," Jack said seriously. "And if we have to protect Rita, we have to include Spencer Cashwell and Ivey Jones."

Ross thought for a moment and then said, "Rita is safe here with me right now and Ivey is in Raleigh. I will call him and tell him to be vigilant and on his guard." Ross blew out a deep breath. "Can you help me with Spencer?"

"We sure are trying, but she's a real enigma, Ross," Jack said. "She's been quiet and low-key since Rita left town and while that would normally be a good thing, Spencer Cashwell with time on her hands is like a weapon of mass destruction. Mack and I have been trying to secretly check on her each night as we head home, but she is holed up in her condo with the blinds closed. I just don't know what is going on now that the inside man at the bank has stopped communicating," he added.

"Since when," Ross asked.

"Since yesterday morning—the state guys haven't had one communication about bank activity since then," Jack stated.

Ross contemplated the information and tried to figure out why, but his thoughts steered to very dark reasons. He sighed and asked, "You don't think we've lost our in, do you? I mean, you don't suppose they're on to him, do you?"

With certainty, Jack said, "No. He's been embedded too long and too deep for that scenario to unfold. He's a complete insider at the bank, Ross. Nobody there suspects a thing. He's had to get dirty with the pigs on a couple of occasions to keep his cover, but he had the full blessing of the department. He's a real adept agent."

"Good, but I am worried about the silence—and Spencer."

"Me too," Jack added, "but that Spencer is a smart one. She knows how to take care of herself at home and Mack and I have her back to and from work. She doesn't even know she has a daily escort," he said.

Ross said goodbye to Jack and hung up the telephone. He felt better, but he also knew that as independent as Spencer was, there were going to be times she was unprotected and alone during the next five days. He would ask Rita tomorrow if she had spoken to her and he almost laughed at the question. He was not a betting man, but he knew that rarely a day would go by that the tight-knit friends didn't speak at least once. The same could be said for Spencer and Ivey and Rita and Ivey.

Ross had a real appreciation for the close relationship Rita had forged with her friends. They had trust, respect and love in and for each other. He suddenly longed for a relationship like that with Rita, but realized that while she trusted him fully, he was holding back some real vital information, really his true identity from her. He could see where she would believe that he didn't trust her. Ross knew that would wound her deeply and that was the last thing he wanted to do.

Ross got up and walked to the window and looked 15 stories down to all of the people in uptown Charlotte scurrying down the sidewalk, going to and from work. He loved this city and couldn't wait to share it Friday night with Rita.

Just thinking about Rita made Ross smile. He had shared his family with her and she would share hers with him tomorrow night. He had also shared his house, his dog, and his bed, but he knew all of that was not enough. If they truly had a future, he would have to share the truth with her about who he really was, what he really did, how the story really started and he realized that he may have already waited too long.

He sighed again. While he was close to cutting off the head of the beast that was trying to devour the bank in Shallotte, and close to confronting a cold-blooded killer, Ross also knew he was close to the point of no return with Rita. He had to protect her. He had to trust her. He had to tell her the truth.

Chapter 80

Lonnie Miller was making the fourth round in the field of hay with the combine when he saw Jeanne and Rita pull up to the fence in his pick-up truck and hail him to take a break. *They sure are a sight for sore eyes*, he thought.

As much as he loved farming and as far as machinery and equipment had brought farmers today, there were still many time-consuming tasks that could not be ignored in the fall of the year. Cutting and baling hay was one of them.

He turned off the combine and got off the tractor to meet them halfway. Rita shook her finger at him with a smile telling him to stay put. She loved the farm and making her pass up the opportunity to climb up on the old John Deere to ooh-and-ahh would just be a crime.

He watched her as she easily and naturally pulled herself up onto the tractor in one fluid motion. She leaned over and hugged his neck and kissed him on the cheek.

He beamed and said, "Hello, Sunshine."

"Hello, Daddy. How's my favorite farmer?" she answered and sighed, utterly content to sit and survey the half-cut field with her 66-year old father. Behind her, Jeanne handed him some sweet tea and a pouch of her famous Callaway Cookies, a secret recipe handed down in her family for oodles of generations. They were delicious and he devoured the salty-sweet creations with pleasure.

"I am fine, banker daughter," he said gently, "I'm glad you're home. Have you got time to help me out around here this week? I could sure use your help with the cattle while I finish up with the hay if you've got time."

"Daddy—I'm on vacation! All I've got is time," Rita stated good-naturedly, "but how will Mom survive without me in the house?"

Lonnie laughed and smiled kindly at his wife who never took offense at their constant teasing of her workaholic nature. "If she will help you, you can do both," he said, and winked at Rita.

He turned to Jeanne and asked, "So, what's for dinner? Are we having beans and rice since we have the king's army coming over?"

"No, I've got chili for lunch in a couple of hours and we're having roasted chicken, mashed potatoes and vegetables for dinner," she said and Lonnie smiled approvingly as his mouth was already watering. Jeanne was a phenomenal cook.

Lonnie took the last swallow of tea in the glass and looked at his watch. He had to get back to work. The gesture was not lost on Rita and she stood and jumped off of the tractor. "Where are the keys to the Massey-Ferguson?" she asked.

"On the first peg in the tool shed," he answered. "One bale at the Lefler barn and one at the main barn will do. The water was changed yesterday at both troughs, but check to make sure it is still to the fill line at both, okay?"

"Okay, Daddy," and Rita smiled broadly, her love of the farm evident in her excitement over such mundane chores. She reached over and patted his foot and said, "I'll handle it. I'll see you in a bit."

"Okay," he said, and he reached to crank the tractor again. As he watched her walk away casually with her mother, he yelled out to her, "Rita!" and she turned to look at him, "I am sure glad to have you home," he finished.

She waved her hand at him and yelled, "I love you too, Daddy!"

He smiled, cranked up the John Deere and watched them get in the pick-up truck. She was his last hope for the perpetuity of the farm, but she lived at the coast and wore a suit to work every day at a bank. He wished she would follow her heart because it would surely lead her back home. She was born to farm, having loved the outdoors her entire life. She was a natural with the cattle, had a green thumb in the garden and was as handy as most men with power tools and farm machinery. Most of all, though, she was a master potter, and her pottery shed was where she was most at home, at peace.

Rita had displayed a gift for scale, size and shape at the pottery wheel since she was nine years of age and begged to go to a pottery camp that summer over in Seagrove, NC. When she returned after her week there, she brought home plates, jars and vases she had made that could have easily been sold at a gift shop or an art gallery. Several of the potters in the area offered her apprenticeships and she studied with a few of the masters over the years. When she discovered sports, though, she put her pottery on the back burner for several years until she came home one summer during college with her heart broken.

As if she had never left the wheel, Rita found her craft again and over the years, she had returned to it over and over. Her gift sustained her, soothed her, and healed her. She was passionate about her work and Lonnie loved to watch her, marveling at how talented his older daughter was.

She was also beautiful, he thought, and he said a silent prayer that she got her mother's extraordinary good looks. His middle child was a great cook, an organizational freak and as thrifty as his father, also a banker. *How can she not be married?* he wondered. The world was obviously filled with fools, he decided.

But he also knew that Rita seemed different today. She was bubbly and relaxed. Obviously, she was happy, but happier than she normally was. Lonnie knew it had been a long time since he had seen her this way. Slowly, a smile spread across his face. Rita was in the Piedmont with her family. Rita was in her element on the farm. Rita was in love with somebody very special.

Chapter 81

Late Tuesday afternoon, I picked up the telephone at Mom and Dad's house and called Ross's direct line at the bank. He answered on the third ring, somewhat out of breath, "Hello, beautiful, hold on for a second," and he put the receiver down. A few seconds later, he was back on the line and I realized I was holding my breath.

"Hi Ross, how's work?" she asked.

"It's busy. I'm trying to finalize the budget today," he said. "How is the farm? Have you had a good time with your family?"

"I've been helping Mom in the kitchen and I fed and watered the cattle for Daddy while he is finishing up baling the hay. I'm going to sleep like a rock tonight, albeit a lonely rock," I said.

"I can tell how much you love the farm by the tone of your voice, Rita," he said. "So when do I get to meet your family and see the operation first hand?"

"Don't go crazy, now," I said. "'Operation' is way too fancy a word for the Miller farm. I'd love for you to come out tomorrow evening and let me show you around the town and the farm and introduce you to Ferdinand and the rest of the family."

"Who is Ferdinand?" Ross asked suspiciously. "I haven't heard about him. He isn't some crazy uncle you keep locked in the upstairs bedroom, is he?"

I laughed and answered, "The bull—Ferdinand; didn't your mother ever read you the book about Ferdinand the bull?"

"Now you're beginning to see how deprived I really was as a child," he teased.

"Yeah, you had it rough, brother," I said with light sarcasm. "We'll eat dinner around 6 pm, but I'd love for you to come out a little early if you can."

"I can't think of anything I'd like better," he answered.

"Really," I kidded—I sure could.

"Really—I'll see you around 4 pm if you'll give me some directions," he said.

So I gave him the less than two minute detail of directions, then I asked him if he would bring some clothes to go hiking. He was intrigued.

"Where are you taking me?" he asked.

"To the Garden of Eden," I replied, "I'll even bring along some forbidden fruit in case you get hungry."

"I won't eat all day," he promised.

Chapter 82

My brother Mark and his wife Shelley arrived first for dinner. Shelley brought a gallon of tea and a huge tossed salad to accompany the feast that Mom and I had prepared to celebrate my birthday. Jan and her crew—her husband Sean and my nephews Cal and Jake—also arrived with food—Sean's famous Brussels sprouts and homemade vanilla ice cream. This scene was the norm, not the exception, for any Miller gathering. We always had enough food to feed the entire student body of our local Pfeiffer University.

But man, did we eat well! Our locally raised free range chicken and homegrown green beans put any chef's creation to shame. We ate dinner and talked, then ate dessert and talked some more. The nine of us completely obliterated the pineapple cake, swearing that Jeannie could sell them and make us all millionaires. Yep, it was that good.

My nephews cleared the table and then retired to the den with the guys to watch television. Shelley, Mom, Jan and I loaded the dishwasher, put away the leftovers and wiped down the table and countertops. Finally, we made a pot of coffee and sat back down at the table to talk.

Jan had recently passed her National Boards as a teacher and was thrilled to have found an extra day in her week as well as an extra couple of hundreds in her paycheck. Shelley stayed busy running the local Laundromat and said if she never folded another shirt or towel again she would be happy, but that she had laundry at home to tackle tonight. As if the entire scene was set far in advance, they all turned to me for my time of sharing. Think crickets, folks.

"What do you want to know?" I asked innocently.

"Aw, come on, Rita!" Jan said. "Who is he?"

I turned to Mom and said, "Who set the grapevine on fire, Mom?"

"I haven't said a word," Mom said.

Shelley added, "Woman, it is written all over your face—M-A-N," and she reached over for dramatic effect and touched each cheek and my forehead. I, of course, rolled my eyes.

"It's not like I've been keeping him secret. He's actually coming over for dinner tomorrow night," I volunteered. Big mistake.

"*What!*" Jan and Shelley exclaimed in unison. I just smiled wider. "Are you trying to keep us away from him," Jan accused.

"Of course I am!" I said. "You two would tell him all those sweet, amusing stories about me and my childhood," I added as I pointed at Mom and Jan, "While Shelley would remind him that I was available and not getting any younger. How could I resist having him join us tonight?" I asked good-naturedly.

"No, no, no," Jan chirped, "I would lie about you to marry you off! I'd tell him you were an ordinary child, an introvert and were being considered for a place beside the Holy Trinity."

"That's sacrilegious, Jan," Mom scolded her.

I snorted softly. I loved to bait my sister and sister-in-law. "Ok, I'll bring him by the farm house to meet you and Mark, Shelley. You, I'm not so sure, Jan," I teased. "Promise you'll behave," I demanded.

"Rita…."

"You want to come over after dinner?" I asked.

"I will be here for coffee and dessert and I'll be on my best behavior," Jan said smartly.

And that's what worried me.

Chapter 83

On Wednesday morning, Spencer sat at her computer, concentrating hard on the financial information she needed to key in order to get the loan application in front of her completed and approved. Immersing herself in her work was the only cure for the anxiety, the anticipation, the excitement and the...well, fear she felt for the fast-approaching evening.

What the hell is wrong with me? Spencer sighed hard. She was heading home early today so she could give her condo the once-over. She needed to get a bag of ice for the beer, pick up the pizza and change her clothes and freshen up after work. *Focus on the tasks,* she told herself.

She was thankful for an abundance of work to do today. The loans on her desk demanded attention and kept her mind off of tonight. They also kept her in her office and away from any more conversations like the one this morning with Greg.

Besides, being in her office kept her away from Dylan Fordham. She would choke the nosy, loud-mouthed jerk if she got close enough to get her hands around his neck. Not that she wanted to get that close to him. He made her skin crawl from a distance. He was always leering at women, skulking around the bank, and trash-talking with the guys.

A couple of the women at her mother's country club thought Dylan was sexy, charming and desirable. The wiser women found him to be sleazy, shallow and repulsive, and Spencer was clearly on this side of the Dylan debate. *Why am I wasting brain activity on the idiot?*

She finished inputting the information on the last loan on her desk, closed the file and stacked it with the others on her credenza. Then, she closed down her computer, grabbed her purse, turned off her light and walked out her door. Repeating her mental list to herself, she was pre-occupied, admittedly, when she rounded the corner and ploughed straight into Dylan. If she had hurt him or at the very least, knocked him to the floor, she would have felt much better. Instead, her purse fell out from under her arm and the contents went everywhere. The thought of a "Dylan Fordham choke fest" seeped back into her head.

"Got love on your mind, Spence?" he said and laughed at his own cleverness.

Spencer retorted, "What is it with you, Dylan? Is your own life so pathetic that the only way you can get your kicks is sticking your nose in other people's business? Boy, have you sunk to an all-time low," she snorted derisively.

She could see she got to him with that remark and she added in her best deep, sexy voice, "Now, if you'll excuse me, I've got some really hot plans involving the grocery store and my condo this afternoon," and she flipped her hair and laughed at what a fool he was as she blew by him.

She could feel his eyes on her as she walked out the door, but she refused to turn around. That's what he wanted her to do, expected her to do. But, of course, he forgot that she wasn't one of his brainless twits that he led on with his money, his cars and his slick, but empty promises.

As she rounded the corner, she shuddered and rubbed both of her arms like Dylan had somehow sloughed off on her. She was running late and she had a lot to do. As she pulled out of the parking lot and headed home, she ticked off the items on her to-do list one by one. She wondered if she had enough time to get everything done. She wondered if she had enough time for a second shower today. She could sure use one about now.

Chapter 84

John Starr sat at his desk, starring out the window, drumming his fingers as he mentally organized what he needed to do next. He had considered almost every possible, plausible and probable outcome of this Patrick Lowers situation. None of them was good—for him personally, for the bankers professionally, or for the bank generally.

One stupid, desperate act by one stupid, desperate individual risked dismantling a highly sophisticated network that had ensured financial security for countless bankers and their families in and around the southeastern part of North Carolina for over 15 years. The saddest part of the impending fiasco is that, until now, nobody had gotten hurt. The extra money that flowed into the bankers' coffers was "created" money from leveraging the depositors' money 10 to 1. Their windfall was just less in taxes the bank had to send to Uncle Sam for some social program that simply took the wealth from the hard-working folks and gave it to the damn "no-goods." This money was simply *their* entitlement.

Or it had been. John could feel the noose tightening daily. Somebody was on the same trail as Lowers, but obviously, the necessary documentation, the proof was incomplete, missing. The disk had not been received, located—yet.

Their team would find the disk. In fact, they were the only ones who knew the disk existed and he was determined to keep the status quo. They were following every hunch, plowing through countless records, destroying endless pieces of paper and deleting old shadow files on the computer. They hadn't been around for all this time by being sloppy, after all.

John considered the possibility that there was no disk other than the one he received last Saturday, but then he asked himself why the disk was a copy. A copy was made from an original. So what did Lowers do with it?

Did he send it to upper management? Those fools, for the most part, wouldn't even know what the disk was, let alone how to open it or understand its contents. Most of the executive management team were so behind the times they didn't even know how to turn on a computer.

The exception was Ross Moore. He was young, technologically gifted by all accounts in the industry and so straight-laced that John was sure that he could hardly relate to the good folks far below his ivory tower. He also had ties to Shallotte and spent way too much time in the area for John's comfort now that he was the bank president.

When American One hired Moore, John had called in as many favors as possible to find out everything he could about President Squeaky. He found nothing. Moore was 43, divorced, had been a CFO at a large computer company, was the number two guy in Washington DC at the General Accounting Office for the government and had worked as the COO at a large, family-owned bank in the state for several years. His father was a retired engineer and his mother was an artist.

He's probably a fag, thought John. Nobody is *that* clean. Unfortunately, his attention was pulled away from investigating Moore to keeping the network from coming unglued. He had to calm the nerves of everybody involved after Lowers was killed—not that any one of the idiots admitted to the crime. If he knew for sure which guy had gone off the ranch, he'd probably off him himself.

Not that he didn't have his suspicions, but now was the time to circle the wagons not strike out alone. His job was to ensure that the team dealt with all of the loose ends and paid attention to even the smallest details. So far, their foot soldiers had meticulously searched the obvious places for the disk while their back-room support washed away the traces of their electronic and paperwork footprints. He was on the team in charge of keeping everybody focused, reminding everybody that they were all in the network together and by choice. Everybody had a job to do because everybody had shared in the reward.

His primary contacts at the SBI had long-since retired, but he had fostered relationships with several of the younger guys over the years as well. Unfortunately, they were not in the loop in this investigation and the silence from Raleigh was deafening. The Shallotte PD knew nothing, the County deputies knew nothing, and John wondered if the lack of communication with the local authorities was because somebody higher up suspected that the investigation efforts at the local level had been compromised.

Damn, I am surrounded by amateurs and idiots, he thought. He momentarily longed for the days of his youth and young adulthood when he was on the team with the white hats. Those days were long gone.

When he first got to the bank, he investigated every missing $20 shortage with such zeal and aggression that he quickly rose to the top. He brought down unscrupulous tellers stealing petty cash to feed their children, an operations manager who diverted excess food stamps over a period of seven year to the tune of $75,000 and a merchant credit card representative who was setting up dummy accounts and running stolen credit card charges through them. John was held up as an example of honesty and integrity.

Somewhere along the way, though, John got lazy. He befriended George Everett and after cultivating the friendship for many years, George let him into his secret kingdom of success. John envied George in many ways. Women loved him. He had homes, cars, took vacations and was planning for retirement next year. John wanted what George had.

So, instead of taking George down, sending him to prison or ruining him professionally, John waltzed right into a highly organized, highly efficient, highly lucrative secret network of bankers that made him richer than he ever dreamed and more unscrupulous than he thought imaginable. Oh well, he thought casually. George called the shots, but he ran the show. George would be the big target and most of the rest would go unpunished because the details were all being erased.

Time to step it up, he thought. He turned back to his desk and made a new checklist of locations to search for the disk. As they searched physical places, the head of the IT department was sweeping Lowers' computer and so far, had found nothing decipherable. All of the information had been permanently deleted several weeks ago and only bits and pieces of account information had been recovered, and then promptly deleted again to further avoid detection.

John was proud of this team. In all his years in banking, he had been to countless seminars, conferences and training about embezzlement, diversion of funds, fraudulent loans and internal theft. Rarely, did the instructors ever touch on collusion because the vast majority of internal bank crimes were perpetrated by a rogue thief. On the rare occasion that collusion was mentioned, the crime typically involved two low-level half-wits working together to steal a twenty here and a hundred there then cover up the missing money. Most of these thieves were caught quickly because cash is so tightly controlled and random audits, unexpected absences or even an astute customer blowing the whistle ends the crime after a very short run.

Their network was one of a kind. It was wide, deep and organized. It spanned multiple departments, included participants both inside and outside the bank and rewarded every member handsomely. Not one invitee had ever refused involvement and that, of course, included him. As a result, the participants were loyal, careful and smart.

In the end, if George went down, he wouldn't give up the rest. John sure couldn't say the same for anybody else, and included himself in this group. As a result, he had to ensure that nobody knew as much as he did and could connect him in any way.

After all, he was the head of security at the bank and that meant he was empowered to protect its assets at all costs. The network was one of those assets and he was prepared to do whatever he had to do to defend and preserve it.

Chapter 85

Dylan stuck his head in Jeff's office. It was five o'clock, and it was Wednesday. He knew where Jeff was headed tonight and he wanted to see what Jeff had planned.

"Got a minute, Jeff?" Dylan asked him.

Jeff looked up and emphatically said, "No."

Nothing more, nothing less, just no. *Asshole,* Dylan thought.

"Aw, c'mon," he whined and he sat down in the chair in front of Jeff's desk. "What are you doing tonight?"

"The asking of the question leads me to believe you already know the answer, Dylan. How are my plans for the evening any of your business?" he asked.

"Really?" Dylan asked sarcastically. "I'm making your involvement with Spencer Cashwell my business."

"Sorry, pal, you're not," Jeff answered. "Now, get the hell out of my office before I throw your boney ass out."

Dylan sat for a moment longer and glared at Jeff. He could screw up everything if he got involved with Spencer, not that he could see for one minute why she would give old, dull Jeff anything to put a bounce in his step tomorrow.

"Quite frankly, I don't give a damn if you get lucky, but you better get smart, Jeff," he said as he got up to leave.

"Stay out of my business, Dylan," Jeff said darkly. Then he added, "Hey, since you can't make smart out of stupid, maybe you just need to get lucky. I'm sure you can pay one of those whores at the beach to help you out."

Dylan fumed and Jeff smiled slyly at just how easy it was to get under his skin. *What a prick,* he thought. As he walked out of the office, he turned back to Jeff and warned him, "You just remember what I said, old man."

"Gotcha, Shorty," Jeff said. His laughter spilled over and as Dylan stormed down the hall, the sound of it followed him every step of the way.

Chapter 86

As Ross drove from Charlotte to Stanly County, he couldn't help but admire the beautiful landscape. The rolling hills of the Piedmont were covered with purple clover, stands of hay, and herds of cattle grazing on the still-green pastures.

When he turned off of Highway 49 onto Wesley Chapel Road, the manicured bungalows along the bumpy, winding road invited visitors to look at their pots of pansies and chrysanthemums as they to struggled to reach the 35-mile-per-hour speed limit. When he crossed the railroad tracks into the university town, it reminded him a little of Bedford Falls in "It's a Wonderful Life." The antique store, the barber shop, the post office and the old stone inn—Misenheimer was picturesque.

Following his hand-written directions, he crossed Highway 52 beside Lloyd's Antiques and drove the mile and a half to the Miller farm that was evidenced by a split-rail fence along the rock driveway. Across the road, Black Angus cattle stood in groups momentarily watching him as he closed his car door and broke the silence of the afternoon. Up on a small hill behind the herd, a white farm house stood proudly against a backdrop of oaks and maples, their vibrant fall colors finally beginning to fade in late October.

As he walked up to the front of the columned brick ranch house, a tall, striking woman opened the door before he could knock, a Halloween ghost in her hands. Not startled at all, she smiled, her face gleaming, and said firmly, "Well, hello—you must be Ross Moore," and as she extended her hand, she added, "Jeanne Miller—but everybody around here calls me 'Jeannie.' Did you have any trouble finding us?"

"None at all. The drive over here is spectacular and your farm is like a picture on a postcard," Ross admired as he shook her hand.

"Thank you, Ross," she said, "Come on in the house and I'll get Rita as soon as I hang up my ghost. It just wouldn't do if we didn't try to scare the children half to death around here on Halloween."

He laughed and walked into the house. As Jeanne disappeared around the corner, he walked over to the wall of pictures next to the foyer and looked at a lifetime of photographs of the Miller family—Rita as a precocious child, laughing and hugging a huge cow; a picture of Rita and a young girl that was obviously her sister singing in a church; a mischievous boy, Rita's brother, throwing leaves at his sisters; and Rita sitting at a pottery wheel deep in concentration as her hands grasped a newly formed vase, her mother and father smiling broadly behind her.

Down the hallway, he heard Rita talking quietly to her mother, her words undecipherable but her voice unmistakable. Surprising himself at the realization, he was nervous and he knew why. He wanted to like her family and he also wanted them to like him.

As Rita came around the corner and smiled at him, she quelled all of his anxiety. She was a vision, even in a baseball cap, hiking boots, a pair of cargo shorts and a light blue oxford rolled up to her elbows over a white thermal Henley undershirt. She had a small canvas backpack thrown over her shoulder. He walked over to her and took the backpack from her to carry and touched her cheek in one motion. He breathed out loud, returned her smile and said, "Hey, Beautiful."

"Hey yourself," and she reached up and kissed him on the cheek. "How was the drive in?"

"Short and scenic," he answered truthfully. "This place is like a Shangri-La."

She smiled again and said, "No—Eden—now come, Adam. I must show you my garden," and she led him out of the house by the hand to an old, beat-up Jeep.

She threw him the keys and climbed in the passenger seat, and said, "Will you drive me over to the farm house?" and she pointed across the road to the quaint white house on the hill.

"Gladly," Ross said. "Whose house is that?"

"My Grandfather and Grandmother Miller built it and lived there for sixty years," she said, "Now, my brother Mark and his wife, Shelley, live there. C'mon."

Ross crossed the road and turned into the driveway which, unlike her parents', was paved. As if reading his mind, Rita said, "Can you imagine driving up this driveway in rain, ice and snow? Paving it was money well-spent."

As they crested the hill, the pavement flattened out and Rita pointed to the right of a huge oak tree for Ross to park. They got out and instead of walking up to the house, she trekked the other way, up a wide path between a small wooden shed on the right and a huge tin garage on the left. Rita was ahead of him and as she walked, she pointed to the shed and commented with a smile on her face, "My pottery shed," then pointed to the garage and said, "Daddy's tractor barn." She was enjoying playing tour guide. Rita stopped at the top of the rise at a heavy metal gate that led to a large, open field and waited for him to catch up. As he walked up, Rita said, "Mark and Shelley aren't home yet. We'll stop in before we go back to the house for dinner, ok?"

"Ok, but which direction are we going?" he asked, trying to get his bearings.

"We are heading southwest—over there," she said and pointed to a hill that peeked above the tree line in the distance as she climbed over the gate and waited for Ross to do the same. Once inside the pasture, they walked quickly but easily up and down small hills, along a small creek that ran through the farm and past a beautiful pond surrounded by an old stand of cedar trees. Ross wondered how somebody like Rita who so loved this land had ever decided to pursue a banking career at the coast.

As if sensing his curiosity, she said, "It's beautiful, isn't it? This is the place God holds in his hand and admires when he needs reassurance about the earth and mankind."

Ross liked that comment and he stopped and looked back to where they had started, seemingly miles below where they were now. This place was special, almost magical, in its beauty.

Rita pointed over to the stand of cedars and said, "That is where I am going to build me a cabin someday. I picked out that spot when I was about eight. Nothing stupid sized, just a small place near my pottery shed that will fit in with all of this," and she spread her arms as wide as the smile on her face as she continued to walk.

Ross could see the cabin right where she pointed, and he knew that Rita's dream would someday be a reality. He wanted to be part of it too, he realized.

Moving on down the path, they began a climb steeper than any on the trek and they both were somewhat winded by the time they neared the top. As he walked up to the top of the ridge, the sight almost took his breath away it was so stunning.

Off far in the distance, the foothills of the Piedmont were perched on the horizon, seemingly floating as the sunlight through the clouds danced, creating a tapestry of shadow and light. The sun, slowly descending down on top of the hills, was a dark orange orb sinking behind the shadowed distant tree line and casting a glow over the grass and the trees around us. *This place surely is Eden*, he thought.

Rita took the backpack and pulled out a cotton blanket and spread it out on the grass. She then took Ross's hand and pulled him down beside her and broke out a bottle of white wine and some curious looking filled crackers. As she handed Ross a glass of wine, she whispered, "It is heaven on earth, huh?"

Ross took her glass of wine and put it aside with his. Then, he pulled her down beside him, silently undressed her and made love to her as the last rays of the setting sun washed over their naked bodies.

Chapter 87

Spencer paced back and forth, fussed over the pillows on the couch, checked the beer for at least the tenth time and retouched her hair and make-up in the mirror in the downstairs bathroom. Stop obsessing, she told herself.

She was nervous, but she was also excited. God knows, she had not had a date in so long, she had almost forgotten what to do, what to say, and how to act. Not that she was a homebody like Rita. Spencer went out with Rita and Ivey for dinner and drinks anytime she could get them to go and she spent an extraordinary amount of time at the clubhouse after she played golf.

She looked at the clock. It was just after 6 p.m. Jeez—almost an hour before Jeff would arrive. Spencer needed to calm her nerves. She needed to talk to Rita. Besides, she hadn't spoken to her since Monday before she left for home.

Spencer called her cell phone and Rita answered on the first ring, "Whatcha doin', fool," she asked playfully.

Spencer laughed and said, "Hey, that's my line! What are you up to?"

"Yesterday, I fed the cattle and ploughed the north forty," Rita laughed. "Really, though, I got home Tuesday morning and thanks to the work carousel that is the Miller house, I haven't stopped. My brother and sister and their families came over for dinner—which, of course, I had to cook. Today, I helped Mom clean the house and cook all morning because Ross is here for dinner. He's in with Daddy talking about something really exciting like farm machinery or crop rotation right now. Whew, I'm so tired I'm going to need a vacation when I get back to the beach to get over my vacation at home."

"Good God, woman, it sounds liked you've been at a prison work camp. What fun," she teased. "I'm home from work and I've been cleaning my condo this afternoon. I'm exhausted too."

"Why are you cleaning your condo on a Wednesday?" she asked Spencer curiously. "You must either be ill or have a hot date!"

"Actually, hot date is a little over the top, Rita," she said almost sheepishly.

"Pardon me? I go out of town and you have a date? What the hell, Spencer!" she said incredulously.

"Crap, I knew you were going to get your panties in a wad," Spencer said. "I just invited one of the neighbors over for beer and pizza."

"What neighbor, Spencer?"

"I invited Jeff Malone over for beer and pizza—at 7, which is forty-five minutes away," she answered.

"*Jeff Malone*? Are you drunk," Rita all but yelled.

"No, but I am a little nervous," she admitted honestly.

Spencer heard Rita let out a sigh and then pause. Then, she asked softly, "But what if he is a really bad guy, Spence?"

"Then, everybody will know he is the guilty party when they find my lifeless body tomorrow. The whole damn bank knows about tonight thanks to Fat Mouth Fordham," she complained.

Spencer could tell that Rita felt better knowing that the evening was not a secret. "So, why are you nervous?" she asked.

"I don't know. It's crazy, Rita. I went into his office after you and I talked on Monday just to see if I could throw him off his guard and we had this kind of surreal conversation. I admit, I was intrigued by him and I know he was by me, too. We just had some kind of...connection. Does that sound ridiculous?" she asked her best friend.

Spencer could hear Rita thinking, could see her in her mind. Finally, she answered, "No, that explanation sounds completely sane. So, again, why are you nervous?"

"I think I want to enjoy tonight. I think I want to continue that feeling I had when I was talking to him on Monday. Hell, I think I want to kiss him or something," she blurted.

"Now we're getting somewhere," Rita said. "Jeff is ruggedly handsome, single and smart. So what do you see in him again?" she teased Spencer.

"Okay, Farmer Smartass, don't make me come up there and beat your butt," she replied and suddenly her tension was gone. Spencer sighed hard. "I'm so glad I called you Rita. I really feel better knowing that you know. Thanks for making me not feel stupid by making me feel stupid. I really love you. And I miss you. So when are you coming back? You are coming back, aren't you?" she asked.

"Yes. Saturday. And I love you too," Rita said. "Hey, will you call me tomorrow and let me know how tonight goes? I really want to know."

"Yes, I'll call you. Enough about me, tell me more about you and Ross? Did you go to Charlotte Monday night? Did it suck waking up alone this morning?" and she laughed at her wittiness.

"Yes and yes," Rita replied. "God, Spence, his house is both gorgeous and comfortable. I loved it."

"You spend a night with the hottest bank president in probably the whole USA and you want to tell me how gorgeous his house is? Rita, you are hopeless. I'll make sure I tell you how many pinstripes Jeff Malone has on his oxford when we talk tomorrow night," she said jokingly.

"No, you won't! Okay, today I gave Ross the 15-minute Misenheimer grand tour after we hiked up to the meadow late this afternoon to watch the sunset. It was so romantic, perfect..." Rita said defending her sexy side.

Boy was that wasted on Spencer and she deadpanned, "Not unless it included a roll in the grass and I'm guessing it did—now that's what I am talking about," and she laughed again. Finally, Spencer sighed what sounded like a nervous sigh and said, "You're a case, but you're also my best friend. I've got to go. Jeff will be here in a minute and you have a bank president to entertain. Bye, Rita."

"Bye, Spencer. Have fun," Rita said then added, "And be careful too."

Chapter 88

Jeff stood on the stoop of Spencer's condo and took a deep breath before he knocked on the door. Within seconds, Spencer opened the door and said, "Hey neighbor. Come on in," and showed him inside. He put the movies on her coffee table and turned around. Spencer was moving toward the adjacent kitchen and asked him what he wanted to drink.

"What are you having?" he asked.

Spencer said, "I'm having a lite beer, but I bought you some of that heavy crap that you and Rita both rave over—Samuel Adams. Want one?"

"Absolutely," Jeff replied, impressed that Spencer had noticed what he drank.

As she handed him the beer, she smiled at him and said, "I've got to tell you I'm a little nervous, Jeff," and she breathed out a huge breath, relieved to have that fact off her chest.

"Why are you nervous?" he asked quietly, "I don't typically bite hard." Spencer studied him quietly as if she was trying to decide whether he was being truthful, all the while Jeff quietly pierced her with his deep blue eyes.

"I'm not sure except that I haven't had a date since Bill Clinton was involved with Monica Lewinsky," she said coolly. "I'm just a little rusty, that's all."

"Come over here and relax," he said, and he took her hand and pulled her down beside him on the couch. "So, what were you up to today? I didn't see you at the bank at all."

"Oh, I was there holed up in my office knocking out about four retail loan approval packages. I left about 2 o'clock to run a few errands," Spencer said honestly. "I had to clean up a place in here so you could sit down, after all. Besides, you may have had to bail me out of jail if I stayed much longer. Dylan overheard me ask you to come over and he couldn't stand not nosing into my business. That man is such a hen, I swear."

"What did he say?" Jeff asked ominously.

"Nothing, he was just being his usual sleazy self," Spencer said. "I think he's a blowhard, personally. He always sounds like he's making up for something he's lacking, but I think if a woman with a brain gave him the time of day, she would scare him to death."

"I'm not so sure he's as harmless as you think he is. He doesn't have a nasty reputation just because of his talk," Jeff said.

"Twenty bucks in Myrtle Beach will buy you a bad reputation if you frequent one place enough," she added, "I know he's been kicked out of more than one place for fondling the dancers."

"Well, I'm not going to defend the little bastard's honor. But I will defend yours, if I need to," he said quietly.

"But you don't really know me, Jeff. Why would you defend me?" she asked warily.

"Let's just say I have good instincts, Spencer," and he sat facing her, never taking his eyes off her.

Spencer got up easily and went and grabbed the pizza and looked at the movies he brought.

She looked over at him and raised her eyebrows. "Have you seen either of those?" he asked.

"No, are they good?"

"'Notorious' is one of the best films Alfred Hitchcock ever made. It's dark and mysterious—but sexy. It stars Ingrid Bergman and Cary Grant. 'Cold Mountain' is based on a book by North Carolina's Charles Frazier. You'll like that one too. It has Jude Law in it, but Renee Zellwegger steals the movie," he said casually.

"You sound like a film critic," she laughed quietly, "Which one do you think I'll like the best?"

"Let's go with 'Cold Mountain' first and see if we have time for the other one later," he said.

Spencer took the DVD out of the case and put it in the player. Her hands were shaking. *What the hell is wrong with me,* she asked silently. She walked across the room and turned on her floor lamp, then turned off the overhead light. In the lowlight, she saw Jeff smile slightly.

She returned to the couch, grabbed her beer and a slice of pizza for each of them and hit 'play.' As the movie's plot unfolded, Jeff slid closer to her, put his arm around her and pulled her back into him easily. Spencer was still nervous, but damn he felt good against her. She tried to relax and found herself really enjoying the movie even though it was intense and bloody at times.

As it neared the end, the love scene was so hot and sexy she felt herself blushing with both desire and discomfort all at once. She could feel Jeff breathing next to her and he touched her arm lightly. She was certain she was either going to burst into flames or have a heart-attack at any moment.

As the movie ended, she said, "Wow," and looked at him. He smiled and pulled her over to him. With their faces inches apart, he reached up and put his hand around the front of her neck. She swallowed hard and looked into his eyes.

"Did you like the movie?" he asked softly, his thumb stroking one side of her neck, his fingers around the other side.

She had lost her voice, so she just nodded. He moved his lips to her ear and whispered, "Did you like the love scene?" and his breath was hot and moved her hair with each syllable. Still breathless, she nodded again. He whispered, "Good," then pulled her mouth up to his roughly and kissed her deeply, exploring every space in her mouth.

Spencer responded and grabbed onto his shirt, her body burning, being consumed with desire. She wanted him, but she also felt a dangerous undercurrent running around her, circling her, waiting to devour her.

When she reached a fevered pitch, he slowly pulled away and looked at her, his breath heavy and ragged, his eyes dark with desire. Still his hand never left her throat and she was sure she was going to faint from a lack of oxygen, wondering if she was even still breathing.

"You are dangerous, Spencer," he said quietly.

"I was thinking the same thing about you," she said, and the comment seemed to surprise him.

"Will you get us another beer?" he asked and as a reply she stood, still somewhat wobbly, and went to the cooler to get two beers. When she came back to the couch, he had turned around facing her.

"I have an idea," he said as she sat back down.

"Shoot," Spencer said, slowly regaining her composure, her nerve, and her bearings.

"We sit and talk for a while tonight then you come over to my place on Friday to watch movie number two. Deal?" he asked.

Spencer searched his eyes, his face, his body language for the right answer, but got nothing. She smiled and quietly answered, "Deal."

For the next two hours, they talked about their careers, their hobbies and their backgrounds easily and comfortably and Spencer let go of the last vestiges of fear and uncertainty she felt around Jeff. Finally, he looked at his watch and reminded her, "If I don't go now, we'll never get to work on time tomorrow. We certainly don't want to throw fuel on Mr. Fordham's fire now do we?" he asked.

"I like toying with him like a mouse in my cat claws," Spencer said, "So it will absolutely kill him when I just give him a smile tomorrow when he starts asking questions—and you know he will."

Jeff stood reluctantly, collected the two movies and walked to the door, his beer still in his hands. Spencer walked to the door with him and turned to face him before she let him go. "I had a great time," she said. "I'm looking forward to Friday."

He put his beer down on the window sill beside the door and stepped so close to her she could feel the heat of his body near hers. He again reached up with his hand and stroked the front of her neck, slowly, watching his fingers as he strummed them back and forth. Spencer's knees felt weak again and he put his other arm around her to support her.

As he leaned down and kissed her, he nibbled her lip and whispered, "I promise Friday will be just as interesting, Spencer. Good night."

Spencer whispered, probably inaudibly, "Good night," and like a shadow in the night, Jeff Malone slowly disappeared into the darkness between her home and his.

Chapter 89

Night had fallen hours ago, and Ross had to work tomorrow. I walked him to his SUV so he could get back to the city before the storm moving in from the west arrived with all its promised fury. The wind was already whipping, and leaves crackled on the trees and rained down all around us. I took in all the sounds of the night around us as we walked in a comfortable silence.

Today had been wonderful. Ross appreciated my love of this land and seemed to thoroughly enjoy our hike, riding around the town and university, and talking and getting to know my family. After the Miller review panel finished with him today, though, I was certain he was tired. I sure was.

As we got to his door, he put his arms around me and pulled me close to him. I rested my head on his chest and closed my eyes. *We just fit*, I thought to myself. Reluctantly pulling myself back, I said, "You better get on the road ahead of that storm—not that I want you to go at all."

He sighed and said, "I know, I hate to leave, but tomorrow morning is going to come early. I had a wonderful day, Rita. Thank you for sharing your family with me."

"It was my pleasure, Mr. Moore," and I reached up and kissed him gently. "I hope you'll come back again soon."

"I certainly will," he promised, "but first, you've got to come to the city and let me show you around. Can you come Friday night? I'd love for you to stay with me. You could leave whenever you want on Saturday—or Sunday."

"Ok," I said. "What do I need to wear Friday night? What do you have in mind?"

"Break out your jeans and something orange," he said cryptically.

"Orange?" I asked curiously.

"Orange—blue and orange—because we're going to a Bobcats game," he said, proud of himself for knowing how much she loved sports. "If you can get to the house around six we can eat and have a few drinks in the hospitality room before the game."

I kissed him again, surprising him with my excitement and he teased, "Hey—you don't have a thing for those svelte young ballplayers, do you?"

"Oh, yeah," I said. "I have a big thing for those guys. Jealous?" I asked coolly.

"Insanely—maybe I just need to take you to the library," he countered.

"I like bookworms too," I said.

"So maybe I'll just lock you in the house and read sonnets to you while I dribble a basketball. How does that grab you, you temptress," he said softly.

"Mmmm, sounds...*hot,*" I said and he leaned back against the door of his SUV defeated.

I laughed softly at his dramatics. "The basketball game sounds wonderful, but I have to warn you I am animated, ok?"

"Yeah, that's really hard to picture," he said and he laughed at his sarcasm. "I've got courtside seats so you can see everything."

"Man, you must be trying to impress me or something," I said with mock suspicion.

"Or something—I'm just trying to return the favor of a wonderful day with you and your family, Rita. Thank you again," Ross said and he leaned down and kissed me.

"You're welcome, Ross. I can't wait for Friday. That is, if I survive one more day of slave labor at the Miller work camp," I added.

"You love every minute of it, farm gal. I was really worried about losing you to Ferdinand when we talked yesterday," he laughed, "but he's not much of a conversationalist, is he?"

"No," I laughed. "You win that comparison, hands down—not that the poor beast has any hands." I looked at the sky. I could feel the humidity rising, foretelling the coming rain. "Go, Ross. I'll see you at 6 p.m. on Friday, ok?" He got into the SUV and rolled down the window.

"It's a date," he said and kissed me one more time for the road. He backed out of the driveway and pulled away down the narrow road toward town and I watched long after the red tail lights of his SUV disappeared around a curve in the road.

Chapter 90

As morning slowly seeped through the windows, Spencer guessed she got about three hours of sleep. She was tired and she was testy. Woe to the fool that causes me grief today, she thought and she knew the fool went by the name "Dylan."

After Jeff left last night, she went upstairs, changed into her sweatpants and a tee shirt, and fell into bed. Spencer was asleep almost immediately she was so exhausted, but dreams both frightening and vague tormented her and she woke up two times panting and soaked in sweat. Both times she got out of bed, changed into another tee shirt, went to the bathroom to grab a glass of water and tried to get a grip on herself before she returned to her bed to sleep.

Finally, the third time, she got out of bed and resigned herself to staying awake so she could sort out all the crap swirling around in her gray matter. She went downstairs, fixed herself a Diet Coke in the biggest glass she owned, and turned on the television to the country music video channel.

Jeff Malone fascinated her and frightened her all at once and Spencer wondered why. He was charming and kind, he was intelligent and well-rounded, and he was sexy in a rugged and seemingly dangerous way. *What the hell does that mean,* she asked herself.

She stood up and wrapped her afghan tighter around her shoulders. The chill of late October had settled in, and reluctantly, Spencer had turned on the heat to take off a little of the nip. As she walked over to the window to look out, images from her dreams seeped into her consciousness—a mask, moving shadows, a silver gun. Accompanying the images were a whole array of intangibles like danger, excitement, lust and fear. What did it all mean?

Spencer looked at the clock on the television. Damn, it was already 7 a.m. She went to the kitchen, refilled her soda and dragged herself up the stairs. She went through her closet three times before she finally settled on a pair of black slacks and a white cashmere sweater, deeming simplicity the winner in her current mindset.

She showered quickly, dressed and put her makeup on and was out the door to work less than an hour later, another huge Diet Coke in hand for the five-minute commute to the bank. As she drove, Spencer rehearsed her reaction and potential response to everybody she encountered this morning—Jeff, of course, Dylan, Greg, Peter, and Tripp, all of whom she was certain knew about her evening plans. She sighed heavily. Thursday was going to be a long day.

As she pulled into a parking space, she checked her hair and face in the rearview mirror and for a moment closed her eyes and just sat still. *Oh, to be anywhere but here today*, she thought. Spencer wished she was on vacation with Rita. Well, not on the farm necessarily, but somewhere at a resort with a wonderful spa and a lush, green golf course. She sighed again, opened her eyes, and almost jumped out of her skin.

Jeff Malone was standing beside the door to her SUV. Her stomach did a flip as she put her hand up to her heart in an attempt to see if it was still beating. Not exactly a scenario she expected on her drive to work.

She slowly took off her sunglasses and smiled at him. He gave her a smile in return, or something that approached a smile anyway, and opened her door so she could get out. As she looked at him more closely, he looked tired and she was sure she looked even more haggard to him. *Oh damn*, she thought. Everybody was going to notice and the rumor mill would be rolling approximately 15 seconds after they walked in the door.

"You look tired, Jeff," she said and she wondered if her would give her an explanation. "Did you not sleep well?"

"No, I didn't," he said. "I guess after I left your place I was too wound up to go to bed. What's your excuse for being so jumpy this morning?" he asked.

"I've been up since 4 a.m.," Spencer answered truthfully. "I had crazy dreams and I got up and didn't go back to sleep."

"What kind of crazy dreams keep you from going back to bed at 4 a.m.," he questioned, a hint of concern in his voice.

"Strange ones," she answered simply. "I'll tell you all about it tomorrow night, I promise," she said.

"I thought we would walk in together to stir the pot this morning," he said playfully. "Are you game?"

Spencer shut the door to her SUV, grabbed her briefcase and moved beside him casually and replied, "Mr. Malone, I invented this game. Come on," and she tossed her hair back and walked close beside him down the sidewalk and into the bank.

Showtime!

Chapter 91

I spent Thursday morning helping Dad on the farm with the hay and cattle and all afternoon helping Mom plant pansies in the large wooden tubs that framed the driveway at the side of the house. The work came with a pact—I would work with her until 3 o'clock, but then she had to go with me to help me find the perfect orange shirt to accompany my favorite pair of jeans for the basketball game Friday night. She was thrilled and even asked me to set the timer on my wristwatch so we could leave on time. Jeannie loved to shop for clothes for me and was really great at finding just the right piece, accessory or ensemble. She could have been a buyer in Manhattan. Unfortunately, none of her fashion sense flowed through my veins and I breathed a sigh of relief that I was home so she could rescue me from a trip to the mall.

We actually got out of the door early and hopped in Mom's minivan for the short 12-mile trip into Albemarle. As we drove, Mom and I sang to the radio some, talked about Stanly County politics and laughed hysterically at Maggie's reaction to the jack o' lanterns on the front porch. My parents' loco pooch growled ferociously, barked like a maniac and bumped them with her nose like she was going to tear them to pieces.

Today had been a great day and I knew it was days like this one that made me long for a life back on the farm, on the land I loved so much, surrounded. by family. Other days, not so much.

Strangely, after Ross' visit, my family had been neither stifling nor inquisitive. After the ribbing they gave me prior to his visit, I certainly knew the whole crew was curious about him, but not one of them had told me what they thought of him after he left last night—no questions, no calls, nothing.

Never one to back away from an issue, I went straight at Jeannie before her reverse psychology actually started working on my brain. "Are you going to withhold your opinion for the first time in history or are you going to tell me what you think of Ross Moore?" I asked good-naturedly.

"Oh, I didn't know you cared about what I thought!" Mom teased right back.

I snorted out a laugh. "Like that has ever stopped you before!"

Mom looked at me for a few seconds that was beginning to feel like an eternity when she finally answered, "He's delightful. He's intelligent, and quite frankly, he's a perfect fit for you."

I sighed and answered, "I know."

Mom broke my dream-like daze and said, "Well, let's get over to Hilda Gannon's to see if we can find the perfect top. You are going to be such a show stopper tomorrow night that you'll make even the cheerleaders' boyfriends green with envy!"

Ever blessed with the gift of hyperbole, I smiled broadly at my mother's compliment and shook my head as we pulled up to arguably the best ladies' clothes boutique in the Piedmont. Hilda Gannon's was upscale but affordable and filled with one-of-a-kind clothing finds from casual to formal and funky to sophisticated. The owner was the store's namesake and she was a lovely, refined woman who was responsible for ensuring the women of Stanly County were finely dressed for over 30 years. She never bought more than one of anything because she knew the greatest fashion faux pas at a social event was looking like a carbon copy of another woman.

My mother, statuesque and striking, confidently walked in and strolled right over to Hilda herself and told her what we were looking to purchase. Within seconds, Mom and Hilda had assembled basically every orange top in the store, several pairs of smoking hot black patent pumps and virtually one of every accessory in the store.

Almost an hour later, I stood in front of a three-way mirror completely blown away at what the pair of fashion mavens had accomplished. The outfit took "jeans and a tee shirt" to a whole new level. The orange microfiber tee shirt had a sweetheart neckline with shirring at the top which accented the bust line beautifully. The shirt was form-fitting and paired perfectly with my favorite jeans and a black patent leather belt. The patent pumps were incredibly sexy and surprisingly comfortable and I knew I was going to spend a lot more money than I had intended on the outfit just on the shoes. They were must-haves.

Mom bought me two long strands of different colored blue glass beads and let them drape at different levels around my neck, and she also purchased the matching pair of earrings. Hilda brought an orange ribbon over and tied my long, curly hair in a very loose ponytail to left and let the hair fall over my shoulder.

I asked Mom to snap a picture of me with her cell phone and I sent it immediately to Spencer with a tag to call me as soon as she got home from work. I couldn't wait for her to see me dressed up...in jeans. I was also dying to hear about her evening with Jeff Malone.

I asked Ms. Hilda to please not say my purchase total out loud for fear that I would keel over. Mom just laughed, grabbed the beautifully wrapped parcels with one hand and me with the other and led me to the door to leave. The afternoon had been a screaming, but expensive, success.

As we got into Mom's minivan, my phone rang. I looked at the caller id and saw that Spencer was calling me. I looked at the time and, sure enough, it was five o'clock. Where had the day gone?

"Hey!" I said half out of breath to Spencer as I climbed back in the passenger seat. "What's up?"

"H-O-T, my sister, h-o-t," she said, "I'm telling you if I was a lesbian, I'd give President Hot Britches a run for his money," and she laughed at herself.

I smiled and asked, "Were you just going to keep me in stitches over your date last night?"

Spencer sighed loudly and answered, "No, I just don't have the words to explain it. It was fun, exciting, dangerous, and scary all rolled into one four-hour evening."

"Huh? Lucy, you got some 'splainin' to do…" I said, doing my best Ricky Ricardo impersonation.

"Ok, but you better get comfortable," she said, breathing out another big sigh.

"I even have on my seatbelt," I said then added, "So drive me slowly down last night's memory lane and don't leave out a thing."

Chapter 92

I am going crazy, he thought. "No!" he said out loud to the empty office. The ferocity and volume of the outburst surprised and embarrassed him and he got up and walked to the door to ensure he was alone now. Satisfied that everybody was gone, he began pacing the floor in his office, turning his Saturday night plans over and over in his mind.

He would play golf as usual that afternoon, finishing up about 4:30 p.m. Then, instead of staying at the bar to brag and have a few drinks, he would make an excuse about having dinner plans and slip away.

Immediately, as the sun was setting, he would park his car at the clubhouse and slip under cover of the impending darkness to the back door of Rita's condo, enter unseen and find that damn disk. He would be very careful, leaving no fingerprints, no trace of his presence, his expedition.

As soon as he located his prize, he would leave as quietly and clandestinely as he had come—out the back door, through the woods and back to his car. It was a perfect plan. Rita's vacation would ensure her absence from the condo so no one would get hurt.

He sighed and ran his fingers through his hair, his dark thoughts turning darker as he paced. And what is up with Jeff and Spencer, he wondered. Jeff cannot be thinking with the head on his shoulders, that's for sure. If he was determined to pursue Spencer Cashwell, that particular piece of ass could cost them all big time.

God, he thought, what a sorry state of existence. He was the only one who seemed particularly worried about the potentially devastating and certainly incriminating information contained on the disk. He had to find it, destroy it and wipe the slate clean. A fresh start, he thought, and momentarily he savored the idea. Just as quickly, though, he dived back into his pit of darkness. Nobody was going to screw up his drive to undo this mess into which he had gotten himself—nobody.

He packed up his briefcase to go home, turned off the lights in his office and went to set the alarm. As he walked through the now-quiet bank he thought, "*This place is my kingdom.*" When he turned to unlock the door to leave, though, his paranoia returned with a vengeance. He turned back around and looked across the lobby of the bank and realized that in addition to being all alone, his domain was completely empty, dark and devoid of life.

Chapter 93

Holy-moly, he thought as he watched Rita through the dining room window walking toward his front door. She was a sexy, blue and orange vision and she stirred him to the core. He was certain the eyes of every man in Bobcats Arena would be on her as they walked to their seats tonight, and he momentarily worried that some athletic Romeo would make a play to steal her attention away from him. He suddenly had the urge to scoop her into his arms when he opened the door, carry her to his bedroom and make love to her over and over all weekend until late Sunday afternoon when she would have to leave to drive back to Shallotte. You selfish bastard, he told himself, but he relished the thought of having her to himself for an entire weekend anyway.

He opened the door before she could knock and she greeted him with her beautiful smile and a hot, wet kiss. He held her at arm's length and slowly spun her around, whistling his appreciation of how well she displayed her team spirit.

"You like?" she asked coyly.

"Oh, yeah," he said, "I like a lot and if we don't leave now, the Bobcats' most beautiful fan will not only miss the game, she won't see the outside world until Sunday," he added honestly.

She smiled broadly, obviously flattered, and asked, "Is that a threat or an invitation?"

He looked heavenward to garner the strength not to ravage her right in the foyer and shook his head. "Let's leave before I make it either one," he said and he grabbed his coat to go. "You really are lovely, Rita Miller," he added softly and bent down and kissed her gently on the forehead.

She looked up at him and just stared wordlessly into his eyes as if she was trying to see deep into his soul. Finally, she replied, "Thank you—you are a tall, dark and handsome devil yourself," and she took his hand and headed to his SUV.

As they drove to dinner, they talked casually about her work on the farm and his afternoon preparing for the board meeting next Tuesday. She told him about her conversation with Spencer and wondered out loud if her decision to engage Jeff was a good or bad idea and whether he was a good guy or a bad guy.

"What does your gut tell you?" he asked her.

"It is strangely silent on Jeff Malone," she admitted.

"Hmmm," he said. "I wonder what *that* means."

"I don't know," she replied then added, "But Spencer and Jeff have plans at his condo tonight for dinner and a movie again."

"Interesting," he answered.

"Yep, it is interesting to say the least. I hope she knows what she is doing," she said and she sighed obviously worried about her best friend's welfare.

Ross reached over and took her hand into his, kissed it and said, "She'll be okay. I'm sure everybody at the office in Shallotte knows where she is tonight so her safety is virtually assured. Besides, Jeff Malone is secretive and enigmatic, but he sure isn't stupid. He would be the obvious target of an investigation if any harm came Spencer's way, Rita." When he looked over at her, Ross could tell she felt better.

They arrived at the arena, parked and made their way to the Bobcats' hospitality room to grab a bite to eat and have a few drinks before the game started. The game was a sellout with the Bobcats on track this year to make the playoffs for the first time. As a result, the parking lot, the arena and the hospitality suite were packed. As they walked through, Rita garnered the attention of every man in the room just as Ross suspected she would.

As she moved through the crowd, she smiled at everybody she encountered. She took getting knocked around by the crowd with grace and there was no shortage of men who reached out to steady her, catch her or brush up against her as she made her way through the gauntlet. They just had to touch the beautiful Rita Miller.

After what felt like an eternity, they arrived at the food table. After they filled their plates, they grabbed a beer at the bar and pushed their way into the corner. Rita was completely at home in this mob scene and she turned her back to the wall so she could people-watch.

"You are in your element, aren't you?" Ross asked.

"Oh, yeah," she said excitedly. "I love pre-game parties—the anticipation, the fervor, the happiness—not to mention the food and beverages. Everybody here for the most part is a huge fan," and she turned and smiled broadly at him.

"Well, you are the most beautiful fan here, hands down," he said.

"Not that you're biased or anything, right," she laughed.

They finished eating, downed their beers and made their way toward their seats. As they walked through the throng of fans, a tall, handsome man yelled loudly to Rita and she turned around at the sound of her name.

Ever the lady, she excused herself and ran over and threw her arms around the neck of the athletic blonde who bent to kiss her on the cheek. *Who is this Adonis-want-to-be,* Ross wondered. They talked for a second and Rita motioned to him to come over to her. Of course, he complied.

"Ross Moore, this is Brian Evans, Brian Evans, this is Ross Moore," she said, making introductions. She turned to Ross and said, "Brian played basketball at the university when I was there. He broke my heart, but I couldn't be happier that he did since he has moved around like a nomad. Brian, Ross is the president of American One. He played baseball at Carolina, so I'll have to dumb-down my orange ball strategy talk tonight. I'll wait until spring to impress him with my love of the boys of summer," she teased good-naturedly.

"Biggest mistake of my life, letting this wild child go, Ross," he said and Ross watched him watch Rita as he spoke, "but she was always destined for a life much larger than mine. It looks like you've found it. You look radiant and happy, Rita."

"I am as happy as you are full of crap," she said to him with a smile on her face. "It is great to see you, Brian. Give your folks my regards, ok?" and she kissed him on the cheek.

"I will, Rita. Ross, you are a lucky bastard," he said and put his hand out. Ross shook his hand firmly and looked into the eyes of a man haunted by genuine regret.

"Nice to meet you, Brian, and yeah, I am a lucky man," he said and put his hand on Rita's shoulder and led her to their courtside seats. As they sat down, he looked back over at Brian and caught him looking at Rita. He didn't look away, though. Ross realized that he was a little jealous of their history, his golden good looks, and Rita's love of this man. He also realized that he wanted that too.

Conversely, though, he didn't intend to let her go, spending the rest of his life wondering what if, but the fear of breaking her heart, losing her trust, lying to her about his true identity suddenly roiled in his gut. He could lose her anyway, he thought, and he silently vowed that tonight was the night he would tell her the truth. He hoped she understood.

He wanted her to trust him. He wanted her to love him. Without the former, the investigation would be a lost cause. Without the latter, so would he.

Chapter 94

Spencer got home on Friday evening, changed into her jeans and a crewneck sweater, grabbed the pail of beer from Wednesday, and headed out the door. As she crossed the courtyard between their two condos, she realized that sometime during the day, the weather had turned colder and a brisk north wind blew directly into her face, causing her to shiver. I should have put on a coat, she thought, but continued on her way, picking up the pace so she could get inside faster.

As she climbed the three steps to Jeff's door, he opened it before she could knock. He pulled her quickly inside and closed the door. "Where is your coat?" he chided. "The temperature is supposed to drop into the low 40's tonight."

"I realized half way over here I needed one, but I was too cold or maybe just too lazy to go back and get one. Besides, I'm sure you've got something here that can keep me warm," she said and as soon as the words left her mouth, she wished she could retract them. Too late—Jeff's smile bubbled up into a full-blown laugh, doubling him over.

"Not the best choice of words," she said, laughing along with him, her face hot with embarrassment.

"C'mon," he said, and he took the beer from her and led her over to kitchen. His condo was incredible with built-in shelves in cherry wood and a matching built-in desk in the corner and a breakfast nook between the den and the kitchen with a table already set for two.

"Very nice place, Mr. Malone," she admired.

"Thank you," he said. "I built the desk, the shelves and the table myself during my handyman phase. I've now moved onto my intellectual phase."

Spencer turned and looked at him, not quite sure if he was kidding or serious—that was Jeff Malone, though. She felt like she knew him better than she did on Tuesday, but Spencer certainly didn't think she had completely figured him out. Undaunted, she asked, "So what does Jeff Malone do in this intellectual phase?"

He smiled and answered very simply, "I read."

"God, you and Rita could start your own book club. She rarely lets a day go by without reading more than 100 pages for pleasure," Spencer said. "I like to read, but I go in fits and starts. If I pick up a good book, I can hardly put it down, but I don't carve out time to read as a hobby," and she looked over at him, hoping he didn't think she was some simpleton.

"So, what do you do for enjoyment?" he asked.

"I golf, I gamble and I get together with friends—like you," she said. "I will never be confused for an intellectual, but I have been deemed the life of the party on numerous occasions."

He laughed again, and said, "That's what I like about you, Spencer—you're genuine, unpretentious and honest," and he reached over and smoothed her windblown hair gently. Then he grabbed each of them a beer and asked, "Are you hungry?"

"Famished," she said with a smile. "What's for dinner?"

"Fajitas—with margaritas," he said.

"Are you trying to get me drunk and take advantage of me?" she teased softly.

Jeff walked right back over in front of her and answered, "I promise I won't get you drunk or do anything you don't want to do, Spencer," and he reached down and tenderly kissed her beside her mouth. Then, he pointed to the chair beside his handmade table and said, "Sit."

Spencer sat down and Jeff waited on her, bringing her all her trimmings on a plate from the refrigerator and a covered dish with tortillas. Then, he made each of them a wonderful salt-rimmed margarita and brought a sizzling cast-iron skillet to the table that had chicken, steak and shrimp to make fajitas. "Wow," she said. "Did you do all of this since you've been home? It looks delicious."

"I prepared most of it last night so all I had to do was cook it up," he said, and he sat down across from her, raised his glass and said, "Here's to new friends and old neighbors. Cheers!"

"Cheers!" Spencer parroted and tapped her glass to his.

They talked easily over dinner, and he filled their margarita glasses one more time before he cleared the table and led her by the hand to the sofa. The television played in the background and he turned to her and asked, "Do you want me to put in the movie?"

Spencer turned to face him. She looked him straight in the eye and answered, "No."

As soon as she answered, he reached over and put his hand behind her neck and leaned over and kissed her deeply. Then he said, "You know you're risking your reputation with me, Spencer."

As she leaned herself back onto the sofa, she pulled him with her and whispered into his ear, "We're in the risk business for a reason, Jeff, and I've got to tell you—I'm a damn good gambler."

With that green light he devoured her mouth, tasting her, exploring her with his tongue. She moaned and pressed herself into him. He was as solid as a mountain and she felt all control and restraint seeping from her body.

He undressed her slowly and she felt like she would explode with desire. He stood to remove his shirt and jeans and she was almost manic at the momentary absence of his body and she pulled him back to her. He lay back down beside her, touching her breasts and running his fingers down her stomach to her legs.

Spencer could feel the heat from his body and she wanted to be consumed by his fire. He moved his lips from her mouth and found her breasts, licking them, nipping them gently with his teeth and she moaned again and arched her back to move into him. When she was sure she could take no more, he rolled on top of her and took her in one easy motion.

She cried out in obvious pleasure and they rocked together, faster and harder with each motion until she felt molten, liquid and hot. Jeff was slick with sweat and he grabbed her hair and pulled her head back and found her mouth as they erupted together. Spencer felt weightless and wondered if she had just spontaneously combusted and was floating piece by piece on the air.

As she cooled and slowly solidified, she entwined her legs around Jeff and she could feel his chest move with breathing as labored as her own. She couldn't speak and, in fact, could hardly breathe. She had seen flashes of light. She had felt the earth move.

Breaking the silence, Jeff said, "Damn, woman. You call *that* rusty?"

Spencer laughed, still trying to catch her breath. "You just oiled me up and made me loose, Mister," she said and rolled over on her side to look at him. "You were just…incredible," she added and he sat up on his elbows and looked her in the eyes to see that she was sincere and no longer joking.

"You were damn good yourself," he said quietly.

"I think we just…fit well, Jeff," she stated.

"You've got that right," he said and he pulled her over onto his chest. She laid her head there and listened to the rhythm of his heartbeat until she drifted off into the dreamless sleep of exhaustion.

Chapter 95

Mack Grissett drove his pickup truck slowly through the condo complex, scanning the courtyard, the trees behind the buildings, and the parking lot for anything suspicious, anything out of place. He saw Spencer's black SUV parked in its space and looked at her condo for evidence that she was inside. The porch light was on, but the lights inside were not.

He looked at his watch and saw that it was already after 10 p.m. Spencer was probably already asleep. He peered over at Rita's place and saw no signs of life, or problems, and decided to call it a day.

Mack had a bad feeling, one of impending danger, and his instincts were rarely wrong. Tonight, though, everything seemed in place and he turned back on the main road. He would check back by again tomorrow morning.

Chapter 96

Saturday morning broke slowly and even at 7 a.m., the sun had not yet risen over the horizon of Jordan Lake in Raleigh. Ivey took his thermos out of the cargo hold of his kayak and took several swallows. He had been up for hours, a deep nagging feeling tugging him from sleep.

He had paced the floor. He had read a business journal. He drank a glass of milk. He was still wide awake. Finally, around 6 a.m., he loaded the kayak, the paddle, the thermos and his fishing gear into his old jalopy and headed to the lake.

He could use the exercise, but more importantly, he could use the solitude and the quiet of a late October morning on the water. The water helped him clear his mind, let him concentrate, and enabled him to mentally de-clutter. The tourists were gone. The teenagers were still asleep. The lake was all his.

Spencer and Rita were on his mind this morning and he knew that after he got back to the house, he would call each of them to catch up. He would ask Rita about her vacation. He would ask Spencer about her golf game. But what he really wanted to know was that they were not in danger.

He felt disconnected here, but after days of recollecting his final months in Shallotte, he knew that there were numerous people feeding the deceptive beast. He also realized that the criminal network stretched beyond the boundaries of Shallotte and the sheer scope of the collusion overwhelmed him and frightened him for his own safety and survival as well as that of his best friends and the bank that employed him.

Taking a deep, cleansing breath, he relaxed and let his mind wander to all of the possible culprits, co-conspirators. There was certainly George Everett, and from his last conversation with Patrick, John Starr. Other likely participants included Dylan, Tripp, Peter, Jeff, Greg and possibly even stretched down to front line employees like Mary Ann and Angie. Somebody, after all, had to process the paperwork.

In addition, there had to be back room help—from audit, proof, loan operations, deposit operations. Documents were processed, shuffled, deleted and destroyed. Red flags were ignored, evidence was buried. The whole affair was incredible in its sophistication, its depth, its tenure.

Rita was safe in the Piedmont for now. He had spoken to Jack Grissett on Wednesday and Jack assured him that he and Mack were keeping tabs as best as they could on Spencer. Jack also informed him that the investigation into Patrick's death and the break-in of his car had been completely silent since the autopsy results were reported on Monday. He told Ivey that Shallotte felt like a powder keg with a match already lit, inches from the fuse. Trouble and danger were imminent.

The conversation with Jack did not reassure him at all, and he told Jack that he was planning to come down on Friday and spend the weekend. The famous Halloween Party was Saturday night. He may not be able to physically protect Rita and Spencer, but he could provide another set of eyes to keep alert, another honest mind to search for avenues out of harm's way.

He felt a tug on his line and reeled in a beauty of a bass beside the kayak. He unhooked the fish, admired it momentarily and then released it. The fish swam away quickly, freed from the hands of his captor, and disappeared into the deep.

Ivey sighed. Satisfied, he paddled back to the lakeshore. This morning had been the best therapy for his worried mind. As he pulled the kayak from the water and hoisted it onto his shoulder to walk back to his old land cruiser, he felt a renewed sense of confidence in the law enforcement professionals, none of whom he knew, working to catch the person or persons involved in all of the crimes at the bank, including the murder of Patrick Lowers. He also thought about the truly honest individuals he knew and knew well who were lending a hand—Ross, Rita, Spencer, Jack, Mack. Collectively, he couldn't think of any smarter, craftier, or more connected people anywhere, but they had to stick together.

Together, they could help dismantle and destroy the criminal network that had operated at Mega unhindered and undetected for years. Alone, though, each of them was in danger of being targeted, isolated and just like Patrick, eliminated.

As soon as the thought crossed his mind, the fear in his gut flared again as his beloved old FJ came into sight. He dropped the kayak and ran to the isolated spot to where it was parked. He dialed 9-1-1 as he ran and pulled his hunting knife from his pocket. The doors of the vehicle were flung wide open, contents were strewn all around and the flames had already consumed the interior and were licking around the engine. The intensity of the heat forced him back to the tree line and he turned, knife in hand, 360 degrees looking for something, somebody.

As he looked back at his beloved vehicle, he noticed that it had been ransacked before it was torched. The FJ was now fully engulfed in flames. It was completely unsalvageable. The ensuing explosion occurred just as the first police and fire responders arrived and the force was so violent that it knocked Ivey to his knees over 100 feet away.

He stood back up, his breathing heavy and ragged. He was stunned. He was angry. He was frightened.

Somebody had driven a long way, gone to a lot of trouble, watched and waited for the opportunity to catch him alone and vulnerable. He took another deep breath to calm down, put his knife away and walked toward the police car. He hadn't seen another soul at the lake, hadn't noticed anything suspicious or unusual, but he quickly came to two conclusions.

One—somebody was looking for something. Two—somebody was sending him a message.

CHAPTER 97

The telephone rang early at Ross's house in Charlotte on Saturday morning and I stirred in the cozy, warm bed, rolled over and realized that I was alone. Morning had broken and sunlight filtered softly through the curtains, encouraging me to wake up.

I felt rested and refreshed. I was also almost giddy with happiness. *What fool wouldn't be?* I thought. The game had been a thriller last night and we cheered and celebrated a Bobcats victory then returned to Ross's house where we made love until the wee hours of the morning. Satisfied and fulfilled, we fell asleep entwined and I slept like a baby wrapped in his arms all night.

I grabbed the robe from the bedpost, wrapped myself in it and rose to go downstairs to join Ross. Before I could get to the door, though, he opened it and came over to the bed where he pulled me back down beside him. Evident by the look on his face, the gesture was not out of playfulness but rather, worry.

Collecting myself, I asked, "Ross, what's wrong?" and I grabbed his hand, anticipating the worst. Early morning telephone calls never relayed good news.

When he answered, "Ivey," I felt like I had been punched in the gut and I struggled to catch my breath, to breathe at all. I felt my hands begin to tremble and I looked up at Ross for reassurance.

"He's all right, but he's been shaken up pretty good," he said. As I released the breath that I had been holding in my lungs, Ross told me what happened.

I listened intently and wished that I could put my arms around Ivey. He and Spencer were my best friends and the thought of anything happening to either of them threatened to unhinge me. I was relieved that he was safe, but was truly sad when Ross told me about his vehicle. Ivey loved that beat-up piece of crap and it suited him perfectly. He had invested an enormous amount of time over the last several years scouring the internet for original parts, spending stupid money just to get it "road-ready." It was the end of an era for Ivey, but I was sure he would transition to a new vehicle seamlessly.

I was much more worried about how well he would bounce back from the scare personally. Ivey was a serious guy and he was almost compulsive about safety in the car, the house, or out in public. I hoped the attack didn't shake his confidence. I vowed to call him later that day and decided I probably should get back home to Shallotte tonight rather than wait until tomorrow.

I reached over and laced my fingers through Ross's and leaned my head over on his shoulder. "I'm going to head home today, Ross," I said, waiting for some sign of reassurance or resistance.

He sighed and answered, "I figured that you would want to go home after I told you the news, but I am going to be consumed with worry over your welfare until this whole sordid affair is over."

"Is it ever going to be over?" I asked.

"Yes, I believe the police are getting close to getting some answers on Patrick's death," he replied, then continued, "and once the killer is identified, the whole bank fraud network will be dismantled and the participants brought to justice. The crimes here are all related, Rita."

"I know, but how do we prove it? How do we identify everybody involved?" I questioned.

"That information is hidden somewhere clever. Somewhere Patrick felt it would be safe and get into the hands of the proper authorities. The honest bankers just have to find the information before the criminal bankers do," he said seriously.

I nodded. Ivey had been identified now as an honest banker. Would Spencer be targeted too? Or would her new liaison with Jeff keep her status to her co-workers in the gray? I knew I had to get back home.

Suddenly, a thought struck me. "Who called you?" I asked curiously and wondered why the president of the bank would be called about a vehicle fire in Raleigh over a weekend.

"The SBI," he answered casually. "They are involved in this investigation since the arson and breaking and entering happened at the state park. I have a lot of friends in the department. Ivey told one of the agents he worked for American One. He told Ivey he knew me and Ivey told him to call me. Probably as much to let you know quickly as me," he said.

"That Ivey is always thinking. He is so observant, so careful. I'm sure this attack on him is a shock," I commented.

"He told the officers he didn't see a single soul before, during or after he was on the water," Ross said. "These people are either really seasoned criminals or really lucky ones. I want you to promise me you will stay close to Spencer all week long," he stated.

"I will," I promised. "I will probably just ask Spence to stay at my place a couple of nights this week and I can stay a couple of nights at her place. I'm going to call her on my way back. When will I see you again?" I asked.

He smiled, kissed me on the top of the head and answered softly, "Not nearly soon enough."

"Can you come down Friday for the weekend?" I asked. "Saturday is Halloween and we have a huge neighborhood party where everybody dresses up and brings foodies and drinks to the courtyard. The kids go around to all the people at the party and try to guess who they are. If they guess right, they get a goody bag filled with enough candy to delight every dentist in Brunswick County. It really is a lot of fun," I added. "Say you'll come."

"I wouldn't miss it for the world," he said. "But I'll have to find a costume. What are you wearing?" he asked.

"I am going to be a mysterious gypsy," I said in my best sultry voice.

"You already are," he said as he pulled me on top of him on the bed. "Come dazzle me, gypsy."

"Alas, one last dance before my caravan moves east," I said dramatically and I untied the robe and let it fall to the floor.

Chapter 98

Spencer initially awakened in the dark of night with her head still on Jeff's chest. She was afraid that if she got up off the couch she would wake him from his sound, even sleep. She rolled onto her side to study him. He was handsome, funny and mysterious. He was smart, rugged and a great lover. She sighed and realized that years had passed since she had been this secure with any man—well, except Ivey, but he didn't count. He was more like a brother.

As if he sensed her staring at him, Jeff reached up and pulled her back to him, never opening his eyes. He was awake, though, because he whispered to her, "Let's go upstairs to the bedroom," and he stood, took her by the hand, and led the way.

He pulled back the covers and let Spencer crawl in first then he got in beside her. He was warm and she snuggled closer to him. He stroked her hair gently and she dozed back off to sleep in a matter of minutes.

She was awakened again, seemingly hours later, by a telephone ringing beside Jeff's bed. He cursed the phone, sat up with his feet on the floor and answered the call. She could hear only the garble of the person on the other line, but whoever it was and whatever he wanted got Jeff's attention fairly quickly. He stood and walked out of the bedroom door, talking quietly as he went downstairs, a sense of urgency in his movements and his voice. Spencer tried to no avail to listen to figure out who was on the phone at this hour and what they wanted with Jeff.

She rolled over and faced the window upstairs that looked out over the courtyard. The sun was up but its heat and light were muted by a thin layer of fog or clouds. Spencer rolled onto her back and looked over at the clock. It was much later than she thought, already after 8 a.m., and she began mentally itemizing the list of things she needed to do today.

She sat up and stretched her arms just as Jeff came back into the bedroom. He had put on his clothes from the night before. Spencer smiled at him and he came over to the bed and stood looking down at her. His mood had changed markedly, obviously prompted by the call and he was distant, dark.

"I have to go to a meeting," he said woodenly.

"A meeting on Saturday," Spencer asked.

Jeff nodded. Then Spencer got it—he wanted her to leave and the realization was like a slap in the face. She felt the heat rising in her cheeks. This day had gone from magnificent to mortifying in record time. She started to push the covers aside to go to put on her clothes, grab her beer pail and head home, but then Jeff sat on the edge of the comforter and she was trapped.

Unexpectedly, Jeff reached over and touched her arm and she looked defiantly into his eyes. "Spencer…" he began, "Do you trust me?" he asked.

After a lengthy silence, she answered honestly, but almost inaudibly, "I don't know, Jeff. I just don't know. Should I?"

He reached up and stroked her neck with his fingers and sighed deeply, leaving her question hanging for what felt like an eternity. Finally, he answered, "You aren't even going to like me, let alone trust me, Spencer."

"I don't understand…" Spencer began, but Jeff got up quickly.

"I've got to go, Spencer. See yourself out, ok," he said.

She couldn't speak so she just nodded. She grabbed the sheet on the bed for cover and stood to follow him out. Suddenly, he turned back to her and kissed her deeply, roughly, and passionately. She wanted to slap him, but before she could react, he pushed away from her and quickly disappeared down the stairs, leaving her naked and alone in his bedroom. After she heard the sound of the front door closing, emotion swept through her and Spencer's deep sobs of hurt, anger and shame echoed off the walls of the empty, colorless room.

Chapter 99

There was very little conversation as, one-by-one, they filed into the conference room at the bank and found a seat around the huge rectangular table. The morning was damp and dreary and a quick look around evidenced that everybody here wanted to be anywhere else.

The room was full—15 in all, including him. There was no small talk, no pleasantries or formal acknowledgements. The discussion went straight to the point. Word from law enforcement informants indicated that the investigation of Patrick's death was expanding and was now focusing on the bank and the employees who worked with him. Brunswick County detectives had been usurped. The SBI, and even the FBI by some accounts, was involved in the case.

He looked around the room. There was some concern. There was some indifference. There was some fear—or perhaps it was just his own. He could taste it like rust in his mouth. He could smell it and it nauseated him. He could feel it as his heart raced and his breathing grew shallow. He thought he might pass out.

He pushed slowly away from the table and leaned over with his elbows on his knees. It helped him breathe a little easier. Everybody was talking, but he couldn't hear them. He was too busy replaying his own plans to recover the damning information contained on a disk. And nobody was asking for his input. Nobody was looking to him to solve the problem.

Screw them, he thought. *I'm going to take care of myself.*

The biggest worry voiced was their recent activity—say, less than five years up through the merger. The questions tumbled out of everybody randomly. Had they shredded enough documents? Had they layered enough meaningless debits and credits to make each money transaction untraceable? Had they taken care of everybody who ensured the success of their shadow bank?

Finally, without feeling his mouth move, he heard himself ask, "But where is the disk?"

Suddenly all eyes were on him. Silence roared in his ears. Was he going crazy? Did he miss the conversation where the disk had been located?

Then, like he had opened the floodgates, the disk became the sole focus of the meeting. Perhaps it didn't exist. Perhaps it was on the bottom of Oyster Bay. Perhaps law enforcement already had it. Perhaps somebody in this room had the disk and intended to use it as leverage. Perhaps it just hadn't been found.

Perhaps my head is going to explode, he thought. Talking is useless. Action was required.

He updated the group on the places that had already been searched. Some in attendance were visibly shocked by the depth and brazenness of the searches. Other seemed resigned that whatever had to be done to keep the investigators at bay and find the disk was fair game.

The participants' involvement no matter how big or small, no matter how long or how recent risked their futures, their families, their freedom. The risks of their involvement had been handsomely rewarded over the years, but the worry etched on the faces in the room answered loudly and decisively whether the reward was worth the risk. It wasn't, but that bell had already rung.

They were all in. They rose to go as silently as they had come. They were spurred to action with one mission in mind. At all costs, they had to find that disk.

Chapter 100

I finally left Charlotte around 1 p.m. Saturday afternoon. Traffic was light as I headed east down Independence Boulevard. After the metropolitan street turned into plain old U. S. Highway 74, I felt comfortable talking on my Bluetooth.

I called Mom and Dad. I told them about Ivey. I told Mom about what a smashing success the Bobcats outfit was. I told Dad how much I enjoyed being back on the farm and helping out where I could. I could hear the concern in their voices over my safety, as well as the safety of my friends. Mom was almost giddy over Ross's reaction to the outfit and even giddier when I told her about seeing an almost maudlin Brian. Dad was appreciative of not only the help I had given him on the farm, but also of my love of it, but he was always quiet when I left, amazed that I could leave it.

I called Spencer. Man, was she in a funk. I couldn't get anything out of her either. She was sad, or mad, or something. She was chippy too, irritated that I kept asking her what was wrong. She told me we would talk when I got back, for me to hurry back. I looked down at the speedometer as I spoke to her. I was going 75 mph. Slow down, leadfoot.

I was eager to get back. What in the world happened between 5 p.m. on Friday and Saturday at 1:30 p.m.? I would get to the bottom of it about ten seconds after I got home. If Jeff Malone had hurt Spencer I would have his ass. Besides, he was potentially not only a jerk, but a crook too.

I listened to the radio, flipping it on the XM dial between ESPN Radio, the classic soft rock of The Bridge and the new stuff on The Pulse. I sang until my throat hurt. I disagreed out loud with the sports guys on the upcoming ACC basketball season. I put back the top of the Miata and let the late-October air run amok through my hair, against my skin, into my lungs. Oh, how I loved autumn.

I was happy with my life and I thought about the people with whom I had surrounded myself. I was a fortunate person. I had a great family, great friends, and a great—what would I call Ross? Boyfriend sounded too juvenile. Significant other sounded too impersonal. I knew what he had really become—he was the love of my life. Corny? Yes, but hey, the truth will set you free.

Damn, 200 miles burns a lot of brain energy, I thought as I drove, finally hitting Maxton, the halfway point of the trip. I stopped at the Hardee's, went to the ladies' room and bought a huge iced tea for the last 100.

When I got back into the car, I called Ivey. I could hear the fatigue in his voice and I was worried sick about him. He reassured me he was taking every safety precaution imaginable and he urged me to be vigilant myself and for Spencer who thought she was invincible sometimes. I promised him I would be careful and keep an eye on Spence when I got back, telling him like I did Ross that we would stay at each other's place for a couple of nights.

I told him I was so sorry about the FJ. He said he was sad to see the end of an era, but he was satisfied he got a lifetime of wonderful memories out of the old hunk of junk and could move on. His sentiment over the vehicle made me laugh. He laughed too when I told him he was going to feel like he got a huge raise now that he wouldn't have to spend obscenely on repairs and old FJ parts.

I asked what time he was coming down on Friday and he said he would be in town around 7 p.m., sure he would be able to leave Raleigh around 4 or so. I was glad he would be around to help keep an eye on Spencer since Ross was coming to Shallotte as well.

After I hung up with Ivey, I drove a while in silence. I turned my thoughts to my career and where it was presently and where it might, or might not, be going. I loved banking, had learned a wealth of knowledge, and had also gained wisdom in how to deal with a myriad of personalities, adversities, and situations.

But where are you going, Rita? I sighed. I no longer wanted to climb the corporate ladder. I no longer wanted to lead the charge for women bankers in the area. I was ready for a new flag bearer. I was mired in an undefined, unappreciated pseudo-branch manager, half-commercial banker role. I had lost my enthusiasm. I had lost my drive. I had lost faith in my profession. Perhaps the farm was really calling me home.

When I turned onto highway 130 off of U. S. 701 in Whiteville, I knew I was almost in Shallotte. The 30-mile finale was beautiful and wild and took drivers through the Green Swamp, across the Waccamaw River and past the now-fallow fields of Bright Leaf tobacco.

I crossed into Brunswick County and as I approached West Brunswick High School, I swear I could almost smell the sweet salt air of the beach. I suddenly wanted seafood—Calabash seafood. I called Spencer to get her to meet me at Captain John's to eat and have a beer. She didn't answer. It was useless to leave a message since she never checked her voicemail.

I drove onto the condo. I'd go get Spencer, buy her some food and a few drinks. A night out with her would cheer her up, satisfy my craving and keep us from being alone and potentially vulnerable. Calabash was a great solution and I pushed the gas pedal harder and drove faster, too fast really. A heavy uneasiness suddenly weighed down on me and the hair on the back of my neck stood up as I called Spencer again.

And there was still no answer.

Chapter 101

Spencer knew she had wasted a perfectly beautiful day. She could have played golf. She could have cleaned her condo. She could have washed clothes. Instead, she had taken an hour-long shower until the water was closer to frigid than lukewarm then managed to pull on her sweatpants and an old tee shirt. Then she sat down on her couch and after almost seven hours, she was still there.

She watched television, she talked to Rita, and she surfed the internet on her laptop all from the comfort of the couch, leaving it only momentarily to go the bathroom or top off her Diet Coke. She was a couch potato. She was idle, physically and mentally.

I am pathetic, she thought. She wished she had a rewind button. She would gladly go back to the yesterday Spencer who hadn't been laid in ages. She wanted to be the unemotional Spencer trying to figure out the good guys from the bad guys. She wondered where good intentions went so awry.

Sounds from next door told her Rita was home, and she was so relieved she almost sprinted out the door. She looked at her watch. It was 4:30. Spencer shook her head. That damn Rita drove like a bat out of hell.

Her mood had lightened considerably and she walked out her door and looked in the parking lot. Rita's car was not in the lot. Hmmm, she thought. She walked back in and got her set of keys to Rita's condo and sprinted down her stairs and up Rita's to unlock the front door.

Rita just couldn't leave the farm in Stanly County. She came back so loaded down with fresh vegetables, canned foods and hand-made heirloom table cloths, napkins, blankets, you name it, that she needed to unload at the back door which was beside the kitchen and the linen closet.

Spencer unlocked the door and went inside. The back door was closed and the lights were off. She walked to the back door and turned the knob to see if she could give Rita a hand. The door was locked.

Fear suddenly swamped her and she turned to go. In the next instant, lights exploded around her and stars shot out all around her. She felt herself failing, almost weightless and in slow motion, to the floor. A black curtain was slowly enveloping her. She was powerless to stop it.

She felt herself slipping slowly away as random thoughts, names and faces raced aimlessly around in her mind—Rita, her impending arrival and subsequent discovery of her best friend's body, Ivey, the old FJ, Rita's front door was open, her mother, what if she had played golf today, Jeff Malone, what had gone wrong. She stopped fighting and let herself go, succumbing to an unconsciousness that felt all too familiar—dark, empty and lonely.

Chapter 102

Jack turned into the condominium complex and drove past the clubhouse, down to the cul-de-sac where Rita and Spencer lived to make sure everything was alright. He and Mack had been here three times today already and it was not even 5:00. Without any discussion, both brothers sensed a lurking danger, a crazy desperation rising in Shallotte. Law enforcement communications had grown scarce and the information they did get was cryptic or vague.

The investigation that once was focused on the death of Patrick Lowers was now fragmented and protracted, providing the killer or killers a golden opportunity to run for cover, destroy evidence or simply disappear. Outside the doors of American One Bank, the chatter was quiet, too quiet.

This morning, Mack had driven by the bank as a matter of routine and discovered several bank employees parking in the adjacent shopping center lot and walking to the bank. They acted paranoid, secretive, and he was curious. He had parked across the street at the convenience store to watch. One by one, bankers arrived, parked at the neighboring lot and walked around to the back door of the bank and disappeared inside. Some he knew, others he recognized, and a few he had never seen before. All total, Mack counted 13 participants, but he wondered if there were already some people inside the building when he arrived. Making the scene even more curious was the fact that there were no lights on and no visible signs of activity inside the bank, either.

Mentally, Mack did a banker inventory and the list of attendees surprised him a whole lot less than those who were absent. There were no signs of Rita Miller or Spencer Cashwell. He perused the parking lot and saw the huge, black pick-up truck that Ricky Jarman drove and wondered if he was in the meeting. Why else would his truck be here? The discovery heightened Mack's concern and he called Jack and asked him to go check on Spencer and Rita's condo. He also called Ross Moore. Ross sounded more than just a little relieved when Mack promised him they would keep tabs on Rita and Spencer. After Ross told Mack about the incident in Raleigh with Ivey, he understood why.

All three times they checked out the buildings and surroundings at the condo complex. All three times, everything was fine. Spencer's SUV was parked out front, lights and televisions were on inside, first upstairs in the bedroom, then downstairs in her den, and Rita's condo was dark and her car was not in the lot. Ross had told Mack that Rita was on her way back and would arrive around 5:30. Jack knew this drive-by would not be his last today.

Dusk was rolling in quickly. The shortened days of the late autumn meant nightfall by 6 pm. He turned on his headlights as he pulled into the parking area in front of the condo building where Rita and Spencer lived.

He barely had time to throw the car into park before he was sprinting toward Rita's open front door silhouetted by the darkness inside. As he ran, he called Mack, certain of trouble, and told him to call the police, call 9-1-1. As he got to the doorstep and pushed the door open wide with his arm, he saw a crumpled, lifeless form at the back door, sure it was Spencer even before his eyes adjusted to the darkness inside Rita's condo.

He rushed over to Spencer's body, terrified she was dead or dying, but determined to save her nonetheless. He checked her pulse. It was very weak and she was unconscious. She was bleeding badly on the right side of her forehead. He got up and turned just as Rita ran in her door. She screamed and came running to help, immediately grabbing a towel from the linen closet. She kneeled down, cradled Spencer in her arms and applied direct pressure to the wound. She spoke softly to her best friend as if she were having an everyday conversation with her. When Jack looked at her, though, tears were streaming down her face and her normally radiant smile was replaced by a trembling, crumbled look that would haunt him for weeks to come.

Spencer lay lifeless in Rita's arms. Spurred to action by the realization, he ran to the door and met the ambulance and the EMTs as they entered. He put his arms around Rita's shoulders and guided her, dazed and distraught, to the side. Spencer was bloody, pale and, unresponsive. Spencer was as close to dying as a person could be.

Chapter 103

Intuition is a powerful thing and as I have matured, I have come to realize that to ignore it is not only unwise, but unsafe. The voice in my core has never been wrong, and I am not a person who uses the words 'never' or 'always' unless they apply as they are intended—unconditionally.

Why didn't I call Jack Grissett after I couldn't get Spencer on the telephone? In all honesty, I was so wrapped up in my own little blanket of bliss that I didn't think about calling for help, sure Spencer would be safe, sure I would be home momentarily, sure I could handle it. I was selfish and discounted the voice inside me telling me to hurry, that something was wrong, that danger was not only possible, but probable. Hadn't Ross told me so just hours earlier?

Jack Grissett had been a friend of mine since I joined the bank. It all began when I had a flat tire, in the dark, in a rain storm, in a cream-colored suit, in heels, 10 miles from the MON (middle of nowhere for you city folks). Jack had driven by in his rollback after responding to an accident and saw me with a ridiculously tiny umbrella in the deluge staring at the side of my car without a flashlight, wondering how I was going to manage the jack, the lug nuts, the flat and the spare. I am sure the whole scene was enormously amusing to a former banker who had traded his suit and tie for a car salvage and repair business.

Anyway, I got his attention and he pulled over in front of me, got out and basically pushed me aside and went to work. He changed my tire, no umbrella, and made me wait in his tow truck. When he was finished, he got in and we introduced ourselves to each other and then talked for almost an hour about sports, banking, photography, Brunswick County and our families. We were fast friends.

As fate would have it, several weeks later Jack's name came up at the bank in conversation with George and Greg at a manager's meeting. George in his blunt, pig-headed manner commented that Jack couldn't cut it in banking so he quit. What a load of horse manure.

Never one to back away from injustice and misinformation, I calmly informed George that Jack's situation was a classic example of racial discrimination. He was too shocked to argue. I further told George that as a white man, he was hardly in a position to understand how getting stepped over and stepped on continuously on the way up the corporate ladder can kill the desire to stay on it. Jack had chosen to get off of it.

I told Jack about the conversation when I called him to go to lunch the next week. He couldn't believe I would defend him to the regional head honcho, George Everett. I would have defended him to the CEO. Besides, I told him, he had saved me without knowing me in the rain. I had just told the truth, set the record straight about a friend. I got the best end of that deal, I said.

Jack has never forgotten, though. He calls me his hero; I call him my comic relief, my phone-a-friend when the corporate bastards get me down. He gives me perspective. We give each other unconditional friendship.

And today, with the sands shifting under me, threatening to pull me under, he was there for me. He didn't give me empty promises that everything was going to be ok, that Spencer was going to be fine. Instead, he handled the situation—showing in the EMT, talking to the police, calling Spencer's mother, driving me to the hospital.

As he drove, he called his brother who had already called Ivey. Then he truly surprised me. He dialed another call and handed me the telephone. He simply said, "Ross Moore—for you." The phone was ringing in my ear and I am certain my mouth was gaping open. I looked down at the screen—the number was Ross's cell phone.

Ross answered, "Jack, what's the situation?"

Just hearing his voice comforted me and I said, "Sorry to disappoint you, but I'm not Jack."

He breathed a loud, relieved sigh. "Rita, I'm on my way down, ok? Just be strong for Spencer. Jack's going to stay at the hospital until I get there to handle any questions. Hey, don't forget—Spencer's a fighter, Rita. She's strong."

I felt the tears rolling down my cheeks, searing hot and salty as they trailed into my mouth. "I feel like I'm falling to pieces," I stammered and looked up at Jack for strength to recover. "First Ivey, now Spencer…it's been a hell of a day," I managed.

"It sure has," he agreed. "I'm near Lumberton. I'll meet you at the hospital."

"Ok, good, be careful," I rambled. "I'm meeting Penny, Spencer's mom, in the ER."

"Rita, I want you to be very careful. Like Jack, I want you to watch everybody that comes and goes, everybody that asks questions, everybody that hangs around. I wouldn't talk to anybody that works at the bank this evening, at least until I get there. Ok?" he asked.

"Why?" I asked.

"We don't know who to trust at this point. They are looking for something they think we have and any information, even unwittingly, may be beneficial to them and detrimental to us," he stated.

"What do they want? We don't have any information! Why can't they leave us alone," I all but yelled, angry, frustrated and scared.

Ross let me vent then he said, "Leave you alone is exactly what I am not going to do. I'll be there in about an hour, Rita. Just hang tough for me and for Spencer, ok?"

"I will. Be careful," I said again and then I reluctantly disconnected.

I looked over at Jack. He looked back and gave me a reassuring smile and reached over and squeezed my hand. As he released it, he said, "You could have told him you loved him, you know."

I looked at him closely and softly questioned, "What do you know about it? And how did you know Ross Moore's cell number? Furthermore, how do you even know Ross Moore?"

Without missing a beat, he countered, "First, I know what I see written all over your beautiful face; second, he gave it to me and third, he and I were in school together before you were born."

"Oh" was all I could think to say.

"Ivey Jones told me you two were close and I was stung that you hadn't mentioned it yourself—not that you've called me in the last several weeks," he gently scolded. "I knew when he put the two of you together you would be good for Ross Moore. I hope he is as good for you."

"What the hell does that mean?" I asked.

"I don't want you to slip away," he teased.

I reached over and put my hand on his shoulder. I looked him in the eye and softly told him, "I can't slip through rock—that's what you are to me. You are my rock, Jack."

"And you are my hero, baby," he said as we turned into the hospital parking lot. "Now, you go in there and focus on getting Spencer to wake up. I'll keep the wolves and vultures at bay, ok?"

You can see why he means so much to me. Jack is just a handler. He is a giver. He is a true soul. He is my friend.

I got out of the truck, much steadier now and a little wired with adrenaline. The two cups of coffee I downed probably didn't help either. We walked into the emergency room entrance and were immediately met by a scattered and scared Penny Cashwell. We didn't stop walking, but I pulled her under my arm as we moved and told her what I knew. It wasn't much.

Jack told us to wait against the wall while he went to talk to the attractive, young woman manning the nurse's station. They obviously knew each other and she obviously wanted to know him better. As they quietly talked, Jack pointed toward Penny and me. Spurred to action by whatever he said, she left the window. The automatic double doors swung open and we were escorted through immediately and back to the intensive care trauma ward waiting room.

We were alone in the little room and I could hear myself breathing as well as Penny and Jack. None of us talked as we waited for the doctor to come update us on Spencer's condition. After the commotion of the main emergency waiting area, the silence was overwhelming.

I felt stir-crazy, and as I got ready to get up and walk around the room to keep myself from climbing the walls, the doctor came in the door to talk to us. After introductions were made, he sat between Penny and me and Jack got up and stood in front of him to hear what he had to say.

The long and short of the conversation was that Spencer was in a coma with some brain swelling from the traumatic blow. Two inches to the left or right of where she was struck and she would no longer be with us. The doctor told us her vitals were improving, the swelling was slowly subsiding and she had lost quite a bit of blood. He said Spencer had been moved into a room in the intensive care unit and there she would be monitored constantly. He finished by telling us the next 24 hours was critical to her recovery.

"Can we see her?" Penny asked.

"Can we talk to her?" I followed up.

"Yes, to both," the doctor said, "But she needs rest too. Her brain activity is good so she can hear you. The coma just protects her from the pain and allows the brain swelling to go down, the body time to heal."

I heard Jack and Penny let out a sigh of relief at the same time I did. Spencer's chances of survival were good.

Jack walked out with the doctor while Penny and I walked over to the ICU and went into Spencer's room. Even after listening to the doctor tell us her prognosis was good, the sight of my best friend hooked up to a myriad of machines and tubes with her head bandaged shocked me and I grabbed one of the chairs to steady myself.

I let Penny visit with her first and I sat next to the window and stared blankly into the woods that stood behind the hospital. I felt like crying, but I was too angry. Questions flared up in my mind. Who would hurt Spencer? Who was in my condo? What did they hope to find there? Why did they think I was involved?

I sighed deeply but silently then I got real. I *was* involved, had, in fact, started this whole series of events by giving Patrick Lowers an opportunity to stop the accounting irregularities I had found by accident. I also knew what the burglar or burglars hoped to find. They were looking for the disk—in my condo. Spencer just got in the way.

Well, I didn't have it! I didn't have the disk. Furthermore, Spencer didn't have the disk, and Ivey didn't have the disk. Leave us alone!

I turned back around toward Spencer. Penny had her head down on the bed beside her daughter, was holding her hand. I got up and walked over to her and put my hand on her shoulder. She pulled her head up and reached up with her free hand and patted mine. She stood slowly from the chair and gave me a tired smile.

"Penny, go get a cup of coffee. I'll sit with Spencer and visit for a little while," I said softly.

"Ok," she almost whispered. She walked to the door and turned back around to look at Spencer. I smiled back at her to reassure her that leaving for a few minutes was fine. She lingered still and finally said, "Thank you, Rita—for everything. Spencer is lucky to have a good friend like you."

I answered truthfully, "No, Penny, I am the lucky one. I'll be here when you get back."

Alone with Spencer, I pulled the chair as close to the bed as I could so I could talk to her quietly, confidentially. I began by telling her about the Bobcats game. I told her about Ivey because I didn't want to tell her on the telephone on my way home and she didn't know. I told her about seeing Brian. Finally, I asked her what had happened with Jeff, what had gone wrong last night. The questions hung unanswered in the air, the only sounds were the occasional beeping of the machines around Spencer and the shallow, but even sound of her breathing.

For now, my questions and Spencer's answers would have to wait. I reached over and grabbed her hand and all of my emotions, dammed up behind a thin façade of strength and dependability, suddenly broke through and I let my tears cleanse the fear, fright and anger from my system. I sobbed for what could have happened to Ivey, for Spencer's current circumstances, and for Patrick's death. I cried until I was completely drained of tears and emotionally numb. Lacking even the energy to pick my head up off of Spencer's bed, exhaustion took hold and I dozed off into a deep, dark sleep.

Chapter 104

Ross arrived at the hospital much later than he had hoped. As he walked through the double doors into the intensive care unit, he saw Jack Grissett leaned up against the wall talking quietly to a doctor. He looked both directions down the corridor, but he didn't see Rita. She must be in Spencer's room, he thought.

When Jack saw Ross, he reached out and shook his hand and introduced him to the doctor on duty. They discussed Spencer's condition, her prognosis and the nature of the injury. Satisfied that Spencer was being given priority care and that she was in critical, but stable, condition, Ross thanked the doctor and let him get back to work.

Alone in the ICU hallway, Jack informed Ross that the burglar hit Spencer in the head with a ceramic vase from Rita's apartment. He also told Ross no fresh fingerprints had been found except for Spencer's, the back door lock had been breached and the SBI and FBI were on the scene. Ross groaned. They would probably leave a bigger mess than the burglar, he thought.

Jack also let Ross know that not one co-worker from the bank had been by the hospital and speculated that perhaps the burglar was hired, perhaps the burglar was acting alone, perhaps the fact that the local police were not the lead in the investigation anymore limited the information that was passed on to the network of bank crooks.

Whatever the reason for the absence of concerned co-workers, only Rita was here with Spencer.

"Where is Rita?" Ross asked.

"Last time I looked in she had fallen fast asleep at Spencer's bedside," Jack stated. "She's had a full day, Ross. First Ivey and now Spencer—she really needs to get some rest. I'm worried about her."

Ross sighed. He turned his back to the wall beside Jack and said, "I'm worried about her too. I know she needs rest, but I'm afraid to let her go to her condo alone. I can't go with her because I've got work to do here."

"Maybe she'll just stay here with Spencer tonight. I would encourage it," Jack said frankly.

"She sure won't get any rest here, though. The nurses will be in and out of that room all night, and Rita has to go to work tomorrow," Ross stated in frustration.

"I could call and see if there are any rooms available at the hotel on the bypass," Jack offered.

"Or I could call Mom and Dad. She could get some rest, and she would feel comfortable there too," Ross said, satisfied Rita would accept an invitation to stay with his mother and stay out of harm's way.

"Do your folks know Rita is in danger?" Jack asked.

"No, I, of course, haven't told them about the investigation. They know I am undercover at the bank, though," Ross confided.

"Well, that's more than Rita knows, Ross," Jack countered. "You need to tell her the whole story. She above everybody else will understand. She deserves to know. You should trust her."

"I *do* trust her, Jack," Ross said honestly, "And I will tell her the truth. I just haven't had time to explain my role, my background to her. It is complicated, you know."

"Well, she's not a simpleton, man," he stated. "The sooner, the better is all I'm saying—if you hurt her, I'm never going to forgive you, Ross. Rita is too good of a person to deceive."

"God, Jack, I'm not deceiving her! I'm trying to head up an undercover federal investigation. I had no idea when it began that the situation would be so complicated, that I'd be where I am now," Ross said.

"And where exactly is that?" Jack asked.

Ross stopped and silently asked himself the same question. He knew the answer and he looked up at Jack. Jack knew too. Finally, he said, "I don't believe I need to tell you the answer to that question, do I?"

Jack shook his head with a smile, slapped Ross on the back and began walking toward the door to meet the police officers that were standing on the other side of the nurses' station. After a few steps, he turned and faced Ross again as if he remembered he had been asked a question. Quietly, he answered, "I don't believe I'm the one looking for the answer to that question either," then disappeared from view behind the double doors.

Chapter 105

I heard the door behind me open, but didn't turn around. Only the comatose could get any rest around here with the constant in and out of the hospital staff. If rest was recuperative, nobody was leaving this place anytime soon, I thought grumpily. I wasn't sure how long I had been asleep, but it sure had not improved my disposition and Spencer was still unconscious.

I felt a hand on my arm and looked up. Ross had slipped in to see me and to check on Spencer. I felt a sense of comfort, safety and relief. He walked over to Spencer, sat down on the edge of her bed, picked up her hand and threaded his fingers through hers. He talked to her easily like an old friend. He told her she had to wake up so he could beat her in a rematch at golf. He promised her we would find the person that banged her on the noggin.

I stood back and watched him. He was good at motivating, nurturing, and coaxing people to willingly give him anything, to want to do anything he asked. For proof, see Rita Miller, Exhibit A.

After he finished his one-sided conversation with Spencer, he turned to me and smiled. He almost whispered, "How are you feeling? You look tired."

"I am tired and I just woke up," I said honestly. "I must have fallen asleep at some point. After I woke up, I realized that everything that has happened today was not just a bad dream. I can hardly comprehend it all, Ross."

"I know," he said and wrapped me in his arms loosely. "Will you do me a favor, though?" he asked.

Remember, Exhibit A…so, I answered, "Anything."

"Let me take you to Mom and Dad's to spend the night tonight. First of all, I am sure your place is a mess. Second, until the burglar is caught, I'm not sure you are safe there. Last, nobody will know you are there and you can get some much needed rest, okay?" he finished persuasively.

I thought it over and remembered how comfortable, warm and welcome I felt with Ross's parents. Right now, my condominium sure didn't feel like home. "Okay," I said, "But only if it doesn't put Marian and Charlie out."

"You've got to be kidding me! They will be thrilled to have you stay with them," he said sincerely. Then he added lightly, "Besides, I know they both have a whole lot more embarrassing stories to tell you about my childhood. Think of the entertainment you will bring to them and the fascination they will bring to you."

I laughed softly, "Okay, okay, I'm convinced," I said.

"Good," he said and he leaned down and gave me a tender kiss. I kissed him back and then put my head against his chest.

Like a comedienne with perfect timing, I heard a croaky, but unmistakable voice deadpan, "For God's sake, will you two get a room? This one is mine."

I all but yelled with delight, "Spencer!" and I rushed to her side.

"The one and only," she said, "But not so loud—my head is killing me."

I felt tears of relief slip down my cheeks. Spencer Cashwell was going to be alright.

Chapter 106

Damn, I hate Mondays, he thought to himself as he unlocked the bank door. He put on his game face, though, and walked inside, locking the door behind him.

One by one, the employees greeted him as he walked to his office. He managed to tell each one of them, "Good morning!" almost like he meant it. He could have won the Oscar, but the 20 yards to his office were like a mile.

He turned on his computer and turned to look out at the traffic on Main Street in Shallotte. Life outside the window was mundane, constant, unfazed by the actions and activities inside these walls. He wanted that life.

Fear followed him home last night. Fear kept him awake because sleeping brought the repercussions of discovery into his dreams. Fear followed him to the bank this morning. He was sick of it!

The memory of last night came roaring into his mind and he thought he was going to be sick. He leaned over and put his head into his hands. He had searched Rita's condo to no avail for that damn elusive disk. Then, everything had gone from bad to worse so quickly. Why, why, why?

He thought about resigning, moving away, starting fresh somewhere new, somewhere faraway. What was stopping him? *Fear, fear, fear*, he thought. Damn, he was going crazy. Get a grip, he told himself and he roughly opened the right drawer of his desk, grabbed a bottle of antacids and chewed up a handful. Choking them down, he drank the rest of his coffee from home, took two deep breaths and decided to brave going to get coffee in the break room.

He rose from his chair and readied himself to go pour the nasty, black poison into his "I am a VERB" coffee mug. In addition to the inspirational words printed there like "communicating," "understanding," and "solving," he wanted to add some new words today. The words "fleeing," "blaming," "hiding," or "ranting" seemed so much more apropos.

Laughing silently at his own cleverness, he felt better and he realized he had gotten the temporary insanity out of his system. He pulled himself together mentally and refocused on projecting his oblivion about the events of last night. He looked at his reflection in the glass of his credenza hutch and smoothed his tousled hair.

He thought again about the coffee killing him and realized there sure were worse ways to go. Mug in hand, he smiled coolly and walked out of his office to see and be seen.

Chapter 107

After sleeping like the dead until the sun had long appeared over the eastern horizon, I showered and dressed quickly then lingered with Marian over coffee on the beautiful front porch of her home. After the string of events that not only impacted the lives of the people I loved and the people with whom I worked but also made me question my own safety, the house on the riverbank was like a safe house, a refuge from it all.

I recounted the madness with Marian, relieved that I could talk about Spencer now in terms of recovery instead of her battle with life itself, relieved that Ivey was only searching for a replacement for his old FJ instead of badly wounded, or worse—like Patrick. None of them deserved such a fate for trying to do the right thing.

Marian seemed truly shocked that so much tragedy had happened in Shallotte so quickly. I feared that I shouldn't have been so forthcoming because I seemed to have upset her and, obviously, Ross had not said anything to her.

As if she just read my mind, she commented, "I'm glad you feel like you can share with me, Rita. I'm not going to fall to pieces and I'm not going to betray your confidence. What is said at this house stays here, but Ross is just like his father—as closed-mouthed as a fresh oyster. He doesn't tell us anything about anything."

I found that particular comment peculiar. Ross had always been forthcoming with me, trusting me enough to introduce me to his parents, but I knew little about him except his title, his reputation at the bank and well, the very personal side of him and his family I had gotten to know over the last six weeks. I would have to ask him why he was so secretive with his parents. I would also have to ask more about his life before Mega.

With Ross on my mind, I began to wonder where he was this morning. Was he sleeping late? I didn't know. Last night, Ross had driven me back to my condo where I got into my car with all of my clothes, toiletries and make-up still there from my week at Mom and Dad's and followed him to his parents' house. I didn't even go inside my condo. Ross had already warned me it was probably a mess after the thorough investigation of the break-in. Furthermore, he knew I needed rest and going inside and reliving the events of the afternoon would only get me all stirred up again.

When we got to the house, it was late and Marian and Charlie had already gone to bed. They had left a note, though, instructing Ross to put me in the guest room. Ross had carried my bags to the room, kissed me goodnight and left me alone to get some sleep. And man did I sleep! I think I was asleep before my head hit the pillow and I slept until my internal clock told me to wake up at 7 a.m., very late for me.

After we finished our muffins and coffee, I asked Marian if she had seen Ross this morning. She shook her head as she swallowed the last of her muffin, then said, "No, Ross left last night and went back to Charlotte. He left a note for you on the counter beside the coffee pot," and she reached in her pocket and took out the note, handed it to me and said, "Here it is."

I opened it and read it out loud. "Good morning, sleepyhead, I had to get back to Charlotte for a briefing at the bank this morning. I will call you this afternoon. I hope your first day back is a good one. I'll see you Friday. Love, Ross," and I sighed. Love, Ross—how could I not? I smiled at Marian and she smiled back as if we had a secret.

Finally, I knew I had to get to work so I rose to go, thanking Marian profusely for her hospitality, her generosity and her friendship. I told her I would come back after work to get my suitcase and toiletries and that I would call her before I came. I kissed her on the cheek, grabbed my purse and briefcase, and headed off to work.

I drove down the highway in silence and cleared my mind of the clutter there. I was certain my office was loaded up with work not done in my absence. Of course, I would also have a ton of e-mails to review and telephone calls to return. Strangely enough, I was still excited to get back to the routine of work, the normalcy of making a living. I had missed the bank.

As I saw the American One sign looming ahead on Main Street, I smiled. I still loved working for the bank. For me, it was honest and satisfying work, a way to help others. I turned into the parking lot, got my bags and briskly walked toward the doors. I was ready to get back to work. Today, I would let others deal with the underbelly of banking. I would let them do their job. They were charged with finding Patrick's killer, Ivey's arsonist and Spencer's assailant. My charge was much more rewarding. I had a bank to run.

Chapter 108

Spencer sat up in the hospital bed and pushed her breakfast tray aside. She was stir crazy and ready to go home. The food was awful, she couldn't get more than two hours of sleep at one shot because some nurse, orderly, or doctor was constantly barging into the room, and last but certainly not least, she was bored and didn't have anything to do. Idle time gave her too much time to think, and her head hurt too much to think anymore.

Her mother would be by shortly, McDonald's breakfast in hand, and she could have some human interaction. Rita promised she would be by to see her after work, and Ivey had already called her to check on her condition. She didn't have a laptop to surf the internet, and her vision was still too blurry to read.

Last night, Rita told her what had happened and Spencer had tried her damnedest to remember anything, but her mind was blank. The last memory she had of Sunday afternoon was sitting on her couch eating an entire quart of Neapolitan ice cream, she thought around 3:30 or so. Rita told her that she was assaulted around 5. *Where did those 90 minutes go?*

She sighed and tried to pull herself out of the funk that had overtaken her yesterday morning. She was lucky to be alive, and she should be thankful, but she just felt…what did she feel?

She felt empty, lonely, embarrassed and sad. She felt like her body was recovering quickly and well from the blow she took yesterday evening, but she wasn't certain her spirit, her psyche, or her heart would ever recover from the blow it had taken yesterday morning.

Get a clue, Spencer, she told herself. You were a roll in the sheets and by now, Jeff Malone had bragged to all the guys about how he had gotten her into the sack. The reputation she had built for over 10 years for being professional and hard-working in the office and enigmatic and off-limits personally was shot. Her credibility would be irrevocably damaged.

She sighed again and asked herself why the whole situation with Jeff bothered her so much. She had tried the self-deception route that he called off the casual affair before she had the chance to call it off, but she knew there was a much deeper, less superficial explanation for the dark fog that had enveloped her.

She had felt a connection with Jeff. She had hoped for a relationship with a partner, a lover, and a friend. In only one week, she had allowed herself to believe that perhaps it was her time to experience being in love, having a soul mate. Now, those hopes, dreams and aspirations were dashed, her feelings discounted, disregarded.

She began to cry. The tears were unstoppable, uncontrollably sliding down her cheeks, around her nose, into her mouth. She let all of the hurt, the disappointment, the anger flow away with her tears until she was free of the inner turmoil, the overwhelming despair inside her.

She had dared to trust, care, enjoy being with Jeff with no barriers to her feelings, her desires, or her soul. She had been completely uninhibited and no matter how he acted or how she felt now, she had liked herself more completely and truly than she had in many, many years.

As the tears slowed, she wiped her cheeks and her nose. If her mother arrived with her eyes red and swollen, Penny would have the doctors re-admit her to the intensive care ward. Spencer got up slowly and walked to the sink. She splashed cold water on her face, and the shock of it seemed to revive her spirit and wash away the dark film that had covered her core. She felt purged. She felt at peace. She looked at herself in the mirror and smiled slightly at her reflection. Perhaps there was hope for her yet.

Chapter 109

Ross left the meeting feeling irritated, anxious and impatient—all very dangerous emotions for a person working undercover and heading up a criminal investigation in tandem with federal, state and local law enforcement. The long and short of the briefing was that they were making progress toward identifying many of the participants in the collusion scheme and were closing in slowly on those involved in the murder of Lowers, the arson of Ivey's vehicle and the assault on Spencer. The noose was tightening.

Pulling the trigger too quickly would inevitably miss some of the details, possibly allowing some of the criminals to slip through the cracks and never face judgment. Waiting too long gave the participants time to destroy documentation, endanger more innocent people who threatened their exposure and avoid prosecution for lack of evidence.

The detectives involved had compiled evidence that indicated the scale of the collusion—a videotape of the bank parking lot from the adjacent convenience store showing a host of bank employees secretly convening last Saturday, a blank surveillance tape of the bank from the same day that was attributed to an equipment malfunction, three years of anomalies in the Shallotte financials that Rita discovered and CPAs had further detailed and investigated.

What they didn't have to complete the investigation and make arrests were the details of where the money went, who committed the crimes, and who benefitted from the scheme financially. The supporting documentation was missing, buried in a convoluted paperwork and ledger wash, or had been long destroyed.

Patrick Lowers told Ivey he had pieced together all the information and sent the information to bank security. Ross was sure he had and that John Starr had received it and destroyed it. The actions of Starr and many of the Shallotte team the day after Lowers' death indicated that the information they received was a copy and they didn't have the original and, in fact, were desperately seeking it.

The criminals had zeroed in on Rita and her close friends for some reason. They had broken into Patrick's car after his death, torn his office to shreds after his death, searched and torched Ivey's vehicle and broken into Rita's condo while she was away. What was so frustrating was that Rita, Spencer nor Ivey had the disk, the information, the evidence that both sides were seeking.

So where was the disk? Ross had no idea, but he did know that the criminals would not stop their pursuit of it until every possible location had been searched, every possible person ruled out. Rita was on somebody's short list and that meant she was in danger.

He felt helpless to protect her 200 miles from Shallotte, but he could not compromise the investigation when he was so close to bringing down the network. He took some comfort in the fact that Jack and Mack Grissett would watch out for Rita after hours at least until he could get back to town on Friday. The investigation team also had a very competent plant inside the bank during the working day.

Would they be able to protect Rita? He wasn't sure, but he knew that Jack and Mack were on watch 24/7 because they felt a rising desperation in the area, an impending danger as the criminals fought to escape exposure and bury their malicious history.

For four more days, Ross hoped their diligence would be enough. For four more days, though, their diligence was all he had.

Chapter 110

After several hours of catching up with the bank staff, meeting with Greg to discuss the state of the budget, and talking on the telephone to George to update him on Spencer's condition, I finally got into the sanctuary of my office about lunchtime. I returned several telephone calls, changed my voicemail and turned on my computer as I stood at my credenza to look at several loan requests and the supporting documentation that had been collected in my absence.

Finally, the computer sprang to life and I turned to sit down at my desk to tackle the task of opening and responding to the countless e-mails in my "inbox." I grabbed a meal bar from my purse and a bottle of water from my mini-fridge under my desk to tide me over until about 4:00 when I was leaving to go check in on Spencer. Remarkably, she was told she may be released from the hospital on Wednesday if she continued to make a speedy recovery.

As I sat down to login to my computer, something felt amiss. I stopped and looked around. Somebody had moved the picture of my grandfather from the right side of my computer to my credenza and the picture of Spencer, Ivey and me from the credenza to the right of my computer. I felt a wave of fear swamp me and I stood and turned back to my credenza and looked at my office with suspicious eyes.

Did the cleaning staff make the switch? Yeah, right, I thought. No one could seriously accuse the cleaners of moving anything to dust or vacuum. No, the switch looked natural, like somebody moved the photos then confused the location of each when putting them back.

Immediately, my mind made the leap to the reality of this discovery. Somebody had been in my office and searched it. They were looking for the disk.

I looked around and grabbed the picture of my grandfather and clutched it to me. I always kept him to my right to remind myself that doing the right thing was its own reward. My grandfather, the respected and honest banker, was probably spinning in his grave.

I felt violated and after the shock of the discovery sunk into my mind, then I got angry. How dare you come into my office and sift through my work, my personal effects, my stuff, I fumed.

I pushed away from my desk, stood up and turned back around to my credenza. I looked at my books. I looked at my manuals. Sure enough, they, too, had been manipulated. My bookends had been moved to the front of the books from the center and the books had been shuffled out of the alphabetical order by author by which I had arranged them. Damn it!

Breathing heavy, I considered what I should do. As I tried to get my anger under control, I heard, "Rita, are you okay?" behind me. I had to calm down—anger or hysteria could be dangerous.

I turned to Jeff Malone, not bothering to veil my contempt. "Just peachy, Jeff," I said, my voice dripping with sarcasm. "Why do you ask?"

He stood looking at me in silence for what seemed like an eternity before he finally said, "Well, you are red in the face and you are breathing hard. You look upset."

"Why the hell would I be *upset,*" I asked, mocking his featherweight description of my mood.

He sighed deeply and answered quietly, "I'm sorry, Rita. How is Spencer?"

"None of your damn business, Jeff," I said seriously, and I looked defiantly and squarely into his eyes. "What do you want?" I asked.

"Nothing," he said. "I'm just glad you're back. This place is a wreck without you."

Well, how do you respond to that kind of comment? I asked myself. So, I took a deep breath and pulled myself together. Finally, I answered, "Well, this place is likely to stay a wreck if I don't get some work done. Thank you for the compliment, Jeff, but you are still on my shit list."

"I know," he said quietly. "Nonetheless, I'm glad you're back," and he turned and walked away toward his office.

Chapter 111

At 4:00, Ross called Rita to check on her first day back at work and verify himself that she was okay. She answered on the first ring, and he felt relief wash over him.

The relief was fleeting, however, when she told him that her office had been searched while she was on vacation. Obviously, nothing was missing because her office, just like her condo, didn't contain the one thing the thieves were seeking—the disk.

Still, he could tell she was shaken up by the discovery and that she was eager to get over to the hospital to check on Spencer. He asked her to call him after she got to the hospital so he could get an update on Spencer's progress.

He was surprised like Rita when she told him that Spencer may get to go home on Wednesday if she continued to recover like she had in the last 24 hours. Until Spencer got home, though, Rita was all alone at the condo complex and he was afraid for her safety.

Broaching the subject of staying with his parents with someone as independent and carefree as Rita, though, was difficult and he thought she would protest. Undeterred, he said, "Rita, I want you to stay at my parents' house until Spencer is back at her condo. It is not safe for you to stay alone, ok?"

Surprisingly, she agreed, probably, in part, because of the break-in at her home and the search of her office. She was smart enough to know she was vulnerable by herself. The other part was that she was completely at ease at his former home on the river, completely at ease with his parents.

He smiled and realized she was already like a member of the family. He could hardly wait until Friday to see her again. She told him she missed him and that she was keeping a journal of all the cute little stories his mother told about him. She said she was sure they would be useful someday. He could hear the smile in her voice and the whole five-minute phone call brightened his day.

Before he disconnected, he asked her to call Jack to check in and let him know about the search of her office. She said she would if he wasn't already at the hospital, checking in on Spencer, but also checking out Lydia, the beautiful ER nurse.

Ross told her to be careful and that he would call his parents to let them know she would be there around 7 p.m. He hung up and sat back in his chair, happier than he had been in his entire life yet riddled with guilt that he was deceiving the woman he loved. One of his lifelong friends, Jack Grissett, had even told him so.

He turned and looked out the window, down on the streets of the Queen City far below. His role at the bank was like his downtown office, high up with a great overall view, but no more knowledge or insight into the everyday conversations, actions or activities of the bank employees than that of the pedestrians on the sidewalk below.

He needed to come clean with Rita about his role at the bank. He needed to be truthful about his background and his life. He needed to be honest about who he really was and how they had met in Greensboro. The meeting that day was not out of luck or chance. Rita was targeted so he could get on the inside of the investigation he was hired to lead.

Ross sighed and realized that his entire future hung in the balance of that conversation. He remembered Brian Evans and the regret he saw in his eyes as Rita walked away from him at the Bobcats game. He didn't want to be haunted that way the rest of his life.

He wanted a future with her, but he wasn't sure it was possible once she knew the whole story. Just as certain, though, Ross knew that a future with her was impossible if she didn't.

Chapter 112

My visit with Spencer on Monday was a welcome relief after the oppressiveness of the office that day. She was smiling and upbeat. As a matter of fact, she was happier than I remembered her being in a long, long time.

I asked her why she was in such a good mood. She shrugged good-naturedly and said, "I feel lucky to be alive, Rita."

I hugged her neck and said, "My world would be a very dull place without you, Spencer Cashwell."

"True that," she said, lightening the mood again. I laughed and sat down on the bed beside her so we could watch "Entertainment Tonight" on the television together. I pulled out the stash of double cheeseburgers and milkshakes I had smuggled into the hospital and we ate and talked about everything and nothing at all at the same time.

Spencer had some tests tomorrow and would be released from the hospital on Wednesday if everything checked out okay. Penny insisted that Spencer stay at her house until Friday when she could go home. Spencer said she couldn't wait to get there. Besides, Ivey would be in town Friday night and she had a Halloween party to attend on Saturday night.

I hated to leave, but it was almost 7 p.m. when Ross had told his parents that I would be back to their home. I kissed Spence goodbye on the cheek and left her room. I found Jack exactly where I had left him, talking to the beautiful nurse Lydia.

He walked me to my car and asked me about work. I told him about the secret search of my office while I was away. I also told him about George's curiosity about Spencer's accident and my strange encounter with Jeff Malone. It had been a hell of a day.

Jack told me to go straight to the Moores' house, and he followed me to the turn off at Shallotte Point. I pulled in the driveway, turned off the car and grabbed my purse. I knocked on the door then went quickly inside and breathed a sigh of relief when I closed the door behind me. I felt relaxed and tired all at once.

I walked down the hall toward the kitchen, saying hello as I went. I was greeted with Marian's warm voice asking me, "Welcome home, Rita. Are you hungry?"

I smiled at her and answered, "No, ma'am, I ate with Spencer at the hospital, but thank you."

She returned my smile, but I could see she was concerned about me. I was certain I looked worn to a frazzle. She commented, "You've look like you've had a long day. Let me make you some tea and you can take it upstairs, have a decadent bubble bath, unwind and get some rest. I imagine the next couple of days won't be much easier."

"No, work is not going to get better until the virus has worked its way out of the bank's system—I sure hope it is only a couple of days. I'm not sure how much more I can stand," I said and I sighed and tried to release some of the tension in my head, neck and back. I felt stiff as a board.

"First, you go up and run yourself a bath and I'll bring the tea to you before you get in. The bath bubbles are under the sink. You need to stay in it until the water is too cold to bear. Then you need to crawl under the covers and go to sleep," she ordered. She sounded so much like my own mother, I laughed.

"That sounds like a perfect plan," I said and I kissed her on the cheek and told her, "I hope you and Charlie don't think I am completely rude and unsociable. I can't begin to tell you how much I appreciate you letting me stay with you."

Marian grabbed my hand as I went by her and said, "I am thrilled to have you here and so is Charlie, not that he has noticed your arrival tonight since he has been asleep in the recliner for over an hour. Now, go upstairs and pamper yourself."

I went, as instructed, and ran the hottest bath I thought I could stand, poured some vanilla-ginger bubble bath into the water, and pulled out my fluffy white bath slippers and my pink pajamas to put on afterward. When I walked back into the bathroom, Marian had left a dainty pink tea pitcher of hot water and matching pink mug, two Earl Grey teabags and a plateful of her delicious scones. I didn't need such pampering, but I sure did appreciate it tonight.

Soaking until the water was cool and my fingers and toes were wrinkled beyond recognition, I reluctantly got out, got ready for bed and disappeared into the comfort of the big queen bed. I felt like a noodle and I lay quietly letting my mind wander from Ross to Spencer to the bank to the farm to my family to Ross's family to having a family.

I intentionally didn't dwell on anything in particular for long for fear that dark thoughts would overtake me and make their way into my dreams. I flitted from the pleasant to the pleasant and, at some point, drifted off into a peaceful sleep filled with, well, nothing.

When I opened my eyes again, dawn was breaking and I looked at the clock. It was 5:30 a.m. I was rested, rejuvenated and restored. I was ready to face another day.

I got out of bed, dressed in my jeans, tennis shoes, and a tee shirt under my sweatshirt to go for a short kayak down the creek. I tiptoed down the stairs only to find the house already alive with activity. Marian was in the kitchen while Charlie was up on a ladder on the porch working on the ceiling fan.

I said good morning to them and asked if I could use Ross's kayak and paddle. She answered, "Of course." Then, she instructed Charlie to put the kayak into the creek for me and tie it to the dock. I protested futilely. Charlie was already on his way.

Marian poured coffee into a thermos and handed it to me with a bag of whole-wheat English muffins with cream cheese. I was being spoiled and I told her so.

She laughed and told me it was her house and she could spoil me because it pleased her. Then she guided me out the door toward the dock. I launched the kayak with Charlie giving me a huge push into the current and a wave goodbye.

The morning was cool and fog rose mysteriously from the top of the water and hovered like a magic carpet just above the surface. Dawn was breaking in the east and the morning sky still shown with the stars directly above me and off to the west. I paddled hard against the current coming into the river and knew the paddle back would be much easier.

My muscles burned as I turned around in the mouth of the Intracoastal Waterway just south of a beautiful spoil island covered in fog and teeming with shore birds. I felt full of life, full of energy this morning. As I headed back into the mouth of the river and back toward the dock, I let my mind take me to the question of where this whole relationship with Ross was headed. I wanted a future with him. I wanted a family with him. I wondered if he wanted the same. I thought he did.

We were so lucky to have found each other at the corporate pep rally that, otherwise, would have been a colossal waste of time. Interestingly, I didn't mind luck, but I had never really been the recipient of it much either. It felt good to be lucky and be me right now.

As I paddled up to the dock and tied off the kayak, I stepped onto the dock, sat down, and watched the sunrise. I poured myself a cup of the coffee and bit into my muffin. I felt the spirituality of the morning as songbirds came to life, the sky dawned with light and the stars faded, then suddenly the bright orange sun peeked over the horizon. I felt small in the world. I felt connected.

After I finished the thermos and the muffin, I stood to go inside to get ready for work. The questions of the universe would have to wait just like the questions about my relationship with Ross. All the big picture things would have to go to the back burner of my life for now.

Right now, I had to concentrate on getting through the next few days, day by day, hour by hour, and perhaps, even minute by minute. I had to get Spencer home. I had to be vigilant for my safety. I had to let Ross manage the Bank overall while I managed the bank on the ground here locally. Neither was an easy task, but both of us were up to it.

I went up and got ready for work and was downstairs in less than 45 minutes, ready to go. I lavished Marian with copious gratitude for the coffee, the muffin and the pampering and I left for work before 7:30 a.m. I drove up Highway 179 into Shallotte in silence, appreciating the sleepy town that had yet to come to life. October cast the coastal towns of Brunswick County in a wonderful light. There was beautiful weather, no traffic and a joie de vivre as area festivals abounded—the Oyster Festival, Festival by the Sea, as well as a variety of fall festivals at the local schools.

Our community Halloween party was Saturday night and was always a lot of fun. This year, I got to share it with Ross. I was excited and wanted to perfect my gypsy costume over the next couple of days. A phone call to Mom was probably in the cards—pardon the pun.

I got to the bank first and went inside, disarmed the alarm and searched the premises. As I went into Patrick's old office, a spooky feeling came over me and I wondered what he did with the disk of damning information. One thing was certain—he had planned the location and its discovery to the nth degree. He was just that anal.

The office felt sterile, cold and lifeless and I wondered just who would fill it in the coming weeks and what the new change in management would mean for me, the office and my co-workers. He or she certainly couldn't be more boorish, demanding or oppressive. Not that I want to speak poorly of the dead, mind you. Patrick was effective in getting results, but it was a hellish existence for the workers, including me.

I set the morning glory signal and went into my office. I called Spencer then I called Ivey. Finally, before I saw the next co-worker, I called Ross. We talked briefly, but I felt even brighter when I hung up the phone. He said he missed me. He said couldn't wait until Friday. He said he wished he could be here with me.

Lamely, all I could do was smile and utter, "Me too." I was whipped and any fool could see it on my face—which was all the more reason not to call him during the day or talk about him at work. He was my wonderful secret—well, mine, Spencer's and Ivey's secret anyway—and he was my sanity, my lifeline through the craziness of this investigation, this unraveling of the tangled web of corruption, this danger.

Ten minutes after I hung up the phone, the bank roared to life as the employees, sometimes one by one, other times in pairs, arrived to begin work.

As the bank filled, the tension built as well, but I refused to be pulled into it, preferring to remain calm, alert and observant.

I intended to survive this fiasco locally and help my bank move beyond the corruption once the bank had cleaned house and the crooks were in jail. I was taking the threat of danger very seriously—to me and to all of the other innocent employees, whoever they were.

So I got down to work on the loans that needed to be closed, the documentation that needed to be filed and the decisions that needed to be made to operate my part of the banking world. Amazingly, the day flew by with very little distraction or interruption and I got a massive amount of catching up and cleaning up done after being out the entire week prior.

At the end of the day, I closed the computer down and headed over to see Spencer before going to have dinner with the Moores tonight at a decent hour. I said goodbye to Angie, the teller supervisor, and told her where I was going in case anybody needed me in the next hour.

I pulled into the hospital parking lot, searching for a parking place, and finally found one at the back of the lot. I didn't mind the walk because I had all kinds of pent up energy and it was a glorious Tuesday afternoon.

I hummed as I walked, but kept alert. The parking lot was devoid of life and I felt suddenly alone. I felt the tension in my neck return and the recoiling of fear in the pit of my stomach. I looked around. I saw Jack's truck and momentarily relaxed. I was among friends.

Before that thought even sunk into my brain, though, a car door closed behind me to my right and I looked around, keenly aware that I wasn't alone, but saw nothing. I quickened my pace considerably.

Somewhere about three-quarters of the way through the maze of cars and trucks, I came around the front bumper of an obscenely large monster truck and ran right into Ricky Jarman. The force knocked me backwards and I struggled to keep from falling to the ground.

Ricky made no attempt to stop my fall and I quickly surmised that he meant to run into me. I decided to play offense instead of defense. I pushed myself up off of the Dodge now underneath me and got in his face with mine and asked him, "What do you want, Ricky?"

He seemed startled for a split second then slowly broke into a sly, sleazy grin. He was busted and didn't give a damn. "Oh, hey Rita," he said, "I just thought I'd come by and check on my buddy, Spencer. How 'bout you? Are you here to see Spencer or are you making a house call on one of them big shot doctors?"

I wanted to punch him in his big, fat red nose, but instead, I smiled back and said sweetly, "Ricky, if you'll get out of my way I can be on mine. I'll give Spencer your regards," and I moved past him, careful to stay out of his reach, coolly and quickly. I saw Jack walking toward me and I wanted to run to him but didn't want to give Ricky the satisfaction of thinking he had unhinged me—the fat bastard.

Jack hadn't seen the collision or the stumble or he probably would have put the big hurt on Ricky, so I didn't say anything. I just put my hand through his arm and walked with him inside. I appreciated the rescue—again.

I wasn't sure how many times Jack was going to save my life, but I was thankful he was here and would be around until this whole bank ordeal was over.

I felt tension in the air at the bank. I felt an aura of mania and suspicion engulfing the town. Without a doubt, Shallotte was beginning to get jiggy.

Chapter 113

Wednesday was a repeat of Tuesday at work with very little distraction or even interaction with the many of the employees of the bank. The situation almost seemed like everybody was trying to lay low, stay off the radar, or keep out of my way. If I cared about what most of my co-workers thought right now, I might have taken it personally, but without a clear knowledge of who was in or who was out of the collusion, I liked being left alone. Besides, I was productive and thorough in my work and I was having a good month from a loan production point of view.

I worked hard all day including through lunch because today was the day Spencer got to leave the hospital. I was going to pick her up after the doctor checked her out one last time. She was scheduled to be discharged around 2 p.m. and I was going to take her to Penny's house until Friday afternoon. Ivey planned to pick her up from Penny's place and take her home to her condo where he would stay for the weekend. We would all go to the Halloween party together on Saturday night. Spencer decided she was going to dress up as a hospital patient to go to the Halloween party. Spencer had even convinced one of the attending nurses to give her a new hospital gown for the occasion. Of course, all this planning was completely subject to how Spencer felt—in Penny's sole discretion. One moan, one groan and Spencer would be stuck at her mom's for the entire weekend.

I was really excited about Friday. Perhaps, Spencer's arrival back home might usher in a return to some kind of normalcy. Spencer hadn't been inside her condo since Sunday, and interestingly, neither had I. Even more interesting was the fact that not being at my condo, i.e. home, didn't bother me in the least. I wondered why. Was I just that comfortable at the Moore's? Had the whole breaking and entering/assault enveloped my condo in a bad karma? Did I just not want to go there alone? Who knew? I sure didn't.

Of course, Friday was also when Ross was coming back into town. He would be here around 7 p.m. he said. I was almost counting the hours. Saturday night at the Halloween party would be a lot of fun too. I would be perfecting my gypsy costume this afternoon with a trip to Alicia Swinson's consignment store to find jewelry, sandals, a peasant shirt and the perfect skirt. I wanted it to be fun, sexy and alluring.

Ross had yet to tell me anything about his costume. I wasn't sure if that was because he wanted to surprise me or if he hadn't decided on one or if he was just not that interested in the whole affair. With or without a costume, though, I knew he would have a good time.

I completed the underwriting on a renewal of a small business line of credit and sent the electronic file up to our centralized documentation department for review. When I finally closed the paper file and placed it in my "out" box on my credenza, I looked at my watch. It was time to go get Spencer!

As I was waiting for the computer to shut down, I looked at my grandfather's picture and remembered with disdain the fact that somebody had rifled through my office. I wondered if the crooks had found the disk. Everything seemed to be at a standstill. The police had not made a move to arrest anyone and the crooks had been decidedly quiet since the attack on Spencer.

Not that I was going to let my guard down, though. I could almost hear the "shark" music in my head telling me that some kind of attack was imminent. Hopefully, I wouldn't be the fool swimming alone in the ocean at feeding time.

I left the office and drove the five miles to the hospital to pick up Spencer. When I arrived at the discharge area, she was sitting at the curb in a wheelchair waiting for me. She was talking to a handsome doctor. He was obviously more interested in her than she was in him. I wondered what the hell was wrong with her. Had the accident knocked a screw or two loose in her head? Doc was hot.

I pulled up to the curb and got out to help load the patient. Spencer pushed all attempts to help her aside and climbed into my Miata. She was in her jeans, a black sweater and her boots. She also had her black glamour shades on. When I closed the door, she flashed Dr. Gorgeous her blinding white smile. I looked at him. He was smitten.

I got in the car, looked over at her and laughed.

"What?" she asked.

"I've got the old Spencer back," I said.

Without missing a beat, Spencer shot back, "Hey, who are you calling old? I'm good as new."

As we drove to Penny's and talked, I thought she was right. I could hear the lightness of her spirit, the calmness in her gestures as she talked about how she had gone from room to room taking her flowers to other patients before she was discharged. She smiled and joked about how physically her mother would nurse her back to health, but that mentally she might need a vacation in a padded room by Friday.

Before I left her in Penny's care, I reminded her to continue to be vigilant. She told me to do the same, reminding me that I didn't have a prison warden in the next room like she did who would protect her charge first and ask questions later. I reminded her that I was staying at the Moore's house until she got home on Friday and that all I intended to do until then was to go straight to their house, straight to work, and back again.

"I miss work," she blurted. "Does that sound crazy?"

I laughed and told her no, but with everything going on it was akin to working at the salt mines lately, especially without her there. We talked for a few minutes about work, what she needed me to do to help her, what I could bring her and how everybody was acting lately. Then, Penny came into the den and told Spencer she needed to rest. Translation: I needed to leave.

I kissed Spencer on the cheek and told her I would see her Friday evening after I got home from work and before Ross arrived at 7. I told her I had to go, and I left for Ms. Swinson's to perfect my costume. As I turned into the parking lot, I looked at my watch. It was 5 pm. Less than an hour later, I was loaded up with a fabulous gypsy outfit and about five pounds of gold jewelry.

I left for the Moore's house around 6 p.m. so I could get there before sunset. As I drove, I turned my conversation with Spencer over in my mind. She had discussed the accident, the investigation, Ivey, Penny, work, her condo, the party, her costume, and Ross—almost everything that seemed to matter in Spencer's world of late. She was funny, quick-witted and seemed completely at peace with the world, but something about the entire conversation this evening, her whole demeanor bothered me. Perhaps I needed to rethink my earlier thought that Spencer was as good as new.

The more I tried to argue both sides of the Spencer debate with myself, the more my head throbbed and I was suddenly tired to the bone. As I pulled into the Moore's driveway, it finally hit me and I knew why I was concerned about her. In the four days since Spencer's accident, she had not only avoided talking about what had happened with Jeff Malone, she had not even mentioned his name.

CHAPTER 114

Thursday roared to life with an unusual late autumn thunderstorm. A loud clap of thunder at 5:15 a.m. startled me to life and I sat straight up in bed, my body awake but my brain still in dreamland.

When I firmly arrived in consciousness, I got up and walked over to the window to watch the display of sound and light over the river. It was an awesome sight. The sky flashed to almost daylight before streaks of lightning zigzagged in every direction. Seconds later, the roll of the thunder would cascade around the room like a timpani drum solo.

I stood at the window until the storm moved out over the ocean, as if the drum corps had marched off into the distance and only the sound of the raindrops tapped their applause on the roof of the Moore's house. Such interactions with nature made me feel small in the world, and gave me perspective that I was only one tiny wheel turning in the intricate clockworks of the world.

The peaceful feeling carried over into my day at the bank and left me upbeat in my interactions and pensive when I was alone. As I finished up the underwriting on the last loan on my desk, I was gathering up the paper files to take to the loan assistants when there was a knock on my door.

I turned to find Helen Marks at my door. I put the files down, walked around my desk and gave her a hug. She returned my affection and held me at arm's length to better look at me. Her beaming smile was infectious and I beamed back.

Helen was a retired librarian from Raleigh and a voracious reader like me. We had struck up a friendly conversation while she was applying for a home loan to buy a condo as a second home several years back before she retired. After discovering our mutual passion for reading, we began trading books with each other every couple months. I had never read a book she recommended that I didn't love. She said the same.

I asked if she could sit for a few minutes, but Helen told me she only had a few minutes because she had a hair appointment, but she wanted to see if I had read the book she dropped off as a belated birthday present. My brain tried to remember if I had seen the gift. I suddenly remembered the gift on my desk on my birthday and I was embarrassed because I not only didn't open it, I didn't know where it was. I covered by asking, "Was that the pretty gift I had on my desk in the brown paper and red ribbon?"

Helen looked puzzled and said, "No, I dropped it off to Spencer while you were away. I'm sorry but I didn't have time to wrap it."

"No, Helen," I said, "Spencer hasn't given it to me yet. Did you know she was injured last Sunday? She was released from the hospital only yesterday," I finished.

After I told Helen what happened to Spencer, she was shocked and reached over and touched my arm and told me to be careful. I told her I would and that Spencer's mother was taking good care of her until the weekend. I also told her I would get the book from Spencer over the weekend and read it. Looking at her watch, Helen said she had to go, but that she would check back with me in a couple of weeks. I told her I would look forward to her next visit and that I would have the book read to give back to her then.

After she left, I began to think about the brown paper package on my desk the morning of my birthday, the Saturday we came into the bank for the announcement of Patrick's death. I was curious and I closed my eyes to reconstruct that morning and what had happened to the gift.

"Are you meditating or daydreaming?" a voice boomed from the door and I jump from the abrupt and unwelcome disruption to my thoughts.

I looked up and saw Dylan standing there grinning like the idiot that he was. He instinctively made me want to hurl, punch him or go get a shower. Not wanting him to get under my skin, though, I smiled back and stayed calm and responded, "Neither, Dylan—I'm trying to remember where I left something. Did you need something?"

"No," he replied casually, "I just wanted to check on you and Spencer and see if you were going to the Halloween party on Saturday."

Who invited you, I thought but didn't blurt. Instead, I answered, "Spencer is fine. She is healing and resting so she can come home Friday then go to the Halloween party on Saturday. Have you ever known her to miss one?" I asked him light-heartedly.

"Well, no, but I wasn't sure that with all that happened if she would even go back home, let alone go to a party there," he said.

"She's a big girl, Dylan, not some shrinking violet," I stated. "Of course, she's going home. Then we're going to find the bastard who broke in and conked her over the head and send his ass to jail." *And that is a promise*, I thought.

"Jeez, Rita," he said, "I didn't mean to get you all stirred up."

"I'm not stirred up, I'm just resolved, Dylan," I added, "Just resolved."

He stared at me blankly for a split second, shook his head like he was trying to understand what the word 'resolved' meant then walked away. Get a dictionary, Dylan.

After all, 'resolved' and 'reject' both start with 'r'.

Chapter 115

I left the bank at 5:15 p.m. determined to find the birthday gift I never opened. I remembered putting it in my purse before Spencer and I left the meeting that Saturday to go to the Waffle House. After that…I had nothing.

I hadn't changed purses. If I took it into the condo, perhaps the intruder stole my present. *Don't be ridiculous*, I thought.

I got in the car and looked around in the back of the car, on the floor—nothing. I needed to go to my condo and look around, but quite frankly, I was a little scared. I was scared to go home alone.

I called Jack on his mobile phone. He answered on the second ring, "You just couldn't go one day without talking to me, huh?" he teased.

"Yeah, I miss you that much," I replied. "Are you busy right now?" I asked him.

"No, not too bad," he said, "What do you need? Your wish is my command, Princess."

"I want to go to my condo, but I'm afraid to go alone," I said, somewhat embarrassed at the admission.

I told him I hadn't been home since Sunday and that I needed to get some clothes, survey the damage or at the least, the mess, and look for a gift that I had misplaced. I was already driving down Main Street. Jack said he was on his way and that he would be there.

When I pulled up in front, he was waiting for me on the front steps. I was nervous and anxious. I know it showed, but Jack didn't say a word. He held his hand out for the key, unlocked the door and walked inside ahead of me.

When I got inside, I turned on the light. My stomach lurched. My home was a wreck. My home was in chaos. My home was a crime scene. I didn't even know where to begin.

But Jack did. He began by grabbing a trash bag out from under the sink and began picking up pieces of broken glass and pottery. I started at the other end of the den and picked up books, magazines, newspapers, and throw pillows. I re-organized my bookshelves, straightened up the furniture and grabbed the vacuum out of the closet so I could get any smaller shards of glass or pottery out of the carpet.

Jack closed the cabinet doors in the kitchen, put the kitchen canisters back against the backsplash and grabbed the mop and cleaned the kitchen linoleum. By 6 p.m., order had been restored, the signs of damage repaired, and the feeling of comfort, warmth and security seeped back into my home.

I thanked Jack profusely and told him I just needed to run upstairs to get an outfit and see if the missing gift was there. As I reached the top and turned right into my bedroom, my heart sank. It, too, was a wreck.

Jack must have heard my sigh all the way downstairs because before I could turn and go downstairs and give up in disgust, he was upstairs in the guest room straightening the mattresses on the bed, closing the dresser drawers, and the closet doors.

I was in my bedroom doing the same, straightening my drawers—God, somebody had been through my lingerie, my gowns, and the rest of my clothes. I made up my bed, put my shoes back in place in the closet, and grabbed my suit for tomorrow.

I had looked all around my condo and not found any trace of the brown-papered package with the red ribbon. My mind returned to the idea that perhaps the intruder had stolen it. Again, I dismissed that notion because I couldn't imagine why a thief would steal a gift that was obviously a book. I also didn't remember bringing the parcel inside. The darn package just seemed to have disappeared.

Anyway, at least my condo was straight and that meant one less thing to do tomorrow afternoon after work. I stood back and surveyed our work. Everything was back in its place. I would clean the upstairs tomorrow.

Jack walked back downstairs with me, checked the back door and ushered me and my clothes out onto the front porch. He, then, turned on the front porch light and locked the door behind us.

I gave him a huge bear hug and he laughed his jolly chuckle and told me he'd see me Saturday night. Of course Jack Grissett would be at the Halloween party. He was the photographer for the evening and would probably net around $500 for the night.

"Please make sure the camera lens is kind to me, ok?" I said.

"Rita, you are a photographer's dream," he replied, and he shut my car door then got into his truck and followed me to the turn off to the Moores' home.

I would ask Spencer tomorrow about the pretty, but elusive package because tonight, Marian, Charlie and I were going to dine on the porch of the house. We were having an oyster roast and I couldn't wait. The salty-sweet local delicacy was celebrated from October until March in hundreds of recipes with different cooking methods; none, though, more wonderful than just steamed slightly opened.

It was a simple, succulent and satisfying event and I hurried into the house to help Marian prepare the cornbread and slaw, melt the butter and set the table. As I announced my arrival, though, Marian met me halfway down the hall with the dishes in her hand and a roll of paper towels under her chin.

She smiled excitedly and told me to go take my clothes upstairs and wash up. We were ready to feast!

The three of us polished off an entire bushel of the tasty mollusks in 30 minutes. We were stuffed and we retired to the comfortable wicker chairs beside the table where we talked over coffee until long after the sun had disappeared below the horizon.

I looked at my watch and could hardly believe it was almost 9 p.m. I needed to get upstairs and pack my bags. I was going home tomorrow, and I was excited and sad about it at the same time. I was ready to return to my home and my "normal" existence, but I also hated to leave the loving warmth of the Moores' idyllic home.

I told Marian and Charlie good night and went upstairs, packed my things and got into bed before 9:30. Alone under the soft, warm quilts, I pulled out my mobile phone and called Ross. He didn't answer, but I was certain he was still at work, even at this hour.

I was so excited about tomorrow—seeing Ross again, Spencer's homecoming, Ivey's arrival—that I was sure I would never get to sleep. I rolled over and put the phone on the nightstand and turned out the light. I watched the clouds roll across the face of the waning moon, almost hypnotized by their constant, but changing motion in the night. I thought about kayaking down the river by moonlight and as I paddled in my mind, I drifted quietly into a restful, black sleep.

Chapter 116

Friday morning dawned softly like a whispered promise that life would soon return to normal, would settle back into a comfortable state of ordinary satisfaction. I basked in the thought momentarily, but then realized that the normal and ordinary of my life six weeks ago didn't include Ross. *Watch what you wish for*, I told myself.

I got up and into the shower before I changed my mind. After I finished dressing for work, I loaded up my carry-on bag with all of my toiletries, my dirty clothes and my shoes then loaded up my arms with my suits on hangers and headed downstairs to get them to my car.

Marian was arranging some beautiful fall flowers in a brown glass vase while Charlie was reading the newspaper in his well-worn, well-loved recliner. I said good morning as I breezed by them so I wouldn't disturb them on my way out. I'm sure you can imagine how well that attempt flew—think lead balloon.

Before I knew what was happening, both of them were wrestling clothes, keys, bags, everything out of my hands. Chaos ensued as I fought their good intentions until finally the keys went sliding across the kitchen floor and half the suits ended up in a hangar-less heap at my feet. Shock at the sight was almost instantly replaced by uncontrollable laughter, and we rested against the walls, bent over and grabbed our knees, and wiped the tears off our faces trying to regain our composure. I loved Marian and Charlie like family. Quite simply, inside these four walls and on the Moores' piece of the earth, I mattered and I belonged.

After we got everything put in the tiny trunk of the Miata, I came back inside and had breakfast and coffee with them before I left for work. I told them again how much I appreciated their hospitality and their company. I offered to cook dinner for them sometime, but Marian would only accept cooking dinner with them. I told her it was a date and that I would call her to find a good time for them in November.

Reminding me that tomorrow was Halloween, she brought me a basket filled with treat bags for any children that came into the bank today. I squealed with delight as I took it and put it on the passenger side floor then asked her if there was an age limit since most of the children would most likely be the men with whom I worked. She laughed and said candy and treats belonged to kids from 2 to 102. I had a feeling I was going to be very popular today.

I tooted the horn as I left the driveway and Marian and Charlie waved goodbye to me. It was like a Norman Rockwell painting of a very special moment in time, but the whole leaving process left me somewhat melancholy.

As I drove on Highway 179 toward Shallotte, I glanced in my rear-view mirror and saw the hanging gypsy costume that Ms. Swinson and I had pulled together and I was almost giddy with excitement for the evening I had planned with Ross. When I looked back to the road, a huge deer was standing 50 yards ahead of me in the middle of the highway and I slammed on the brakes, closing my eyes in fright or as a prayer that I didn't kill the poor creature or destroy my little car. When I opened my eyes, I was stopped and the deer was gone, but my purse was in the floor on top of the turned over goody basket.

The sight slapped me like a hand across my face and I suddenly remembered the slamming on brakes in Shallotte with Spencer on my birthday on the way to Waffle House. Today, my purse was zipped. On my birthday, it was not and crap had flown around this car like a tornado.

I pulled off the road at the Baptist church on Highway 179 and parked in the paved parking lot behind it. Leaving the car running, I leaned over and put my purse back on the seat and straightened the basket on the floor. Then, I opened my car door and got out, pulled the seat forward and stuck my hand as far under the seat as it would go. My hand touched the wrapped package and I pulled it out.

I sighed with relief and smiled at my luck—I was having a streak of it. I found the present, I didn't hurt Bambi and my car was still in one piece. I untied the red bow and tore the brown paper off. As I suspected, the gift was a book—*Shakespeare Favorites*. Now I was really curious.

I opened the leather-bound book and gasped—yep, out loud. Patrick Lower's handwriting screamed at me from the book's title page. I reached out my index finger and ran it over each word of the inscription as I read it out loud. "Rita, you are the only one who will appreciate the contents of this book as much as I do. Happy Birthday. Patrick."

I began to cry, and I clutched the book to my chest and sobbed until all of the sadness of his untimely death, the loss of his presence as a husband and father and the sacrifice he had made out of honest loyalty to our bank was depleted from me. I remembered his enthusiasm, his confident demeanor on the last night of his life. Perhaps that night he was as close to happy with his life as he had ever been and I realized that was the way I wanted to remember him.

He had quoted Shakespeare to me that night. What had he said? It was from "All's Well that Ends Well" and I looked at the Table of Contents page and turned to page 279. This time, there was no gasp because I was certain

I was no longer breathing. My hands began to shake and I fumbled clumsily to lock my doors as I felt suddenly alone and vulnerable.

I reached down and tugged gently at the envelope I found taped to the play's title page and slowly turned it over. On the back of it in Patrick's handwriting were those infamous last words he had uttered to me at the golf tournament—"Why then tonight let us assay our plot!" I opened the flap and pulled out a simple white computer disk.

The magnitude of the discovery overwhelmed me, and I held the disk flat in the palm of my hand and pondered its power. Once opened, careers would be destroyed. Families would be destroyed. Lives would be destroyed. I wasn't sure I was ready for it all, but I also could not put the disk back into hiding either now that I had discovered it. Instead, I realized I had opened Pandora's Box, and my banking world would never be the same again.

Chapter 117

Ross had been in meetings last night until after midnight. He had missed Rita's call and she had not left a message. It was strange how he had come to count on hearing her voice before he went to sleep and when he didn't, he slept fitfully. He would call her at 7:45 a.m. if she didn't call him first. He missed her and couldn't wait to hear her voice or to see her tonight.

He was dressing up as the Phantom of the Opera to go to the Halloween party on Saturday. Ross had called Julia Basco, a friend of his from his Chapel Hill days. Julia worked with Charlotte's Neighborhood Theater now and he called her to solicit suggestions and advice. She obviously heard the desperation in his voice and told him to come see her. He did and she had hooked him up in a big way.

Julia loaned him the cape, the mask and a white bowtie and told him to put on his tuxedo. When he tried on the ensemble that evening, he admitted to his reflection in the mirror that the outfit suited him perfectly. First of all, he was living behind a mask. Second, he operated in a shadowy, foggy world with a diverse cast of characters. Last, but certainly not least, he had dragged Rita into his dangerous underworld. He hoped his fate was far less tragic, however, than the phantom's. He wanted to end up with the heroine, free from the mask, and make a life with her filled with honesty and clarity.

Ross hated his career at times, never more so than right now when he had to keep his cover and protect the integrity of the investigation. *What about my own integrity,* he thought as he sighed and ran his fingers through his hair.

He knew the investigation was beginning to move now that the computer whizzes he had on staff had recovered and reconstructed several years of deleted electronic files from Mid-Atlantic Bank. The evidence was slowly coming together, but the process could take much longer before they were ready to make even the first arrest. For every recovery of evidence they made, he was certain an equal amount of destruction of evidence was occurring to deter them. Ross wondered if the bad guys had found the disk. He hoped that good would prevail over evil this time.

If the good guys found the disk, the investigation would move into overdrive. Arrests would be made, the network would be dismantled. That kind of victory meant the FBI had done its job, the bank could turn the page and operate more profitably, the criminals responsible for Patrick's death, Spencer's assault, Ivey's arson and Rita's breaking and entering would go to prison, and Ross could make that clear, honest life he longed for with Rita.

He sighed again. Oh, how he wanted that disk.

Chapter 118

I pulled into the bank parking lot at 7:30 a.m., the first to arrive. I had returned the disk to the envelope and secured it back inside book exactly like Patrick had. I put the book under my arm and carried it with me. Since the crooks had already searched my office, they certainly wouldn't think to look again since they had no idea I knew about their clandestine snooping.

I walked in alone, checked the premises and set the morning glory signal before I retreated to the sanctuary of my office. I sat down and took in the silence of the bank. My hands were still shaking, my nerves still raw. I was a wreck.

I picked up the telephone and called Ross, and he answered on the first ring. "Good morning, my green-eyed gypsy," he said smoothly.

I took a deep breath and tried to find my voice. "Oh, Ross," I whispered almost inaudibly, "It's so good to hear your voice."

"Rita, are you ok?" he asked, his voice suddenly filled with concern.

"No," I said simply. I looked around outside my window warily, I was alone. Nonetheless, I continued to whisper, "I've got it."

I was certain the silence that followed was Ross attempting to grasp the full meaning of those three words. He whispered back, "Oh my god…with you?"

"Yes, yes, and I'm scared to death," I said and then told him the story of how I discovered it.

I could almost hear him thinking and I imagined him pacing back and forth in his office gathering his thoughts. "Rita, where is the disk right now?"

"It is right where Patrick originally hid it," I stated matter-of-factly.

"Ok, don't move it and keep that book in your sight all day long," he said. "I'll be down around 7 p.m. tonight. I want you to go straight home after work. Don't linger at the bank either. Better yet, make an excuse and leave early. Go home and go see Spencer and Ivey. I hope you greet me with your castanets," he said, trying to lighten my spirits.

I smiled and said, "I will. I wish I could just fall asleep and wake up at 7:00."

He laughed softly, "Don't do that! Stay alert and vigilant today. That disk is the beginning of the end of this whole fiasco, Rita."

"I will," I said then added, "I sure hope you're right about the beginning of the end. A return to normal around here is long overdue." I sighed hard and I started to feel scared again, and I wondered if the fear would be obvious enough to alert the crooks that I had discovered the disk. I sure hoped not and silently vowed to try hard to conceal it.

As if he could sense my anxiety, Ross said, "I'm going to unload you of that disk this morning so I want you to relax. I'm going to call Jack and have him come by with his bank bag, make a deposit and come into your office. Give him the disk and leave the rest to law enforcement."

"Ok," I said, "As long as Jack will be safe."

"Jack will be safe and he will get the disk into the hands of the right people—the good guys," he promised.

Ross assured me that the disk would be the end of the criminal collusion at American One and that all of those involved would be brought to justice. I was confident that he was right and I was relieved that in only a few hours the dismantling of the network would begin, but I also had mixed feelings about the toll the whole process would take on the friends and families of those involved as well as the entire Shallotte community.

I told Ross that I couldn't wait to see him tonight, and he said he couldn't either. Then, I reluctantly disconnected the call to get to work. I looked at the full basket of goodies Marian had prepared for me this morning and then I looked at the clock. I sighed out loud. It was just before 8:00 a.m. on the day before Halloween.

It was going to be a frightfully long day.

Chapter 119

By 8:30, the bank was in high gear. As I suspected, I was very popular with the employees today because of the basket of goodies on my desk. Greg, Dylan, Peter, Tripp and Jeff all paid me a visit to tell me hello, ask about my weekend and Halloween plans and chit-chat under the guise of collecting their very own bag of wonderful baked goods. They were so transparent.

I found myself talking too much, filled with a nervous energy to pass the time, to cover the fear of my discovery, and I wondered how many of my co-workers and which ones were involved. I tried not to scrutinize or guess. The fact is I refused to look at the contents of the disk so I wouldn't know who was involved. I would know soon enough.

In a moment of solitude, I wondered what time Jack was going to arrive. I glared at my desktop clock, mentally willing it to move faster. I'm sure you know how that worked out for me.

After the goodies were exhausted and my office was no longer social central, I finally got down to business. I returned several telephone calls, scheduled a few appointments for loan applications for the following week and called a couple attorneys to check on upcoming loan closings. The clock demanded my attention again. It was only 10:30.

I was sure Jack would be here any minute. I had saved a treat bag just for him as the means to lure him behind my desk. I would slip the book and the treats into his bank bag. I had moved the book from my credenza to the corner of my desk under the goody bag.

As if he read my mind, I saw Jack Grissett at the door to the bank. He looked at me, casually threw up his hand, and strolled over to Angie to process his deposit. They chatted cordially and he never looked my way. *He is one cool customer*, I thought.

I feigned busyness and stared blankly at a loan file, randomly pulling sheet of paper, stacks of financials from within it as if I was on an underwriting roll. When I felt almost maniacal in my acting as if I couldn't continue this façade anymore, Jack mercifully rapped on my door. I breathed a huge but inaudible sigh of relief.

Jack smiled at me and I saw the concern in his eyes as sure as he saw the fatigue in mine. He broke the silence and said, "Hello, Princess!"

"Back at you, Mr. Grissett—I have something special for you. Come here," I said in a seemingly confident voice that belied my nervousness and fear. Jack walked to the corner of my desk. I continued, "You can have this goody bag, but you can't eat it until later today or it will spoil your lunch. How about I put it in your bank bag?"

"Aw, and my mouth was watering for one of those cookies," he said, playing along. He unzipped the bag and I quickly slid the book in first and put the treat bag on top. I looked into his eyes and found the reassurance for which I was looking. His body shielded the truth of the exchange from the bank lobby and as long as this morning seemed, when he partially zipped the bank bag, revealing only the orange and black cellophane of his goodies, I knew this part of the ordeal was over.

He reached down and kissed me fondly on the cheek. He squeezed my forearm and said simply, "Thank you! I will see you tomorrow, my dear. Stay safe from the ghouls and ghosts until then, ok?"

I breathed out another heavy sigh, "I will, and Jack, you too."

"You know I will," he said and then looked at his watch. "I've got to go. Bye, Rita."

"Bye, Jack," I said with a smile on my face, but I felt tears trying to well up in my eyes. He shook them away with another squeeze on my arm then turned and walked away with his cool, casual and unhurried gait. I watched him all the way through the lobby, through the doors and out to his tow truck.

I turned around, closed my eyes and took several deep cleansing breaths. I looked at the clock. This day was in slow motion, in some kind of unbelievable time warp. The exchange of the disk meant employees at this bank, long-time co-workers of mine would be going to jail, and their families would be destroyed. The exchange of the disk also meant the network of collusion, crime would be dismantled, the bank would be rid of its criminal element and justice would be served for Spencer, for Ivey and especially for Patrick. It was 10:40. The entire exchange had taken less than 10 minutes.

Chapter 120

Behind the locked door of his office, he closed his eyes. He was falling to pieces. He felt like he was going to cry. He slid down the wall of his office into a heap on the floor.

Rita was as much of a wreck as he was this morning. She was too talkative, too nervous. She had a secret. She was hiding something.

He had to think—think! His hands were shaking. His breathing was ragged. His chest hurt. Maybe he was having a heart attack.

He lay back flat on the floor, opened his eyes and stared at the blank, white ceiling above him. He breathed methodically in and out. Reason slowly returned, and he admitted what he knew.

Rita had found the disk. All attempts made to prevent that very discovery from happening had failed.

He rose slowly to his feet, went to his desk, sat down and picked up the receiver of the telephone. He made calls, one after another. His message to each was simple, "The disk has been found. You are on your own." He was oddly calm now.

He would deal with this fiasco himself. He would take charge of his own fate. He knew he had to destroy all the evidence against him. He had to get rid of both the information and the possessor. Simply put, he had to get rid of that disk. He had to get rid of Rita Miller.

Chapter 121

Less than two hours after Jack Grissett delivered the original disk to Ross's FBI field manager at the Brunswick County Sheriff's Office in the county seat of Bolivia, NC, the law enforcement collaborative of the Shallotte Police Department, the Brunswick County Sheriff's Department, the SBI and the FBI marveled at the vastness of the collusion at American One. In the estimation of every man and woman present, the sophistication, the depth and the duration of the fraud was unprecedented. Furthermore, the network ran the gamut from fraudulent loans to huge overdraft losses to phony expense reports to kickbacks from paid invoices for work never performed. The participants were bank officers, department heads, hourly front line employees, vendors and customers. They were fathers, grandfathers, sons, daughters, mothers and grandmothers. They were church deacons, community volunteers, and civic club members. The sheer numbers of people involved, of dollars involved was mind-boggling—15 people who had bilked the bank out of over $15 million dollars over at least the last 15 years. And those were just the numbers they had documented so far.

Law enforcement teams were assembled, and plans for arrest were devised after further consultation with the detectives who brought the forensic evidence to ensure today's arrests would lead to convictions in the courtrooms. The teams would waste no time.

Arrests of the banker thieves would start immediately after the bank's Friday closing time of 6 p.m. By 6:15, most of the culprits would be in custody. To prevent any of the participants from leaving early and possibly escaping arrest, the president of the bank—Ross Moore—was calling a mandatory conference call at 5:45 p.m. for management and department heads at American One. By 5:00, law enforcement would be in place to arrest anybody involved who went home early as soon as they walked outside of the bank. All of the people identified on the disk and implicated in the fraud were working today and if they somehow missed apprehension at the bank, procedures were in place to make arrests at their homes.

Assignments were also made for the arrests of those involved externally. They too were verified to be in the Shallotte area and were being located and rounded up.

Today was the day to put the plan into motion. Today was the day the fraudulent network would finally be dismantled. Today was the day of reckoning.

Chapter 122

At 3:30, I decided I had had enough fun for one day and I was calling it quits. I shut down the computer, grabbed my purse and turned out the lights. I never left early on Fridays, but today, I was making an exception. Besides, I had permission from the president of the bank.

I walked over to Greg's office and knocked on the door, he answered, "Come in."

I opened the door and he looked up, seemingly surprised to see me. I told him, "I'm going home. It has been a hell of a week. I'm tired and Spencer is coming home tonight around 6. Are you coming to the Halloween party tomorrow night?"

He smiled and answered, "Probably not. We'll probably stay at home for the trick-or-treaters. I guess you didn't get the e-mail about the conference call then?"

My heart sank. "What conference call?" I asked. "I was working on loan spreadsheets all afternoon, and I didn't check my e-mail. Not very smart, huh?"

"It's ok, Rita, you're tired. Executive Management has scheduled a conference call for 5:45 this afternoon," he said then added, "They are probably going to make some announcement about an acquisition or something. Go on home. I can fill you in on the details later. Have a good weekend and Happy Halloween."

"You too, Greg," I said, relieved, "And thank you. You're the best."

I left his office and went around to the teller line to tell Angie I was leaving. Finally, I got out of the door around 4 p.m. and got in my car. I put back the top, popped in my new Eagles CD and put on my sunglasses. Then, I pulled out of the parking lot to go home. The sky was bright blue with only a handful of small cirrus clouds creeping in from the west and I knew that the weather for the party tomorrow night was going to be fantastic. I looked over at my gypsy costume and smiled. I was excited about seeing Ross, having Spencer back home and Ivey's arrival. I could hardly wait.

I drove down Main Street and turned left on highway 179 to go home. I looked down at my gas gauge. I was almost on empty. I pulled into the Scotchman, turned off the car and got out to fill up my car's tiny gas tank. I also knew I had not purchased the first bag of candy for tomorrow night so I went inside to purchase several bags and pay for my gasoline.

When I came out of the store, a huge black SUV was parked opposite of my car on the near side of the pump. The sight was almost comical. The obscenely large vehicle dwarfed my little white car and I chuckled at why anyone would need something that big. Overcompensation, I guessed. God, the gas alone would bankrupt me.

I looked down to pull my keys out of my purse and walked around the front of the monstrosity to get to my driver's side door next to the pump. As I looked up to open my door, a massive human paw grabbed my arm and I looked up, shocked by the contact.

Fear and repulsion quickly replaced my shock. Ricky Jarman stood in front of me, his arm preventing me from getting into my car. I covered my fear with irritation. "What is your problem, Ricky?" I asked, exasperated and tried to pull my arm away.

"I don't have a problem, Rita. You do," he said, and he pulled me by the arm toward the SUV.

I think I screamed and I tried with all my might to kick the crap out of his shins and hit him with my free hand in his fat face, but in my frantic attempt to fend him off and free myself, I didn't hear, didn't see the person behind me. A cloth covered my mouth and nose, muffling my cries. I immediately felt dizzy, sleepy. My Miata began to fade from my sight and then, the whole world went dark.

Chapter 123

Ross arrived at the command center in Brunswick County at about 3 p.m. on Friday. It had been a crazy day ever since he answered Rita's phone call this morning before 8 a.m. He had called Jack Grissett and told him about Rita's discovery of the disk and asked him to retrieve it around 10:30 a.m. and deliver it to Weston Carter at the county complex. Then, Ross had contacted Weston, the head of the Shallotte team collaborative, and let him know that Jack would be delivering the disk before lunchtime to him personally.

Weston Carter was a Special Agent in the Coastal District for the SBI, and he was trustworthy and diligent. He had worked to develop relationships and ties in Brunswick County for years on a mission to bring down the Jarman family. Every time he got close to a breakthrough, though, his efforts were somehow thwarted and he never was been able to implicate them in anything due to lack of evidence, missing evidence, and dead ends. Weston knew they had help from somewhere, but never could pinpoint the source until he met and began a discussion at a state banking commission conference in Raleigh, NC with one of the bankers at American One. After cultivating the meeting into a friendship, Weston later hired the banker as a special agent to work on the inside of the bank after he finally got the blessing of the North Carolina Banking Commissioner. Together, they had slowly been building a solid case piece by piece for several years.

When the FBI got into the investigation, Weston could have been indignant or territorial, but he wasn't. He wanted to take down the Jarman cartel of redneck criminals so badly, he simply asked what he could do and how he could help.

Ross had taken an immediate liking to him and while the FBI was clearly at the helm now, he tapped Weston to coordinate the efforts in Shallotte. The move gained Ross instant respect from Weston and helped foster credibility from the rest of the agents at both the state agency and the Brunswick Sheriff's Department. With Weston leading the local effort, Ross also didn't have to wonder who to trust or how to establish communication with the former banker informant, now embedded agent, inside the bank.

After hanging up the phone with Weston, he phoned his parents to let them know he would be in Shallotte today, but he couldn't tell them what time or if he would be arriving at their house. He asked his dad to meet him in the parking lot of West Brunswick High School at 2:30 to pick up Jinx. He asked his mother not to say anything about his arrival to anybody, especially

Rita if she called. He could feel his mother's disapproval even though she didn't say a word.

Finally, he called the CEO of American One to update him and let him know that the criminal enterprise was on its way to being shut down. The CEO, Will McAdams, had contacted the FBI and Ross almost a year ago about some inconsistencies in the Shallotte office and agreed to allow Ross to come in undercover as the president of the North Carolina Bank. All of their hard work was going to pay off today, Ross thought. He hung up the telephone and sent an e-mail that called a mandatory management meeting at 5:45 p.m. to ensure that all the culprits were in their offices to more easily be located by the agents when the trigger was pulled. At 11:20, Ross left Charlotte for Shallotte.

Due to the highly sensitive nature of the investigation at the bank and the fact that the extent of the problem and the people involved were unknown, only McAdams as CEO, Ross as president, the FBI, the state banking commissioner and accordingly, the SBI and investigation team of local agents knew that Ross's bank position was a cover for his true profession at the bureau. The operation was top secret and accordingly, any leak could compromise the success of the investigation.

As soon as he got to the command center, Ross began having one-on-one meetings with each team leader to discuss strategy for the arrests, the processing of the suspects and their subsequent interrogation. Ross also reviewed each member of the team with the leader to discuss trust, history and role in the operation. After the leader meetings, the group would meet collectively in the conference room at 3:30 p.m.

After the final team meeting but before the commencement of the operation, only 10 people, including Ross, across three forces knew about the impending crook roundup. The other nine were above reproach. Even the deputies being pulled from the Brunswick County Sheriff's Department didn't know who or what they were targeting this evening. That information was being provided only to the team leaders.

Finally at 3:30, he convened the briefing and handed out final assignments for each stakeout and subsequent arrest plan. The team broke at 4 p.m. to go set up surveillance at their assignment points, and as they left the conference room, a message for Weston was taped to the door. The inside plant had called with an important message.

Weston showed Ross and he went immediately to the nearest phone to make contact. Ross was right beside him when he dialed the number. There was no answer. Weston looked up at Ross and shook his head. He called the main phone line at the Shallotte office and asked for the undercover agent/banker by name. Weston was told that banker had an emergency and had to leave suddenly. He hung up and told Ross.

Ross instinctively knew this information was bad news. The criminals were feeling the heat and were circling the wagons. He used his mobile phone that was forwarded from his office and called Shallotte Main and asked for Rita. He was told that she was gone for the day. He called her cell phone. Her voicemail immediately answered. Rita's phone was turned off.

He sighed deeply and told Weston. "I'm going to go check her condo," Ross said, his voice thick with concern, but he knew he had to focus on the overall operation right now. "You've got a band of brothers to arrest," he said. "Go get them, Special Agent Carter," he said respectively.

"Yes sir," Weston said, and then added, "She'll be alright, Ross."

Ross simply nodded then said, "I'll see you back here tonight."

Alone to collect his thoughts and grab his car keys, Ross felt his worry deepen. Not prone to either despair or panic, though, he remained calm and methodically thought through what he needed to do. He got into his undercover car and drove toward Shallotte. He called Spencer on her mobile.

She answered, "Hello, Mr. President." Spencer made him smile and he momentarily relaxed a little.

"Hello, Spencer. How's your noggin?" he asked.

"Never better, so don't be surprised tomorrow night when I'm all bandaged up again, okay? What's up?" she asked.

"Have you talked to Rita this afternoon? She's not answering her cell," he said lightly, masking his concern.

"No, I haven't," she said. "She's probably at the grocery store grabbing candy or up at Aurelia's store perfecting her costume. Ivey's on his way from Raleigh tonight to pick me up and take me home from Sing-Sing. We're supposed to meet Rita at her condo at 8:30," she finished.

Ross felt some relief after the conversation and he disconnected after telling Spencer he would see her tomorrow night. He turned off the highway onto Smith Avenue and then turned right onto Main Street in Shallotte. He slowly drove by the bank and the parking lot where, because of his trained eye, he saw one of his command teams moving into place for the impending arrests at the Shallotte Main office of American One.

He continued down Main Street past the old drugstore and crossed the Shallotte River and pulled into the turn lane to turn left onto highway 179. Suddenly, he saw a white Miata with the top back parked almost behind the convenience store on the corner. He turned in warily and parked beside the car and got out.

When he walked to the back, his heart sank. The tag read "RI'S MI." He walked around the car and looked inside and outside of the car. Rita's cell phone was on the driver's floor board. Two bags of Halloween candy in a bag from the convenience store appeared to have been thrown on the passenger seat.

Ross ran quickly into the store and tried to talk to the clerk who acted put out and didn't have time for questions. Ross grabbed his lapel and got his attention. Ross described Rita and told him about the candy she purchased. The clerk remembered her and said that she got gas and the candy about 45 minutes ago and left. The self-service pump was behind the attendant. He didn't see a thing.

Ross rushed out of the store. He was breathing heavy. He was worried, but worse, he was angry with himself. During the entire planning process for today's operation, Ross never once called Rita. Honestly, he didn't even pause to consider that she may still be a target, be in danger. Foolishly, he himself had told her to go home early, not even thinking about the fact that she would be alone and vulnerable.

Now, he had to figure out what to do. He looked at his watch. It was 4:45 p.m. Ross had one hour before the conference call. One hour before he would know who was on the call and who had left early. He called Jack Grissett, told him the situation and asked him to help. Jack was on his way over.

Ross took a deep breath and tried to calmly assess the situation. Rita had obviously been abducted and her fate was potentially in the hands of a killer. He didn't know who had her. He didn't know where she was. Rita was in trouble, and Ross didn't have a single clue where to begin.

Chapter 124

As they rode down Highway 130 East toward the Green Swamp, he reached into his pocket, casually pulled out his cell phone as if he was checking the time and activated the GPS. He had no idea where they were going, but at least now Weston could find him, find them.

He looked down at Rita slumped over against him. She was out cold. He hoped she stayed out for a while. This band of crooks was now fraying rapidly at the edges, increasingly desperate and more erratic by the minute.

He wondered what measures he might have to employ to protect Rita and his own identity and ensure their safety. Besides, there was only one of him against three of them. It had been a long time since he played the part of the good guy, the hero. He wondered if he was up to the task. He wondered if he would remember how. He wondered if he would survive today.

Chapter 125

At 5:30, Ross arrived back at the command center conference room to set-up the 5:45 conference call. The call would take only 15 minutes like he had promised in his e-mail. That was all the time he needed. He would begin by taking attendance at the North Carolina offices as they called in. Then he would ask each if everybody was in attendance. He would concentrate on the regional departments and regional headquarters in Wilmington and, of course, the main office in Shallotte. Fifteen bank employees would be arrested today along with the four Jarman brothers.

At 5:37, he called in as the conference administrator and waited for the participants to join into the call. The next few minutes felt like an eternity. Raleigh was the first to join. All but one officer was present and she was on vacation. Next, Asheville joined with all present. Winston-Salem chimed in with two out of place—one on maternity, the other sick with strep throat since Wednesday.

All the department heads were on the call. One by one, the 32 main offices joined until only Shallotte, Nags Head, and Greensboro remained. At 5:44, Shallotte and Greensboro joined almost simultaneously. Greensboro was all present. When Shallotte joined, though, only Tripp and Peter were on the call. Ross asked lightly, "Where is everybody?"

As Peter stuttered out that Greg, Dylan, Jeff and Rita were out of the office, the Nags Head office finally called in to connect with only one officer missing due to a planned vacation. Ross let the Shallotte situation go because he had the answer he needed.

He proceeded to discuss rising loan losses from the current economic slowdown and how the recession was putting pressure on the bank's profitability and capital. Ross detailed several new reports that would help the bank track borrowers under pressure and he urged all of the lenders—commercial, small business, retail and mortgage—to be proactive in recognizing the warning signs.

He announced that all loan production goals were being immediately suspended. This decision would allow the lenders and the offices to more importantly spend their time tracking borrowers who were past due in their payments, identifying and analyzing larger credits where the value of the collateral had been significantly diminished and working with builders and developers who were sitting on large amounts of real estate inventory who may need to slash prices to move the lots and houses.

On the deposit side of the bank, Ross discussed the new strategy to retain only checking accounts, savings accounts and certificates of deposit where the owner had either a checking account or loan relationship with the bank. Effectively, the bank was no longer going to pay higher interest for hot money that moved in and out depending on which bank had the highest return. These depositors had no loyalty to American One. The funds were costly and put pressure on the bank's profit margin. The bank would let them go elsewhere as these funds matured.

He wrapped up the call by telling the participants that supporting documentation would follow in the coming week. Ross also told them that if they were thinking that the bank was effectively shrinking the balance sheet, they were correct. The bank was simply putting the loans under pressure on the front burner and keeping only the inexpensive deposits in place to match those loans.

At 5:58, Ross asked if there were any questions. Susan Gillings from Hillsborough asked if the deposit goals were still in effect. Ross clarified that checking, savings and money market goals were still in place but that certificates of deposit and overall deposit growth goals were effectively eliminated.

With no other questions, Ross wished the callers a Happy Halloween and told them to have a great weekend. Then, he disconnected the call and immediately went to work to figure out where Dylan, Jeff, and Greg were and what they had done with Rita.

He called Weston on his secure phone line. Ross told him that Jeff, Greg and Dylan were not on the call and that Rita had been abducted. Ross told him that Jack Grissett had taken Rita's car to his lot for them to pore over later. He heard Weston sigh. Ross knew the sigh meant more bad news.

Weston's team assignment was to arrest the Jarman boys. Roger, Ronnie and Robert were in custody. "Ricky is missing though, Ross," he said. "It can't be a coincidence that he is MIA along with the rest of those guys."

Ross agreed, "No, I'm sure it isn't."

"Well, I do have some good news for you, Ross," he added. "Our mole has activated his GPS. He's heading east toward Whiteville as we speak."

Ross felt a glimmer of hope. "May I join you?" he asked.

"You bet," Weston said. "Meet me at the corner store in Ash in 15."

"I'm on my way," Ross said and he hung up the phone, grabbed his keys and made like lightning to his car.

Hold on baby, he said to himself as he thought about Rita. *Help is on the way.*

Chapter 126

Outside his huge, tinted office window, he saw his impending demise slowly unfold and spring into action. George looked at his watch. The time was 6:03 p.m. There was a contingent of armed officers heading for the back door of the bank. They were coming for him.

He casually walked over to his credenza and pulled out the bottle of scotch he kept there. He took out a glass, walked over to the ice maker beside the sink and poured himself a stiff drink.

He had had a great run. He had lived high on the hog. It was a pure shame he would never get to enjoy retirement in some ways, but in the end, he was somewhat relieved that he didn't have to watch his influence wane year after year until he became the pathetic old fart that tried to throw his weight around just to get noticed and be heard. No, George Everett was going out on top.

He heard the commotion in the lobby. He walked over to his desk. He sat down, finished his scotch and opened the bottom left drawer.

He smiled one last smile as he lifted the revolver to his head and pulled the trigger just as the agents burst through the door. George Everett's final conscious thought of victory was sprayed all over the windows behind him along with the rest of his brain.

Chapter 127

Most of the arrests happened as planned with no fight or fanfare. At the Shallotte Main Office, Peter and Tripp were handcuffed as they walked to their cars two minutes after the end of the conference call. The only surprise among the team of agents was that it took the pair that long to leave on a Friday afternoon.

Angie Potts was truly shocked by her arrest as she left the bank at 6:15 with the rest of the tellers. She began to cry inconsolably as the agents half walked and half carried her to the squad car hidden behind the auto parts store next door. The rest of the tellers watched the spectacle with sadness until Angie was out of sight then they disbursed quickly, ready to begin their weekend.

Elsewhere in Wilmington, John Starr was apprehended trying to flee through the basement exit at the bank with his laptop in tow. He was taken into custody by none other than his former colleagues at the SBI, a fitting end for his abandonment of the ideals and principles that the agency held dear.

Over at the operations center on 23rd Street, the regional auditor, Chip Hunt, the regional general ledger accounting manager, Phyllis Eury, and the head of the loan processing department, Ella Massey, were arrested too. All three spouted hysterically about how they were innocent, that there was some kind of mistake as they were hauled away in handcuffs through the departments over which they had presided for years.

Kelly Patterson, the regional facilities manager, was arrested at home just as he was sitting down to dinner with his girlfriend while his wife and three children were away on vacation in Charleston, SC. He didn't fight at all. He told his girlfriend to go home and call his attorney to meet him in Bolivia. He handed her his card then put his hands behind his back to be cuffed.

By 6:15, the government center in Bolivia was a busy place. Most of the participants were charged with crimes under federal law. They were interrogated and booked locally but would then be sent over to Wilmington for a hearing at the federal courthouse on Monday morning. Some of the participants were released after posting bond while others were denied bail because they posed a flight risk.

All in all, eleven of the participants were in custody, the kingpin was dead from a self-inflicted gunshot and three other suspects were still at large. The government center took on almost a festival-like atmosphere as the media from the area arrived in force, waiting for a salacious sound bite, a flashy headline that somebody important was either indicted or dead.

For now, though, the county public relations manager stonewalled them well enough to keep them at bay, but encouraged them enough to keep them from leaving. As soon as the ongoing operation was complete, a press conference would be held. Stay tuned, folks.

Chapter 128

I felt like I had been sleeping off a three-day drunk. My head felt heavy, my eyelids were operating in slow motion. I felt so tired and I was completely disoriented.

Where the hell was I? What was going on here? I shook my head slowly and tried to regain some measure of coordination. It was dark in here—wherever "here" was. My eyes didn't need long to adjust to the dim shadows surrounding me.

"Wake up, sleepyhead," a voice whispered in my ear, moving the hair over my ear with each syllable of breath.

I suddenly felt sick and leaned forward to quell the tremors inside my gut. I was in a chair. I was tied to it, my hands behind me. The realization of my situation then gained some clarity as the scene at the convenience store replayed in my foggy mind.

I was a hostage, abducted in broad daylight at the gas station in Shallotte by Ricky Jarman. When I connected the voice in my ear with his name, I felt the nausea begin anew. I leaned over again, sure I was going to be sick.

Then, I felt my head being pulled backwards by my hair and right in front of my face was Ricky's pudgy face and sour breath. I gasped for breath and turned my head to wrestle my head free. He laughed and I leaned over again and promptly threw up on his shoes.

Being sick had never been so wonderful. He jumped back and yelled, "You stupid bitch."

I sat up and smiled at him. "Glad to oblige, you bastard," I said.

He slapped me across the mouth with the back of his hand, and I tasted the blood at the corner of my mouth even before I felt the searing pain that followed.

Jeff Malone stepped forward and said, "What the hell is your problem, man?" Jeff leaned down and dabbed at the corner of my mouth with a cloth. I looked him straight in the eye. He didn't look away and instead matched my gaze with his piercing, dark eyes.

I was also fully awake and aware now of my surroundings. I looked up to my left. Greg Hardy was pacing the floor, back and forth, back and forth. He looked disheveled, nervous, and just a little crazy. I sighed and felt completely deflated. I didn't want Greg to be involved, but he obviously was.

To my right leaned against a post was Dylan Fordham. He was cool, detached, and still. He looked as if he was waiting on a friend to bring him another beer from the bar. He stepped forward from the shadow shielding his face. He was almost smirking. I wanted to slap the crap out of him. I glared up at him. "I'd say I was surprised to see you, but I'm not a liar, Dylan," I almost spat out.

He chuckled and said, "I'm happy to see you too, darling." I thought I'd gag again. He stepped a little closer and leaned down as if we were going to have a personal conversation. All of the humor and sarcasm left him, though, and I saw his face grow serious before he asked, "Where is it, Rita?"

I looked at him defiantly and paused for effect then slowly enunciated each word of my reply, "I don't have it anymore." Then I smiled and shook my hair back over my shoulder.

Greg quickly came forward, completely out of control and almost yelled, "Where is it? Where is it?" and he grabbed both of my arms with such pressure I could almost feel the bruises forming under my skin.

He was like a wild animal with jerky, uneven movements, his eyes darting from one object to another and I felt sorry for him and a little afraid of him at the same time. I looked up at him, almost tenderly, and softly said, "I gave it to the authorities this morning at 10:30."

He jumped back like he had been stung, betrayed and began pacing again and repeating, "Oh, God" over and over. Dylan looked over at him with disgust.

"Get a grip on yourself right now, Greg," he snapped, and then he turned his attention back to me. "You made a foolish choice, Rita, a very foolish choice," he reiterated.

"As opposed to giving the information to you," I said and looked him in the eye, "Or you, or you?" I asked, looking at first at Jeff then over at Greg. "Right…" and I shook my head for impact.

Dylan stepped forward over me and grabbed my hair and yanked my head straight back as he stood over me. A calm, but pure evil visage peered down at me. "Guess what? You are useless to me now and that's a shame. Sweet little piece of ass like you…" and he reached up and roughly traced my chin with his finger.

I turned my head away in disgust. I had a plethora of wonderful retorts to his dream, but I realized there was no need to bait him. Instead, I urged them to just flee while there was time. "Look, you just said you didn't need me, so just go. Slink off to Columbia, Lebanon or Abu Dhabi while you still can," I stated.

"Maybe she's got a point," Jeff commented.

"That's exactly what the authorities are waiting for us to do, man," Ricky said. "You know damn well those guys have every inlet, marina and transit dock on alert in addition to airports all over the east coast. They're not stupid."

"Bunch of wusses," I mumbled under my breath. The comment was not lost on Dylan, though, and he turned on me suddenly and hit me with such force across the side of my face that not only did I see a flash of light followed by a galaxy stars, but I also slid completely off the chair suspended above the floor by my bound hands. My face throbbed, my wrists burned and for the first time since I regained consciousness, I wasn't certain I was leaving this place alive.

Chapter 129

It was almost completely dark by the time Ross arrived in Ash to meet Weston and his 5-man team of agents and officers. When he got out of the car and walked over to them, he saw an aerial map of the Green Swamp spread out under the lights of the gas canopy on top of the hood of a state trooper's car.

As he looked at the map, a red circle marked a heavily wooded area about halfway between Ash and Old Dock down near the Waccamaw River. A clumsy, old wooden building sat on the edge of the east bank of the river. Ross looked up at Weston, silently asking him if he believed Rita was there. Weston simply nodded.

An old army truck was parked on the edge of the road beside the store. The agents had all been supplied with camouflage, were dressed and awaiting the word to go. Ross and Weston huddled and planned to enter the road as quietly as possible, block access just out of sight of the hunting lodge and surround the building. Depending on the layout of the lodge, they could enter through the back and front simultaneously or pop tear gas through one of the windows and flush out the occupants. There were risks either way. Ross and Weston agreed that they would better assess the risks once they were on sight. They were wasting valuable time.

At 6:15, they piled into the truck and made their way east on highway 130 for about eight miles until they saw the old logging road off to the left. Weston was driving since he was much more familiar with this part of the county and as he made the turn off of the highway and onto the narrow, overgrown road, he turned off the lights.

They drove slowly down the barely discernable path, their eyes adjusting to the dark as they traveled toward their destination. They were focused on reaching the end of the road and making the final arrests of this operation. The end of the road seemed both near and far at the same time. Neither spoke a word. They left each other to the hopes and doubts that filled their minds. The reality of the situation was simple. Tonight could end poorly or end well or it could end a hundred ways in between.

Chapter 130

Dylan's violent treatment of me startled Greg and made Jeff angry. I could tell Greg wanted to help me, but he was too immobilized by fear to move. Jeff, on the other hand, came over, quickly turned Dylan around and punched him squarely in the nose. Dylan dropped to the floor in a heap. Jeff stood glowering over him and said, "Didn't your mother teach you not to hit a woman? You spineless pussy—she's tied up too. You and Ricky better keep your damn hands off of her. Understand?"

He turned back toward me and winced when he saw my face. He grabbed a beer from the cooler and wrapped it in a towel and put it against my face. I'm sure I looked like Rocky Balboa by now. "Skip the chivalry, Jeff," I said then added, "Saving yourself from a second murder conviction won't help when you get the needle for Patrick's murder. It only takes one of those to do the trick," I said.

"No, that was the brilliant work of Greg and Dylan here," he said sarcastically and motioned with his head toward the two. "They couldn't even wait long enough to give Ricky time to call some of his buddies in Shallotte to pull Patrick over for DWI. They just got lucky the blow to his head from the drop of the bridge was fatal."

"Shut-up, Jeff," Greg warned. "You were just too gutless to do anything. The idea of being somebody's bitch in the federal pen must be a lot more appealing to you than the rest of us."

"No, I don't intend to be caught," Jeff said.

"What, are you just going to flap your wings and fly away, little bluebird," Dylan said smartly.

"No, I'm walking out of here, then going over to see a friend who is going to take me to the airstrip in Whiteville where we will be flying in his Cessna to a private airstrip in Florida. Then, I am catching a yacht over to Freeport then onto the DR," Jeff said. "Did you guys think I was going to wait on you to come up with a plan for me? Get real."

Nobody could call Jeff Malone stupid or unprepared and I could feel the tension in the room building. Ricky was getting nervous, Greg was completely unhinged and the normally unflappable Dylan was in shock that he hadn't devised a clever plan like Jeff. Quite obviously, he didn't have a plan at all.

Jeff pulled his cell phone out of his pocket and looked at the time. It was 6:15. He put the phone back into his pocket, sighed and began walking toward the door.

"You can't just leave us here," Greg cried and he ran over to Jeff and grabbed his arm. "Please take me with you, Jeff, please."

"No, Greg," Jeff answered simply.

"Let him go, Greg," Dylan said. "If he doesn't get eaten by a gator or a bear, he'll probably starve to death when he gets lost in the Green Swamp."

Ricky laughed and added, "Yeah, that's a hell of a way to go."

Jeff looked at me and for a second, I thought I saw him waver in his decision to leave. He said, "Goodbye, Rita. You're a class act," and he grabbed the front door knob to go.

Without any warning, Greg completely snapped and screamed, "No! No!" and suddenly everything seemed to happen in slow motion. Greg had a gun in his hand, it went off randomly and Dylan and Ricky dove for cover. Jeff came running toward me and pushed me to the floor, cradling my head in his free hand as my chair of captivity fell to the floor.

Wide-eyed and scared, he had a gun in his hand as well. Jeff whispered, "Everything is going to be okay. The authorities are on their way."

Greg was walking around shooting the pistol at random. Dylan yelled to him, "Put the gun down you maniac!" Greg turned, raised his pistol again and shot Dylan Fordham in the forehead, killing him instantly.

I screamed, and Ricky broke for the door. He tore it open and ran outside, and found himself instead staring right into the barrel of the AK-47 in the hands of a federal agent.

Greg was weeping now and my heart hurt listening to him. His cries were filled with profound sadness, regret, and loss. I felt a tear fall down my cheek and I wasn't sure I could bear the sounds much longer. Jeff untied my hands and told me to stay put.

I watched him, confused as to what he was doing and what his role in this madness was, but I nodded my head. He stood up and called out to Greg. "Ok Greg," Jeff said calmly, "It's just you and me now. What do you want to do? Do you want to go with me? Or do you want me to go and leave you here alone?"

Greg didn't answer, he just continued sobbing and repeating, "I'm sorry, I'm sorry…Oh, my family, my children. I'm so sorry."

Jeff tried again, "Come on, Greg, let's get out of here. We can follow my plan then you can send for your family when we get to the Dominican, ok?"

That line of reasoning seemed to reach Greg momentarily and he raised his head from his hands, considered it and began to melt down all over again. He stood, raised the gun toward Jeff, and pulled the trigger. The sound of the gunshot rang in my ears, and I felt rather than heard myself scream as he fell backward. Greg walked toward me and I began crying uncontrollably then. I was crying for him, with him, and because of him. I was crying for the loss of him.

I looked up at him, and he was completely vacant. Greg was gone, and I knew I was too. He raised the gun toward me and I shook my head, crying loudly, and closed my eyes. The gunshot rang out and I felt myself scream again. I fell backwards, but I felt no pain.

Commotion ensued and I slowly opened my eyes and touched my trembling hands. I was alive. I had not been shot. I looked around confused. Men in camouflage had appeared out of nowhere and were seemingly everywhere. The smell of gunpowder filled the cabin.

Greg Hardy lay dead on the floor in front of me. Jeff Malone reached over from beside me and weakly squeezed my arm. Stunned he was still alive, I scrambled over to him. He was shot in the right shoulder, and he had lost a lot of blood. He just held onto my arm and said, "Good, good."

I began to cry again and I felt myself nearing hysteria. I recognized I was in shock, but I was powerless to ask for help or even to move. I looked around and Ross was in the cabin. I knew I had to be hallucinating. I must have fainted because the next thing I knew I was in an ambulance. I had no idea how I got there or how much time elapsed in between. Ross was right beside me. I could see him. I reached out and touched his arm. He was real.

He smiled and I looked at him confused. How did he get here? He put his finger to my lips then reached down and kissed my cheek. He got out of the ambulance and the EMTs shut the door. They gave me a sedative and I succumbed to the chemically-induced relaxation. A blanket of darkness covered me slowly and softly, and I slipped under to a place that was warm, black and welcoming.

Chapter 131

Ross called Jack Grissett from the crime scene in Ash and told him as calmly, quickly and succinctly as possible what had happened, and he asked Jack to personally go to Spencer's condominium to tell Spencer and Ivey what had happened and to meet Rita at the hospital. Ross could hear in the silence after he stopped talking that Jack was deeply concerned about Rita and that he would not be satisfied that she was safe until he got to the hospital to check on her for himself.

The depth of love that Rita shared with her unlikely and diverse cadre of friends was amazing to Ross. They were fiercely loyal, wildly protective, and brutally honest. They shared not only a genuine love for each other, but a deep respect as well. Having known Jack Grissett practically his whole life, Ross knew he didn't give that respect without it being earned.

After Jeff Malone and Rita were transported by ambulance from the gruesome scene to the Brunswick County Hospital, the county coroner arrived and pronounced Dylan Fordham and Greg Hardy dead. Their bodies were being transported to the county morgue. Their families were being notified by the Brunswick County Sheriff's Department. Ricky Jarman was on his way to the command center to be interrogated, formally charged and booked. He was already singing like a canary, but little would save him from prison at this point.

Ross looked around the tiny hunting cabin that was now a crime scene. The place was a mess. Blood was everywhere and the air in the cabin was suffocating from a mixture of dust and mustiness, gun smoke and death.

The investigators documented and photographed every inch of the cabin and the huge black SUV parked outside. Ross talked to the agents investigating and got a timeline for their reports and findings. He walked outside and found Weston.

Weston was talking to the coroner beside the ambulance when Ross walked over to them. Ross listened to the coroner's initial findings and they certainly reinforced what Ricky Jarman said. Greg Hardy had apparently had a psychotic break. He had shot and killed Dylan Fordham, then shot Jeff Malone, intending to kill him as well. Finally, as he was preparing to shoot Rita, Greg himself was shot and killed by one of the team of agents who stormed the cabin.

When the last of the agents and investigators had left the scene, Weston and Ross jumped back into the front of the army truck and rode back to the Ash convenience store. They got into Ross's undercover cruiser and rode back to Bolivia to the command center. They rode in silence as each took the necessary time to process what had just happened and the aftermath of the events.

Ross was glad the massive collusion scheme had been dismantled. He was glad to give Will McAdams, the CEO of American One, his bank back. More than anything, though, he was glad Rita was safe from harm. He breathed a huge, audible sigh of relief and he looked over to see if Weston had heard him. Weston met his gaze and said quietly, "It's over, Ross. Rita's going to be ok."

"I know," Ross replied, worry creasing his forehead. "I know," he said again and breathed another heavy sigh.

They turned into the government complex and pulled around the back of the sheriff's department and went inside. The whole department was busy, but it was no longer electric, excited, or energetic. Instead, the atmosphere was serious, subdued, almost sad as the collective team of local, state and federal agents attempted to digest the events that had transpired in and around Shallotte, NC and logically explain them in writing.

What had begun years ago with an agreement between a corrupt banker and a crooked borrower—Ron Jarman, the father of the four Jarman criminals that were now locked up in the county jail—ended with four dead bankers, two more at the hospital and fifteen people in custody. Thank goodness two of the three survivors from the scene of the madness in Ash were innocent. The fact is that both Rita and Jeff were lucky to be alive.

Weston looked at the clock on the wall. It was almost 10 p.m. and well past visiting hours at the hospital. He knew the time wouldn't stop his boss and friend from checking in on the woman he loved at the hospital. He reached over and put his hand on top of Ross's shoulder and said, "We've got the situation under control here. Why don't you go check on Jeff Malone and Rita Miller before you go get some sleep? You look like a zombie and it's not even Halloween yet, Ross," he said.

"You know, Weston, I think that's exactly what I'm going to do. I'll see you tomorrow morning," Ross replied and he turned to get his coat and go. As he walked toward the door, he turned around and said, "Thanks, Weston, really…"

Weston threw his hand up, smiled slightly and said, "Go—I'll see you tomorrow," and Ross returned the gesture and walked out the door.

He got into his SUV and drove in silence to the hospital. It was a long three miles. His thoughts raced as he drove. What would he say to Rita? How would he explain everything? Would she understand? Would she forgive his secrecy? The doubts and fears that had been building inside him for the last several months now threatened to overwhelm and consume him.

Ross knew he would stop at nothing to preserve his relationship with Rita, and tonight could certainly determine how difficult or easy that task was going to be. He had secretly involved her in a federal investigation and let her get pulled into the criminal enterprise onto which she had accidentally stumbled. Her honesty had pulled her into the whole sordid affair when Patrick recognized that she above everybody, really anybody else, could be trusted. Her honesty had almost gotten her killed today too.

He took a deep breath after he parked at the hospital and turned off the car. For just a few seconds he sat in the car trying to collect himself and his thoughts. God, he needed her, he wanted her, and most of all he loved her. Ross needed to tell her, but he hoped that he had not come to those realizations too late to matter.

Ross admitted Rita Miller was much more to him than a lover or a girlfriend. She was his soul mate. She was his future.

Chapter 132

Spencer paced back and forth in the hospital waiting room trying to make sense of what Jack Grissett had told her. Greg was dead. Dylan was dead. George was dead. Jeff had been shot and Rita would have been shot had Greg not been shot first. Eleven more of her colleagues and the four Jarman brothers were all in the custody of law enforcement. They weren't in some damn crazy Hollywood action film; they were in Shallotte, NC.

Maybe her head was still screwed up because she didn't feel like crying, she felt like punching somebody. She stopped pacing momentarily and looked over at Ivey and Jack. They were huddled together talking quietly. Ivey saw Spencer stop pacing and looked up at her. He got up and went over to her.

"Are you ok?" he asked and reached out and took her hand in his.

"I don't know," she said honestly. "The whole world has gone crazy. I mean, Greg shot and killed Dylan. He almost killed Jeff and was going to kill Rita too. I…just don't get it."

Ivey could hear the fear and the shock in Spencer's voice. She seemed to be on the verge of depression. The loss of Rita and seemingly even Jeff would have sent her reeling. Depression was manageable. Destruction was not.

"Hey," he said quietly, concerned, "We survived this fiasco, okay? You, me, Rita and Jeff—we've got to be strong for our bank, for Shallotte, because we're all the management Ross Moore and Mega has left."

Spencer considered his words carefully and she realized he was right. She was a survivor of this crazy ordeal along with her best friends and Jeff. She wasn't sure how she would label her relationship with him. She wasn't sure who he was, what he was or how he was involved in this madness, but she sure was going to find out.

She wanted to see Rita. She wanted to see Jeff too, but she wasn't as sure what to say to him. What was taking so long anyway, she wondered? She looked over Ivey's shoulder toward the nurse's station. Ivey knew she was not going to be put off any longer.

Jack saw Spencer's resolve as well and he was already up ahead of her running interference with nurse Lydia. Spencer would not be easily stopped if she was determined to find Rita. Spencer followed Jack out of the waiting room and as she turned the corner, she ran right into Ross.

She was both surprised and relieved he was here. She knew with everything that had happened at the bank today, he had not stopped since he had the conference call this afternoon. His bank in Shallotte was currently in shambles with numerous officers detained for bank collusion and several others shot dead. His girlfriend was in the hospital and Jeff Malone was injured. She sure was glad she was not the bank president.

"Hey Mr. President," she said kindly and hugged his neck. After all, she reasoned, he was her best friend's boyfriend. That relationship meant they were almost kin as far as she was concerned.

"Hey yourself, Spencer," he said and smiled warmly as he looked at her at arm's length. Satisfied that she was really almost mended, Ross believed she could now care for Rita as Rita had cared for her when she was here only a week ago. God, last week seemed like ages ago now.

Ivey walked over to Ross and shook his hand. Ivey looked him in the eye and found reassurance that everything was going to be okay. He saw in Ross a confidence that the bank and his employees would weather this madness. The strength of Ross's resolve was evident in the things he said and did and it overshadowed the fatigue he carried from this hellish day. After everything that had happened at the bank today, Ross cared enough for Rita, for all of them really, to come here to console them, support them, and just check on them. He was here in many roles tonight—leader, friend, president and lover. Ivey's admiration for the man continued to grow.

Ross asked them if they had seen Rita since she arrived.

"No, I haven't seen her yet," Spencer said and as she looked at him in the light of the hallway, he looked worn to a frazzle. "You look like hell, Mister," she added.

"I know," he answered. "I wanted to come by and see Rita before I went to Mom and Dad's to get some sleep. I have another busy day tomorrow."

"God—I can't imagine," Spencer said. "Another in a long line of busy days, I'll bet."

"Oh, it won't be so bad," Ross reassured. "Mega has some great employees," he said fondly and winked at her. "Come on. Let's go find Rita."

She looped her left hand through Ross's arm and her right hand through Ivey's and they headed down the hall. Nurse Lydia and Jack Grissett stood at the end of the corridor waiting for them. As they approached, she just shook her head. "Y'all are becoming such regulars here I'm going to get you name tags," she said lightly. "Come on. Rita is back in the emergency area. I think we might release her and let her go home tonight," she added.

Almost in unison, they breathed a sigh of relief and they followed Lydia to the emergency area. As they walked, Spencer walked next to her and asked her softly, "Lydia, where is Jeff Malone? Is he in a room yet? Is he alone?"

Lydia reached over and squeezed her arm to assure her of his safety then she said, "He's just gotten out of surgery. He's in post-op and will be in a room shortly. Yes, he's alone right now, but I'm sure he'd be happy to have you there when he wakes up, Spencer."

Spencer felt tears sting her eyes and she simply nodded her head in thanks to Lydia because she knew if she spoke she might just completely break down. She fell back in step with Ivey and Ross and put her head down on Ivey's shoulder. Ivey pulled her close to him and kissed the top of her head. He knew the emotion he saw flaring in Spencer was a good thing. He would be sure to get her over to Jeff Malone's room as soon as he and Spencer were convinced that Rita was going to be alright.

"Ross," Ivey said, "If Rita is released tonight, will you take her home? I think Spencer is going to stay here with Jeff for a while and I am going to wait on her so I can drive her home."

"Of course," Ross answered, "I will take her home as long as you will check on her early tomorrow morning. She is certainly traumatized and will probably need some professional counseling, but nothing is going to help like you and Spencer just being there for her to sit and stare, talk and cry, scream and vent."

"Well, we'll certainly be there for her," Ivey said. "We always have been and always will be."

"I'm counting on it, Ivey," Ross said seriously. "Rita is going to have more doubts, more questions, and more pain in the days, weeks and months ahead as trials begin, funerals are held, and faces change around the bank. She may even want to take some time off from work. God knows, she's due."

Ivey had not really considered all of these aspects of Rita's recovery, but he realized Ross was right. They walked up to the door of Rita's room. Ivey looked in the window at his friend. She had a black eye and a swollen lip. He felt anger rise in him suddenly and he turned to Ross, ready to question what the hell had happened. Ross quickly pulled Ivey and Spencer back toward the wall beside the door. He momentarily forgot that they didn't know everything that had transpired at the cabin. He needed to tell Spencer and Ivey how bad the scene really was, prepare them for what they would see and what they might hear.

"Look, Rita has been badly beaten, and she has blood from Dylan and Jeff all over her. Both of them were shot within feet of where she was tied to a chair," he said seriously. Spencer put her hand to her mouth and tears spilled over onto her cheeks. "She is bruised around her wrists from the ropes, on her arms where she fell to the floor. She is also dirty from head to toe. The hunting lodge was filthy," he finished.

Spencer walked over to the window and looked at Rita. She was staring blankly into the black of the night through the tiny square window beside the bed. She was wrapped in a blanket. She was everything Ross just described and more. She looked haunted, vulnerable and spent. Spencer walked into the room without knocking. Rita turned stiffly, saw Spencer and patted the bed beside her. Spencer walked over, wrapped her arms around her and let tears of relief roll silently, but freely.

They had gotten through this nightmare together and they would close this chapter and move on together as well. Spencer felt strong and she knew she would be the shoulder on which Rita leaned first and most in the coming days and months.

Surprisingly, though, was the other feeling that filled her. Spencer may not have even recognized it had it not been so powerful, so sure. There was hope here. Hope for the future, and hope for today. Rita always said that hope was not a strategy, and most of the time she was right. In this case, though, hope was nothing more, but nothing less than a simple faith, a real possibility that tomorrow would be better. Right now, better was all they had, but better was achievable and tonight that was enough.

Chapter 133

When I saw Spencer walk in the door, I knew exactly how she felt, having been in her shoes just one week ago in this same emergency ward at this same hospital. I saw fear and relief cross her face and just like I was last week, Spencer was overcome by the sheer power of those emotions, helpless to stop her physiological response to them.

As much as I needed reassurance and comforting myself tonight, I felt much more inclined to reassure and comfort my best friends. After all, Spencer and Ivey were as much in the thick of the insanity of the criminal enterprise inside our bank as I was. Fortunately, both of them were one or two steps more removed from the catalyst of the network's demise than I was. They didn't possess the disk.

"I'm ready to go home," I said to break the silence, "But I'm still groggy or something. At one point, I swear Ross was right there in the cabin while all of the madness was unfolding."

Spencer pulled back and looked at me curiously then said, "Rita, he was there, and he is here right now waiting for Ivey, Jack and me to see you first. You weren't imagining him."

I stood shakily and went over to the window. I was glad he was here. I loved Ross Moore. He was the president of American One Bank. So what was the president of an $18 billion bank doing at the scene of a law enforcement sting? Something just didn't fit. I sighed and turned around to Spencer, choosing to let the questions churning inside me go unanswered for right now.

"So, have you been to see Jeff? He's my hero, you know," I said honestly. "Spencer, he saved my life."

"I knew he wasn't rotten to the core," she offered simply. I noticed tears welling up in her eyes and I walked over and rubbed her arm. "I haven't seen him yet. I don't know if he's in a room, he was still in surgery up until just a little while ago," she added, her voice shaking with every syllable.

"Is he going to be alright?" I asked.

"I hope so," Spencer said. "God, I hope so. You know I wished he was dead after that last night we were together," and I heard her sniffle softly. "Jack said he was involved in all this crap, but only because he had to be, whatever that means. I'm going to go visit with him in just a minute. Lydia said he doesn't have any family," she finished.

I gave her a hug and whispered, "Go—you sure aren't going to find the answers in here with me. All I have are questions at this point, Spence."

She nodded and replied, "And you don't need to have all of them answered tonight either. You need to just be thankful you're alive and for God's sake, get some rest." Then she stood, wiped her eyes and added, "Besides, we've got a Halloween Party tomorrow night. Life does go on after all. Ivey and I will come get you tomorrow morning for breakfast, but not early. How does 9 o'clock sound?"

"Sounds great," I said. "Now go to Jeff because he needs you right now more than I do. I have a whole entourage outside that door to see," I told her.

Spencer kissed my cheek and said, "I'm glad you're okay, Rocky...I mean, Rita. I don't know what I would do without you."

"I don't know what you'd do either," I said continuing to lighten the mood. "Now vamoose!" I added, and I pushed her toward the door.

When she got to the door, she turned again and almost whispered, "I'm scared, Rita."

"I know, Spence, but isn't Jeff Malone worth the risk of a broken heart?" I asked just as quietly.

She nodded her head and answered, "Yep, he is, but here's what scares me—what he did for you, Rita, was brave and wonderful and completely instinctive. What he'll have to do for me, though, is a whole lot harder, takes a whole lot longer and is damn sure almost as dangerous," and she sighed then added, "And I'm not sure anybody is that heroic," and with that remark, she pulled open the door and walked out into the hall.

CHAPTER 134

Ivey visited me next, but he didn't stay long. He told me I needed to scrap the gypsy outfit tomorrow night and go instead as the second place boxer in a heavyweight title bout. I hugged him and laughed. Only Ivey could tell me I looked like hell in such a caring, kind way.

He confirmed that he and Spencer would come over at 9 tomorrow morning to go grab breakfast, and he told me to get some rest. Then he said, "I'm going to let you off the hook tonight, but we're going to talk about this fiasco tomorrow, ok? You need to digest what happened, to understand the facts, and if you want, talk about how you feel about it all."

As he got up to go, he squeezed my hand then leaned over and kissed me on the cheek. "Jack is going to come in to see you next. Then Ross wants to drive you home. The hospital is processing your release right now," he said. "If the doctor gives you meds to sleep, take them and get some rest. You don't need to sort this craziness out alone or re-live it tonight. I'm sorry for what you've been through, Rita, and I wish like hell that I could have prevented it from happening—especially to you. You're one of my best friends and I love you. I'm glad you're going to be alright. I'll see you tomorrow morning," he said.

"I'll see you tomorrow morning and I love you too, John Michael," I replied and he squeezed my hand again, and turned to go.

As he opened the door, I looked into the hall, hoping to catch a glimpse of Ross. I didn't see him, and I wondered where he was. Before I could start down that thought path, though, Jack Grissett stuck his head in the door.

I smiled broadly and opened my arms wide for him to come give me a hug. He walked over and gently threw his arms around me. "That black skin around your eyes is turning me on, woman," he whispered in my ear, and I laughed. I loved this crazy fool, too.

"Jack, I'm so glad to see you," I said, and I squeezed his neck a little tighter.

"I'm glad to see you too, but I understand you had a close call. I'm sorry. I should have been there to protect you. I didn't know you were leaving early, Rita," he said.

"I don't think anything could have stopped them," I assured him.

"I damn sure tried," he replied softly.

"I know, and I can't tell you how much that means to me," I said.

"But you're my hero, baby," he answered, and he pulled away from the hug and sat down instead on the edge of the bed. Then he sighed and said, "I only have a few minutes before the man you were searching for in the hallway comes barging in your door."

I looked at him, surprised he caught me, but more surprised that he seemed to understand the depth of my yearning. I could hear it in his voice. "Is he waiting to see me?" I asked.

"Of course he is," Jack said. "He just stepped down the hall with Lydia to check on Jeff Malone's condition. He just came out of surgery."

"Oh," I said and I suddenly felt the urge to fire off dozens of questions to Jack about Ross. "Jack?"

"Hmm?" he answered and by the way he was looking at me, I was sure he knew I was going to interrogate him.

"Tell me about Ross," I began. "What was he doing at the scene tonight? Why was he here? How did he know?" I questioned.

He shook his head slowly and held my gaze. Then he answered quietly and seriously, "It is not right for me to answer for Ross Moore. You need to ask him, Rita. But I will tell you one thing—if you ask him, you need to be prepared to accept his answers. He is a good man and he will tell you the truth."

I heard what he said, but I didn't really understand what he meant and it scared me a little. "Yeah, you're right, of course. He's the president of the bank, and I know his position is filled with responsibilities that I don't even begin to fathom," I rambled.

I looked up into Jack's very serious eyes. He leaned closer like he was going to tell me some deep, dark secret and said, "Rita, sometimes things are not as simple as they seem on the surface and when you dig deeper, you don't find any answers at all, just more questions."

"What the hell does that mean?" I whispered back.

"Just when Ross answers your questions, don't be angry when they aren't the answers you were seeking. The truth doesn't always set you free, Rita," he said and he got up to leave. He kissed me on the cheek tenderly and told me, "More than anything, you love him and he loves you," and he put his index finger on my lips when I started to interrupt, "Love can, and in fact should, overcome doubt, hurt, confusion and even trust. You just remember how much you love him in the days to come. Will you promise me that?"

I was so moved by his earnestness, so perplexed by his words that all I could do was nod. It was enough for Jack. He smiled, winked at me as he got to the door and slipped out into the hallway, leaving me alone momentarily to carefully weigh what questions I should ask Ross or whether I should pose any at all.

CHAPTER 135

Lydia walked Spencer up and down a maze of corridors and hallways until she finally stopped outside a wooden door clear on the other side of the hospital. Spencer heard the sounds of monitors and machines beeping and whirring inside Jeff's room through the closed door. Her heart felt like it was in her throat and she was certain she would choke on it. Her hands were shaking visibly, and she was sweating profusely.

Spencer took a deep, steadying breath and looked into the room through the window in the door. Jeff was hooked up to a myriad of machines, and he had tubes and wires protruding from both sides of his body. He looked fragile.

She forced herself to look more closely, and when she finally got past the medical equipment and tuned out the sounds, Jeff simply looked like he was sleeping. From this perspective, he looked peaceful and Spencer breathed a little easier as she pushed on the door and went inside.

As she walked over to his bed, Spencer remembered watching Jeff sleep in the middle of the night when they were together only one week ago. She had watched him breathe, his chest moving up and down, his lips slightly parted, his forehead stress free. That night, she had put her head on his chest to draw him near and listened to the rhythmic sound of his heartbeat as she fell back asleep wrapped in his arms.

Tonight, though, she pulled the chair to the left of the bed as close to him as she could, grabbed his hand and laid her cheek on top of his hand so that she could watch him sleep now like before. Spencer couldn't hear his heart, but the monitor marked each beat with a green blip on a black screen and was accompanied by a soothing tapping sound. She sighed and laced her fingers through his.

Tears welled up in her eyes, spilled over onto her cheek, then rolled across her nose and onto Jeff's hand as Spencer realized how much she wanted him, how much she needed him. She hoped Jeff wanted and needed her half as much, and she was overcome by the sheer power of her emotions.

She sobbed silently and held onto his hand, refusing to break the connection between them. At some point, though, Spencer dozed off, exhaustion finally rescuing her from the nerve-wracking drama that had unfolded in the last twelve hours.

She awakened slowly to her long, blond hair being stroked gently, then the warmth of a hand on her cheek, strumming it lightly. The sounds slowly penetrated her consciousness and she opened her eyes.

Jeff was awake and was looking at her. Spencer grabbed his hand again and stood up and leaned her head down to his, her hair cascading around him. Tears again flowed down her face and she met his gaze and smiled at him. He smiled back.

"Hey, mister, if you wanted some attention, you should have just asked," she said quietly.

Jeff chuckled and said hoarsely, "I damn sure got more than I wanted, Spencer, but I'm glad you're here. How's Rita?"

Spencer relaxed and sat down on the bed beside him, choosing to keep his hand in hers as they talked. She told him that the hospital had released Rita and that Ross Moore was taking her home. Then she asked him, "Jeff, what is your role in all of this madness?"

"How much time do you have, Spencer? It's a long, sorry saga," he said somberly.

"I have all night or at least until the docs or Lydia kick me out of here," Spencer answered.

"Well, come up here beside me and get comfortable and I'll tell you the whole story," he stated, and he patted the space on the hospital bed beside him.

Spencer got up, put the side rail down and snuggled up to him, careful not to tangle or undo the tubes and wires hooked up to his hand and chest. She turned and looked at him and with great relief said, "I'm really glad you're okay. This day was horrible, but it could have been much, much worse if it had been you or Rita on a slab in the morgue instead of Dylan, Greg or George."

"George?" Jeff asked, surprised.

"Yeah, the coward blew his brains out with a pistol he had at his office when the feds went in to arrest him," Spencer said quietly. She realized he didn't know everything that had happened since that fateful ride to the hunting lodge after Rita was abducted. "Let me tell you what happened at the bank and then you can tell me how it all happened," she added.

For the next few minutes, Spencer detailed the arrests of the bankers, the Jarman brothers, and the discovery of the disk, the relay to authorities, the conference call, George's suicide and John Starr's attempted escape. While she talked, Jeff alternated between nodding and slowly shaking his head in disgust. He didn't seem shocked by anything he heard, but he did seem sad.

He sighed and quietly said, "This whole situation was destined to end poorly, Spencer. Over the years, the petty criminals became monsters, the once-honest bankers turned into greedy bastards, and the desperate and guilt-ridden just fell to pieces."

Jeff pulled Spencer closer and told her about meeting Weston Carter by chance years ago in Raleigh at a banking conference and how they kept in touch and became friends. He told her that he after he expressed some concern about the Jarmans and their cozy relationship with George Everett and many other bankers at Mid-Atlantic Bank how Weston offered him a job undercover working for the SBI at the same time he kept his job as the senior credit officer at the bank. Spencer was stunned by the revelation, amazed at the intrigue at their local bank.

Over the next half hour, Jeff told her about how he infiltrated the group by agreeing to overlook some discrepancies on a loan to the Jarmans in exchange for a kickback. He was included in the bounty going forward but he was never able to detail the full extent of where all of the money was coming from or how it was being washed out of sight of audit, security, or loan review. He had no idea that so many people were involved.

Jeff discussed Patrick's death and how he knew Greg and Dylan were responsible for his death and that Ricky Jarman was involved as well. Spencer told him how she and Rita overheard someone talking to Ricky the night of the golf tournament telling Ricky to get rid of a problem and how she and Rita knew the problem was Patrick when he turned up dead that night.

Jeff nodded again as if everything made sense now. He then explained how the duplicate disk was sent to John Starr through interoffice mail and how it tied up all of the loose ends of inflated work orders by the Jarmans' companies, overdrafts cleared with small, unsecured loans that were subsequently charged off without alarm because they were too small to be reviewed. Jeff said that John Starr informed the group that the original was missing and everybody got scared.

"Basically, that's when the wheels came off the wagon and Greg and Dylan and Ricky and George were desperate to find that disk," he said. "They just got crazy about being arrested, being labeled what they were—crooks."

"So who conked me over the head?" Spencer asked.

"Oh, that was Greg," he said disgusted. "He just snapped after we had a meeting in Shallotte the morning after you stayed at my place. He sent Ricky to Raleigh to search Ivey's vehicle and when it wasn't there or in Patrick's office or safe deposit box or Rita's office, he assumed that Rita had it at her house. You just got in his way." He reached over and grabbed Spencer's hand and squeezed it and continued, "I met with Weston that day for lunch in Southport and I had no idea until late that night when I came back to our condo complex what had happened. I was sick over it—sick," he said.

Spencer squeezed his hand in return and said, "Hey, Jeff, you didn't know. I never knew what hit me. Thank God for Jack Grissett," she said.

"Yes, he's how I kept up with you. Rita wouldn't give me the time of day. She was certain I was a real crook," he said. "Jack, Weston and Ross were the only ones who knew what I was doing."

"Why did Ross know?" Spencer asked.

Jeff sighed and seemed to struggle with what to say next. Finally, he shrugged his shoulder and answered, "Spencer, Ross is a special agent with the FBI out of Charlotte. He's a plant of the highest order."

Spencer was dumbstruck. She didn't know and she knew that Rita didn't know either. Before she could ask the question on her tongue, though, Jeff answered it. "No, she didn't know. She couldn't know, Spencer. This investigation was a federal covert sting. He was the lead agent. Ross's identity could not be compromised."

"Damn..." was all Spencer could muster in reply.

"Ross will tell Rita tonight, I'm certain. The secrecy has been bothering him for several weeks," Jeff answered. "At least, that's what Weston said."

"I hope she's up to it tonight. She is struggling right now. She is quiet and introspective and that's a bad sign in Rita," Spencer said.

A knock at the door got their attention and they looked up at a scowling Lydia standing in the doorway with her hand on her hip. "Spencer Cashwell, I just got you out of one hospital bed and here you are back in another one. Visiting hours are over, missy," she said good-naturedly, but firmly.

Spencer sighed and rolled her eyes. "Yes, Nurse Ratchet," she said and got off the bed as gently as she got on it. She leaned down and kissed Jeff on the lips and told him, "Good night, Jeff. Are you up for a visitor tomorrow?"

"I will be crushed if I don't have one," he said, then added, "I'd hate to spend Halloween alone."

Spencer said softly, but loud enough where Lydia would hear here, "I'm dressing as a hospital patient. Do you suppose I could share a room with you?"

"Hmmm," Lydia growled as a warning.

Spencer winked at Jeff and squeezed his hand. "I'll see you tomorrow afternoon. I'm so thankful you were there for Rita and that you are safe."

"Me too," he said quietly and continued, "And we'll talk some more tomorrow if you have time."

I'll have time," Spencer said, and she walked out the door with Lydia and waved to Jeff one last time through the window in the door. She sighed and hoped tomorrow came quickly. She had a lot more than time to give Jeff Malone. Spencer had the rest of her life.

Chapter 136

When Jack came out of Rita's room, he walked past Ross sitting on a bench in the hallway and put his hand on his shoulder as a steadying gesture and said, "Good luck, Ross."

Ross nodded and took a deep breath to ready himself to talk to Rita. He looked down the hallway and after Jack turned the corner out of sight, Ross was alone. He closed his eyes momentarily to collect his thoughts, his words, and his feelings. He didn't remember a time in his life where he had so much to lose. More importantly, there certainly hadn't been a time where he cared so much about what he had to lose.

Ross stood to go into Rita's room. It was now or never, he thought, and he walked to the door and pushed it open slightly before he knocked. He stuck his head inside, and she was on the bed looking at him. She was smiling slightly, but she looked so sad that Ross thought his heart would break.

"Come in," she said kindly.

Ross walked over to the bed and sat down. He reached up and put his hand on her cheek, the dark blue bruising stark against her olive skin. She looked him right in the eye unflinching and maybe even defiant. "God, Rita…" he said, groping for words to describe the enormity of the relief he felt that she was ok, the heartache he felt for what she had witnessed and lived through. Words seemed so inadequate.

She put her hand over his. "It's been a hell of a day, Ross Moore. Will you take me home?" she asked quietly, but seriously. "I need to get out of here. I need to get some air," she added.

"Come on," he said and he grabbed her hand. He reached over and picked up her purse off of the bedside table. Jack had thoughtfully remembered to bring it to the hospital with him since he got it out of her car before he towed her Miata to the car lot to be investigated and then to her condominium. Her purse had her keys in it so she could get into her house when she arrived.

Ross pushed the room door open with his free hand, and they walked silently down the hospital corridor, past the nurse's station where Ross had already handled the discharge paperwork for Rita and the bank, out the front doors of the hospital and into the dark autumn night. The air was crisp, cold even, but still. Millions of stars dotted the black blanket of sky overhead and Ross pulled Rita closer to keep her warm since she didn't have a coat.

He opened the passenger door of his unmarked car for her. She stopped, silently looked at the car momentarily, then got inside and put her seatbelt on as he walked around to the driver's side. He got in, cranked the car and pulled out of the parking area and onto highway 17 southbound back toward Shallotte.

"Rita, I have a lot of things to tell you," Ross began, and he looked over at her quickly to gauge her reaction to his preamble. She continued to stare straight ahead. "First of all, there are many parts of my life you have never seen."

Rita turned her head toward him slowly and answered softly, "It's more than what I haven't seen, Ross. I don't know who you are at all."

Ross sighed. This conversation was not going well. "Rita, that's not true. You know *exactly* who I am, just not what I do. I am a special agent with the Federal Bureau of Investigations, based out of Charlotte, NC. I handle cyber crime and white-collar crime. I was hired by Will McAdams to find the source of the losses at American One in the southeast region. Only four people initially knew who my true identity and what I was doing there, including Will and me. The other two were Weston Carter of the SBI, and my boss in Washington, DC. I was sworn to secrecy," he said. "Not even my mother and father knew what I was doing."

When he finished, silence fell again and Ross wondered if Rita was going to say anything else. He wanted to know how she felt, what she felt, or if she felt anything at all. "Rita, say something…" he said, his voice trailing off.

"Ross, I'm numb, I'm tired and I am heartbroken over the loss of so many members of my bank family. I just cannot process one more feeling tonight. I'm sorry."

Breathing a sigh of relief and silently cursing himself for being such an inconsiderate bastard, Ross said, "God, Rita, I'm the only one here who should be sorry. I am an insensitive, selfish clod." He squeezed her hand tighter and asked, "Do you still want me to come over tomorrow evening for the Halloween party or do you want to go alone or just skip it altogether?"

She smiled just a little and said, "Life goes on, Ross. Thank God I'm alive to enjoy the fun and fellowship of my neighbors and the children. I think we should go. Have you got a costume?" she asked warily.

"I do," he said. "You are going to love it…it's apropos."

Rita simply looked at him and raised an eyebrow. Ross wasn't sure what she considered apropos and he certainly wasn't going to ask.

He heard her sigh as they turned into her condominium complex, and when she saw her car at her front door, she seemed to relax just a little. When he pulled up beside her car and looked at her profile, she looked tired, distant and hurt. Ross felt almost sick, and he wished he could do something to help, something to soothe.

He got out of the car and went around to her car door and opened it for her, held out his hand to help her out and put his arm around her to keep her warm as they walked the very short distance to her door. She reached into her purse and retrieved her key, unlocked the door and opened it enough to turn on the porch light and the den lamp.

Rita looked at her condo with yearning eyes and Ross remembered that she hadn't stayed here in weeks—since before she left to go to her parents' house, in fact. He knew she was glad to be home and that she needed the night and the condo to herself.

"Promise me you will go inside, get a bath then get in the bed and get some sleep," he said.

"I don't know that I have a choice," she said gently. "I'm home, I'm nasty and I'm so tired I feel like my legs may not make it up the stairs."

"Want me to carry you?" Ross asked playfully.

Rita laughed softly, but sadly. "You've already got your arms around enough, don't you?"

Ouch, he thought, but he simply added, "Touché."

"Sorry, my sense of humor is tired too, Ross," she said and she put her hand on his arm. "I obviously need to retreat to pull myself together. Can we talk tomorrow?"

"Of course," he said, "I've still got so much to tell you."

"Why don't you come by tomorrow around 5:00," she said then added, "In *full* costume, okay?"

"Okay," he said, and he leaned down and tenderly kissed her on the right cheek because it was much less blue than the left one. He lingered next to her ear and added softly, "I'm going back to the hospital to check on Jeff Malone. I'm forever indebted to him you know."

When he stood back up, her green eyes were glistening and they seemed to bore into him, searching, silently questioning. She breathed out lightly and whispered, "He saved my life and I haven't had the chance to thank him yet—not that I understand his role in all of the madness either—maybe tomorrow," and she sighed, hugged him tightly, and turned to go inside. She paused and looked back at him again and said almost inaudibly, "Good night, Ross."

Ross was helpless and he felt like he was losing her. He felt the sickness return to his gut and he sighed lightly to quell it as he answered, "Goodnight, Rita. I'll see you tomorrow."

After she closed the door and he returned to his car and pulled away, he realized that the career he had chosen, the profession on which he had relied most of his adult life to keep him focused, driven and satisfied no longer lit the fire inside him. Suddenly, the dream from a month ago came to his mind. Rita was a gypsy telling him not to let his career jeopardize his future. Her remember watching her walk alone into the woods then hearing the gunshot. The hair stood on the back of his neck.

His career had sustained him for existence; Rita sustained him for real living. His profession had kept a fire burning when his world had been lonely, but facing the rest of his life without Rita, Ross realized an important truth. A career could provide a living but it was no life. A career could fire ambition and motivation, but it sure couldn't keep you warm at night.

He remembered Brian Evans from the Bobcats game, and he wondered why men were such classic screw-ups. Making the same mistake that a sad, former lover made when you vowed not to make the same mistake clearly puts you in the camp labeled "Idiots Only," Ross thought. He looked in the rear-view mirror and introduced himself to the reflection—meet Idiot Camper Extraordinaire.

Chapter 137

When the door closed behind me, I leaned up against it and slid slowly in a heap down to the floor. All of the emotion welled up inside of me broke through and I cried, draining every bit of the energy I had left. I cried for the loss of co-workers, husbands, fathers and sons. I cried for being used so thoroughly. I cried as I recognized how close I came to being killed and what my death would have done to my friends and my family. I cried for being angry, for being naïve, for being in love.

I cried finally for the loss of love I had for my profession and I realized that I would probably never go back. No career was worth risking your life for being good, honest and helpful. I just didn't want this life anymore.

I had no more tears left in me, or so I thought, until I realized that mom and dad didn't know what had happened today. The whole sordid situation would be the headline of the nightly newscast all over the state, the region and the nation. My heart sank and I disintegrated again thinking about having to relive the nightmare to some damn reporters amped up on energy pills and caffeine so they could break the survivor's story tomorrow. Tonight, though, they would report on all of the gruesome details of the deadly drama with no concern for the why. My folks would be watching the 11 o'clock newscast on WBTV out of Charlotte, NC.

I looked at my watch. It was 10:43 p.m. I took my blackberry out of my purse that was flopped over beside me right where it fell and dialed home—childhood home, I mean. Mom answered, "Hello," on the first ring.

I felt the hot tears of relief, fear, hurt, and probably a dozen more feelings bubble up in my voice as I tried to respond. Finally, I said, "Mama, it's me…"

"Rita, what's wrong, honey?" she said, concern creeping into her voice.

I couldn't talk, so I just cried for a few minutes. All the while, she patiently listened, soothed me by telling me she was there and ensured me I was going to be okay. I finally took several breaths and told her very generally what happened over the last eight hours or so between sobs. Mom yelled at Daddy who was obviously still in the den, "Lonnie pick up the other phone…" I heard him pick up another receiver.

As I told them about the hunting lodge, Mom's words turned serious and scared and she kept saying, "Oh, Rita, are you alright? Do I need to come tonight? Do you want us to come down to Shallotte tonight?" By the time I finished, Jeannie was crying with me, hurting with me, and reassuring me without words just how much she and Daddy loved me. Daddy was silent, but I sensed anger and I knew he was going to get some answers and hold somebody accountable for hurting me.

I could hardly talk I was sobbing so much, but I told them that Ross was coming over tomorrow along with Spencer and Ivey and that we were going to go to the community Halloween party. I felt like the children needed us and I didn't want to let them down.

Mom said, "Rita, you are so considerate of other people, but you need to think about yourself some here. You need to rest."

"I know, Mom, and I will on Sunday," and I began to cry again. "Can I come home again for a while?" I stammered. "I think I'm going to take a break from the bank, from banking in general," I said.

I immediately felt better just asking, and I could almost hear the enthusiasm in their voices as they answered, "Of course!" in unison. Daddy continued on, "I'll even clean up your pottery shed for you so that it is spic-and-span when you get here, princess."

I thought my heart would burst with the fullness of their complete and unconditional love and I could hardly speak as I sobbed, "That's exactly what I want to do, Daddy."

When I hung up the phone, I realized that I had just made a huge, life-changing decision. I got up from the floor, dragged myself up the stairs, and tried to figure out how I felt. I got out a long-sleeved sleep shirt, turned the shower on the hottest bearable setting and got under the soothing water.

I washed away the blood, the grime and the tears of the hell that was today. I refused to look in the mirror, preferring to towel off my battered face and body in the steam trapped in my shower. When I got out, I slipped on my shirt, combed my hair and braided it in a long braid over my shoulder and walked to my bed.

I turned off the bedroom light and crawled under the covers. I needed sleep and the sheer exhaustion that overtook me when I became still was incredible. I felt like I couldn't move another inch, couldn't utter another syllable, couldn't think one more thought.

The blackness of sleep propelled my mind forward and I could see my future life—light, peaceful and sure. The life behind was dark, hurtful and filled with uncertainty and I was pushing it out of my mind. I drifted into a deep sleep, satisfied that while I might not understand all that had happened over the last several months in my career and in my personal life, I was turning the page, beginning a new chapter. The new chapter had not been written, and the page before me was blank, clean and unblemished.

Chapter 138

When Spencer and Ivey pulled up to the condominium complex at 11:30 p.m., Rita's condo was dark. They had talked about her the whole way home from the hospital. They were worried about her, but they didn't want to wake her, especially since they were going to breakfast at 9 tomorrow morning.

They were both tired, too, and they said their "goodnights" to each other as soon as they walked into the condo and went to bed without turning on the television or sitting down to talk. Besides, neither really knew where to begin a conversation tonight.

Saturday dawned with a stiff northwest wind rustling the remaining leaves out of the trees and onto the ground. It was crisp and clear outside. It was Halloween.

Spencer woke first, and she tiptoed down the stairs and looked at the clock. It was 7 a.m. *What is wrong with me?* She chided herself for getting up at such a ghastly hour on a weekend morning. She could have slept another hour.

Awake now, she walked to the kitchen, quietly filled an insulated tumbler with ice and poured herself a Diet Coke. She drank almost all of it immediately and filled it again. She was parched. The refill in hand, she walked to the back door and gently pulled it open and let herself out onto her back porch. The air was cold, but it was like a splash of cold water, exhilarating and refreshing, not bone-chilling.

She looked over at Rita's porch and there she was, coffee mug in one hand, book in the other. Just like last night, she was quiet, almost withdrawn and she stood staring at Spencer with a hint of a smile on her face. The smile didn't reach her eyes, though, and the left side of her face was blue and swollen. Rita looked sad and distant, but didn't say a word.

Spencer walked over and sat down at the chair to the right of Rita around her teak table. She softly whispered, "Good morning."

"Good morning, Spencer," Rita said, and she reached over and squeezed Spencer's hand.

Something in the gesture touched Spencer and it brought tears to her eyes. Still holding Rita's hand, Spencer leaned over to her and asked her quietly, "Where are you, Rita?"

Rita released Spencer's hand and pushed a flyaway curl behind her ear. She sighed and looked into the woods as if she could see miles away and was watching something very interesting, engrossed but not involved. Finally, she answered, "Somewhere not here…."

Spencer shook her head and quickly wiped a tear away that had slipped out. She struggled to find the right words, not sure if there even were any. "I understand needing to get away, Rita," she said, "You've been through a hell of an ordeal."

Rita's head snapped around to Spencer, and she looked her right in the eyes and answered, "I'm not talking about getting away, Spencer. I'm talking about moving away."

The clarity of the words echoed in the air as Rita turned back to stare into the woods. Spencer was speechless, stunned and she wanted to argue, to offer a rebuttal, but she had nothing.

Spencer's back door opened, and Ivey stepped out into the morning with a cup of coffee. He looked first at Spencer whose eyes were full of unshed tears. Then he looked at Rita, or at least at her profile and her eerily serene smile. Her face was bruised, and he was unsure if the swelling around her left eye was from the blows she took yesterday or the tears she had cried. Rita had obviously made peace with where she was, what she wanted and where she was going. She just wasn't happy about it.

Ivey walked over and put his arm around Rita, and they stood side by side, staring off into the stand of trees. She put her head on his shoulder and sighed. Finally, Rita pulled her head up and went back to the table to sit down, silently inviting Ivey to join her and Spencer.

She sighed, and looked at Ivey then Spencer. Both knew she was about to say something important, something well-considered, something final. Ivey felt the hair on his neck stand. Spencer let the tears spill undeterred onto her cheeks. Life as they knew it would never be the same.

"I'm leaving the bank," Rita said. "I've decided to go back to Misenheimer for a little while and figure out what to do next. Maybe I'll find some clarity there, some direction."

Ivey nodded and Spencer reached over and took her hand. "That bank won't be the same without you, Rita," Spencer stated.

"That bank won't be the same, period, Spencer," Rita replied. "I won't be the same either. I've lost my passion, lost my drive for this work. Worst of all, though, I've lost my faith in it, too."

"Oh, Rita…" Ivey said. "You make me sad. What can I do? What can I say? How can I help you get past all of these feelings?" he asked.

"You can't," she answered.

"What will you do?" Spencer inquired.

"I'm going to hole up in my shed and figure it out," Rita replied. "Shaping clay is extraordinarily therapeutic for helping shape a plan for the future. I'm not sure why, but it has never failed me."

Spencer and Ivey looked at each other. They were not going to change her mind.

"What about Ross?" Ivey asked. "Where does he fit into all of this?"

"I don't know, Ivey," Rita said, "I don't know who he is, let alone how I feel about him."

"Oh, bull crap!" Spencer said sharply. "How can you not know who he is? He's the man you love, Rita."

"I love the Ross Moore he created for this investigation. He's not that guy, Spencer," Rita said. "He's a fed, a g-man, a special agent with the FBI."

"I know," Spencer replied.

Rita whipped her head toward Spencer. "Did everybody but love-struck Rita know?" she asked sarcastically. "Why didn't you of all people tell me then, Spencer? I feel so used."

"Wait a damn minute now, sister," she said hotly. "I found out last night from Jeff who only found out recently because he was undercover too—a statie, an s-man, a special agent with the SBI. Don't you dare accuse me of hiding anything from you! I wouldn't do that, and I am stung that you'd even think that I would," Spencer added and the tears of anger, of hurt continued to stream down her face.

"Spencer, I'm so sorry," Rita said and she put her head down on the table and sobbed silently, her shoulders wracked with grief.

"Hey, now," Ivey said calmly and softly, "Let's take a breather and let cooler heads prevail here. It's 8 o'clock. Let's go get a shower and then go get some breakfast."

Rita pulled her head up at the comment and looked at Spencer, and slowly they started laughing. Ivey was perplexed.

Spencer said, "Ivey, if we all went to get a shower, we'd have to call the paramedics to come revive you, mister."

"Yeah, was that an invitation or a fantasy?" Rita giggled.

"God, y'all suck!" Ivey protested good-naturedly. His face was red, and he got up slowly to regain his composure. Then he added, "I'm going to go get a shower, but each of you needs to get one too. The gutter is a dirty place, ladies," and he smiled broadly and shook his head as he walked back to Spencer's place.

Chapter 139

Working at the Brunswick county Sheriff's Department on Saturday was like working in the salt mines. Ross got at the base camp around 7 a.m. knowing that he would be able to put in a full day's work and still get back to his parents to change into his costume and be at Rita's by 5 p.m. The "full day" part was the challenge here. The processing of paperwork, compiling information and writing reports was tedious, grueling work that had never yielded much satisfaction to an action guy like Ross. Sitting at a desk on a computer was akin to torture in his world.

Even still, he plugged away through the morning, through lunch and into the afternoon. When he finished his last arrest report on Ricky Jarman, he looked at his watch. It was 3:21 p.m. He had filed the arrest report on Ricky and read the other 14 reports, reviewed the coroner's reports on Dylan, Greg and George, and detailed the events that led up to and triggered the shootings at the hunting lodge. He was mentally fried.

He grabbed his coat off of the chair and walked around to the office at the end of the hall to see if Weston was still there. When Ross saw him sitting at the desk, he was startled at how worn out his friend looked. He was sure he looked worse. This career took its toll on the body, mind and spirit at times. This investigation was clearly one of those times.

"I'm off to go trick-or-treating," Ross joked. "Go get some rest, Weston. You look like hell."

"Have you looked in a mirror? Your face could damn sure pass for a mask of horror. You'll scare the kids to death," he replied.

"I hope a shower will help. I'll skip the candy and go for the caffeine instead. Good night, Weston," Ross said.

"Good night, Ross. I'll see you on Monday," he answered.

Ross drove to his parents' house, and went upstairs to get a hot shower after he stopped in the kitchen and begged his mother to make him a super-sized, super strong mug of coffee. Twenty minutes later, he was downstairs in his tuxedo with his hair slicked back with gel. Marian was speechless and questioned his garb simply with the raising of her eyebrows as she held the piping hot mug of Joe out to him.

He laughed and said, "It *is* Halloween, mom. This is part of my costume, but I need your help. I need you to 'doctor' my face on the right to look like I was burned with acid. This mask covers the right side of my face," and he handed her the phantom mask.

"You haven't dressed up for Halloween since you went as a chainsaw killer to that party when you were in middle school. Where are you going?" she asked curiously.

"My, my—aren't we *full* of questions tonight," he said smartly, but gently to his mother. "I'm going to a party for a while then I am going to take my beautiful gypsy somewhere we can talk." His voice turned very serious and he added, "She's been through quite an ordeal in the last couple of weeks, particularly the last 24 hours, Mom. I don't know where we go from here, where she goes from here. I just want her to go there with me."

Marian took his hand into hers and looked up into his eyes. "Then tell her just like that. Don't waste time, don't mince words—just tell her so. If you love her and she loves you, that feeling alone can overcome hurt, pain, anger and uncertainty." Ross sighed as Marian pulled her art supplies out of the closet. "Now, let me see what I can do with that face of yours," she said, and she went to work creating a phantom's face out of her grown son's.

When she was finished, she turned him around to look in the mirror in the den. The transformation was amazing, just like the hands that created it. He leaned down and kissed his mother on the cheek. "I love you, mom," he said sincerely. "Thank you."

Marian put her hand to her cheek and smiled, then she pointed to the door and said, "Go!"

The ride over was nerve-wracking and he felt nervous, excited, anxious and scared. He felt like he was a defendant going back in the courtroom after the jury has reached its verdict. He knew his life was in the balance of how tonight unfolded, but the events that led up to the decision couldn't be changed, argued, mitigated or undone. Waiting was awful.

As he turned into the complex, the entire driveway had been transformed for the party. Jack-o-lanterns lined the both sides of the road. Spider webs hung from the oaks. To the left of Rita's building, black, orange, white and green Chinese lanterns were hung in the courtyard and a bonfire had been lit. Tables were set up and a stage and games had been set up near the back. The neighborhood was ready for a party.

He parked his SUV and put the finishing touches on his costume. He attached his cape, put on his mask and put a red boutonniere on his lapel. He looked at himself in the rearview mirror. *Who the hell are you,* he silently asked himself, and the real meaning of the question was not lost on the phantom in the reflection. He took one more deep breath and got out of the vehicle.

He knocked on the door and waited. The door to his left opened instead of Rita's and Spencer stuck her head out, "Damn, man! You look good even as a pasty old, sewer resident with a nasty scar! Come on in…Rita's over here."

Ross relaxed and smiled. Spencer had her head wrapped in gauze with a big red spot on it. She had on a printed hospital gown with white circulation socks and bedroom shoes on. She looked authentic, but Ross was worried she would freeze with the evening chill. As he followed her in the condo, he saw the three or four blankets beside her and realized she would have those on to keep warm. Spencer hadn't forgotten a thing.

As he walked in, Ivey stood, smiling and came over and shook Ross's hand. Ivey admired Ross's get-up, but he was obviously quite pleased with his own. He was dressed as Daniel Boone. He had on a coonskin cap, a leather pair of lace-up moccasin boot, a matching leather jacket with fringe on it and blue jeans. He had a musket and a gunpowder bag. The best part of the outfit, though, was a string of obviously fake animal pelts slung across his shoulder.

"How long have you been working on this costume, man?" Ross asked him, laughing.

"Since last year, of course," Ivey answered. "Spencer's much more spontaneous than I am."

"I was wondering where she got her inspiration," Ross teased.

"Admit it," she yelled from the kitchen, "I look good."

"You look marvelous," Ross chuckled. "Where is my gypsy?" he asked, wondering where Rita had gone.

"Here," Spencer said and she handed Ross a beer. "She wants to make a grand entrance. She's been working on that gruesome bruise for almost an hour. We got some scar make-up to cover it. Hey, you want some," Spencer replied then laughed at her own cleverness.

"My mask covers mine quite well, thank you, Patient Cashwell," Ross replied.

Spencer walked over to the stairwell and said, "I'll be right back."

When Spencer walked upstairs, Ivey walked over to Ross and said, "Rita's in a strange state, Ross. She's got a lot of questions to which there may not be any answers. She's too calm, too okay, almost like she is empty of emotion and devoid of feelings. She freaked Spence and me out this morning. We've been working on her all day, but she's still stoic."

"Thanks, Ivey," Ross said. "I've got a lot of explaining to do. I can't undo what is already done and I can't unsay what has already been said. I can tell her the truth from the beginning and tell her who I am, what I do, and how we got to where we are. It may not help, but she needs to know the truth."

"It may not help immediately, but Rita has a good head on her shoulders. She may just need some time, Ross. You need to be prepared for that," Ivey stated.

Ross sighed loudly and said, "I know. I keep telling myself I am, but are you ever ready for a decision like that?"

"No," Ivey said.

Ross looked over at the foot of the interior stairs and he saw Spencer come bounding down first. She hurried over to a barstool so she could watch Rita and Ross's reaction.

Ross breathed deeply to try to steady himself. His stomach was jittery and he felt jumpy. He was a nervous wreck.

When Rita sashayed around the corner, she nearly took his breath away she was so beautiful. She jingled and jangled, her neck loaded full of gold necklaces. She had castanets on her fingers. Her olive skin glistened along the untied neckline of her white peasant shirt. Her long, curly hair was tied back off of her face with a kerchief and loose curls brushed her cheek and her neck. The bruises on her face were barely visible under her sexy makeup and she looked exotic, mysterious, even dangerous.

She had large gold hoops in her ears and the long red and black patchwork skirt brushed just above her still-tanned ankles. She had a pair of gladiator sandals on her feet. Ross was sure his mouth was gaping open.

"Damn, Rita," Ivey said, "You clean up pretty good."

Rita just smiled. "Hello, Phantom," she whispered.

"Hello, beautiful," Ross said back to her. "You look incredible."

"Thank you," she answered. Spencer walked over and handed her a beer and she said, "Thank you, crip."

Spencer laughed and turned to Ross. "I went to the hospital to see Jeff today—dressed like this," and she spread her arms wide and spun around. "I had nurses and doctors asking me where I was going, telling me to go get back in the bed, asking me if they could help me. It was a real riot."

Rita rolled her eyes. Ivey chuckled. "They were afraid to tell me visiting hours were over. That is, until Nurse Lydia, chased me out of Jeff's room so he could get some rest. She's a real drill sergeant," Spencer said. "Jeff told me to make pictures tonight so he could enjoy the party." Without any warning, she snapped a photo of Ross admiring Rita, the flash blinding everybody in the room momentarily.

"Now I blind and maimed," Ross retorted.

"Come on y'all," Spencer said. "The party can't start until we get there! Ivey, you and Ross grab that cooler, and Rita and I'll grab the foodies and the picnic blanket. Let's roll, people," she ordered, and they walked with their hands full to begin the Halloween festivities.

Rita walked behind the guys with Spencer and a comfortable silence fell between the two. Spencer looked across the courtyard at Jeff's condo. Rita put her arm around her and said, "I know you wish he was here in body, but he's here in spirit. I'm sure they'll be a lot more parties for you two in the future."

Spencer slowed a little more so that she and Rita were out of earshot of

Ross. Rita looked at Spencer with concern when she slowed almost to a stop and said, "What's wrong?"

Spencer sighed and said, "What I really wish, Rita, is that *you* were here in spirit and not just in body. Your future is at *this* party, woman." She took a deep breath and looked Rita straight in the eye, "You're my best friend, so I'm not going to sugarcoat anything for you. Stop your pity party, get off your pedestal and look at what's staring you in the face—he loves you, you love him, blah, blah, blah. It's enough—period. Now, come on Griselda. There's a party waiting for us."

Chapter 140

In spite of the stinging but true comments from Spencer on the way over to the party, I had a really good time. I thoroughly enjoyed all of the squealing, laughing and running by the children there. They lifted my spirits, made me smile and took my mind off of the brutal honesty laid bare by my best friend.

I watched Ross and he was having a good time too. He loved terrorizing the children for Halloween. He would fit in well with my mother in that regard, and I started to ponder a Halloween in Misenheimer with Mom and Ross. Then I stopped myself—no sense indulging in that futile fantasy—and decided to just enjoy the moment, tonight, the party.

About 8:00, Ross brought me another beer. He was winded from running around and playing games with the kids, but he was beaming from ear to ear. I looked at him in profile as he sat down on the blanket beside me. Ross Moore was a beautiful phantom.

He turned and looked at me full in the face and said, "Would you read my palm?" He held out his right hand.

I studied his face for a second or two and decided to indulge him. I took his hand. Using my worst Hungarian accent, I began, "I see a grand future for you—great fortune, success, fame. Your head line, here," and I pointed to the center line on his hand, "is deep and long. This line represents your work, your career. Now this line is your life line," I said pointing to the bottom line on his hand. "It is wide and far away from the thumb," I continued and ran my finger along the line. "This line means you are generous with your time with other people and that you are giving. Finally, this line up here," and I moved to the heart line at the top of his hand, "this line is near the center of your hand. You are very controlled in matters of the heart. And see," I said as I moved my index finger along the line, "it moves up toward the Jupiter finger. That lines means you are very reasonable when it comes to love, but kind." I stopped and looked up at him. He was speechless and perhaps a little stunned too—and not in a good way.

"I don't like your reading," he said quietly, "because it sounds like I'm either doomed to a life full of work or a life light on love. That's not the grand future you promised first."

"The hands don't lie even when the heart and head do," I said in my own voice.

He looked back at the party as if he was trying to gather his thoughts through the commotion. Finally, he looked back at me and asked, "Can we go someplace a little quieter where we can talk?"

"Do you want to walk back to my condo? We can talk there," I said then added, "or we can go over to the beach and sit at the gazebo or the sand or walk out on the pier. Come on." We stood and I folded up the picnic blanket then walked over to Spencer and Ivey who were manning the "Go Fish" booth.

"We're going to go somewhere where we can talk," I said and immediately regretted my choice of words. Spencer's eyes lit up and Ivey smiled. I simply shook my head to dismiss their overoptimistic hopes. "Will you bring the cooler home?" I asked Spencer.

"Of course," she said. "Call us when you get home—even if it's tomorrow morning," she added. I rolled my eyes and walked off. They were so transparent.

I walked back over to Ross and smiled at him. He was a great phantom. He reached down and grabbed my hand as we walked. My heart hurt because I wanted…this. "So you think this costume is apropos, huh? Want to explain why?" I asked a little too sharply.

Ross pulled me closer and almost whispered, "It is, and yes I do." We walked over to his SUV and he pulled out his keys as he walked to the passenger side and opened my door for me, "The beach is a great choice—and my gondola is out of service," he said.

I got in and watched him walk around. When he got to the driver's seat, he took off his cape and his mask and put them on the back seat. Then he took off his coat and his bowtie and rolled up his sleeves. Finally, he took off his shoes and socks and reached on the floorboard behind him and grabbed his flip flops and expertly put them on. I smiled at his organization and planning skills, a definite strength most men lacked.

He looked at me and smiled back. "Once a boy scout, always a boy scout, I guess. I'm always prepared to go to the beach. I never take my flip flops out of the car," he said.

"I like that," I said honestly. "It shows you know how to be spontaneous, frivolous, and flexible. I wasn't sure you had those things in you, Ross."

"Oh, Rita…" he said sadly. "You don't think much of me right now, do you?"

"On the contrary," I said softly, "You're all I think about right now."

He sighed and seemed to accept my comment as a glimmer of hope. We crossed the Ocean Isle Beach Bridge in an easy silence. The night was black and clear and the crescent moon shone down from high above, casting its reflection clearly in the dark liquid expanse of ocean in front of us. The waves were flat and rolled gently in and out on the narrow strip of sandy shore. Stars twinkled above and bounced light in little pin pricks across the water. The autumn with its low humidity and mild temperatures was a magical time at the south Brunswick beaches.

We turned right onto First Street and drove west on the island. We parked in the public access parking lot and I grabbed the picnic blanket as we got out. We walked across the wooden walkway over to the beach. The tide was out and we walked up high in the soft sand next to the dunes walking west away from the pier. I stopped and took off my sandals and threw them over my shoulder once I buckled them together.

The sand was cool and almost completely free of shells and it oozed between my toes. The wind blew my hair lightly and was cool and dry. I shivered with the exhilaration of the beach. The feeling never grew old.

Ross took my hand as we walked. He looked energized by the beach too and I caught him with his eyes momentarily closed enjoying the breeze on his face. He looked sexy and sure, but somewhat sad too. After about 500 yards or so, Ross stopped and turned to look at the ocean. "Let's sit here," he said.

I opened the blanket and spread it out easily on the sand. We had stopped in an area that was almost like an alcove, further back and higher than the other sand, but still not in the dune line. Ross took off his flip flops, took the sandals off my shoulder and put them next to the blanket in the sand and sat down. I joined him and he leaned back and pulled me next to him. I heard him sigh, and I suddenly wanted to stay here all night, as long as we didn't have to talk and ruin the silence of the beach's beauty.

I realized I was being ridiculous, though, and I sighed too and fired the first salvo when I said softly, "So when I asked you 'why me' and you answered 'I guess it was just my lucky day,' luck really had nothing to do with it that day at the pep rally, did it?"

He breathed in deeply and answered, "No. I had checked you out in the organization. Your reputation is as solid as a rock. You are considered independent, hard-working and honest by former employees, peers, your supervisors and executive management."

"How did you get an answer without compromising your investigation?" I asked.

"I looked at annual reviews, commendations, and personnel files," he stated. "I also used my own gut instincts. The touch with 'Rita Hayward' really got my attention that day and told me I was spot on about you."

I continued, now on a roll. "So, you targeted me before that day, but how did you know I would blow off the meeting or go to the car?" I asked.

"I didn't," he said emphatically, "that's what I've been trying to tell you—luck was definitely on my side."

"Lucky for you, maybe," I said cynically.

He sighed and said, "Definitely lucky for me, Rita." Ross turned and faced me and he looked me in the eyes. He was serious, intense and I wasn't sure what he was going to say or do next. After what felt like an eternity, he finally said, "Here are the facts, Rita—I needed you for the investigation, I got to know you, I enjoyed being with you and then I fell head over heels in love with you—so yeah, it was definitely lucky for me."

I was speechless and I felt tears well up in my eyes and spill over onto my cheeks. He loved me. I loved him too—so what the hell was wrong with me then? I silently asked myself. "I love you too," I whispered.

"So why are you crying and why do I feel like I'm losing you?" he implored. "I don't want to lose you, Rita. I want this relationship. I want a life with you."

The tears continued to roll down my cheeks and I looked up into his eyes, "You didn't trust me, Ross, you just didn't trust me!" I sobbed twice uncontrollably and then took another deep breath and managed, "Even the constant bastard Patrick trusted me," I cried and I put my head down to try to regain my composure.

Ross stroked my hair. Gently he put his chin down on the back of my head and quietly whispered, "I'm sorry, Rita. Secrecy was paramount to this assignment. It was my duty."

"I know, but I'm still devastated by it," I stated. "I want a relationship and a life with you too, but what future is there for a relationship built on a lie?" I asked and began crying again.

"I hope a long, happy, stable, child-infested one," he said passionately. "Promise me you'll take some time off to heal, to consider and to weigh everything before you write me off, Rita—promise me."

I reached up and put my hand on his face. I loved him. I wondered if it was enough like Spencer said and her stinging words reared up in my mind and wounded me all over again. Maybe I was being a fool. I suddenly wanted to be in Misenheimer. "I promise you," I said. "I'm going to take a sabbatical from the bank—and it may become permanent."

Surprised by my statement, Ross asked, "What are you going to do, Rita?"

"I'm going back to the farm, to my pottery shed for a while. I can think clearly there. I can heal there," I answered calmly now and I smiled up at him, and continued, "At least until I die of boredom, am worked to death by Jeannie or am institutionalized for insanity thanks to my family. Any one of those things could happen sooner than later."

He smiled and said, "At least you have a plan. Can I call you?" he asked.

I wanted to answer yes, but I knew I needed time to figure out what I wanted and where I went from here so I said, "I'll call you, ok? When I'm ready, I promise I'll call." I looked lovingly into his eyes and he nodded. I don't know what in that gesture made me feel so sad, but I felt the hot tears in my eyes tumble onto my cheeks again. I reached up and kissed him. I tasted the urgency in his kiss and I wanted to give myself to him completely right there on the beach. I felt the passion rising in me and I ran my hands down his back.

I heard him sigh deeply and then he slowly pulled away. "I want you to heal, to think clearly and to want me…us with all of your being, Rita." He kissed my forehead then my lips softly then added, "Let me take you home."

I nodded and we rose in silence, folded up the blanket and walked back up the beach the way we had come. The even ebb and flow of the waves soothed me, the beach air dried my tears and the wind at our backs eased us to our destination gently. As we got back into Ross's SUV, I felt relaxed, but also drained, and I simply looked out the window at the Intracoastal Waterway and the lights of the mainland as he drove me home.

When we got to the condo, Ross got out and walked me to the door. He leaned down to kiss me, barefoot and still in my gypsy garb. I threw my arms around his neck and held on tight. "I do love you, Rita Miller. Don't you forget it, either," he whispered.

"I won't, Ross—I promise," I answered.

He kissed me again, this time much more passionately, then he stroked my right cheek gently with the back of his hand and said, "Goodnight, gypsy."

I took the scarf off my hair and tied it around his neck, "Good night, phantom," I said softly, and he reached up and touched the scarf, looked me in the eyes then kissed my forehead and walked back to his SUV and drove away.

I stood on the porch long after his lights had disappeared from sight. I realized that I was all alone and that I didn't want to talk to Spencer or Ivey tonight. No, what I wanted was gone, and I stood shivering in the night air simply staring off in the direction Ross had driven away, longing for him to come back, and wondering if he ever would.

Chapter 141

Lonnie Miller saw the light on in Rita's pottery shed as he parked the tractor in the barn. Night was upon him much more quickly than he expected since the air felt much more like September, warm and moist, than November's cold, dry evenings. He got off the tractor, turned off the overhead lights and walked over to see his older daughter.

It was Saturday night, and he and Jeanne were going to go to Salisbury to eat dinner like they usually did. It was their date night and had been for the 38 years they had been married. He would invite Rita to go, but he knew her answer. She would politely decline after she pretended to consider the offer for a few seconds. He sighed, frustrated that Rita was back to withdrawn, pensive, and sad in spirit from where she had been just a few weeks ago—outgoing, interactive and happy.

He wished he knew how to snap her out of her funk. She had told her mother what had happened with Ross. He didn't understand what her problem was. The man had a job to do. He did it and did it well. Along the way, Ross fell in love with his daughter. *Why in the world was that not enough for Rita*, he wondered. Jeanne said Rita's feelings were hurt, that Rita felt like Ross didn't trust her. *Baloney*, he thought. "And the greatest of these is love," Lonnie remembered from the Bible. So why didn't Rita give it the greatest consideration?

He had mulled all of these thoughts over and over all week, but he had held his tongue. Lonnie was tired of holding his tongue. He had to get through to her—and soon.

Rita had been here for almost two weeks. Lonnie was sure glad to have her home, but when he looked at her, he hurt with the pain he saw in her eyes, especially when she didn't know he was watching her. He stood in the doorway now, watching her masterful touch on the shapeless clay on her wheel. Rita worked the mass with her hands lovingly, a fluted vase almost magically taking shape. She had a slight smile on her face and her head was slightly tilted as she worked smoothing, shaping and manipulating her work of art.

He looked over at her shelves. Rita had turned out more than a dozen pieces since she had arrived home. Many had been completed—glazed and fired in the kiln. Others were glazed and not yet fired. The rest had been turned and were waiting for color, texture. She had certainly been on a tear.

"That's a beautiful piece, honey," he said in the doorway.

Rita looked up at him and smiled, "I'm going to make this one red and green for Christmas. I'll have lots of gifts this year."

Lonnie looked back over at the shelves and said, "You keep up this pace and you'll have the next dozen Christmases taken care of."

Rita followed his eyes to the shelf and seemed to realize for the first time just how many pieces she had made. She simply nodded.

"Come walk with me for a minute," Lonnie said, and he held out his hand. He watched her waver between staying and going. Finally, she turned off the wheel off, washed and dried her hands at the sink and walked over and took his hand.

They walked in the dark toward the pasture gate for a few minutes in silence. He pulled her close to him and asked quietly, "Are you going to let me take you and your mother out for dinner tonight? You know if you don't go, I'll never hear the end of from your mother."

Rita laughed softly and said, "I'm sure you can find something more interesting than my eating habits to discuss, even after 38 years, Dad."

"Probably not," he answered, "Jeannie possesses an endless fascination with the lives of her offspring—especially you. You're her new pet project."

"God help me then…" Rita moaned.

"Rita, I've been meaning to ask you something and I'm not sure how to ask you or whether I should ask you, but I'm going to ask you nonetheless," he rambled. He had stopped walking momentarily and turned to face her as he talked.

She had a confused, concerned look on her face, but she nodded and said, "Okay…"

"I know that Holt Barden moved to Shallotte a couple of years ago, and I know he came to see you at the bank," he said. Lonnie stopped for a second and sighed then he continued, "Well, old Holt has moved back here and he came to me and wants to buy some of my old farm machinery. He has asked me to finance it for him."

"Okay…" Rita said again, this time a little more tentatively.

"What I am asking is did Holt borrow money from you? And if he did, did he pay you back on time and as agreed? Also, what rate of interest did you charge him and what were the terms of the loan?" he asked her.

Now, Rita's mouth was all but gaping open in shock. She looked at her Dad and seemed to be searching for what to say to him. Finally, she said quietly, "Daddy, I can't answer any of those questions for you. That information is private."

Lonnie pressed her more. "Rita, I won't tell anybody, though. Please tell me. You can trust me, honey," he said intensely.

Rita was wringing her hands and she was wrestling hard with doing the right thing and trusting her dad. After a long few seconds, she answered in angst, "I can't, Dad. I just can't tell you. Privacy is a basic tenet of my career. I have a fiduciary responsibility to Mr. Barden to keep that information private. I'm sorry." Lonnie looked her right in the eyes. They were misty, troubled.

He wasn't trying to hurt her more, but she was making an argument for her actions that was in complete contradiction with what she expected from Ross. Rita was being unfair.

Lonnie stood looking at her, waiting for the reality of this discussion to sink into her conscience. He knew it would. Sure enough, after less than 15 seconds of silence, he saw the dawning.

He crossed his arms and waited for the barrage, the explanation, the justification. Rita was almost angry and he was ready for her reaction. "It's not the same," she seethed.

"It is the same," he argued, "unless what's right for you is wrong for anybody else."

Her eyes filled with tears, and she seemed at a total loss for words. "Oh, Daddy…" she wailed, and she turned and began retreating back to her pottery sanctuary.

"I'll see you when we get back from Salisbury," he called after her gently. She threw up her hand, but she didn't turn around. Lonnie knew she didn't want him to see her crying. Rita was broken-hearted again—this time thanks to her father making her realize she was a hypocrite.

He walked to his pickup truck. Lonnie hated tough love, but damn, he thought with the beginning of a smile on his face, it sure was effective.

Chapter 142

I stood looking at the shelves in my shed. They were nearing capacity and I started at the top and looked at each of my works carefully, mentally deciding to whom I might give it. Each piece was a window to my mood, through color and shape, form and flow, at the moment of its creation.

I had cried myself numb. Daddy was right. Before him, Spencer had been right. I had been a real sanctimonious bitch. I had raised the bar after I fell in love impossibly high, expecting perfection, ensuring failure. I had been in my own way, blocking my own path to happiness, and successfully sealed my fate—Ross was gone, and I was alone.

After I pulled myself together, I tried to call Ross. He didn't answer and I fell apart all over again. It was Saturday night. He was probably out on a date with a woman who could enjoy his company and didn't take herself so seriously. What the hell is wrong with me?

I started up the pottery wheel again, wiped my eyes and nose and sat back down. I didn't really want to create any more pottery tonight, but I was seeking therapy and solace, not chasing inspiration. I put my hands around the cool, damp clay. I closed my eyes and felt the excess clay ooze through my fingers. The feeling reminded me of the cool sand between my toes on Halloween and I opened my eyes, now upset, even angry, at my incredible stupidity.

I was breathing heavy and I felt a simmering fury rising inside of me. I stopped the pottery wheel from turning. The clay silently called for me to touch it, so I did. I reared my fist back and brought it down on top of the beginnings of what had been a beautiful vase. Not now. It was just a formless blob and I punched it again and again, ridding myself of all of the frustration, anger, and sadness that had camped inside of me for the last two weeks. *Damn*, I thought, and then I picked up the clay and hurled it toward the door.

Suddenly, I felt like I was having a heart attack and I couldn't breathe. I fell back onto my stool and grabbed the splash guard around my wheel to steady myself. Ross Moore was standing in the door, only inches from where the orange blob of clay had made contact with the doorjamb. I put my hand up to my mouth in sheer horror at what I had done and how I must have looked.

The look on Ross's face was one of pure shock, though. Slowly, though, he started to laugh, and said, "Damn woman, Carolina could have used you in the bullpen!"

I began laughing, and my embarrassment, shock and surprise took a backseat to the hysterics that followed for the next few minutes. We laughed, composed ourselves, then laughed some more. Ross walked over and threw his arms around me and I held on so tightly that he probably was a little afraid for his life—at the very least, his health.

I looked up into his eyes and said, "I love you, Ross Moore. Will you forgive me for being so unreasonable and so harsh in my judgment?"

"I'll forgive you anything," he said, and then added, "Especially with a ball of clay in that hand of yours."

We disintegrated into silly laughter again until finally, I said, "I'm starving! Would you take me to Cripple Creek Tavern to get a pizza?"

Ross stepped closer and said, "I'll take you anywhere you want to go, Rita. I love you and I'm sorry for the pain and loss you've been through lately, some of which is my fault. I'll spend the rest of my life making up for it by making you happy if you'll let me."

"I want that very much," I said to him. "And where I want to go with you right now is for pizza," I tried to add seriously but I burst into laughter once again.

"You've got a deal, Rita Miller. I offer you Paris, Jamaica and you choose pepperoni and Cripple Creek Pizza. You're my kind of woman," he said, laughing.

I washed my face and my arms and hands, took off my apron and hung it on the hook on the back of the door, then turned off the light. By only the light of the moon I took his hand and we walked down the hill toward his SUV. I wrapped my arms around him and he pulled me against him.

Tonight was the first night of our forever, and I shivered with exhilaration at the thought. Ross and I had so much to discuss, but I knew now that our future included each other. We shared passion and attraction. We could laugh at and with each other. We had definitely proven that tonight with our crazy laughter over a flying ball of unformed clay.

What we had was also special, deep and sustaining. It wasn't perfect, but it was true. Tonight, over beer and pizza at the local tavern we would begin our life together. We wouldn't solve the world's problems, and we might not even figure out everything related to our careers, homes, friends or families, but tonight we would start. We had a future to build—one filled with excitement and built for endurance. I loved Ross Moore and he loved me, and as a silent response to Daddy and Spencer, I finally realized that this love, above all else, most certainly was enough.